Shadow Play By: Christie Palmer

She reached up to cup his face. Leaning forward in his arms, she pressed her lips to his. This time he couldn't stop himself. He let her slide onto her feet and pressed her against the side of the cave, his hands roaming all over her amazing body. He memorized every magnificent inch he could manage to touch. He slid one hand down to cup her ass, pulling her into him. He then pulled her leg up and wrapped it around his hip. He pressed himself into the center of her femininity. She rewarded him with a slow and throaty moan.

Her taste was intoxicating. He sucked on her bottom lip, memorizing the taste and feel of her. He felt her body respond as she pressed against him. Her hands slid up the inside of his T-shirt. He jerked when her cold hands touched his stomach and moved up his chest.

"You're so warm," she moaned. "I can't get close enough."

Ryder wanted her so badly, he couldn't see straight. The gland in the back of his throat shot a volt through him and produced the extra saliva to mark her as his.

Shadow Play

Christie Palmer

Other Books by: Christie Palmer

Lost in Time -- Book 1 of the Fallen Spring 2013

Book 3 – Summer 2013

Jinx Fantasy Fiction LLC
Salt Lake City, UT
www.jinxfantasyfiction.com

Edited by: Jennifer Sommersby
Cover Design by: Jaycee De Lorenzo of Sweet N' Spicy Designs http://jayceedelorenzo.com/sweetnspicy/new-page.html

ISBN: 978-0-9885557-1-6
Manufactured in the United States of America
First Edition December 2012

Dedication:

This book is dedicated to my amazing husband and two children who believed in me even when I didn't believe in myself. Thank you just doesn't seem to encompass all I feel for you.

Also to my mother who taught me the value of reading, this wouldn't be possible if you hadn't made me read when I was a kid.

Chapter 1

Grisly pictures of a mutilated female body stared up at him from where his brother had tossed them at his feet it had been a woman now ripped apart. Her remains resembled a plastic baby doll with its arms and legs torn off and haphazardly flung away. Ryder knelt down and gathered up the pictures before turning to his brother.

"You needed something?" Ryder asked.

"How long are you going to ignore Max's request for help?" Lykar asked waving the pictures he still held at Ryder.

"It's a Mortal issue." Ryder rose to his feet and handed the pictures back to his brother. He had seen them already. Ryder did not do Mortal issues, regardless of the person requesting the help.

Besides, he had not ignored Max's request. He had looked over the information Max had sent, and he didn't want anything to do with what was going on. He was sure that Max would be able to figure out what was going on and take care of it. The killing could be Mortal, but he doubted it. The entire issue reeked of Other, and he wanted nothing to do with it. Hundreds of years of following his instincts had kept him alive. Although he owed Max, and the injustice of turning his back on a friend clawed at his conscience with sharp talons.

Lykar waved the pictures in Ryder's face. "A Mortal is not capable of doing this …" He stammered, "This type of torture, mutilation … it just isn't right."

If anything, Mortals would be just as capable of this kind of horrifying act as Others, and they both knew it. Ryder raised one eyebrow. "Tell me you're kidding." He pushed past Lykar in order to leave the study.

"The Council thinks it is unusual. Something they have never seen before. They are worried the Tribunal will get involved." Ryder snorted at Lykar's ominous pronouncement. It is problematic, Ryder thought. But with his mind set, he would not get involved. "The Council does nothing these days unless it benefits them."

"The last victim was only fourteen." Lykar's voice dropped low and solemn, making Ryder hesitate for just a fraction of a second before slamming through the door and into the hall. Lost innocence no longer affected him; the emotion of sentimentality is something an imMortal Tracker shouldn't dwell on.

He didn't want to get involved. Why did it have to be him? "Because," his conscience whispered, "Max asked for you."

"You are the only one who is capable of tracking this." Max's proclamation haunted him.

The last victim had only been fourteen, way too young to have her life snuffed in such a brutal manner. Could it be a Mortal? Or an Other? Five women in three months. It could be a serial killer. He tried to pull the cold-hearted warrior back into place. Nevertheless, he faltered, leaving him swearing at himself for caring.

"Son of a bitch." Ryder slammed a fist into the wall, leaving a gaping hole in the paneled wood. Lykar opened the door of the study and looked from the hole in the wall and back to Ryder. A smile played at the corner of his lips.

"Where is Marlee?"

"Just sent her a text. She'll meet you at the airport."

"Of course she will." Ryder rolled his eyes, his annoyance ratcheting up a few notches. "If this is some reckless Mortal serial killer, I'm going to tear him to shreds and feed him to Marlee."

"Whatever." Lykar shrugged. "Just take care of it before the Tribunal gets involved. There are several different communities of Others in the region."

Ryder glared at his brother. "And when have the lives of Mortals or Others meant anything to me?" Beside his brothers and a select few, Ryder couldn't give a rat's ass for anyone else. His brothers often accused him of not having a heart, but it had never paid off to be sentimental, so he just didn't bother with it.

Lykar stopped him as he headed up the stairs. "Um, by the way, Marlee isn't happy about this, with the full moon only having been last night. Also, my information says the Council is sending someone else in. If the Council picked him, whoever he is won't be able to tie his own shoes without help, so I wouldn't worry about him. Just be aware you might not be alone."

"No shit," Ryder muttered, more to himself than to Lykar. Stopping halfway up the stairs, he said, "Tell me why you aren't doing this."

Lykar gave him a serious look, "'Cause, bro, you're the best."

Yeah he never failed to complete a track, never brought feelings or emotion into play. If it defined him as heartless, he could live with it. He did his tracks with skill and precision, no feelings involved.

Kyra sat for several minutes after she'd pulled over, waiting for the Honda VTX to cool. She listened and she hadn't liked what she heard whispered on the breeze. The air barely rustling within the trees, as if in doing so the trees themselves would be punished. Evil hung in the air like the blade of a guillotine, hovering moments before its plummet through silent air toward its victim's fragile throat.

Kyra swung one leg over the seat of her motorcycle and looked out into the woods, the trees so dense she could see only several feet into the forest before it closed in, hiding its secrets from peering eyes. The overhanging trees and thick moss covering rocks and roots shrouded the malevolence like a blanket.

She planted her feet into the dirt path and soaked up the senses of the earth below her, taking several deep breaths, trying not to gag from the filth suspended in the air.

Kyra focused all her Elemental powers, blocking out the sounds of screams and the smell of old and fresh blood.

The surrounding air started to whisper to her, she shuddered at the pain it emanated there. So much pain and loss, years, even centuries choked her. Whoever had perpetrated the killings chose well. This forest thrived on the darkness and secrets held within its shadows. Surroundings where murder and pain had been committed unfettered.

Kyra gazed through the thick branches. The sun just peeking through the shroud of branches, creating a halo of light in the exact spot where she stood. She tilted her face up to the sun soaking up the light, pulling it into her chest and deep into her soul. It fueled her power and chased the shadows away.

Holding her hands out, she felt a shiver pass over her as she phased into a smoky and mist. A power Air Elements had. They gave her the ability to flow with the breeze over the rough earth, letting the air and gentle wind take her where she needed to be. It pulled her forward around and through some trees, the path uncertain. The air she floated on stopped suddenly. Cold air tickled her nose, sending chills down her spine as she came to a halt.

Her feet settled into the earth as she rematerialized, her biker boots sinking into the moist soil. Everything in her recoiled she wanted nothing more than to pull her feet back as visions of what had passed assaulted her. Shadows of things done: clips, whispered screams, mumbled pleas, and vindictive horrifying laughter, both male and female. Frightening and unclear, without any substance, the horror of it churned her stomach. Kyra was shocked at the state of the problem facing her, it was Other, but now what? Visions assaulted her; she felt the horrors happening to her. Unable to control herself, she doubled over and retched into the bushes, adding to the damage already done to the area. Swearing, she spat and wiped the back of her hand over her mouth. Still nothing moved. Even the air held its breath.

This type of action wouldn't go unnoticed for long by Mortals or the Tribunal. Kyra didn't have a lot of time to get information back to the other Elemental Enforcers and the

Council. She soaked it up, committing it to memory for her report.

Kyra had learned darkness and a brutalizing type of death would taint a place, would steal the air and life. She looked up through the shadows, trying to find a shred of light. To feed her starved Elemental senses.

"What did this?" she asked the shadows, not expecting an answer. Darkness held and kept its secrets.

When a Shade appeared, Kyra stepped back in surprise, stumbling. The Shade's transparent body bled through the bushes Kyra had just emptied her stomach into. "He comes!" the Shade shrieked, pointing toward the woods behind Kyra. Kyra covered her ears, the shriek loud and overpowering.

Kyra shook herself and examined the woman in front of her. She wore a long white dress, which meant she could be lingering from one hundred years ago, or one of the latest victims. Shades seldom shared why they lingered in the Mortal plane. They differed from ghosts, which held memories of people and how they had died. Shades, on the other hand, had substance, knew they no longer lived. However, something about this Shade made the small hairs at the base of Kyra's neck stand on end.

She looked over her shoulder in the direction the Shade had pointed. Reaching out with her Elemental senses, she sensed something, but couldn't place it. Human or Other? At its current distance, it wouldn't be a threat. Trying to ignore the Shade Kyra moved past her to continue to look for evidence.

Angered the Shade stepped in front of Kyra. "You must run," she wailed, pulling at her curled brown hair hanging in waves around her shoulders. Kyra reached forward and put her hand into the chest of the screeching woman.

"Who did this to you?" Kyra asked the apparition she closed her eyes trying to see what secrets the Shade held. Images assaulted her, nothing she could focus on. Nothing to give her any idea of who or what had happened. Just snatches of pain and dissolution.

"Run!" the Shade screamed, making Kyra jump back in surprise. The Shade shoved her farther into the bushes. Kyra yelped in pain as she fell back into a thick bush, the small branches scratching at her face and neck as she fell back landing on her back.

"Bloody freaking hell," Kyra cursed. Rolling out from beneath the bush, she froze. All her Elemental senses going haywire: the nonhuman, non-Other entity she had sensed miles away now stood in the clearing ahead of her. Power radiated from whatever stood within killing distance to her. Kyra knew this meant trouble. She remaindered herself there happened to be a murderer in the woods, and she may have just stumbled onto whatever it might be.

Taking shallow breaths, Kyra steeled herself before looking up. Several yards in front of her stood the largest man she'd ever seen. Short dark hair cut close to his scalp, shoulders so broad, Kyra would be unable to wrap her arms around him and touch her fingers in the back. He looked as if he could snap her in half without even trying. Jean-clad legs spread wide in a fighting stance. A black t-shirt stretched over a broad chest. He radiated power, control, and deadly intent.

Kyra pushed herself to her feet and stood and palming the Glock strapped to her back. She didn't pull it out, but if the man made one move toward her, she had no qualms about firing it into his beautiful face. He may not be Mortal, but that didn't necessarily mean imMortal. The way he looked at her made her want to shoot first and ask questions later.

"Who are you?" He tilted his head at her in such an animalistic way, it gave Kyra the chills.

"Who are you?" she fired back.

He stared at her with black eyes, nostrils flaring. Recognition tickled at the back of her mind, but she pushed it aside. Trying to figure out what type of creature he was didn't rank at the top of her list.

Kyra scrambled trying to figure out what to do next. "Can I help you?" she asked in her most adult voice, a voice her brother Eric always laughed at.

A low growl surged from deep within his chest, raising the hackles on the back of her neck. When he did speak, it rumbled, like a thunder cloud. "I only ask once." He stepped forward, sucking up all the air between them; Kyra couldn't control her involuntary step back.

If her brother Eric could see her now, he would laugh his ass off. She couldn't remember the last time she'd backed away from anything, Mortal or otherwise. But damn, the guy stood six and a half feet tall and just as broad. Muscles no guy outside of a bodybuilding room should have rippled as he rolled his shoulders. It looked like an involuntary movement. And then he took a breath, drawing in the smells of everything around him. His eyes narrowed as if making up his mind about her. By the look he gave her she had somehow come up on the losing side.

Kyra planted her feet and squared her shoulders, refusing to move another step back. She didn't know of a creature capable of moving with his speed he had moved up on her without her notice nothing she knew of had that type of ability. She reached out again and faltered when she felt a Lycan moving in fast on their location. Kyra wished she had received a proper invitation to the party this had turned out to be. The only question? Whose side would the Lycan be on? Kyra would bet it wouldn't be hers. It was just the way her day had gone.

Fiona had sent Kyra to find out all she could and bring back information to the Druid Council. The mission did not include stopping the killings. This was to be a simple fact-finding mission. What could be easier? She felt the need to kick something. Why did things just not work out the way they should? The way Kyra wanted them to?

She had been sent to gather information and bring it back to the Enforcers, and then a plan would be made. Kyra hadn't come to fight, but didn't mean she would back down from a fight if cornered. After all, she had been raised as an Elemental Enforcer. It didn't mean she could retreat until she better understood her foe. It just meant living to fight another day. And she hadn't come to cause more unnecessary deaths. Especially her own.

"So, would you like to tell me what you're doing here?" she asked, trying to decide if she would shoot him or not. Maybe it would help decipher what type of creature he was. Most importantly, whether or not he could be killed.

The thought whizzed through her brain just as the Lycan stepped through the trees, freezing Kyra in absolute shock. Kyra shook her head, sure she was seeing things. The Lycan, stood around six feet tall, wore skinny jeans, a tight T-shirt which read "I'M THAT BITCH" printed in black across her ample chest, and red stilettos, the heels sinking into the soft earth. She relaxed into a casual stance looking like she totally belonged, as if everyone dressed in such attire while tracking and killing helpless women. Kyra wondered how the hell she traversed the soft earth with those shoes. The Lycan stood with her hands on her hips and looked from Kyra to the man. She didn't look happy. Kyra could smell the irritation rolling off the woman. Unhappy didn't begin to encompass the Lycan's feelings.

"Ry?" the Lycan asked, her painted lips taking on a practiced pout. It made Kyra want to rub her beautiful face in the dirt. Nobody should look as good as this Lycan did.

"Shut up," the man growled. The Lycan bristled, but closed her mouth.

"He keeps you on a short leash, doesn't he?" Kyra asked, knowing Lycan's had very short fuses. Getting this one riled up would be an easy task and a perfect distraction.

Kyra barely telegraphed his launch as he growled low, sending shivers up her spine. She phased out just in time, but still felt the breath of his hands close around her shoulders. When she reappeared several feet back, the woman hunched down into an attack pose, her breathing heavy. Her red fingernails dragging in the soft earth.

"What are you?" the man asked.

"What are *you*?" Kyra threw back.

"I'm your worst nightmare," he said, crossing his arms over his chest. Nightmare isn't the category she would put him in. His voice resonating deep in her chest. The saner side of her brain marked him dangerous as hell, but she wouldn't classify him in the nightmare category.

Kyra let the corners of her mouth turn up. "Cliché' much? Besides I've been told something similar before but ..." She raised a palm to the sky in a shrug. "I just don't seem to scare easily."

"I'm really going to enjoy killing you," the woman snarled.

"I could say the same to you." Kyra didn't even turn to look at the woman, keeping all her attention on the large man several feet away.

Kyra hated to disappoint the woman, but she didn't have any plans on dying today, or any other day. Instead Kyra pulled her gun out from behind her and pointed it at the woman, her eyes steady on the man.

"My silver bullets say otherwise, sweetheart, so back the hell off."

The Lycan bared her teeth. "I don't believe you." She glared at Kyra before exchanging a look with the man they shared a moment of silent conversation before the Lycan stepped back still growling.

Kyra heard the growl and shook her head as she pulled the trigger, planting a bullet into the dirt within an inch of the Lycan's left hand. The show of dominance died a quick death as the Lycan realized Kyra did, in fact, have silver bullets in her gun. When you dealt with imMortals of all kinds on a daily basis, you always came prepared for a fight. Silver could hurt and kill a substantial number of Others. Kyra refused to shoot any other kind of bullet.

"Short leash," Kyra said, again wanting to keep the Lycan on edge because she didn't yet understand the man in front of her. She needed to keep the pieces of this puzzle moving, and keeping the Lycan pissed would be a good start. As long as she kept the pieces moving, she had different plans for escape. Once the pieces stopped moving, she hoped to be in an advantageous position.

"Kill her now," the Lycan snarled between her teeth. Kyra wondered if she would start foaming at the mouth soon if the man didn't make a move of some kind.

"Are you the one who has been killing the women?" he asked Kyra using a voice which bounced off the inside of Kyra's skull, making her want to run screaming into the woods. She blinked refocusing on the man in front her. What the hell? She wanted to spill her guts about everything she had seen in her mind's eye since arriving in the cursed place. Kyra shook her head again and blinked. Clamping her mouth shut around her traitorous tongue, drawing blood in the process.

"What are you?" Kyra asked, her voice sounding weak even to her.

"I'm the one asking the questions. And if you'll remember, I only ask once. So if you want to answer my questions, now would be a good time." He leveled the words at her, his black eyes swirling with gray. His words burned into her brain like lava. Kyra felt each word as if it was being etched in her the small lines of her brain making her wince in pain.

The hand holding her gun started to shake and she feared dropping it. Something trickled from her nose, and she realized she was losing this battle. The pieces of the puzzle screeching to a sudden and furious halt. Kyra glared at her two unknown opponents, before using everything she had left to Shift away. Reappearing next to her bike, she wiped the blood from her face and pulled on her helmet.

What type of creature had those abilities? Kyra thought as she climbed onto her bike and took off.

She searched her brain for a species with the power to control someone with voice. But her head hurt and she could barely keep her bike on the road. Nothing came to mind, which only pissed her off more. It disappointed her that this situation would require a call to Fiona for further information before moving forward.

The question seemed to taunt her as she drove down the road, ignoring the posted signs. Kyra felt the urge to wrap her bike around a pole. She had either just made contact with whatever had been killing the women here, or she had stumbled onto something else. She hoped it would be the latter. If these two were the ones doing the killings, Kyra didn't know if she had enough fire power on her own to stop them.

"You need to get the hell out of there," Fiona barked into the phone so loud, Kyra almost dropped it. The fact that Fiona was freaked out spurned Kyra into action. She grabbed her saddlebags and threw everything she had into them.

"What is he?" Kyra asked as she packed.

"Tracker," Fiona said, but the word froze Kyra in her steps.

"But Trackers are extinct." Kyra breathed the words. She scrambled through everything she knew about Trackers, everything she had learned while in training, which was little. The things she did know, they had an extraordinary sense of taste, touch, and smell.

"The only species with voice compulsion are Trackers. And not even all of them have that ability. I believed them to have died out several thousand years ago." The last Fiona mumbled more to herself.

"You can't fight him alone," Fiona said.

"Have they been known to be murderers? Monsters who would kill helpless women?" Kyra asked.

"I will need to do some further research. Get moving and come home now." She grabbed her bag at Fiona's rushed words and headed for the door. "How long until you are a safe distance?" She barked.

Based on the limited knowledge she had about Trackers, Kyra knew she wouldn't be able to hide or get away from him. She only hoped she hadn't been in contact with him long enough for him to get her scent. Maybe he wouldn't be able to track her because of her ability to Shift. You can't track something that's not there, right?

"How long?" Fiona asked again. To Fiona, it would mean enough of a distance so the Tracker couldn't locate Kyra.

"Give me twenty-four hours. If I need to, I'll ditch the bike and take a plane."

"Ditch the bike and get on the damn plane. Forgo everything else. Just get back to the Haven." Her urgency made Kyra's head pound harder.

"I'm going, I'm going." Kyra threw her bag over her shoulder and headed for the door.

With one hand on the doorknob and the other holding the phone, she was lifted off her feet as the door and part of the wall exploded, it picked her up and threw her into the opposite wall of the motel room behind her. She rolled to her side, gasping for air and getting a lung full of smoke and debris.

"What the fuck?" Debris, smoke, and fire rained down all around her. She covered her face and head with her arms.

"Kyra?" Fiona screamed from the phone but rubble and dust made it impossible for Kyra to see where the phone had landed. "KYRA?"

"Do I get to kill her now?" a female voice asked from somewhere over her head.

"Fuck." Kyra muttered, pulling out one of her guns. She pointed it into the thick smoke, waving it around as she tried to pick out movement. But the edges of her vision started to get fuzzy. She blinked, forcing herself to stay conscious.

"No, not until we have the information we need," the male from the woods said, somewhere to her right. Kyra scrambled back, hoping the smoke and remnants of the room would camouflage her, hoping for the few more seconds it lasted, they would be as blind as she.

She watched as two figures emerged from the dusty plume. Kyra didn't hesitate to pull the trigger, and bullets flew at the couple. Her aim off, the three shots went in different directions, going left when they should've gone right. She shook her head again trying to hone in on her attackers.

The male shook his head in disgust. "The room is on fire. Get her out of here."

Kyra snorted smoke and coughed. "No shit, Sherlock. You just blew a hole the size of a train into my room. I hear explosions cause fire." She snapped lowering her guns as her vision blurred again.

The Lycan kicked the gun out of Kyra's hand and leaned down so they were face to face. "Hello again."

"Fuck you," Kyra spat. At least now every part of her body felt as miserable as her head.

"Tsk, tsk. It will go so much better for you if you just stay quiet," the woman said, placing her index finger against Kyra's lips. She pressed until Kyra tasted blood, proving she and her freaky ass companion had complete control. "Now isn't that better?"

Kyra kept her mouth shut, instead glaring at the woman. The Lycan stood and arched a perfectly shaped brow at her companion. "If looks could kill."

"You'd have died a hundred years ago," he quipped before bending down and picking up Kyra. He leaned her against the wall. Kyra couldn't hear Fiona screaming from the phone any longer and new the old Druid had stopped to listen, to gather any information she could. Fiona never stopped when one of the Elements could be in danger. It defined who she was.

"Are you going to come with us?" the male asked. His voice vibrated over her skin and sunk deep into her brain. At the moment, she would do anything if he would never ever use compulsion on her again.

As she no longer seemed to be in control, Kyra clamped her mouth shut. If the Lycan didn't want her to speak, she would keep quiet.

"Have it your way." He leaned close and whispered the next part into her ear, making her shiver for a different reason. "But remember I told you, I only ask once." She didn't see what knocked her out. But blackness swept up and swiftly consumed her. Kyra welcomed it, sinking into oblivion.

Chapter 2

Marlee's neck popped audibly as she rolled it. "What do we do with her?" She asked Ryder waving smoke from her face. Her glossy red fingernails waving in the air like a beckon.

Ryder looked down at the unconscious woman. They needed to find somewhere quiet and secluded to question her. Taking her back to the house Max had set up for them was out of the question. By the sounds of the commotion coming from outside of the room, time was running out to go around unnoticed.

"Let's get the hell out. I hear sirens." He didn't like the big show of busting through the door like they had. He was sure a knock would have sufficed. Marlee, however, had refused. Said she needed to release some frustration. Now, though, he was second-guessing the idea. The motel was on fire. If they got caught, they'd have a lot of explaining to do. And Max was not going to be happy.

He flung the woman over his shoulder. She moaned, and the sound went straight to his groin. He almost dropped her on her head. Ignoring his reaction for the moment, he settled the woman over his shoulder, grabbed her bags, and headed for the door. "Don't forget her guns." He was glad she had been packed it would save them the trouble of having to clean up after her. Now they could just walk away.

People were starting to gather, murmuring about the scene. Several were on cell phones—just what he didn't want. Ryder took several steps and realized nobody had looked their way. He was a large man, and although he did everything possible to go unnoticed, his height and bulk made him stick out.

Maybe the woman had a charm on her to draw attention away? She was turning out to be full of tricks. He had never met an Other or Mortal with the ability to withstand his compulsions. He looked at her sideways and wondered what type of creature she was. She didn't smell like anything he'd ever come across before. Again, another shot of lust went straight to his groin as he inhaled her scent, making him stumble.

He took a deep breath and cemented her smell to memory, trying to make it not affect him sexually. She smelled like a refreshing clean breeze with a muskiness that was all her and unlike anything he had ever smelled before. Although she had disappeared into thin air in the woods, it hadn't been hard to follow her scent. She smelled incredible and it wasn't a smell he was going to forget anytime soon.

He tossed her in the back seat of the car and slammed the door. Glad body contact was over with. "She doesn't look like a killer to me," Ryder said as he climbed behind the wheel. Taking advantage of the fact that nobody was paying any attention to them.

Marlee climbed into the passenger seat backwards and leaned over the seat to look at their new passenger. "What does a killer look like? 'Cause she looks better than the demon we took out down in Fiji." Marlee swung back around and pulled a pack of gum from an inside pocket. She chomped on it, loud, the way she did everything else with a zeal that left people dazed. If gave him a headache. He often took all her gum away from her but no matter what he did, Marlee always seemed to end up with a new pack.

"Ew." Her mouth formed a perfect 'O'. "How about the crazed vampire in South Africa? Or the pygmy in Mexico? Now *that* thing looked like a killer." *Chomp, chomp.*

The last thing he needed was to rehash all their past Tracks. "Can we just concentrate on the job at hand?"

"We can't take her back to the house." *Chomp, chomp.*

Ryder took a steadying breath. He was not going to fight with Marlee. "I saw a cabin up in the mountains. Let's take her there. In case we have to dispose of her, we won't be doing it in Max's territory."

He was surprised when Marlee shut her mouth and leaned back resting her head against the headrest it was her way of saying she agreed with his plan. Marlee always had an

25

argument ready, but she just nodded and leaned her head back and closed her eyes. Within minutes, her even breathing told him she was sound asleep. Ryder shook his head and wondered why he took the Lycan with him anywhere? Half the time, she was a loose cannon, the other half a raging bitch. Yet when it came to getting something done, she was spot on. And according to her, dealing with her other shit was just an added bonus.

The woman in the back seat moaned again. Ryder adjusted the mirror so he could see her. Even from the front seat, he could see long lashes that swept over her high, rounded cheekbones. Dressed in black leather from neck to ankle, she looked like a wet dream. A long, strawberry-blond braid stretched down her back, though half of it had come undone and splayed across the seat. He had dealt with some of the worst creatures in the world, and she didn't look or act as if she was capable of murdering anyone. There were a lot of things he could imagine about this beauty, but killing like they had come across? She couldn't be responsible.

Ryder knew she must be one the Council had sent. If she had just cooperated with him in the beginning, none of this needed to happen and they could be working together. Instead he had blown the motel to bits and knocked her unconscious in the process. He was making a wonderful first impression.

Why should he care what type of impression he was making? If she was with the Council, he doubted she would want to work with him now. On the contrary, if she were the killer, he wouldn't hesitate to do what needed to be done. It was what he did. And nobody could argue that he was anything but excellent at what he did. She moaned again and he caught himself hoping that she wasn't the killer.

When Kyra was able to put two thoughts together, she realized one truth right away: everything hurt. It might have to do with the fact that someone was shaking the hell out of her. Kyra felt each move with a jarring that made her teeth rattle.

"Ack," she moaned, trying to throw her hands out to stop whoever was shaking her. Alas, her hands were bound. Not a good sign.

"I'm awake," she said in an attempt to stop the shaking.

Water splashed into her face. She spat and peeled her eyes open. "Good freaking hell! Stop already!"

"What's your name?"

Kyra looked toward the voice and into black, emotionless eyes that sent a shiver down her spine. She squinted and tried to remember what was going on. How the hell had she had gotten here? Something bounced around in her brain painfully.

"Kyra." The answer to his question tumbled out before she could stop it.

"What's going on? Where am I?" she asked, her voice as weak as she felt.

"Who are you?" he asked.

"You're breaking your rules." Where the hell had that come from? Kyra stared at the man. Blinking she tried to remember where she knew him from, but she came back blank. He growled, the sound so menacing, it took her breath away.

She bit her tongue, knowing she wasn't supposed to answer his questions, even though her tongue and lips moved to form words.

"What are you?" she asked instead, wishing she hadn't when the pain cracked through her skull like a lightning bolt.

Someone backhanded her. She let her head fall to the side, instantly dizzy and sick to her stomach. She heaved but nothing came out, causing her head to ache more. Which she honestly didn't think was possible.

"Don't hit her," came from the male voice.

"Since when do you care about how we get answers?" a woman asked.

"Just don't hit her again."

"Why were you in the woods today?" he asked. Though his voice was gentler, his words still bounced around inside her skull, making mincemeat of any coherent thought. The only thing that made sense was that she had to answer him.

Kyra focused on the large man, blinking several times. She tried to figure out exactly what had happened to her.

"Shit, Fiona and Eric are going to blow a gasket." She said instead of an answer.

"How the hell is she doing that?" the female screeched the sound causing lightening sharp pain to shoot right through her skull. "What type of creature is able to withstand your compulsion?"

The man grunted and leaned down. Kyra breathed, trying to figure out what was going on. How she'd come to be where she was. The last thing she could remember was waking up in the motel.

She looked at the man standing over her. She had to admit that it looked as if she had been compromised. For the love of all the Gods, she wished she could remember what had happened. She shook her head again ignoring the pain.

"What did you do to me?" she muttered, spitting out blood from biting her own tongue.

Were these the ones who were killing the women in the woods? If so, why was she hog-tied and being questioned? None of this made any sense.

A stunning woman knelt down, and into her line of vision. She turned Kyra's face into the light, and muttered something Kyra didn't quite hear. "I think you knocked her on the head a little too hard, Ry. What is the last thing you remember?" she asked Kyra still holding her chin up.

"Waking up in my motel room." She thought for a moment. Closed her eyes and concentrated. "It was Thursday morning."

The woman laughed, but there was no humor in the sound. "Yep. A little too hard, and the mind-fuck shit you do has turned her day to dust. Great job, big guy." She released Kyra and stood patting the man on one broad shoulder.

The man's voice rumbled low and the sound moved around her like thunder. "Why were you in the motel room?"

His questions were starting to get old. And the fact that she wanted nothing more that to spit out the answers to everything he asked was starting to piss her off.

"Because it was the room I rented when I came to town," she said with as much sarcasm as her screaming head would allow. "To sightsee." She threw in just to irritate them.

The man pulled one of her guns out from behind him. "You always sightsee with a loaded Glock?"

Kyra forced the pain aside and smiled. "A girl can never be too careful. Safety first," she said in a singsong fashion, even though it cost her, pain shooting through her body.

The woman laughed and flicked her in the forehead with one long red painted nail. "You're a smart one, aren't you?" She threw glossy pictures into Kyra's lap. Kyra looked down and felt bile rise in the back of her throat. They were pictures she had seen already—pictures of a young woman who'd been mutilated, the fifth killing in the last couple of months. Fiona knew there were no solid leads.

Kyra's intel said that the Tribunal hadn't yet been notified. It was getting to the point where they would find out, and that was what she was trying to avoid. When the original Intel had come, it had been assumed that it was rogue Lycan or escaped Demon. Because it was an Other, it was being kept as quiet as possible. This was a need-to-know-basis issue. Looking at the large man and his beautiful sidekick, Kyra was pretty sure neither was on her list of the need-to-know.

In fact, Fiona hadn't wanted to get involved at all, but a small group of Druids lived in these mountains. If the Tribunal started poking around, the very existence of those Druids was on the line. The Elemental Enforcers had worked for centuries to keep the Druids and other Elements under the radar. They weren't about to let that all go now.

She shifted her legs and let the pictures fall to the floor. "What do you want?" She wasn't going to pretend she didn't know about the murders. It wasted time. She reached out with her senses and recognized the female as a Lycan, but the male?

He was something all together different. He exuded pure power Kyra couldn't place. Something tickled at the back of her brain, but her head hurt so much, she couldn't pin it down.

The male leaned down and pierced her with his black-gray eyes. "If you are the creature doing this, say so now, and I will kill you swiftly. Despite what you did to those women," he said as he pressed her own gun to her temple.

Kyra wondered how many people he had given that ultimatum to. How many had taken it and been granted a quick and easy death. She trembled, thinking of what this large, muscular man was actually capable of.

Something flickered over her vision. She shook her head. "Just give me a second," Kyra pleaded with her best damsel-in-distress voice. "I'm not the person you're looking for." She wasn't, but neither was she willing to give out anything that she should not. Her brain felt like scrambled eggs. She just needed a minute to try and piece together what the hell was happening, how the hell she had ended up here so she could get the hell out.

He stood and moved off with the Lycan. As they whispered in the corner, Kyra focused her thoughts on the room they were in. She closed her eyes and concentrated, tendrils of her Elemental powers flowing from her into the room. She felt the air whisper across the skin on her neck. A draft from behind her, and the air smelled fresh and clean, with wet moist earth. It was smell she recognize as woodsy. They were in the woods. That didn't bode well for her; those women had all died in the woods, torn apart like animals. Her powers snapped back in reflex to her sudden anxiety.

Kyra opened her eyes and looked at the two individuals in the corner, their heads bent in conversation. If she wasn't the killer, it was possible that these were the killers. A chill worked down her spine.

Kyra felt the air movement around the room and with her abilities; she was able to picture in her head the exact layout of the room. She exhaled, releasing some of her tension. Understanding her surroundings comforted her.

Now to figure out what had gone so horribly wrong with her day? Kyra reached back in her mind to when she had woken up. Remembered the feel of the scratchy carpet beneath her feet as she climbed out of bed.

Out of the blue, the image was overlaid with the woods and blood and carnage. She shook her head, trying to remember. She saw an explosion in her motel room. The man standing over her seemed to be tattooed on the back of her eyelids. She examined him, taking note of everything. He was one of the largest men she'd ever seen. And sexy as hell. She wondered what he would feel like under her hands, his muscular chest and strong arms holding her close.

Forcing that thought away, she took a steadying breath and peeked her eyes open. A possible concussion from the explosion in her motel room would explain some of her memory loss.

She focused for a moment on her feet and was happy to see her right foot Phase. She was regaining some of her abilities. She looked around. If she could figure out where she was, she could Shift out. But the power was a hindrance as much as a gift. Without knowing where she was and where she could end up, her ability to Shift was useless. And Phasing only got her so far. Kyra closed her eyes and focused again on the smells of the room. She could smell the Lycan. If she wasn't mistaken, and she seldom was, she was a Wer but not a warrior class, which was good for Kyra. The Wer Warriors tended to kill first and ask questions later.

The male, Kyra couldn't place. She smelled the air that drifted around him, drawing it in so she would be able to sense him in the future. He smelled like old leather and something animalistic and utterly male, she couldn't help but be drawn into his smell.

As an Air Element, she smelled things that most people missed and this man's smell enthralled her. She felt swallowed by it, as it settled deep in the pit of her stomach, spreading through her bloodstream like warm honey. She tried to push past his smell, but it held her like a vise grip. Kyra took a couple cleansing breaths. Tucking his smell into her memory for later.

Shaking her head, Kyra refocused herself, only to feel something dark surround her. Like an invisible cloud it wrapped itself around her. She would've gasped for air if she could move, but she froze. Now superimposed over the small room a vision of the clearing became evident. A Shade stood several feet from her, dark hair blowing in the breeze. The smell of death and the destruction of souls swirled around Kyra making her gag. She reeled back from the stench and the Shade.

The two in the corner stopped talking. However, they were a peripheral substance just outside her line of vision as the Shade and the clearing took shape.

"He's coming," the Shade whispered, the breeze almost stealing the words.

"Who?" Kyra asked.

"He's coming." The Shade turned and looked in the direction of the Lycan and the man still in the corner of the room. The hair on Kyra's arms stood on end as the woman turned back to her.

"It's too late he is here." The words were torn from the Shade. Pain and fear flavored the air of Kyra's vision as the Shade reached out. Her pale hand extended toward Kyra, the flesh falling away. The bones elongated into sharp talons, reaching forward to sink into Kyra's chest.

Kyra yelped and Phased as the fingers pierced her chest, and she tumbled back Phasing through the chair and her bonds. Gasping for air, she landed on her butt behind the chair. She kicked and scrambled back as the Shade flickered above her. Eyes glowing, a glimmer of something passed through the dark depths of the Shades eyes.

Ryder blinked a couple of times. The woman had turned to mist and sunk right through the chair, landing with a grunt on the floor, her bonds undone.

"Holy crap," Marlee gasped. "She pulled that damn trick in the woods. What creature has that ability?"

Ryder grabbed Marlee before she could leap on their captive. The woman lay on the floor, gasping for air. They'd been trying to decide what to do with her when her eyes had gone from blue to silver. She'd looked around the room, as if seeing something different, and then yelped and misted out.

He walked over to her and kneeled down. The time for answers had come. She had a terrified look on her face and scooted away from him, as if the devil stood at his back.

"What the hell just happened?" he used compulsion.

"Tracker." Trackers were close-knit and associated with very few people. After thousands of years, they were nomads and mercenaries. To know of the Trackers meant you knew too much. If she knew what he was, she wouldn't be walking out of this cabin. Especially if she could ignore his compulsion. She didn't know it, but it sealed her fate. Ryder hesitated for just a moment; he didn't want to see her hurt. That thought alone drove him to act. He didn't let himself care, caring was for fools.

He exploded to his feet and pulled the gun from its holster at his waist. Aiming for the middle of her forehead he pulled the trigger. She misted out again and the bullet went right through her, embedding in the floor where her head had been. He pulled the trigger again and again, and each time she avoided it by turning into mist.

"Neat trick. Now tell me what the hell you are!" he shouted. The raw power of his compulsion bounced off the walls of the cabin and made the entire structure shake. Marlee groaned from behind him. Ryder kneeled on the floor, grasping Kyra on either side of her head. He looked deep into her blue eyes.

"Element," she moaned, blood trickling from her nose right before her eyes rolled into the back of her head.

"Element?" Marlee whistled from where she stood next to him. "They are about as mythical as you are."

"She isn't the killer," Ryder concluded. He had known Elements before. Over a thousand years ago, they were many things, and like any race, they had their bad apples. Their type of corruption, however, blackened the soul. Ryder would've been able to tell. Unlike Mortals, when an Element was evil, they exuded so much dark power, it poisoned everything around them. If she were a killer, he would've been able to sense it.

"Right, because the Elemental race is so pure and righteous," Marlee spat. "So now what? What would an Element be doing here?"

"She has to be the one sent by the Council." Ryder raked a hand over his short-cropped hair. If the Elements were getting involved, then things were much worse than they had thought. He pulled his phone from his pocket and dialed Max.

"Who else have you asked to come and look into this issue?" Ryder barked.

"No one. I wanted to keep it quiet," Max explained.

"Well, then, why the hell is there an Element lying unconscious at my feet?" Ryder looked down at the woman.

"A what?" Max asked, so incredulous Ryder knew he hadn't sent her. "Is she from the Council?"

The woman moaned and her eyes flickered open. "I'll call you back," Ryder snarled.

"Who sent you?" he asked, kneeling down so that he could look into her face. Blood ran from her nose. She wiped at it with the back of her hand. Her eyes were glazed over, more silver than blue. It turned her face almost angelic. Like at the motel, his damn body reacted to her.

"Fiona," was her only answer.

"Did the Tribunal send you?" The thought of them getting involved made Ryder's skin crawl. They would come in and kill everyone and everything.

"No, trying to keep it from the Tribunal," she moaned, looking him dead in the eye. Now that he knew what she was, he felt guilty for the pain he had inflicted upon her. A feeling as foreign to him as not knowing what she was. The whole

34

situation irritated the hell out of him. Add that to his body's reaction to her, and he felt at a total loss.

"The Tribunal must not find out." Her words were laced with pain. She sank back and closed her eyes, falling into unconsciousness again.

Ryder picked her up and placed her on the only bed in the small hunting cabin. He didn't go around looking for help, but if she was here to investigate the murders, he wouldn't turn down her assistance. Keeping her close felt right.

Besides, once this was done, everyone could go his or her separate ways without the Tribunal knowing any different. From what he knew of the Elements, they were as secretive about their existence as the Trackers.

As a general rule, he didn't pick up strays. Marlee had been the one exception to the rule, and some days, he even regretted that. But given what little he knew about the Elements, Blue here could be very useful in finding out what was going on. He just had to find a way to get her to work with him after everything he'd done to her. He ran a hand through his hair again. This wasn't going to be easy.

This time when she came to, she was lying on a bed. But she felt like hell. Swinging her legs over the edge, she tried to rise but dizziness swamped her. Kyra wavered for several seconds before sitting back down with a thump. She was going to need a few minutes before she did anything.

"Here. Drink this." The woman offered her a bottle of water.

Kyra couldn't even manage a nod as she took the bottle and swallowed a long swig before screwing the lid back on. She reclined on the bed and put the cold bottle on her forehead. "He really needs to never do that again," she muttered, more to herself than to the woman.

"Yeah, you could ask him to stop. Let me know how that goes for you." The other woman's sarcasm wasn't lost on Kyra.

"Who are you?" Kyra asked, ignoring the spike of pain it caused. She might not be a prisoner anymore, but she wasn't sure that they weren't the killers she had come looking for.

"Marlee."

"And him?"

"Ryder."

"Do you have my phone?"

"Nope."

Not much of a conversationalist, Kyra snorted. "This has been some kind of mistake. Just take me back to the motel and we can go our separate ways. If I don't call in soon, they will come looking for me."

Kyra was pretty sure that Fiona had already sent somebody for her. That didn't bode well for the Lycan. However, the Tracker, was a different story altogether. When Marlee chose not to respond, Kyra felt her anger ratchet up a notch.

Kyra didn't like being ignored. Despite the pain that swept through her, she pushed herself to her feet. At least she remembered what was going on now, which brought her very little comfort. She needed to go back to the motel and find out if any of her stuff had survived the explosion so she could call in. None of this should have happened. She shook her head, irritation coursing through her entire body.

When the female Shade appeared again, her talons extended, Kyra Phased out of the way not wanting to play this game again, as the Shade screamed, "He's coming!"

"Yeah, I've heard that one," Kyra said as she re-solidified a foot from the bed, her legs shaky.

The door swung open and Ryder stomped into the room, both guns drawn. Kyra felt a moment of panic. Was he going to shoot her again?

"Something is coming," he said to Marlee who narrowed her eyes and looked from Ryder back to Kyra.

Ryder noticed. "What's going on?" he looked from one to the other.

"She was just muttering to herself like a crazy person," Marlee said, pulling her own weapon out. She went to the window and moved the curtains aside.

"Do all Elements talk to themselves or are you special?" Ryder asked, tossing Kyra's guns on the bed. He walked through the wailing Shade as he crossed to her. "Point them at either me or Marlee, and I'll kill you."

She didn't know how he planned to do that since she was capable of eluding any weapon he branded against her. But the threat stuck, and for some reason, she knew he could do just that. But he had returned her guns so she decided to let the comment go for now.

She checked them, and then strapped them to her back. Feeling more like herself, she sat back down on the edge of the bed and closed her eyes. She forced herself to breath. In through her nose and out through her mouth. Quietly counting as she read the air surrounding her.

"What the hell is she doing now?" Marlee groused. Kyra ignored her. She didn't care if they thought she was mad as a hatter. She didn't need their approval. Kyra focused her breathing and tried to hone in on what was coming. Her head pounded in unison with her breathing. She cursed. Kyra could feel something just out of reach. It was blackness and evil and pissed as hell. But her head was pounding so hard, she couldn't focus.

Kyra opened her eyes and pierced Ryder. "Hey, asshole. Next time, mind-fuck someone else." She rose to her feet and drew her guns, wanting very much to kill something, though still unsure who the enemy was. At the moment, Ryder was at the top of her hit list. She had to admit—he was likely one of the good guys.

She threw open the door and stepped into the dark night. Being outside made her feel better, her Elemental abilities taking solace in the fresh air of the mountain. The cool breeze surrounded her like the comfort of an old friend. She drew in the clean air and felt her strength returning. The pain in her head started to recede and she walked toward the darkness approaching. The Shade fell into step beside her, screeching to bring down the heavens themselves.

Kyra held up a hand, hoping to stop the noise. "Yeah, yeah, he's coming. I got it." Kyra rolled her shoulders and glared at the woman. "Don't push me, sweetheart. I'm having a bad day."

The Shade continued to wail without so much as changing the pitch.

Kyra's mouth snapped closed. The air stilled and a unearthly quiet surrounded her. Not a single sound came from the woods. A shadow black as ink oozed from between the trees several yards away. She thought for a moment she might be seeing things, that the light was playing games. But she couldn't deny the blackness that now pooled and shaped itself into a man.

"I need my soul," it burbled, causing the Shade to waver in and out of sight. The shadow gurgled, the sound making bile rise in the back of Kyra's throat. It took several menacing rolls forward. Kyra had had just about enough.

"I don't think so." Kyra pointed one of her guns and fired into the black mass. She had no idea what it was or how to kill it. But it obviously hadn't showed up to wish her well, taking the offense she fired into the darkness. Her bullets caused the Shadow to bubble heartily. It dissolved, pooling in the dirt before re-solidifying so fast, she might've missed it if she'd blinked. Kyra stepped back as it advanced, and then it opened up and her bullets came flying back at her. One entered her shoulder before she could Phase out. It tore through the soft flesh, right through her shoulder. She screamed in pain.

"The soul," it bellowed, its mass growing as it moved forward.

Kyra Shifted back into the cabin. Ryder and Marlee stood with strange looks on their faces. "Don't shoot at it."

"No shit." Marlee rolled her eyes.

"Are you hurt?" Ryder asked.

Her arm was killing her, but she wasn't about to show either of them any weakness. They had already seen her weak. She wasn't going to give them another demonstration.

"I'm fine," she lied just as the shadow tore through the door. Teeth the size of her forearm ripped into the wood like it was paper, devouring what had been the front door and half of the front of the small cabin.

"It was promised to me!" it shouted.

The three of them scrambled to the back of the cabin.

"Now what?" Marlee barked over the sound of the mass of darkness now eating its way through the cabin to get at them.

"I think I might have pissed it off," Kyra admitted.

"What does it want?" Ryder snarled.

"Souls," Kyra said. Ryder and Marlee looked at her incredulously. She shrugged, causing pain to shoot up her arm and neck. "That's what it said."

"So you're on speaking terms with it?" Ryder asked.

"If you mean when it screams, 'Souls! Give me my souls!' and I happen to listen to it, then yes, we're on speaking terms," she replied sarcastically. She had never in her life wanted to hit another person as much as she wanted to hit Ryder at that moment. Instead Kyra searched for another way out of the cabin but they were backed into the corner with no escape.

"Well, it can't have mine. I'm not done with it yet," Marlee said, firing her gun into it.

Kyra flipped the one table over and hid behind it as Marlee's bullets whizzed back at them. "What part of don't shoot at it didn't you understand?" Kyra yelled.

"Time to leave," Ryder bellowed as the mass advanced. Kyra watched in shock as he kicked through the wall behind him, opening up a sizable hole. He grabbed Kyra and tossed her through like a rag doll. Marlee landed on top of her and he stepped through just as the mass attacked the table they had been hiding behind only moments before

Marlee bounded to her feet. Ah, to have the agility of an animal, Kyra thought.

"Where you planning on staying?" Ryder asked, picking her up by the collar of her leather jacket. He half dragged, half carried her to a car parked at the back of the cabin and then threw her into the backseat. Kyra had to admit; she was getting sick of being manhandled.

"Knowing you had an escape plan would have been nice." Kyra said pulling herself into a sitting position as Ryder climbed behind the wheel of the care.

"What did you think we walked here?" he asked.

Ryder jumped into the driver's seat, swearing. This was turning out to be a much larger problem than Max had explained. Turning the key, he slammed on the gas and watched from the rearview mirror as the inky blackness consumed the cabin before soaking back into the woods.

"What the hell was that?" Marlee asked.

"I have no idea. But I think we might've found what is killing the women here," Ryder said.

"I need a phone."

Ryder looked at the woman in the backseat and slammed on the brakes, causing Marlee to hurl uncontrollable forward and hit her head on the dashboard.

"What the fuck?" she shouted as Ryder climbed out of the car and pulled the first-aid kit from the trunk.

He climbed into the backseat. "You drive," he said to Marlee who was still rubbing her forehead.

"One of these days, I'm going to slam your head against something. Just you wait and see if I don't, you inconsiderate, heartless bastard. Remind me again, why I even stick around?" She snarled as she climbed behind the wheel.

"Let me see." Ryder hadn't realized how bad Kyra's wound was. She was bleeding pretty heavily and had to be in considerable pain she didn't show it. He had to give it to anyone who had that much control, considering everything he'd put her through.

"I'm fine." She moved, positioning herself as far from him as possible, her hand stuffed against her shoulder.

"I don't ask twice," he said, grabbing at her.

"Yeah, you mentioned that," she said, still refusing to move an inch toward him. "But you also broke that rule. If I remember correctly."

Ryder snarled and shook his head, "Don't make me do it again, Blue."

He wasn't going to play this game so he reached out for her. They ended up wrestling for a moment. In the end, he got her leather jacket off and ripped her T-shirt so he could get to her shoulder. By then, she was too busy trying to keep herself covered to fight off his first aid.

"You don't have anything I haven't seen before," he said, holding gauze to her wound. He pulled her forward and looked at the back of her shoulder. "It's a good thing it went right through. Otherwise, I'd have to dig it out."

She paled, and sweat beaded on her forehead and upper lip. "I'll heal, thank God."

"Elements are not immortal. How fast will you heal?" She would be no use to them if she was laid up with a gunshot wound.

"I'll be healed within a day." She looked at him, her blue eyes dark with pain. It was a color he had never seen before, something between dark blue and almost purple. He couldn't bring himself to look away. He gentled his movements as he cleaned the blood from her shoulder. He let his fingers graze over the top of her breast, soft as silk against the back of his fingers. Ryder couldn't stop himself from doing it again. She sucked in a breath and his eyes shot to hers. They were still that deep color but now silver ran in lazy swirls. He had to admit, it was one of the sexiest things he had ever seen. And he couldn't help but wonder what color they would turn when she was in the depths of passion.

She was the one to break the eye contact. And it took everything he had not to reach forward and pull her face back to his, to look into those eyes and sink into her. He wondered what color her eyes would be when he did that.

"Are you done?" she asked her voice icy. It made him smile because he could smell her attraction. Her pheromone level had surged, and damn if he didn't like the smell of her desire.

Marlee pulled him out of his lustful thoughts when she snorted from the front seat. She had the nose of a Lycan and she could probably smell what he smelled. "Do you want me to pull over?" she asked, giving him a conspiratorial look in the rearview mirror.

"Shut up," Ryder went back to dressing Kyra's wound, ignoring the knowing look Marlee leveled at him from the front seat. He made a point of keeping his hands to himself except to administer the medical treatment.

"Does it hurt?" he asked his voice gentler. Another snort from the front seat. Ryder slammed a boot into the back of the seat. Marlee bounced forward and into the steering wheel.

"Fuck you," she snarled and reached over the driver's seat to swat at him with her hand.

"The two of you have a very strange way of communicating," Kyra muttered moving so that Marlee's wildly swinging arm didn't hit her. Ryder was able to avoid her without even trying.

"Yeah, love to hate," Marlee groused.

"You should be fine, as long as it doesn't get infected." Ryder sat back and crossed his arms over his chest controlling the urge to reach over and gather her into his arms. What was this woman doing to him? He contented himself with just watching her as she tried to cover herself with the remnants of her shirt. Her smell had taken a dramatic turn from sensual to irritation. He marveled at the levels each emotion emitted. Her face said nothing, but her smell … Well, that was something altogether different.

"Upset?" he asked unable to stop himself.

Her head snapped up. Her blue eyes had turned to aqua. "Why would you ask that?"

"Because you look upset." For just a moment, he thought she was going to take a swing at him, which amused the hell out of him.

"Let me see…" Her voice dripped with sarcasm. "I've been knocked unconscious, had compulsion used on me until I passed out, shot, slapped, had water thrown in my face, tied up, and manhandled. Does that about cover it?" She ground her teeth together. "All in the span of twenty-four hours. Please excuse me for being just a little off." She ended her voice a higher pitch then when she started.

"Sorry about the slap. Sometimes my bitch comes out." Marlee shrugged from the front seat as if that would explain and apologize for her behavior. "Didn't know at the time whose side you were one. A girl can never be too careful, you understand." She threw Kyra's words back at her.

"And last but not least, attacked by a black shadow gurgling about souls, and shot with my own bullets. Upset doesn't begin to cover it." Kyra closed her eyes and took a deep breath, trying to envision being in the gardens at the Haven, walking with Eric. Instead, she got a whiff of the man taking up more space than he had a right to. She pushed the button to roll down the window and inhaled deep breaths of the cool night air that rushed in to surround her. She was in control, she said to herself, she said it several times hoping it was true.

Growling, she opened her eyes and glared at the man next to her. "Do you have a phone I can use?"

She tried not to notice how his muscles rippled or the way his hips thrust forward as he reached into his jeans pocket and pulled out his cell. Or the way he looked at her as he offered her the phone. Kyra told herself he wasn't giving her bedroom eyes. That he hadn't caressed her breast while he cleaned her shoulder. That he wasn't the sexiest thing she had ever seen on two legs. The sooner she saw the back of him the better. She probably had brain damage, and it was all his fault.

It was the only answer to the way she was reacting to him. Besides, there was just no way—after everything that had happened, no way he could be thinking about sex. But, every inch of him had the look about him and it infuriated her. She took the phone without touching him, and dialed Fiona.

"Where are you?" Fiona barked.

Kyra sighed and looked around. "I have no idea."

"About eight miles outside of Marshall," Ryder provided.

She glared at him. "About eight miles out of Marshall."

"I heard him," Fiona said, a little more calm in her voice. "Are you hurt?"

"Shot in the left shoulder, concussion, scrapes and bruises," she admitted. "For a fact-finding mission, this has turned into hell on wheels."

"I'm on my way. I should be there by midmorning," Fiona said without addressing her wounds. Kyra didn't expect anything different.

"Stay with him," Fiona said. She had to mean Ryder. Kyra turned to him. He'd leaned back and closed his eyes but wore a smile on his lips. She added excellent hearing to her list of Tracker abilities and another reason she hated him. The smug smile told her he'd heard every word that was being said.

"Why? What does the Tracker have to offer us?" Her words wiped the smile off Ryder's face. She didn't care if she was attracted to the man; he'd tried to kill her. Several times as a matter of a fact. Irritating him was a bonus she didn't know she didn't know she would enjoy.

"Just stay with him," Fiona said.

"I'll see you in a couple of hours," Kyra said, hanging up. She tossed the phone into Ryder's lap. "So, why so upset at the word Tracker?"

A vein started to tick at his temple, which, for some sinful reason, made her smile. What was wrong with her? She was usually so laid back and calm.

"We keep to ourselves, and when you say Tracker, it means that we aren't doing our job at staying below the radar."

His voice rumbled low, it vibrated through him and into the seat. She imagined she could almost hear his voice, and it was seductive as hell.

"I've never met a race that tried to kill someone for knowing who they were before." She didn't want him to forget that he had shot at her when she had first mentioned the word Tracker.

"That means you have never met a Tracker before. By the Way I apologize for shooting at you." He didn't even open his eyes as he spoke.

Kyra turned to watch the scenery. So much had happened in the last day. She tried to let everything sink in so she could process it. All she wanted at the moment was a shower and a place to sleep, though she doubted that a shower or nap was on her schedule anytime soon.

With Fiona coming, she would have the backup she needed. But that didn't mean there wouldn't be time for rest. She knew from past experience, rest was something that came after a mission was complete.

They pulled up to a small house just outside of town. "What are we doing here?"

"Home for now," Marlee said, climbing from the car.

"How long have you been investigating this?" she asked Ryder.

"Not long." Ryder climbed out of the car and slammed the door.

Kyra was torn between screaming and kicking that arrogant man's ass. Instead, she climbed from the vehicle, knowing she was stuck with them until Fiona showed up. Then she would never have to lay eyes on either one of them again.

Ryder watched her as she made her way to the house. She didn't quite walk as much as she glided, moving with a fluidity that hitched his breath in his chest, it was intoxicating to watch. He leaned against a tree trunk to do just that. More to the point, he needed a few minutes alone. Her smell had driving him nuts. He had been sitting in the back of that car in physical pain. He'd never smelled something that drew him in like her smell did. He had ignored it at first, thinking it was just his tracking skills kicking into overdrive. But all he wanted to do was smell her, taste her, and draw her essence into him. Which was a bad idea. She was a bad idea. Sexy as hell, but still a bad idea.

She was an Element, and they weren't the "fuck 'me and leave 'me" type. She was dangerous. If he had any brains in his head, he would avoid her as much as possible. Let her go with her other Elemental friends that were on the way and never look back.

Ryder closed his eyes and drew in the sweet scent of the clean mountain air. He tried to clear her out of his system. But no matter what he did, her smell lingered. Yep, he needed to put some distance between them.

So why was he trying to figure out a way to keep her around, just so he could have that smell with him more? He'd lost it. That was the only explanation.

Chapter 3

"So, what exactly was it?" Marlee asked for the hundredth time. As she paced in front of the desk where Ryder sat working on his laptop. She was anxious and it was wearing on everyone. Ryder and Kyra had stopped responding to her over an hour ago. It didn't seem to stop the Lycan from asking the same question.

Ryder was doing something on his laptop that had Marlee leaning over his shoulder every few minutes. Whatever it was seemed to appease her. Eventually, the bombshell got up and left the room.

"She talks a lot," Kyra said.

"And you don't talk enough," Ryder said, leaning back so that he could look at her. "What exactly was that back there?"

"Argh. You too? Why am I the one with the answers?" She shot to her feet and headed toward the door. Maybe she needed a break as well. "I have no idea what it is. And if that answer isn't good enough for you, you can go to hell."

Ryder stopped her before she made it out the door his words halting her in mid-step. "Why don't we work together on this? We're obviously trying to accomplish the same thing."

Kyra gave him a hard look. She couldn't figure out why he would even make the offer. After all, he'd tried to kill her. "Why do I have the feeling that you don't work well with others?" she asked.

"Elements are supposed to have died out a thousand years ago," he countered.

"Trackers even before that," Kyra said. "So two mythical creatures standing in the same room. What are the odds of that?"

He raised one cynical brow. "My point exactly. Whatever is in that mountain needs to be taken care of before the Tribunal comes in and wastes this entire region. Why not work together? We would both benefit from it, Blue."

"What did you just call me?" Her hands flew to her hips and she leaned forward as if she hadn't heard him. Fire shooting from her beautiful blue eyes.

"Blue. Your eyes," he shrugged.

"My name is Kyra. Kkkkkyyyyyrrrraaaa." She drew it out for him.

She didn't even see him move, and then she was pressed up against the door. His warm body pressed tightly against her. From chest to toes she felt every inch of him like a scalding shower raining down around her. She couldn't help but notice that they fit together almost too well. "I know your name, Blue. But I've come to realize I really like the color of your eyes, hence the Blue."

Kyra pressed on his chest, trying to get him to move. But it would've been easier to move the house itself. "Is there a point you're trying to make?"

Ryder leaned down and buried his face in her neck. "Yes," he murmured.

Kyra couldn't help it. Her head fell back to give him better access. She was rewarded when she felt him smile against her neck. "And that would be?"

"Working together could be interesting." She felt the words rumbled through his chest and into her hers.

Kyra clamped down on the moan that was building up from deep in her chest. She needed to get away from him. "I don't do interesting."

He chuckled, the sound vibrating through her. This time she couldn't stop the moan. "Don't you think you could make one exception?"

"And then what?" Kyra said with the last of her strength. If he continued to push her, she was going to fall to her knees and beg him for sex.

Ryder finally moved away, and she was able to take a breath that wasn't exclusively him. "We've barely met, Kyra. There is no *then what*."

Now that she was able to breathe again, her indignation flared. "Great. So basically, you want a sex toy during the job and that's it."

Ryder shrugged and moved back to his chair. "A little release does wonders for a person."

Kyra was so furious for the moment she was helpless to do anything other than stand there with her mouth hanging open. Callous much? She wanted to scream. "How do you plan on meeting up with your backup?" he asked, changing the topic before she blew up at him.

Fiona would find her wherever she was. It was something she did. Of course she had her motorcycle, or did she? She threw her hands in the air. "Where is my motorcycle?"

"Motel, as far as I know," he said, turning back to his computer.

Kyra then did something she couldn't remember ever doing before in her life. She stomped her foot in sheer and absolute irritation. Ryder looked up, a smile playing at the corner of his lips. He gave her a deliberate look from her feet to her eyes, making her stomach roll with tension at least she told herself it was tension. She decided then and there that his eyes were trouble. She took a deep breath, trying to calm herself before she did or said something she was going to regret.

"Why am I getting the feeling you're enjoying this?" she ground out between gritted teeth her hands fisted at her sides.

His eyes had gone a soft gray. "I think we would work well together," he said again, but this time, it was a statement instead of a question. "You should think about it, Blue. We could make a difference here." He stood and moved to stand in front of her again, crowding her up against the door.

She bristled at him calling her Blue. "Don't call me that."

All Air Elements had blue eyes. Hers weren't special. But the way he said it made it sound like it was something noteworthy, almost an endearment.

"What if I said I don't work well with others?" If her words came out a little breathless, she would never admit it. But damn, he was pushing all her button, and it was impossible to ignore the very large erection pressed against her stomach. Her mind went haywire for a moment as she imagined touching and caressing it. Doing things with him that she had no right imagining.

He laughed, and she could feel it deep in her chest as he pressed up against her. "Neither do I."

For several seconds she had no idea what he was saying. Did he just roll himself against her? Kyra felt her legs weaken slightly. "What are you trying to prove?" she demanded.

"Only that we would work well together. Regardless of what you might think," he whispered.

"The Tribunal is knocking at the door, ready to rain down death, and you're hitting on me." She wanted to turn away from him but she couldn't.

Ryder shrugged but didn't move back. "Pretty woman, I'm not blind."

Kyra bristled. She needed to put more than just physical distance between the two of them. "Go sniff up the skirt of your Lycan. You're not my type. Unlike you I am here to do a job. Save the innocent people and all that…"

He stiffened and stepped back, his eyes changing from a bedroom glow to a flat black. "Is that what you think you are? The one that is going to save the town from certain death? Do you honestly think you and your other Element friends will be able to track that monster and kill it?"

"I know how to do a job without getting personal." She pointedly looked at his groin as she said it. "So if the shoe fits?" Kyra smiled. "You said you've been working on the problem for a couple of days. I got here yesterday and I've made more progress than you have." That really made her happy. But Ryder's dark gaze made her regret throwing it in his face like she had.

"Listen, sweetheart, the last thing I need is some freaking air fairy to come in and help me out. I was offering you my help. If you aren't smart enough to take it, then no skin off my nose." He turned and walked back to the table and his laptop. "Get lost, Blue. My offer has officially been rescinded."

"Right, because you never ask twice? I remember now." She tapped her temple, as if her memory was still a little faulty from what he had done to her.

He shrugged. "If you had admitted who you were at the beginning, I wouldn't have had to resort to what I did. So from where I stand, that little bump on the head? Your little headache? That's your fault."

"Weren't Trackers descended from cavemen and barbarians?" she asked, trying to piss him off.

His nostrils flared. "And didn't the Elements lose the Element of Light, causing the gates of hell to open up and release the Element of Darkness?"

Kyra was so angry, she didn't know what to say. "She did it to save her love, and not one person could control that kind of power."

He shrugged again. "Put whatever romantic, sentimental spin on it you like. But the result is the same, Blue. You guys blew it."

She stormed out, the sound of his cynical laughter ringing behind her.

"Where is the Tracker now?" Fiona asked.

"No, I'm fine, thanks for asking," Kyra said as Fiona climbed into the car Kyra had commandeered, which might have been a lousy idea. But she was so pissed, she didn't actually care. It wasn't like he couldn't find her and the car whenever he wanted. "The wound in my arm is healing, and the several bumps on my head are all but forgotten."

"I'm glad to see your still standing with all those wounds." Simon said climbing into the back seat.

Kyra was surprised to see the other Enforcer, "You needed back up in the field, Simon will be perfect for this mission." Fiona said in answer to her unasked question.

"We will need the Tracker. Where is he?" she asked.

"Why?" Kyra asked. "We don't need him. He's a Neanderthal." A sexy, drop-dead-gorgeous Neanderthal who made her want to either kill him or fuck him. She wasn't sure which she felt at the moment. Probably take advantage of him and then kill him. She couldn't get the feel of that large cock pressed against her belly out of her mind.

Fiona shook her head. "What exactly happened between the two of you?"

Kyra shrugged. "Oh, he just tried to kill me a few times. We don't need him," she demanded, more because she didn't ever want to see him again. Seriously, she didn't know how long she could stand to be in his presence before killing him. Besides, she had stolen the car—she might have burned that bridge. Which, of course, she didn't care about one little bit. Right?

Fiona closed her eyes and took a deep breath. "What have you done, Kyra? Because we'll need his help."

"It would've been nice to know that." Before she had stolen his car, but she didn't say that to Fiona.

Fiona shook her head. "I told you to stay with him. What did you think I meant by that?" The older woman shook her head. "And then you wouldn't have burned that bridge, am I right?"

Kyra nodded sheepishly. She flipped the car around and headed back toward the house. Where the arrogant bastard was probably waiting. Crow was not her favorite dish.

"So, how long has she been with you?" Fiona asked, nodding toward the Shade sitting in the back seat with Simon. She had shown up the moment Kyra had taken the vehicle, though she hadn't uttered a single sound. Kyra was thankful for that one reprieve.

Fiona hated Shades. Kyra didn't know why, but she had heard rumors that one had haunted Fiona for almost a century, making the old woman skittish around them.

"I first saw her in the clearing. Didn't see her again until the cabin." She told Fiona everything that had happened since leaving Illinois.

"Can the Tracker see her?"

"He didn't act like he could. Walked right through her at one point." She doubted that he could see her. And this thrilled Kyra, knowing something the arrogant bastard didn't. He was far too full of himself.

"That could definitely work to our advantage," Simon said. Kyra smiled at the man. She was glad Fiona had brought Simon. He was levelheaded and had a little thing for Kyra, so she was able to get away with more when partnered up with him, things she wouldn't normally get away with. Not that she liked to break the rules, but she preferred to do things her own way.

Simon was an Earth Element who worked well with everyone. He had an easy smile, and it drew people to him. Kyra had once thought that they could make a go of it, but she also knew she'd walk all over him. Simon deserved more than what she had to offer. She could be crabby and tended to take it out on the people around her. That was why she and Eric got along so well. They both looked at the world through a decidedly cynical lens. It was a rare point of view, for an Element. Most Elements were easygoing, their attitudes loving and peaceful. Regardless, she and Simon worked well together. At least now she had a partner she could count on.

Kyra could feel him on the other side of the door. She looked around for something she could smash against the door or better yet, against Ryder's thick skull.

"Why does this Tracker have you so tied up?" Simon asked, watching her pace through the room.

"You haven't met him or his psychotic sidekick, so you might want to withhold judgment until then." Kyra muttered.

When Ryder had answered the door, the smug, gloating look firmly planted on his face, she realized that he knew they would be back. It infuriated Kyra. He hadn't said a word but held out his hand. She had dropped the keys in his palm and pushed past him. To top it off, Fiona asked to speak with him privately, cutting Kyra off at the knees. She turned to the door and glared.

Simon laughed and she turned to him. He tossed a small figurine to her. "You look like you need to break something." He sat back relaxed, obviously ready to watch a fight.

Kyra gently placed the figurine on a side table. "This isn't my house and although I would enjoy smashing that over his head, I'd feel terrible for breaking someone else's things."

Simon laughed. "That's one of your idiosyncrasies that I like so much. You care way more about everyone else than you should. You do what you do because you want everyone to have a happy life. When will you allow yourself that kind of happiness?"

She was saved from answering when Fiona opened the door and smiled. "Kyra, can you join us, please?"

She bristled, desperately wanting to say no or stomp her foot like a petulant child, but she could do neither. "Yes."

Ryder was sitting in a chair behind a desk by the window, his fingers steepled under his chin, a smug smile on his lips.

"You two will work together on this matter," Fiona declared as soon as the door was closed behind Kyra.

Kyra felt her mouth fall open. "What about Simon?"

"Come on, Blue." Ryder smiled; showing straight white teeth that made her want to run her tongue along them and kick herself at the same time.

"Don't call me that," she snapped, glaring at him. She swung back to Fiona. "What exactly does he want from me?"

"He refuses to help us unless you ask him personally to be your partner in trapping and killing whatever is out there killing innocent women—before the Tribunal steps in. You must also apologize for stealing his car." Kyra wanted nothing more than to punch the man in the face.

"Kyra, we have a great deal at stake here. It is only a matter of time before the Tribunal is notified. These killings are not going to go unnoticed. He has a unique set of abilities that will end this sooner rather than later. It could be the catalyst we need." Fiona folded her arms over her chest. She gave Kyra that mothering look that she couldn't say no to.

Kyra turned back to Ryder and leveled him with a stare. "Don't you already have a partner? Are you working on your supernatural harem? How will the Lycan bombshell like me stepping in on her territory? I'd hate to have the bitch come back out, not sure my head can take much more trauma."

"She isn't my Lycan. She is a partner. There is no need for you to worry about her. There is plenty of room for more partners." He smiled, again flashing his straight white teeth.

"Did he happen to mention how he gave me a concussion and caused me to nearly forget the entire day? How he tried to kill me, several times?"

"Now, now, Blue," Ryder said with forced calm. "No need to be petty. We both said and did things that we regret. Can't we put the past behind us?" His eyes held a warning that Kyra couldn't mistake. She was not to air any further dirty laundry for Fiona to inspect.

Kyra's eyes narrowed. She did not want to play this game with him. Something in her screamed that nothing would ever be the same once she did. Just the thought scared the hell out of her. "I won't do it."

Ryder moved so fast, he was a blur. He stood behind her, his breath brushing against the back of her neck as he spoke. "You can't do it without me, Blue. Now we both know my rule of not asking twice, so how about you ask me real nice instead?"

Kyra glared at him. "How do you move so damn fast?" she asked petulant at being pushed into a corner. She was going to take a really long vacation after this. Might take the next century completely off. Screw the world and all its bullshit.

She was going to sleep in and not strap a gun to her back every morning. Maybe get a tan, spend some time outside and just relax. Plant a garden at the Haven. Be an Element—just an Element, not an Elemental Enforcer. She would forget about this Tracker. This enigmatic man who had gotten so thoroughly under her skin, she couldn't begin to figure how she would ever get him out.

The worst part? As he pressed against her back, she wasn't sure she wanted to. And then she did it again. She stomped her foot like a child. Fiona looked at Kyra's foot as if the woman had never seen one before. Kyra knew exactly how the old Druid felt. She'd been in this constant state of confusion from the moment she'd laid eyes on Ryder.

"Will you help us?" she said between gritted teeth.

He moved away from her as quickly as he had come at her. In a blur, he was back in his seat in front of his laptop, as if he hadn't moved an inch. "Yes."

Kyra stomped toward the door, but he stopped her.

"Have you forgotten something?" he asked.

She turned and gave him her brightest smile, fluttering her eyes at him. "Can you please forgive me for stealing your car?" she said with her sweetest I can't get enough of you and please be my knight in shining armor smile.

For half a second, she thought maybe she had pushed him too far. Fire flared in the depths of his eyes and his nostrils flared. If she didn't know better, she would've bet that he wanted nothing more than to launch over the desk and strangle her. He nodded curtly and she turned, slamming the door behind her so forcefully, she was surprised it didn't fall off its hinges. She did the same to the front door.

"Kyra? What's going on?" Simon asked, following her.

"He said he would help us. But I'm not sure exactly why we need his help." She took a couple deep breaths that didn't seem to help, so she took a couple more. Simon moved behind her and massaged her shoulders.

"Just relax. Let's just get this done and then you'll never have to see the man again." She knew he was right, but was still unable to ease the agitation and the feeling that Ryder had somehow planned this.

Ryder smiled to himself. He knew working with the Elements was going to get this issue resolved faster. Plus it was going to give him some time to figure out what it was about Kyra that made him so crazy. Her smell, those blue eyes … from the first moment she had looked up at him in the forest, there was something about her that made him just a little nuts. The only problem? He didn't know if it was a bad omen or not.

He had to be honest with himself. She wasn't like the other women he'd worked with. She was a fighter and held herself proudly. Other than Marlee, he hadn't met a woman who could hold his attention for longer than it took to fuck them. But there was just something about Kyra that pulled at him.

Once this was all done, he would take her to bed. Work her out of his system. Until then, he was going to have fun with her. That was, unless, she looked at him like she had right before leaving the office. The force of his attraction to her had nearly driven him to be the Neanderthal she'd accused him of. He wanted to leap the desk and take her right there on the study floor. He calmed himself and finished his business with Fiona. But he couldn't wait to get the taste of Kyra on his tongue, to mix it with her smell. Touch her bare skin, get to know her physically. The thought made him hard all over again.

With that in mind, he left the study and went in search of her. She wasn't in the living room or the kitchen. He checked the couple of rooms on the ground floor before hearing voices from the front porch.

He opened the door and came to a dead halt. A man stood with her—and the bastard had his hands on her! He was rubbing her shoulders, and for the love of the Gods, she was leaning back into his hands. The smell of the man's arousal was potent. Ryder bristled with anger.

Kyra stiffened and pulled away from the man as he stepped out onto the porch.. It had never crossed Ryder's mind that she may be attached to someone. Well, that would change nothing. What moron would allow his woman to go off on a dangerous mission like this alone? Someone who didn't deserve her. That pretty much settled the issue in his mind.

"We have work to do. Marlee is out scouting the woods. Let's discuss how we're going to kill this thing." He stood back so she could walk into the house. But when the man made to follow, Ryder stopped him. "Who the hell are you?"

"All you need to know is that I am with her." He nodded toward Kyra, not even flinching when Ryder growled primitively at him. "Does that usually work to frighten people away?" Simon asked casually.

"No, but the beating that follows pretty much hammers home the point." He was about to follow through on the threat when Fiona stepped between them.

"He is with me, Tracker." Her voice was so calm, it instantly relaxed Ryder. He knew it had something to do with her Elemental powers. Part of him was furious, but the part that was in control stepped aside and let the man through.

Once Fiona released him, he snarled at her. "Don't use your Elemental powers on me again."

"There is no point in arguing between each other. It will cause dissension, and slow our progress." She had a point, but he wouldn't abide being controlled by another person.

"I agree, but never use your powers on me." Fiona nodded in agreement. "And I said I would work with Kyra. You didn't mention anyone else."

"Ryder, you can't possibly think that I won't be bringing in everything possible to take care of this issue. We can't afford to have any more innocent people injured." Again her voice was calm but Ryder didn't sense anything change within himself, so at least she wasn't calming him. "I will do whatever it takes to stop this before the Tribunal gets wind of it. Simon is an Earth Element and he will come in handy. I guarantee him."

Ryder didn't really want to believe her, but he followed her into the living room. "Simon is with me, and that is nonnegotiable."

He would hold out judgment until later. He did know one thing, though. If Simon put his hands on Kyra again, Ryder was going to beat him to a bloody pulp.

"Marlee is out scouting. I am hoping that if we find where the beast hides, then we might be able to trap it and kill it," Ryder offered when everyone was in the living room.

"I'm not sure if following a predator of that sort into its lair is a good idea," Simon said.

"Really?" Ryder asked. "And just what is your plan?"

Both men bristled and glared at each other, waiting. Simon was the first to blink, which pleased Ryder immensely. "We need to find out more about what it is before we go in, guns blazing."

"Yeah, guns blazing would be the wrong thing to do," Kyra said.

"See?" Simon motioned to Kyra. "We have to have a well-thought-out plan. Who is your contact here?"

Ryder glared at Simon and Simon glared right back. He may be forced to work with him, but that didn't mean he had to like him. "His name is Max. He's a Shapeshifter. Works in Marshall as the sheriff."

"Is there a way I can speak with him?"

"No, but Kyra can speak with him," Ryder said, just to be contrary. He stood up and left the room. Pulling his cell out, he called Max.

"Hey, buddy," Max answered.

"Got some time to come over and go over the case with me?" Ryder asked.

"What more do you need to know?" They had talked when Ryder had gotten there several days before.

"I've picked up some partners. They want to interview you."

Max swore. "The more people we get involved, the bigger chance the Tribunal will get wind of this."

"Chill, Max, they're here to help," Ryder said calmly.

Max snorted. "Since when did you become a diplomat?"

"Leave it."

Another snort. "The only thing that ever gets you to deviate from a plan is a woman." Ryder smiled. He had to give it to his old friend—he knew Ryder well.

"They're Elements, Max," Ryder said, hoping to lead his friend in a different direction.

"Yeah? What kind of Elements?"

"Do you have time to come over or not?"

"Yeah, but if there's a woman involved, I'm going to kick the shit out of you," Max said.

Ryder laughed. "Bigger men than you have tried and failed. But bring it on, old friend."

Ryder hung up and walked back into the living room. "You realize you Elements think way too much. Sometimes a straightforward attack is the best course of action."

"Yes, because going in shooting without thinking has worked so well." She motioned to her shoulder.

"I agree with Simon that some recon and research is needed before we decide what should be done next," Fiona added.

"Whatever. Max is on his way. Question him till you're satisfied. I'm going to get some sleep." He knew everything that Max was going to tell them and he also knew that the next couple of days were going to be rough, so getting some sleep was a good idea.

Kyra liked Max the minute he walked into the house. He had a military-style haircut, graying at the temples, and the kindest brown eyes she'd ever seen. Breathing him in, she knew he only wanted what was best for his people.

Kyra smiled brightly at him. "You're Max?" She extended her hand.

Max looked her up and down and shook his head. "Yeah, that's me. Ryder needs his ass kicked."

Kyra couldn't help but laugh. "I think you're my new best friend."

Max snorted as Kyra introduced him to Fiona and Simon. "So, where is the bastard?"

"He went to get some sleep," Kyra said.

Max snorted again. "Sleep, my ass. He's somewhere listening to every word that's being said. If he had any balls at all, he'd come out and face me."

Kyra found Max fascinating. "Exactly what has Ryder done to deserve your wrath?"

Suddenly, Ryder was standing between the two. "It doesn't concern you," he said over his shoulder to Kyra, shoving Max in the chest. "Is it possible for you to make any more of a racket?"

Max raised a questioning brow. "Actually, yes. Where's the bombshell fire starter? I assume the explosion at the motel was her?"

"Sorry, Max. You know how Marlee is with explosives."

"Put a leash on her before I do," Max said.

"You know what?" Kyra joined the conversation. She stepped around Ryder and took Max by the arm, linking it with hers. "I really, really like you. Are you married?"

Ryder threw his hands in the air and stormed off.

"Have you known Ryder long? 'Cause if you can get him so frustrated he walks away within the first two minutes of a conversation, we need to spend a lot more time together. Is he always so grumpy?" Kyra said.

"Only when he's awake," Max said with deadpan seriousness. Kyra couldn't help it. She threw her head back and laughed. "And most women fall at his feet." Max offered.

"Oh, now that I believe. So would that be before or after he kicks their asses?" Kyra asked.

"I never kicked you," Ryder bellowed from somewhere in the house.

Kyra laughed even more and leaned forward. "Not for lack of trying. I'm sure that if he had been given the chance, he would have."

"I never kicked you," Ryder bellowed again.

Max gathered her up in his arms and hugged her. "I like you," he rumbled.

Kyra leaned into him and laughed. "I like you too."

Max answered all the questions they had, giving them an idea of what was happening. Three of the women were married and, from what Max understood, had just up and walked out of their homes in the middle of the night. Another had left a family party, and the fifth had never made it home from school. There were no signs that any of the women had fought off their attacker. They had nothing in common that would suggest the killer was going after a particular type of victim.

"None of this makes any sense," Kyra said, looking at the file again.

"That's why I called in Ryder. He's the best. If anyone can track what is doing this, he can," Max said with confidence.

"You have a lot of faith in him," Fiona said.

Max nodded. "You don't know a lot about Trackers, do you?"

Fiona shook her head. "Their history is about as hard to come by as the Druids and Elements."

Max snorted. "The only written history is the history you want leaked to the world. Same for the Trackers, except they chose to not release any."

"Ryder is the best at what he does. Even his brothers would recommend him. I would trust no one else," Max explained.

"Are you done talking?" Ryder demanded, walking into the room. He'd listened to enough, especially once Max started talking about his brothers. It was time to end the conversation.

"Yes, I think we have enough now to go into the field," Simon said, standing.

Ryder glared at the man. "Fine. Then let's go out and find Marlee. We can start your recon and research. But don't blame me if it all goes up in smoke."

Max pounded him on the back. "Find it and get rid of it."

Ryder nodded. "It's what I do."

Max then hugged Kyra. "You, I like. Feel free to stick around as long as you like. I'm not as old as I look." He winked at her.

"Are you done?" The Shapeshifter needed to get his hands off Kyra before Ryder removed them for him.

Max, of course, sensed that and kissed Kyra on the top of the head in a fatherly manner.

"Old man, I only owe you so much," Ryder snarled.

Max smiled. "Yep, and there aren't any women involved," he said, slapping Ryder on the shoulder as he walked out.

"Are you ready?" Ryder said to Kyra.

"Yes, Simon will be going with us." Kyra reached for her weapons on the tabletop. She holstered them in a special harness that crisscrossed her stomach so that the guns were actually strapped to her back.

He couldn't help it; she was the hottest thing on two legs. The holster cinched everything just right. Best thing he'd ever laid eyes on. His body responded and it took a great deal of control to not give into his reaction to her.

"Let's get moving."

Ryder pulled his car into a clearing just outside the valley where Kyra had first stopped. She eyed him warily; he'd been acting strange since leaving the house. Given she wasn't all that familiar with him, she didn't know if this was normal behavior. It was different than the cocky, gun-toting psycho she'd grown accustomed to in the last day.

She sighed. Had it really only been twenty-four hours since this whole thing started? Granted, she'd been knocked out for several of those hours. Nevertheless, it still felt like days.

Kyra was pulled from her musing. "When I tracked it earlier, it stopped about twenty yards into the tree line," Ryder said. "Circled around and then took off. For some reason it won't cross the tree line here."

"When did you track it?" Kyra asked, shocked. As far as she knew, he'd been with her since they blew off her motel room door.

Ryder gave her a black look. "None of your damn business."

Kyra sighed. So this was pissed-off Tracker? His mood had changed; she made a mental note. She tried to pinpoint exactly what had caused his current mood. It didn't matter. Ryder's moods were none of her business.

She had to admit that his tone and words stung. What happened to working together? Being partners on this? More questions than answers, she sighed, and that pretty much explained her last twenty-four hours.

They climbed out of the car. Ryder opened the trunk and threw her saddlebags at her feet. Kyra stared at them for a moment. She thought they'd been lost in the motel explosion. Did Ryder go back to get them? Or had he had them the whole time and was a total asshole? She went with the latter because it made more sense. She'd been wearing a torn-up, bloody T-shirt for hours now. Damn him.

Grabbing a set of clothes, he walked to the edge of the tree and whistled.

"What the hell is he doing?" Simon asked from beside her.

"Calling his dog," Kyra muttered as a large red-brown wolf loped out of the woods. In seconds, it morphed into Marlee, a very naked, very beautiful Marlee. With her long red-brown hair flowing around her shoulders, she looked like a Lycan Goddess. It made Kyra gnash her teeth. She'd learned a long time ago that you couldn't compete with a woman like that.

"I need to get a dog," Simon said, obviously enjoying the view.

"Shut up." She glared at him and then turned back as the other woman pulled on a pair of jeans and the black T-shirt Ryder handed her. Kyra thought the shirt could be a size or two bigger as it was pulled tight around Marlee's large breasts.

"Show off," she muttered, more to herself than to anyone else. But Marlee looked up and smiled at the other woman. Kyra ground her molars together before speaking again. "Are you done with the show?"

Marlee shrugged her shoulders like this was an everyday occurrence, which it probably was. "There is a set of tunnels all through these mountains. I smelled that thing everywhere. It's going to take some time to go through them all."

Kyra raised her hand like she was in school and when everyone was looking at her, she asked, "Did you say tunnels? Just how are we going to do this recon and not be attacked?"

"We will do it very carefully," Simon said, trying to sound reassuring. "Can you track it or sense it?" he asked Ryder.

"Both," Ryder said. "Tracker, remember?" He pointed at himself.

"I sense it as well," Kyra offered.

"And I can smell it," Marlee said flippantly. "What can you do, pretty boy?" She turned to Ryder. "By the way, who the hell is he?"

"He's with me," Kyra said in defense of Simon. He'd been getting a lot of shit since he'd shown up. He didn't really deserve it.

"No shit, sweetheart. Still doesn't tell me who he is, and I'm not going anywhere with him in tow until I know who he is. I don't back up just anyone." Marlee pulled a pack of gum from her pocket and popped a piece in her mouth.

Simon stepped forward and extended his hand to Marlee. "Hello, I'm Simon. I came with Fiona to be of assistance with the investigation. I am also an Earth Element."

Marlee stopped chewing her gum for a moment before extending her hand. "No shit. Another one?" Her next question was directed at Ryder. "Just how many more people are there going to be in this investigation?" she said. "Why don't we pull up a short bus full of sightseers while we're at it?"

"'I'm interested in finding out exactly how we are going to go about doing this recon without handing ourselves up on a silver platter. Can we concentrate on that for a moment?" Kyra shook her head in frustration.

Marlee glared at her. "Sure. Why the fuck not. I don't have anything better to do."

"Perfect. With all our unique senses, we will be able to know if it is anywhere near us," Simon said cheerfully. Kyra gave him a stunned look and then reminded herself that he hadn't dealt with the grueling black shadow that consumed souls.

"So, let's just hypothetically say we sense it. We'll be vulnerable, in its territory. We aren't really sure what it is or how to hurt or God forbid, kill it," Kyra threw out.

"Job just keeps getting better," Marlee muttered. Kyra couldn't agree more. "What the hell did you do while I was running all over the mountain?"

"Don't even ask." Ryder muttered. Kyra glared at him.

"Well unless anyone else has a better idea what about using bait?" Marlee asked the group.

Kyra hadn't thought about that. "How do we know what to use as bait? Do you have a busload of souls? Or perhaps another cabin not in use?"

Marlee gave her a broad smile. "Sweetheart, Ryder and I have been here for two more days than you. Haven't seen a damn thing. The only time we saw anything was that night at the cabin when it talked to you."

"Oh hell no." Kyra shook her head in frustration. Marlee wanted to use Kyra as bait. Wasn't it enough that the thought of going down into tunnels was making her want to run screaming in the opposite direction? Now she was being considered as bait? It was official. She needed a drink, a strong knock-you-on-your-ass drink.

Marlee snarled. "So we're just going to risk it and walk right into those tunnels without knowing exactly what we're going to face? I'd rather take on a slathering coven of vampires."

"Then you be the bait," Kyra suggested.

Marlee smiled. "I go with Ryder."

"I want to know which entrance and exit it uses the most," Ryder said thoughtfully. He pulled a map from the trunk and laid it out on the hood. "How many did you find?"

Marlee leaned over the map and pointed to different areas. Ryder marked them. When they were done, eight Xs marked a ten-mile radius throughout the mountain range.

"Let's stay together for now." He pointed to the Xs he had in mind. Ryder wasn't about to let Kyra out of his sight for the moment. "Let's start with the farthest and move forward. You going to run in your leather pants?" Ryder asked Kyra without taking a breath or looking up from the map. The look she leveled at him could've killed. He hadn't event looked up from the map as the spoke. Why her choice of wardrobe was any of his business, she couldn't guess.

Ignoring him, she went back to her bags and pulled some black khakis and a simple black T-shirt.

"Don't you own anything but black?" Ryder asked, looking over her shoulder into her bag. Kyra couldn't help but jump. He moved so fast, it was discombobulating. She hadn't felt or heard him move but there he was, standing at her back again. He seemed to be her kryptonite. He could kill her anytime he wanted. The thought left a lump in her stomach.

"Can you please discontinue popping up at my shoulder like that?" she said with more anger then necessary. He answered with a grunt, which gave her absolutely no clue as to his answer.

"And it's none of your damn business." She threw his words back at him. Kyra looked up into the sky and checked her watch. "We have a couple of hours before nightfall. That should give us a good idea of what we're dealing with. I don't think hanging around in the dark with a creature of shadow is a good idea."

"I agree," Simon said.

"Bloody hell," Marlee screeched from the back of the car where she was waist deep, digging through the trunk like a badger. Everyone moved to where she was tossing things out right and left. "I swear, Ryder, one of these days, I'm going to really fuck you up. Do you understand me?" She pulled her head out to nail him with feral red eyes, and then turned back to the trunk of the car.

She finally pulled herself free, a shoe in each hand. "Where's the gum?"

"What happened to the piece she was chewing?" Simon whispered to Kyra. Kyra had given up trying to figure the woman out and shook her head in confusion.

Ryder shrugged as if he had no idea what Marlee was talking about. "Fine, but I'll have my day. Just you wait and see." One thing was for sure—that was definitely the Lycan's mantra. Hopping on one foot, she slid a shoe on and then the other. She screeched again, but this time in glee.

"Does she do that a lot?" Simon asked the group at large.

"She hasn't shut up since I met her," Kyra said.

Ryder again only shrugged, but Marlee was ignoring them all as she pulled off the shoe and shook it. A pack of gum fell from the inside. Marlee raised one eyebrow in utter domination, as if she had won something very important. Ryder shook his head and walked away.

"They are the strangest couple I've ever seen," Simon muttered.

"You have absolutely no idea." Kyra couldn't agree more, they were perfect for each other. She looked around for a place to change. She wasn't quite up to Marlee's morals of being free and naked in front of strangers. But there was nowhere to change so she gave Simon a pointed look. He nodded and turned away.

Ryder, on the other hand, leaned up against the trunk of a tree, arms folded over his chest as if he had all the time in the world. He acted like he meant to spend that time watching her change her clothes. Damn him and his peeping Tom, bedroom eyes. If he thought watching her change her clothes was going to upset her, he had another thing coming. She'd been raised in a houseful of men, for God's sake. One Tracker watching her dress wasn't going to bother her. It didn't matter that when he looked at her, it made her stomach roll like cresting a rollercoaster.

She pulled off her leather jacket and her tattered T-shirt, leaving her black lace bra on. And just to be flippant, she pulled off the leather pants. She'd always been proud of her body. She tried to work out every day, not just cardio but with weights too. She had a complex about being thought less of because she was female, so she put in extra time at the gym, and her body reflected her hard work. However, after seeing Marlee naked, she couldn't hold a candle to the Lycan, so what did she have to lose? She ignored Ryder as she pulled on her khakis and T-shirt.

Marlee was the one to break the silence. "I like your holster design. I haven't seen anything like it before."

Kyra slipped the holster over her shoulders, crisscrossing her stomach so that her guns lay flat against her back ribs. It freed her to have fluid movement with her arms, and with any kind of jacket, the guns were undetectable. Nobody would expect her to be armed. Xavier had custom-built her equipment for her, including the wrist gauntlets that she also pulled on, each concealing a deadly knife.

Kyra eyed the other woman suspiciously. "I had it designed specifically for me."

Marlee stepped up. "You know, Kyra, we could be friends, you and me. Women in this line of business should stick together, don't you think?" Marlee smiled and gave Kyra the once-over, leaving Kyra feeling as if she'd been groped. Marlee continued, "The men don't deserve all the credit all the time. We women need to step up and show them whose boss once in a while." She winked.

"Um, okay." Kyra was so shocked by Marlee's olive branch that she was incapable of any other response.

Marlee smiled brightly. "The two of us could kick some serious ass," Marlee said, more for Kyra's ears than anyone else's, leaving Kyra wondering for a moment if Marlee was hitting on her.

But before she could think more on that, Marlee sauntered off toward Ryder who stood still as marble, and then shook his head, as if he'd found something interesting. She ignored him and pulled on her running shoes.

When she was all dressed, she rejoined the group at the edge of the woods. "How far?"

"Four miles."

Ryder looked up. "Looks like we're running. Do you think you can keep up?" He directed the question to Kyra and Simon.

Simon snorted and Kyra bristled. "Why don't you try to keep up with us?" She motioned for Marlee to lead the way and they took off.

They didn't stop or slow the pace once, and it wasn't easy going. Kyra had been trained from the age of seven to be exactly what she was: an Element Enforcer. That meant grueling cardio on a daily basis. But Ryder and Marlee took running to a whole different level. Several times Ryder, who ran directly behind Marlee, turned to watch Kyra, a satisfied smile on his face as she stumbled to keep up with them. She almost fell several times, but each time Ryder caught her before she tumbled back into an unsuspecting Simon. He would release her, making sure to graze a breast or hip as he did it. It was getting to the point that she was stumbling just to get him to touch her again. Damn, she needed to get herself under control.

She desperately wanted to stop so she could throw a rock at the back of his arrogant head. Kyra was sure he was pushing them harder than he needed to see if she could keep up. By the time they reached the mouth of a cave, she was gasping for air. She deliberately slowed her breathing, not giving into the urge to lean over and gasp.

"It splits off about sixty yards in." Marlee offered a bottle of water to Kyra, who took it gratefully.

Ryder looked around. "You two search out here, and Marlee and I will go in and see what we can find."

Kyra nodded. She was fine with that idea. She found the thought of going into a tunnel or cave or whatever the hell it was abhorrent. The air was stagnant and thick with memories. It was where air went to die, taking with it the memories of everything it had passed.

She knew that if she spent too long in a place like this, it could drive her mad or simply kill her. She shuddered at the thought.

"Are you cold?" Simon asked.

"I'm fine. Let's see what we can find." Simon nodded and bent down, burying his hands in the dirt. Kyra moved off to the side and allowed herself to phase out as she took several deep breaths. Memories and images played like a movie in her mind with only a couple glimpses of the black shadow.

Opening her eyes, she looked at Simon. He was sitting cross-legged in the dirt. "You get anything?"

"No." But he kept looking at her.

"What?"

"You glow. When you phase and you're reading the air. You glow. It's absolutely beautiful." His voice had dropped to a quiet, almost reverent pitch. "He seems pretty focused on you," Simon said just as quietly.

"Who? Ryder?" Kyra asked, not really wanting to have this conversation with Simon. "Yeah, I think he gets a kick out of irritating me. Knocking me out. Using compulsion on me until my head almost explodes. He's a joy to be around. Give it twenty-four hours and I'm sure you'll like him as much as I do." But there was something about him that made her warm all over, and that part scared the hell out of her. However, that wasn't something she was going to share with Simon.

"Right …" Simon drew the word out.

"He doesn't even like me, Simon. Ryder has tried to kill me several times. He actually shot at me." She wasn't sure what Simon was seeing, but from her perspective, it didn't look like a match made in heaven.

"He doesn't need to like you to take you to bed."

Kyra stood still for a moment, trying to decide the best way to handle this situation. "Haven't we had a conversation very similar to this before?"

Simon shrugged. "Old habits die hard, and sometimes, Kyra, I …" He didn't finish. Kyra was more than happy that he left it unsaid.

"Simon, it's just not meant to be. One day you're going to find a woman who is going to make you happy. Keep you safe and warm. Not some gun-toting Enforcer who isn't smart enough to know what's good for her." Kyra's mind instantly pulled up a picture of Ryder. "One day you're going to leave the Enforcers. You've said it yourself that this isn't what you want to do for the rest of your life. You'll leave the Enforcers and be happy. That is what I want for you, not this life."

Simon climbed to his feet and cupped her face. "I think you are way too hard on yourself. And I know we've had this conversation before, so we don't need to rehash it here. But you can't blame me for holding out a shred of hope, Kyra."

She didn't want to hurt him. She never wanted to hurt him. Simon was one of the kindest, most honest, selfless people she knew. She cared for him a great deal, but it would never be enough for him. She could never be what he deserved, and they both knew it. Simon needed to accept the fact that she wasn't going to change. She also knew that if she were to give in to him, she would kill some of that selflessness and kindness that he gave out unconditionally. Because she was so hard. That was just something she couldn't bring herself to do.

"What's up with you and the little Element?" Marlee asked as soon as they were out of earshot.

Ryder grunted. "Not sure yet." Marlee knew him about as well as his brothers did.

She laughed quietly. "You're not sure if you want to get her into bed, or not sure if you want to kill her, or you're not sure if she is useful, or you're …"

Ryder held up a hand. "Do I have to have a plan regarding her today?"

"Just not like you," Marlee said, sniffing the wall. They both could see perfectly in the dark. "You always have a plan, always."

Ryder sighed and pulled Marlee to a halt. "What's not like me?"

"You don't share. When you're tracking, you're utterly focused and you don't share. Now you're working with a group of Elements. Just not like you. And I have to ask myself if it has something to do with the woman. I see the way you look at her. I smell your reaction to her. I just don't want to have to kill her if she hurts you." Marlee shrugged.

"And what if it was about her?" Ryder asked.

Even in the dark, he saw the cryptic look on her face. "Then I would tell you to fuck her and send her on her way. We have business to take care of. Otherwise, she is going to get in the way, or Gods forbid, get her damn self killed. And as hard as you are, if she were to die on your watch you would never forgive yourself."

"It's not using this tunnel often," Ryder said, heading back toward the opening. He wasn't ready to evaluate what was going on or not going on between him and Kyra. And Marlee was hitting too close to home at the moment. He didn't want to evaluate how Kyra made him feel.

"I'll have your back, you know," Marlee said, following him. "Regardless."

Ryder stopped and turned to her. "Damn straight, you will, or I'll feed you to a pack of slathering Wers."

Marlee punched him directly in the nose. Blood gushed from the broken appendage. "Not funny," she said with just a hint of seriousness.

Ryder laughed. "My bad." He pulled a bandana from his pack and pressed it to his face. The exchange pretty much summed up their relationship.

"What happened?" Kyra asked, rushing up to Ryder as they stepped from the entrance of the tunnel. She brushed his hands away to look at his wound. Ryder was so stunned by her compassion he was unable to move away as she inspected him. She poured water onto the bandana to clean up the blood. "It's stopped bleeding. You heal incredibly fast." She looked up into his face, her aqua blue eyes filled with amazement. He wondered what it would be like to see that look on her face more often. It was a cross between shock and awe.

"Ran into the wall in the dark," Marlee said, chomping on her gum. "Let's get moving." She headed back into the woods, Simon behind her.

Ryder took the bandana from Kyra and wiped the rest of the blood from his face. "Thanks for the concern."

She shrugged, uncomfortable. "You're no good to us if you don't heal fast," she said, again throwing his words back at him.

"Nice to know you're listening to every word I say," he said, smiling.

He instantly felt the change in her, which only amused him more.

"Shall we?" he asked. Kyra nodded and tossed her backpack on. She took off, following Marlee and Simon, promising herself she wouldn't look back to see where Ryder was behind her or if he was checking her out.

The next set of tunnels they checked held less than the first. Kyra was exhausted. They still had to check one more cave before starting the nine-mile hike back to where they'd left the car. She took several deep breaths as she steeled herself for the last cave, pulling strength from the air around her.

When they stopped and walked into the small area in front of the cave, they froze.

Kyra tried not to gag on the stagnant air pouring from the black opening. Images assaulted her so quickly that her brain couldn't process everything. She stumbled back, trying to move far enough away so that the air from the tunnel didn't assault her so terribly.

Simon dropped his pack, taking her by the arm. "Kyra?"

She held up a hand. "I'm fine," she said, looking deeply into the darkness of the cave. "Something terrible is going on in there."

Everyone turned to the opening. Kyra thought she saw something. Wasn't sure if it was a light or shadow. A voice drifted on the air. "Help me." It was so remorseful, it tore at Kyra's heart. She instinctively took a step forward, toward the movement deep within the cave.

"Do you see that?" she asked the group at large.

"I'm getting nothing," Simon said.

"All I can smell is death," Marlee said between her teeth.

Kyra wanted to turn and hush them. Something was in there. She took several steps forward. A light burned deep in the cave's shadows, a tiny glow moving away from the tunnel entrance. Words and horrible images danced unencumbered through Kyra's mind.

Something in her cracked at the pain she felt. She was almost inside the tunnel when a hand on her shoulder stopped her.

She turned to Ryder. "Can you hear it?" she begged, her heart breaking for the pain she read in the air.

Ryder's eyes were black and he looked over her shoulder. "I hear nothing."

Everyone stopped when an ear-shattering scream pierced the darkening evening. Kyra grabbed her head as pain lanced through her. "Something horrible is going on here!" she shrieked, doing her best to stay on her feet.

She turned back to the cave. The light faded. She knew she had to get to that light before it disappeared. Shaking off Ryder's hand, she Phased and ghosted into the darkness.

"Bloody hell," Ryder turned to Simon and barked. "What the fuck?"

Simon shrugged and started to follow her, only to be pulled to a halt by Ryder.

"I have no idea what's going to happen or what's in there. Go back to the car. If we don't return in an hour, get back to the house," Ryder said to Marlee.

"Are you insane? I'm not going to leave Kyra," Simon snapped.

"I'm not asking," Ryder barely controlled the shout. "If he resists, knock his ass out." Marlee nodded and Ryder knew she would take care of the situation. He took Marlee's pack, swinging it over his shoulder. He might need the extra supplies. He knew she'd have extra ammunition—and if he knew Marlee, explosives.

With the supplies, he took off into the cave, ignoring the argument starting at the entrance. Kyra was his only concern at the moment.

Kyra ignored the stagnant air as she turned down another passageway, the light leading her deeper into the mountain.

Images of mutilated men and women assaulted and flooded her mind. She finally stopped to take several deep breaths but the urge to keep moving forward pushed her onward. The air closed in around her and the light went out, leaving her in total darkness with only the voices of the dead to lead her on.

Screams echoed through the darkness. She bounced off walls, cutting and scraping herself. She pushed forward, knowing there was something she needed to do.

Ryder followed the scent that was uniquely Kyra. Screams echoed through the dark, and after several minutes, her smell changed. Tinged with the metallic taste of blood. Anger perfuse him in a way he couldn't understand. He ended up at several dead ends frustration making him careless. He knew Kyra obviously stumbling blindly through the caves. Regardless he felt he was getting closer; her scent stronger. He halted when he finally entered a large cavern. And froze, trying to take everything in. Then he saw her, her blue eyes sparkling in the dark of the cavern. He didn't move as her eyes darted around, stricken and panicked.

"Kyra?"

Her head swung in his direction but he knew she couldn't see as well in the dark as he could.

"It smells like death," she whispered. "It's choking me." She clawed at her throat, causing small scratches that started to bleed.

"Kyra, are you hurt?" he asked, stepping toward her slowly. He didn't know what had prompted her to take off like she had, or why she now sat curled up in a ball.

She shook her head no, and he could see tears streaking down her cheeks to mix with the bloody scratch's on her throat. "Did you know that air holds memories, Ryder?" she said frantically. "Holds pictures, visions, life, and death, stories of what has come, what has gone. Lives it has touched. Death's it has witnessed."

Ryder hadn't known that. He couldn't imagine hearing and seeing what could be trapped in the air. As a Tracker, he knew the air held many things, things he explored as a Tracker. But as an Air Element, the air did something completely different to Kyra. And at the moment, it looked like it was trying killing her.

"The air," she looked around the dark cavern, "is trapped with the souls and lives of what happened here." Her body stiffened and then convulsed her limbs shaking and tense. Her eyes rolled back as her body writhed on the cold floor.

Ryder rushed over to her. Once the convulsion stopped, her tired eyes focused on him. Her blue eyes glowed in the dark, beautiful as ever. "Terrible things have happened here," she gasped in pain.

Kyra clutched at the front of his shirt. "There isn't any air down here, Ryder. I'm an Air Element and this air is dead" She shook her head, struggling to take a full breath. "I can't breathe down here." Tears ran down her face and he brushed them away.

"Then let's get out of here." Ryder offered her his hand. Something in him snapping into place. Her pain and fear palatable.

Kyra closed her eyes and leaned her head back. "There isn't any air down here and something horrible is going on. Look around! The souls are trapped. The screams held in the air are desperate to be heard. But they aren't because there isn't any air!" she bellowed.

Ryder stood and looked around. Several tables sat littered with things you would find in a laboratory—microscopes and incubators. A generator rested in one corner. "What is this?" Metal fridges hung open, the contents spilled all over the floor.

Kyra grabbed his pant leg. "Someone is doing something very, very wrong. Creating things, living and dead." She looked around frantically as if someone would stop her next words. "Mostly dead, and they hurt," she cried. "They hurt so badly."

More screams pierced the darkness, and Ryder thanked the Gods they weren't from Kyra. He sent up a prayer for the poor soul. Kyra wrapped her arms around her head, as if that would stop the sound. Kyra was right—something horrible was taking place in this mountain. And they needed to find out exactly what it was. But at that moment, his main concern was Kyra.

"Make it stop," she moaned. "Something very, very bad is happening down here," she said again.

Ryder couldn't agree more, but he had to get Kyra out of there. "Can you walk?" he asked, bending down again. "There isn't any air down here. How can anything live where there isn't any air?" She cried, "It hurts." She clutched at her chest. "She is being tortured." More screaming from the tunnels.

Ryder wrapped his arms around Kyra and picked her up. "There is something very wrong with this place," she whispered, wrapping her arms around his neck. She pressed herself against him. "I am an Air Element. I can't breathe down here." She emphasized it by taking short little gasps. "It kills us, drives us insane. We need to be able to breathe air, fresh air."

That information would've been nice to know before they'd gone looking in the caves in the first place. He was going to kick someone's ass over this. Kyra should never have been brought here. Just being in the caves was deadly for her. Damn it. She'd just become a liability. And he didn't do liabilities.

"Why?" Ryder asked her. "Why would you come into this place knowing that?"

"The lights and the voices," she whispered her breath catching as she tried to breathe. Kyra looked up at him. Her eyes had turned silver. It was an eerie color that made her look unearthly. "Ryder, I can't breathe."

Ryder knew it was a bad idea, but he couldn't help himself. "You can breathe." He whispered the words against her lips and she inhaled the breath he offered. "See?" She nodded slightly and he gently blew into her slack mouth. Her eyes closed and her head leaned against his shoulder. Before he knew it, his lips were pressed against hers. He told himself that he was just helping her. Pulling away, he drew in more air and inhaled her beautiful scent. He nuzzled her neck and just behind her ear, inhaling deeply where her scent was the strongest. Kyra tilted her head and breathed in his exhalation. For Ryder, it was the most erotic feeling in the world; he would breathe out and she would inhale, pulling it deeply into herself. They breathed like that until Kyra had relaxed against him. He held her close, his lips brushing against hers several times. His tongue dipped in to taste her, and he stumbled against the wall, one hand going out to catch himself. Her taste went straight to his head, like alcohol. If another scream hadn't erupted through the cave, he would've lingered longer, exploring every part of her mouth, her taste, her smell.

He pulled back still concentrating all his exhales to feather across her face. He stopped for a moment and looked around the cavern, taking everything in. He breathed it in, solidifying the smell in his brain.

"We'll fix it," Ryder promised as he moved out of the cavern.

"I don't think we can," Kyra said quietly. "The darkness down here is suffocating. Way too much pain. Nobody can fix this."

Her breathing shallow, she was pale as death. But the moment they turned into the opening of the cave, fresh air hit her. She filled her lungs with several deep breaths, the fresh air causing her skin to glow. Her eyes drifted open. They were more silver than the aqua color Ryder had become used to. But the brilliant blue was bleeding back in and taking over the silver.

She reached up to cup his face. Leaning forward in his arms, she pressed her lips to his. This time he couldn't stop himself. He let her slide onto her feet and pressed her against the side of the cave, his hands roaming all over her amazing body. He memorized every magnificent inch he could manage to touch. He slid one hand down to cup her ass, pulling her into him. He then pulled her leg up and wrapped it around his hip. He pressed himself into the center of her femininity. She rewarded him with a slow and throaty moan.

Her taste was intoxicating. He sucked on her bottom lip, memorizing the taste and feel of her. He felt her body respond as she pressed against him. Her hands slid up the inside of his T-shirt. He jerked when her cold hands touched his stomach and moved up his chest.

"You're so warm," she moaned. "I can't get close enough."

Ryder wanted her so badly, he couldn't see straight. The gland in the back of his throat shot a volt through him and produced the extra saliva to mark her as his. He swallowed it, but it burned a path down his throat and churned like poison in his stomach. It was better than a cold shower for a Tracker.

He pulled away from her, his body rejecting the movement. He was glad when he had to hold out a hand to steady her; she was shaky on her feet. Her hands slid down his chest and stomach before they fell loose from his shirt. He felt the loss of her touch like a blow to head.

"Kyra." He breathed her name, everything in him screaming to touch, taste, and drink her in.

Aqua eyes stared up into his, rimmed with desire and need. It was almost his undoing. Screw everything. This was the woman he wanted like he had never wanted anything else in his long life.

"Thank you." She shook her head weakly. "I think this may even the score. You've saved me as many times as you have actually tried to kill me. Thank you." Her words, whispered and weak, held just a little self-deprecation. "I'm so tired." She wavered for a moment, then her eyes drifted close and she sunk into his arms again.

Ryder swore under his breath and looked down at the woman in his arms. What the hell was he doing? What the hell was he going to do with her? He couldn't look at her without wanting to tear her clothes off and make her his forever. The problem was he wasn't sure which scared him more—the thought of wanting her, or the thought of keeping her.

Chapter 4

Ryder cradled her in his arms as he came through the front door of the house.

"Is she all right?" Simon asked, rushing forward.

"Yes. Did you know how she was going to react to the caves?" he asked, shoving past him and moving into one of the bedrooms.

Simon followed close on Ryder's heels. "Air Elements react differently to caves and closed-in spaces. I had no idea how she would react, or that it could be so extreme."

"Someone has a lot of explaining to do," Ryder barked, his words making the entire house shake. "Because Kyra has now become a liability. If that thing is using those caves to traverse through that mountain, she is completely useless to us." He was going to have to bring in some more men, further complicating the issue. Just what he wanted—more Others gathering together around unexplained deaths. It was bound to attract the attention of the Tribunal. Just as Marlee had alluded to, this was getting a lot more complicated.

This time when Kyra woke up, she felt unusually rested, as if she'd slept for a week. She lay there as memories of the night before cascaded through her mind. Groaning, she pulled the covers over her head as everything came back to her. She had flipped out in the caves. Had lost herself among the smells and visions of death. Somebody had done some things they really shouldn't have done. Women and men alike had died for some sadistic reason.

She remembered visions and tried to sink further into the mattress. She never wanted to climb out again. Didn't want to face Simon or Fiona, or Gods, the very thought of having to look into Ryder's hard, dark eyes. It made her skin prickly with embarrassment.

However, in the darkness, he had been there. Ryder had breathed for her, kissed her. She vividly remembered wrapping herself around him only to have him pull away. The idea of a vacation was sounding better every minute. If she could just figure out where and how everything had gotten so far out of her control, she might be able to change it. She heaved a heavy sigh. Even she knew there was no way to fix this, no spell or magic that would be able to undo what had been done.

"Hiding?" Ryder asked from somewhere near the bed. Of course he was there, and of course she didn't sense him. Damn him. She groaned again. He was watching over her. After all, he'd been the one to find her hiding in a corner of a cave. Why not torture her a little more by watching over her? But, part of her screamed with glee that he'd stayed with her. Too bad she wanted to throttle that part of her.

"Hiding doesn't fix anything. And my sexy little Element, you have some questions to answer." He thought she was sexy? Kyra shook her head. She had thrown herself at him; it was clouding his judgment. Then she'd passed out. Eric would laugh his ass off. Ryder was just being nice.

"But this is so much easier than facing you," she whined into her pillow. "I am an Elemental Enforcer. I do not break down in a cave during an investigation."

The covers jerked free from over her body. She curled up, hugging her knees to her chest. "Why do you insist on torturing me?"

"You have some questions to answer. And I haven't begun to torture you." His last words terrified her.

"What?" She sat up, some of her temper taking over. "I made a mistake. Aren't people in your world allowed a few mistakes?"

"NO. Did you know you were going to lose it down there?" His voice vibrated over her.

"I knew if I went into the caves, there was a possibility of air sickness. It's when an Air Element is deprived of fresh air. I hadn't planned on actually going into the caves." She glared at him. "And you don't have to use your compulsion. Aren't we past that yet?"

"You said she was being tortured. Who is *she*?" Shit. She had said that. She felt like slapping herself in the head. And of course, he asked it using that damn voice again.

"Ryder, there were people—men and women both— who were tortured in that mountain. Experimented on, killed. The air down there pulsates with the deprived souls of innocence lost. This isn't something that just started a couple of months ago. The death there is centuries old," she answered, but didn't, hoping he wouldn't notice.

"You said it like you were speaking of someone specific." Damn, he was like a dog with a bone. Impossible. And any warm feelings she had for him for sitting with her and calling her sexy flew out the window.

"I think it's the Shade of his last victim." She looked down at her hands, knowing he really wasn't going to like that answer. But he'd demanded one, so she gave it to him. Let him stew on that for a moment.

Ryder stood up so quickly, his chair flew back. Kyra cringed. "And do you happen to be in contact with this Shade?" he asked using compulsion. Kyra felt the words bounce around her skull, but since she planned on telling him the truth, this time it didn't hurt.

"She came to me that first day, but I thought it was residual energy," she said in her own defense.

"And now?"

"She hasn't admitted it, but I think she might know more than she lets on." Kyra offered.

"Did it ever occur to you that this Shade might be working with that monster?" Actually, Kyra hadn't thought that. Shades didn't help their murderers. The look on her face must've given her away.

Ryder roughly raked his hand through his short hair and walked toward the door. He stopped and turned back to her. "Stay in bed. You need to rest." His words, though said gently, belied the anger that stiffened his shoulders as he slammed the door behind him.

Kyra lay there in shock for all of thirty seconds before swinging her legs over the edge of the bed. She headed toward the shower. If he thought he could tell her what to do, he had another thing coming.

"Is that really a good idea?" Marlee asked as Kyra came into the kitchen where everyone had gathered.

"This isn't something we can do on our own. The evil in that mountain is going to take more than us." Ryder glared at Kyra as she took a croissant from the tray next to the sink. She sat down at the table beside Simon. He smiled and patted her on the shoulder.

"You feeling okay?" he whispered.

Kyra smiled back. "Couldn't be better. What's going on?"

"They're arguing about whether to bring in reinforcements," Simon said.

"Why?" Kyra asked, looking back to Ryder. He was still glaring at her. She felt the urge to stick her tongue out at him but shoved a large chunk of croissant into her mouth instead.

"I thought I told you to stay in bed."

"I'm not going to hide in bed just because I had a little trouble in those caves. I will not let that monster beat me like that." She glared back. "Now what is going on?"

"I've called one of my brothers."

That shocked Kyra speechless for a moment. Until two days ago, she'd thought they were an extinct race, and now he was bringing in more? Fiona was going to have a ball questioning them. Her next thought—were they as good-looking as Ryder?

"If you can't handle yourself down there, then we need people who can." If he had struck her, he couldn't have hurt her worse.

Kyra bristled. "It won't happen again."

"Really? Can you promise me that? Or are we all going to put our lives on the line hoping you won't lose control?" She was so incensed, she was unable speak.

She stuttered and tried to regain some of her control. Before she was able to say or do anything, Ryder continued. "You will concentrate on how to kill it, and how to get rid of that Shade. And you will stay above ground. The issue is not up for debate," he said with absolute finality. He glared at her, daring her to contradict him.

Kyra was so mad, she was unable to form coherent words. All she wanted to do was throttle the overbearing ass. He'd assumed control of this crazed mission. She was saved from doing something stupid when Max came through the back door. Kyra felt bad for the man. He looked so tired.

"Thanks for coming, Max." Ryder thrust out a hand.

"Yeah, I owe you," Max grumbled.

Ryder snorted. "You sure as shit do. Because the shit your little town is facing is bad."

The man paled slightly. "Tell me what you found. Because another woman went missing last night."

It could've been her they heard screaming. Ryder had chosen to save Kyra instead of saving the woman.

"Has the body been recovered?" Marlee asked.

Max looked from her back to Ryder, sadness etching deep wrinkles around his expressive eyes. "Not yet. I'm putting the town on lockdown. Demanded that everyone stay out of the woods."

"Marlee?"

Marlee nodded and stood. She rolled her shoulders. "I still think bringing Lykar here is a bad idea." Then she pulled off her jacket and headed for the door.

"We'll have the body by nightfall, Max." Ryder patted the man's shoulder.

Simon joined the conversation. "From what Ryder saw in the cavern, it looks like someone has been doing something they weren't supposed to."

"Meaning?" Max asked.

"Someone tried to play God and failed," Kyra put her croissant down not hungry anymore.

"If we can figure out who created it, what was done to it, then we'll have a better idea how to kill it." Ryder grunted and rubbed a hand over his skull, redirecting everyone to the real topic. Kyra realized this was his one show of irritation. His face gave away nothing that he didn't want seen, but he rubbed his head when he was irritated.

"My brother is on his way. It doesn't leave a lot in the way of being able to track it, so having more Trackers will enable us to cover more ground. I'm hoping to trap it." Ryder sighed heavily. "Kyra is going to figure out a way to kill it while we try to figure out a way to lure it out of the mountain."

Fiona interrupted them all when she walked into the room, a man following close behind her. Kyra and Simon jumped to their feet, garnering a glare from Ryder. It wasn't Fiona, though—it was the man behind her who had brought Kyra to her feet.

Marcus smiled and Kyra couldn't help but feel her heart melt just a little. He was beautiful, exuding so much light and goodness that it was almost painful to look at him. How could someone so amazing have fallen from the heavens? One day she was going to get her answer, but for right now, it was enough that the fallen angel was here.

Marcus moved over to Kyra, hugging her, and placed a gentle kiss on her cheek. "It is good to see you again, Kyra."

"Who the fuck is this?" Ryder said, stepping forward. Kyra glared at him over her shoulder.

Marcus laughed softly, and extended his hand to Ryder. "I am Marcus."

"Holy hell," Max swore, taking a step back from the larger man. "You're the Fallen."

Marcus turned his smile toward Max and nodded imperceptibly. "Not 'the' Fallen, but a Fallen nonetheless."

Ryder threw up his hands. "Just what we need. A Goddamned fallen Angel to round out our merry group." He stomped from the room. Kyra thought about throwing something at him. Hadn't he just said they needed more people?

Marcus laughed softly. "It's a good thing I'm not here to gain his approval."

"Why are you here?" Kyra asked. Not that she cared why he was there. He was beautiful and kind and she loved working with him. They'd worked together several times and had grown close. He was one of the most gorgeous men she'd ever laid eyes on with his honey-colored hair and high cheekbones, those full lips that often smiled, though she knew they could also be cruel. Unfortunately, Marcus had taken a vow of celibacy five hundred years ago. And he fought personal demons that he didn't speak of. She would never try to persuade him to tell her something he didn't want to.

"I hear you have an interesting tagalong." He looked around the room. "But I see nothing."

Kyra shrugged. "She comes and goes."

Marcus gave her a hard look. "She is sentient?"

"She acts as if she isn't, but I think she is." The Shade didn't act like lingering energy. Kyra didn't offer that the Shade might be working with the monster they were all here to kill.

He extended his hand to Kyra. "Shall we go find her?"

Marcus might've fallen from the Elysian Fields where the Angels held court, but he still held the aura and goodness of a pure and golden soul, and Kyra was not immune to him.

"Of course." Kyra smiled.

"What about the Tracker?" Marcus asked.

"I'll handle him," Max offered, standing. He stopped as Ryder appeared in the doorway.

Ryder was strapped to the hilt with an array of weapons that boggled Kyra's mind. "Let's get this done. Lykar will be here by nightfall."

Kyra's mouth dropped open. "What are you expecting to find out there?"

Ryder's eyes were black as death as he looked at her. "Something that is tearing women apart. So I'll need whatever it might take to destroy it. Does that answer your question, Blue?"

"But is all of this really necessary?" Marcus asked.

Ryder grunted. "You have no idea what is needed. You just got here."

Marcus nodded. "That may be so. However, the darkness that I sense in the mountain is something not even I have seen or heard of before. How can you know if your weapons will have any effect?"

"If you can sense it, why don't you do something about it?" Ryder asked incredulously.

"Oh, right …" Ryder drew it out. "You Fallen do nothing that doesn't benefit you."

Marcus shook his head. "We are fighting our own war, Tracker. One you could never begin to understand."

Ryder got in Marcus's face. "You have no idea what I can comprehend. Now let's get this over with."

He pushed past Marcus and slammed through the back door. Marcus shook his head. "That man has a chip on his shoulder. If he's not careful, it will prove to destroy him."

Kyra had the strangest urge to defend Ryder. Instead, she bit her tongue. Ryder had been kind and gentle, but he had also knocked her out and shot at her. She couldn't decide whether she liked him or if she would rather see him dead. He was such a contradiction, it was making her crazy. And that was all before she had thrown herself at him in the cave. Yeah, he was a complicated, angry man, and she wished to the Gods she could figure him out.

Nobody spoke as they made their way up into the mountain. They stopped in the same clearing as before. As they exited the cars, the Shade immediately appeared next to Kyra, screeching like a banshee. Simon and Marcus both took reflexive steps back. Kyra, on the other hand, had had enough.

She stepped right up to the Shade so they were nose to nose. "Stop!" Kyra bellowed at it.

The Shade immediately shut her mouth as if Kyra had stuffed a sock into her open gob.

"What makes you think that screaming like that is going to change anything?"

As the Shade looked around the group, something passed in her eyes. Again, Kyra almost missed it. A look of shock was quickly replaced with calculation.

"You're not like the usual Mortals who come to see what is haunting these woods. Besides, isn't that how the dead act? Shaking chains and moaning, screeching for redemption?" the Shade looked at the group.

Kyra laughed. She couldn't help it. "Honestly?" Kyra shook her head. "I have no idea how the dead act. I haven't had that much contact with them. But I do know the screeching has got to stop."

"This doesn't feel right," Ryder growled.

"He isn't a very happy person, is he?" the Shade asked. "You should get rid of him."

Kyra shrugged, choosing to ignore Ryder's comment. "What is your name?"

"Sophie," the Shade replied.

"Who did this to you?"

"I thought he cared about me." She drifted for a moment before solidifying again. "He said he did."

"Who?" Kyra asked. This could all be solved if she'd just tell them who was doing this.

"I can't remember his name," Sophie said sadly. She shimmered with the sun, fading and then forming again.

"He lied to her. That information left her when she died because it wasn't true," Marcus said. Moving forward, he stared at Sophie. He shook his head and walked around her. Sophie watched him with calculated eyes.

"What?" Kyra and Sophie both asked at the same time.

"She's tethered," he said, looking behind Sophie toward the dark shadows of the mountain.

"Something is coming," Ryder glared at the tree line.

"Oh, don't worry. It can't move past the tree line," Sophie said. She turned in a circle, trying to see what Marcus was talking about.

"How do you know that?" Kyra asked, watching the tree line. She wasn't exactly sold on believing what Sophie had to say.

"Because he was trapped there," Sophie said. She then turned to Marcus. "What do you mean, I'm tethered? What are you? Actually, what are any of you? None are Mortal."

Marcus gave her a sad look before turning to Fiona. "Something isn't right. She's not a Shade …" He left the rest hanging. "She should be dealt with before she becomes a burden."

"Okay." Kyra couldn't agree more. "How exactly do we do that?"

Sophie started to rock back and forth on her heels, softly moaning.

Marcus turned to her. "She's not what you think she is. Are you?" Sophie's eyes narrowed but she said nothing. "Until she shows her true identity, I am unable to help. However, I do know that she is putting you all in danger. She had a direct connection to the darkness in that mountain."

Kyra grabbed hold of Marcus as he moved off. "What do you mean you can't help her? What is going to happen to her?"

Marcus lowered his voice. "She will be consumed by whatever has her tethered. Or she will wander for eternity in the form she now has." He looked back at Sophie. "Maybe this is the Gods punishment for her."

Sophie's moaning grew louder and made the hair on Kyra's arms stand on end.

"She is not a Shade. Her entity is older than what is going on here. Don't trust her," Marcus said so that only Kyra could hear.

"What exactly are you?" he asked the Shade.

Kyra looked at Sophie who was again quiet. She no longer looked like the lost soul she'd been playing for days.

She glared at Marcus. "I will not remain trapped like this forever," she uttered, her voice an unearthly, guttural snarl.

Marcus took a deep breath and leaned into Sophie, his head tilting to the side as if he was trying to place something that he had forgotten. Sophie immediately backed off; Marcus nodded, as if her movement confirmed his answer.

"Be that as it may, you are not in the in-between. You are tethered by whatever darkness did this to you. You cannot move on until it is killed or your soul is devoured. You are trapped." As Marcus spoke, Sophie's eyes widened until they were the size of saucers.

Kyra felt sadness for the woman. She obviously didn't want this. She started to wail again.

"I promise we will find a way to get you released," Kyra promised. But as the words passed her lips, something deep within the mountain moaned and the clearing shivered.

Everyone stopped when a horrifying sound screeched through the woods. Kyra had never heard anything so menacing. The blast shook the earth under their feet and sent branches flinging at them in the clearing.

The ground shook harder. Marcus tried to grab hold of Kyra as they stumbled around, but they were both thrown to the ground. Kyra felt pain slash through her upper left arm and couldn't quite control her scream of pain.

Ryder bellowed in rage, almost matching the menace of what was coming from the mountain. Between the bellowing of the men around her and the growls and moans now coming from the woods, Kyra was unable to make heads or tails of what the hell was going on.

Ryder was suddenly next her, standing between her and the mountain. She grasped his strong arms for balance, glad he was there, until he spoke. "Get in and stay there." He said dragging her over to the side of the car.

"It can't come past the tree line," she argued. Besides, she wasn't about to hide from it. She might've had a bad couple of days, but she was ready to kick some ass. Ryder stopped in his tracks and gave her a hard look.

"Are you sure?" He looked from her to the tree line and back. "How do you know?"

"That's what Sophie said." Kyra nodded to the screeching Shade.

"Oh, for the love of all the Gods," Marcus swore and cuffed the woman upside the head. She immediately dispersed in wisps of black smoke. "That's better. I don't know about you, but I couldn't stand to listen to that for another second."

The thundering from the woods stopped the moment Sophie disappeared. Everyone turned to look at the border of the trees. Nothing moved, not even a breeze to rustle the leaves.

"They're linked. Are you sure she isn't working with him?" Marcus asked.

"It hadn't occurred to me that she might be working with whatever that thing is. But the evidence is starting to mount against her," Kyra said, knowing it was exactly the conclusion Ryder had come to.

"But what is it?" Ryder asked, eyeing the tree line. Everything had gone quiet. Nothing moved or made a sound. She noticed she was the only one with a wound. She closed her eyes and took a steadying breath, trying not to curse the Fates. Did it have to be her?

Ryder grabbed the first-aid kit out from the trunk and pulled her over so he could dress her wound. Again.

"You seem to be doing this a lot," she said.

Ryder didn't look up. "Who saved your ass before me? Because I have no idea how you've remained alive."

His words stung worse than her wound. "Up until this job, I guess I've just been lucky." She pulled away the moment he was done and moved over to Simon and Marcus.

Marcus shook his head. "I've never seen anything like it before. Someone is playing creator. I think he missed his mark. The mere fact that the creator has trapped it says he failed at what he was trying to do. Find a way to kill it."

"I think that's what we're here to do," Kyra said with more sarcasm than she intended. Which only made Simon and

Marcus give her a hard look. Now she had pissed off all the men with her. Just want she needed.

Thankfully, Marlee loped out of the woods fully dressed, which Kyra was thankful for. The Lycan threw up her hands. "That was an awesome show. Let's not stick around for the encore." She headed toward the cars, but stopped when no one else moved. Marlee eyed the group as if collectively, they were all insane. "Then at least tell me you have a fucking plan."

"I think we might have bait," Ryder said, eyeing Kyra.

She didn't like the way he was looking at her. "Whatever you're thinking, stop. I'm not bait," Kyra spat, unable to control her temper. If that was all he thought she was good for, then he was sorely mistaken. She was more than capable of taking care of herself. Not that she had proved it to him. So she might've been wrong about Sophie. But that didn't mean she was going to play bait for him, or anyone else for that matter.

Ryder only grunted before pushing past her. Another damn grunt and God only knew what that one meant. Her temper flared, burning the edges of her sanity. She didn't know what a bullet would do to the Tracker, but she was willing to find out. Before she thought better of it, she had pulled out her weapon and aimed it directly at the center of his arrogant back.

A hand settled on her forearm and she turned to Marcus, who was smiling sadly at her. "This action will only take you from the light. It won't kill him, but it will make you into something you don't like. Honestly, do you really want to see him hurt like that? He's not all bad."

She lowered her weapon. "I'm pretty sure it would make me feel a hell of a lot better."

Marcus threw his head back and laughed. "I'm sure it would, my little Element. However, the world would be a worse place with one fewer Tracker. And for that matter, the light that you bring it with your fierce attitude and strength."

"You said it wouldn't kill him," she said petulantly and holstered her gun.

"I found the body," Marlee said, breaking into her conversation.

Marcus shook his head. "Mortals are so fragile. It saddens me to see a life snuffed out prematurely."

"We need to collect it," Ryder said, his voice gruff.

Max shook his head. "I'm really sick of having to tell town members that their wives, daughters, or sisters are dead. And that we have no idea what happened to them."

Kyra's heart went out to him; his job wasn't an easy one. She followed the group as Marlee led them to the body. The scene was so much more gruesome in reality. The photos she had seen gave her a sense of disconnection. There was no way to disconnect herself from what lay on the forest floor in front of her. It was much worse than she could've ever imagined. She promised the poor soul that she wouldn't rest until this monster was destroyed.

"Wait." Max held out his hands to the group. Everyone stopped. "Marlee, did you do anything with the scene at all?"

Marlee rolled her eyes. "Of course not. This isn't my first rodeo, sheriff."

Kyra focused all her senses on the air around them. It was heavy, almost alive, the woods deathly silent.

"Trap?" Simon whispered.

"Something isn't right," Max said, stepping forward cautiously. "How close did you go?" he asked Marlee over his shoulder.

"Didn't get this far. I smelled it and came back for you guys," Marlee admitted.

Max sniffed the air. "Something is very wrong."

Ryder stepped in front of Kyra, pushing her back.

"Hey." She shoved back. Ryder didn't even turn around to acknowledge her. "Would you please stop doing this?"

"I just don't want to have to rescue your ass again so soon," Ryder said over his shoulder.

"I should've pulled the damn trigger," she muttered to herself.

Ryder finally turned his eyes black. He leaned down so that he was speaking into her ear. "If you ever point a gun at me again, pull the trigger. Because you won't get a second chance." He then pulled away, but not before licking the shell of her ear. Shivers raced down her spine to settle deep in the center of her back. Spikes of desire pierced through her body.

He was watching her, his dark eyes saying nothing. "Don't we have a job to do?"

Simon kneeled down and buried his hands in the earth, closing his eyes. Marcus jumped up into the trees. Kyra watched in amazement as he walked nimbly from branch to branch, as if weightless. Marlee shifted into wolf form, blending into the undergrowth.

Kyra looked at Ryder, who was still staring at her. "And what's your superpower?" she asked sarcastically, hurt and frustrated.

Ryder finally smiled, a dangerous, predatory smile. "I have many." And then he moved, so fast she didn't see him. One moment he was standing there and the next he was gone. She only rolled her eyes; he was totally showing off now.

Max had blended into the woods as well. She felt utterly alone. She closed her eyes and breathed deeply, drawing the air into her lungs. She reached out and was bombarded with images. A blond woman running through the woods, tears streaking down her face. She didn't cry out. As though she knew no one would hear. She stumbled and Kyra reached out as if she could do something to change the outcome.

Blackness swamped her, hiding what was being done to the woman. Kyra had a feeling if she could hear anything, it would be terrorizing screams. She had to admit, she was thankful to be spared that much. Kyra stepped forward as the darkness dissipated and a man stepped forward. For half a second, Kyra thought it was still a past image. Then Marcus bellowed something and Kyra realized she had walked straight into the trap.

Chapter 5

Her first thought was, she had just handed Ryder a reason to rescue her ass again. She wanted to stomp her foot but was too busy assessing the situation with every single Elemental sense she had.

She looked around, waiting for the others to do something, anything. But they all seemed frozen, not moving.

"Great. Just great," Kyra muttered to herself. She was on her own.

The man in front of her smiled slowly. "They cannot reach you, little one." He whispered the words and they moved over Kyra like an icy wind. Frost glistened on her eyelashes and her breath billowed out in frozen, smoky puffs.

He was good-looking, in an "I'll kill you if you get too close to me" sort of way. Raven hair hung down over pale skin; eyes as black as night burrowed into her. Black slacks and a black shirt made him look even paler than he was.

She heard gunshots and felt the air around her shiver. Kyra watched in amazement as a bullet shot toward the back of the man's head, but it came at him in slow motion before coming to a stop and whizzing back to where it had come from. Several other bullets did the same.

"What are you?" she asked, backing up a step. Her mind reeled with possibilities and what exactly her next move might be. When her back slid against a cold surface, she turned to see a wall of ice so thick, it distorted the woods beyond. She jerked back and the ice faded and disappeared. Experimentally, she reached out and touched a finger against the barrier that surrounded her. The ice barrier reappeared.

She turned back to the man. "That's new. What exactly are you?" She was so happy her voice didn't break, because she was shaking from head to toe.

Broad shoulders shrugged. "I am not supposed to be."
He sounded as if it hurt him to admit it. I search for peace,
Kyra. Can you give that to me?" He moved toward her fast, his
hands reaching out for her neck.

"How do you know my name?" Kyra asked, dodging
from his reach at the last second. She wasn't Mortal, and she
wasn't going down without a fight.

The man shimmered before answering. "I know more
than you think I do." He advanced again.

Kyra dodged the attack and dropped to the ground,
rolling out of his reach. She grabbed a fallen tree limb the size
of her own arm as she came back to her feet. She held it as a
weapon. Not using her guns was killing her, but she already
knew how well those worked with this thing.

"I don't think you're really searching for peace," Kyra
said as he swung at her. Kyra ducked but felt the power behind
the blow. She was certain she wouldn't be able to withstand
many of them. Elements were not imMortal, and this thing
knew it, picking her out as the weakest link in the group. Kyra
would just have to prove him wrong.

He stopped for a moment and tilted his head to the side
as if in thought. "Aren't we all searching for peace of some
kind? Mine requires the souls of others. We must all do what is
necessary in order to survive and find peace." He lowered his
chin and glared at her with sightless black eyes.

He attacked again. Kyra spun out of his grasp,
slamming the tree limb against the back of his head as he went
by. He seemed to absorb the blow and let fly an elbow that
slammed into Kyra's chest. It took her off her feet and she hit
the dirt, the breath knocked out of her. Gasping, she opened her
eyes only to see the thing descending upon her. Kyra rolled
away, barely keeping out of his hands. Rolling to her hands and
knees, she continued to gasp for air. She went through
everything she could do and decided that hand to hand conflict
was the best option at the moment.

As for the thing, it stood looking down at her as she climbed to her feet, as if waiting to give her a moment so that the fight wouldn't be cut short.

"Bastard," Kyra muttered.

Kyra watched closely, trying to telegraph his movements. Her only warning was a twitch of a muscle as a hand slammed into her chest. She flew back and the cold wall stopped her. She struggled for air and looked up through the frozen wall. Ryder stood on the other side, screaming and pounding against the barrier. Kyra pulled herself to her feet and put her hand flat against where Ryder pounded helplessly. She then turned back to the thing. The muscle twitched and she phased out just as a hand reached into her chest. She reappeared behind him and swung the tree limb at the back of his head with every ounce of strength she had.

He crumpled to the ground and she pulled one of her guns from its holster, pointed, and pulled the trigger. The bullet entered the back of his head. Kyra watched in horror as the wound closed as quickly as it opened. How the hell were they going to kill this thing?

He turned into a mass of inky black shadow before solidifying again, standing directly facing her. He backhanded her and she collapsed to the ground, her face on fire. Stars danced around the edges of her vision as she barely held on to consciousness. Her mouth bloodied, she spat and staggered back to her feet. If the thing was going to kill her, she would die on her feet, damn it.

"It will be a pleasure to devour your soul, Kyra. You have such passion, such strength. With your soul, I will be able to break through the barrier, and finally be free." He grabbed her by the neck and squeezed. Kyra dropped everything and clutched at the hand that held her throat as he lifted her several inches off the ground.

He pulled her forward, still not allowing her feet to touch. He leaned forward and rubbed his nose against her cheek. It felt cold and dead. "I think of all the souls I have devoured, I will enjoy yours the most. Think of me while you futilely try to destroy me. I'll be thinking of you." He licked her cheek, his tongue like slime gliding over her skin. She barely controlled the urge to throw up.

And then he was gone.

Kyra lay in the dirt gasping for air. Action burst around her, but she didn't notice any of it. Never before in all her time as an Enforcer had anything frightened her as much as his last words. She made it to her hands and knees, only to stumble to the side and tumble back into the dirt.

"Damn it all to hell." Ryder slid to a halt next to her.

Kyra held up a hand. "Keep it to yourself." She wasn't ready to deal with Ryder.

He grabbed her by the shoulders and pulled her so that she was facing him. "Where are you hurt?"

"Everywhere." Kyra jerked away from him, forcing herself to stand on her own two feet, even though her legs wanted to give way. "I don't need your caretaking," she choked.

"Are you okay?" Simon asked.

"Yes," Kyra spat.

"We saw what was happening but we couldn't do anything," Simon said. "It was like you were in a glass box or something."

"Well, that would explain the lack of help," Kyra said.

Marlee appeared next to her, pulling on her T-shirt. "Shit, girl, some of those blows looked like they freakin' hurt. I thought Ryder was going to go bat-shit crazy. Never seen him so out of control before. Couldn't decide what was the better show—you getting your ass handed to you or Ryder going gonzo."

Marcus stepped forward. "What did he say to you?"

"That he wanted to eat my soul."

Marlee snorted. "No offense, but better you than me."

"Shut up, Marlee," Ryder snapped.

Marlee shrugged her shoulders and turned back to the woods. "I'll follow it, but I think it's just going back to its lair."

Marcus stopped her. "Regardless of what we saw, I'm sure that she injured him. He is going to ground. There is no use following him." Marcus looked into the woods in the direction the thing had taken off. "We know where he's going. And we now know what he wants." He turned back to Kyra, a sad look in his eyes.

Ryder was so furious, he couldn't see straight. Marcus and Simon were stuck to Kyra like glue after the attack, not letting her out of arms reach until after the body had been collected and Max had left. Then they flanked her in the backseat on the drive back to the house. If Marcus touched her once more, Fallen or not, Ryder was going to grind him into dust.

Once they were at the house, Ryder took off on Kyra's bike, which he'd gone back to the stupid ass motel for. And she hadn't even noticed.

He was an idiot. He wasn't sure whose ass he wanted to kick more—Simon, Marcus, or his own. His attachment to Kyra was driving him mad. He was losing control. Watching her take that beating when he couldn't help? Never in his life had he felt so utterly helpless. Not when his father had died, or his brothers and sisters. None of those occasions had left him feeling so helpless. Impotent fury had eaten at his gut while watching her fight that thing.

Ryder finally stopped just outside of town and climbed off the bike. He desperately wanted to hit something, wanted to have some sense knocked into him. Even he could tell he wasn't acting like his normal, heartless self.

He forced himself to think about a way to take his focus off Kyra and direct it on the monster instead. Regardless, his mind kept going back to the fact that he'd left her in the house with Simon, who wore his love for Kyra on his sleeve. And Marcus, who just looked too damn good. Damn Fallen drew people to them like moths to a flame. They just couldn't help themselves. Others and Mortal combined—it seriously irritated Ryder.

"You look like hell."

"Yeah, well it could be worse. I could look like you." Ryder turned to his brother. Lykar was his exact opposite. Blond with golden eyes, women fell at his feet and he sucked it up like a dying man offered a glass of water. Casanova had nothing on Ryder's younger brother.

"You would be so lucky." Lykar punched him in the shoulder.

"What are you nannies going on about?"

"Things couldn't possible get any worse now, could they?" He turned to Skylar. His one brother that he desperately wanted to have a relationship with but the past had come between them and neither of them knew how to get past it. You never really knew which side he was on, or if he was even going to be nice.

To prove that point, without warning, Skylar threw a punch as his way of saying hello. They *had* left on bad terms the last time they saw each other. The hit laid Ryder out in the gravel, bleeding from the nose.

Ryder launched to his feet and leveled Skylar with a backhand. Skylar attempted to block the blow but wasn't fast enough. He was on his own back, blood trickling from a split lip.

"At least you're learning. Nice attempt at a block," Lykar laughed, helping Sky to his feet. He slapped Ryder on the back. "Are the two of you done?" he asked.

Sky laughed, spitting blood. "We haven't even started yet."

"Why the fuck did you bring him?" Ryder demanded.

"He was the only one not doing anything." Lykar shrugged. "Besides, he thrives on weird and freaky."

"Yeah, because he is weird and freaky," Ryder said, which only made Skylar smile.

Even though they all dealt with weird and freaky on a daily basis, Sky was the one who excelled in it. It might have had something to do with the fact that he'd been a mercenary for a bloodthirsty madman for over a century.

"Either of you ever work with Elements before?" Ryder asked, heading back to the bike.

Sky spat again. "Yep, a couple of times, but it's been centuries. I actually thought they had all died off. They aren't the best race to work with, secretive little buggers. Is that what we are hunting?"

"I have no idea exactly what we are tracking, but the Elements want it as well. So we're working with them." Ryder watched closely his brothers' reactions. They didn't disappoint him.

"The hell you say?" Sky barked.

"We don't work with others. Just the fact that you put up with that crazy Wer is enough. Anything more is not an option," Lykar argued.

"Oh, and apparently, they've brought in a Fallen," Ryder said, smiling. Irritating his brothers was actually making him feel better. Sky took a swing at him, but Ryder moved out of the way. "Getting slow in your old age."

Instead of throwing another punch, Skylar launched himself onto Ryder. Ryder welcomed the fight; he needed this. He hoped that Sky was able to knock some sense into him.

"What the hell happened to you?" Kyra's mouth dropped open as his brother's drug him into the house between them. "Were you attacked?"

He couldn't tell if she was concerned or annoyed by his appearance. He secretly hoped it was concern. He could use someone to take care of him, if only for a moment. His second thought was that his brother hadn't beaten him hard enough because he still wanted the damn woman.

"In a manner of speaking, yes," he muttered through swollen lips and lifted a bottle of vodka he and his brothers had been working on. Kyra shook her head but didn't move.

Ryder pushed past her and walked down the hall into the room he was using. He threw himself on the bed. He would sleep it off and tomorrow, the world would make sense again.

Unfortunately, Kyra and his brothers followed him.

"Excuse me!" Kyra scrambled back as Skylar pushed her aside so that he could lean against the wall. He promptly slid to the floor. "Who is this?" she demanded of Ryder.

Lykar gave her a bright smile. "I am Lykar." He nodded toward Sky. "That's Skylar. We're here to help."

Ryder watched Kyra's reaction from beneath lowered lids. She narrowed her beautiful blue eyes. "Well, you aren't going to be much help in your current condition." She looked over at Ryder and then back to his brothers.

Lykar bowed his head, smiling. "Yes, well, we heal fast. And you must be Kyra?"

Lykar gave her the once-over, which seriously pissed Ryder off. "Go find a bed," Ryder growled. Lykar smiled at his brother, swung Sky over his shoulder, and left.

"Those are your brothers?" Kyra asked. He listened to her move around the room and then she was pressing a wet cloth to his face. He froze as she wiped the blood from his cheek. Her hands were so gentle. It was different from the women he had come to know lately, and it left him slightly breathless. The kiss from the cave haunted him, and he wanted nothing more than to kiss her again.

"Is there a reason you fought with …"

"Skylar?" he supplied. "Because Skylar is an ass. I would bet money that by the end of tomorrow, you'll want to kick his ass too. He has a warped sense of humor."

He saw her smile. "Don't you think that's the pot calling the kettle black?" she snorted. It was an endearing sound, one he wouldn't mind hearing from her more often.

"Something like that. By the way, how are you feeling? I see you've lost your two body guards," Ryder said.

"I'm fine. A little sore, but I'll survive," she said, still cleaning the blood from his face.

He reached up to hold her hand against his cheek, soaking up the warmth she exuded, the luminescence that was unique to her. "I'm really not all that bad, you know."

One of her eyebrows rose in obvious disbelief. "Of course you're not. Just because you've tried to kill me a couple of times shouldn't ruin my view of you."

He had to give her that one. "I'm not trying to kill you right now. I've saved you several times too. Don't forget that." Those words made her stiffen.

"I don't need you to save me, Ryder."

He reached up and cupped her cheek, unable to resist. "I like saving you. You have the bluest eyes. Do you know that?" he muttered.

She jerked away from him. "All the Air Elements have blue eyes. It's nothing special."

"But they are special, no matter what you say." He wasn't going to argue the point with her. She had beautiful eyes. If he stared long enough, he'd be able to see eternity through them.

"You look like hell." He knew she was trying to change the subject.

"How old are you, Kyra?" he asked, ignoring her comment.

"I'll answer that if you answer a question for me." She was pushing it, but he nodded agreement. Too damn tired and worn out to argue with her. "I was born in 1836. When we go through the Changing, our aging slows down."

"So not imMortal?" It was more a statement than a question. So she could die? He wasn't sure why, but that scared the hell out of him, sobering him slightly. He wanted to immediately lock her up in order to keep her safe and wondered if there was a basement under the house.

She shrugged. "No, not imMortal, but long lived. Fiona is several hundred years old. We have natural immunities to the illness in the Mortal plane. How old are you?" She tossed the now-bloodied cloth on the bedside table and sat down, tucking her legs under her. She rested against the headboard and looked as if she might stay awhile. And damn it, he wanted her to. For the first time in as long as he could remember, he felt comfortable and relaxed.

"I'm older than you," he offered, not really answering her question.

"ImMortal?"

"Yes, so it really doesn't matter what year I was born, does it?" It was a number, after all, and like the Elements, when they reached maturity, they stopped aging completely.

"But I would like to know," she pressed.

"432."

"Current or past century?" He had to give it to her—she was smart.

"Past," he said.

Her eyes bulged. "Damn, you are old." She giggled. "Did they even have the wheel back then? Fire?" She barely finished her sentence before bursting out laughing. "Oh my God, I can just imagine you in a Conan the Barbarian outfit—furry underwear and swords across your back, storming a village." She laughed harder. "Now that I would pay to see."

Ryder ignored her, but only because she wasn't that far off. Besides, the sound of her laughter was making him feel better, rolling over his wounds, both inside and out, like a soothing balm.

He was just about to drift off when she calmed herself and asked another question. "If you are imMortal, then there should be hundreds of Trackers in the world. But you are the first I've met."

"You're the first Element I've met. How many of you are there?"

She snorted and shook her head. "But we die, we get old and die. You're …" she poked him in the shoulder with an index finger, "imMortal. And like huge, scary, and invincible."

Ryder didn't know if he should feel complimented or insulted. Being imMortal wasn't all it was cracked up to be. Although, he had to admit, he enjoyed who and what he was.

"We can't die by natural means like old age, Kyra. That doesn't mean we can't be killed or that we don't die." He had watched the majority of his people die and refused to watch one more Tracker die by foul, or fair, measures. They would protect each other to the death. It was the one thing that they all agreed upon without a shadow of doubt. He would always have his brothers' backs, and they in turn would have his.

"So, the rumors are true, then?" she asked quietly. Ryder knew exactly what she was referring to but wasn't in the mood to talk about it. He swung himself to the other side of the bed so he could get away from her. This was not something he or his brothers discussed.

"And what rumors are those?" he asked, his voice laced with steel. He walked into the bathroom and splashed water on his face, washing the remaining blood away. He had a cracked rib and was bruised, but by morning, he'd be good as new.

When he finally walked back into the room, Kyra was still on the bed. She gave him a sad look. Fury erupted through him and it took everything he had to not lash out at her. But it wasn't her fault that his race fell in love, and that it could potentially kill them. It was the fault of Fate. The only thing that could be done about it was for the Trackers to keep to themselves.

"It's true what the books say about Trackers? That if you fall in love, it could kill you? Your own body slowly poisons you to death. Unless the one you fall in love with is an Other and can withstand the venom of your bonding kiss?" she shook her head sadly.

"It must seem very romantic to you. A race of hunters and warriors reduced to lovesick, whipped dogs." He raked his hand over his head. It was the reason he'd lost his four sisters and one brother. It was why he, Skylar, and Lykar had made a pact to never fall in love. Then they had met up with Falcon and through the centuries, picked up more. There were eight of them now, all brothers. Fighting for each other till the deadly end. No love, no death.

"No, it seems like a horrible fate. I couldn't imagine what that would be like. Never being able to let anyone in for the fear of losing everything. Hasn't there ever been successful mating?"

"Of course. And if you think I'm secretive, try to figure out who they are." He knew of four couples who lived happily, but they didn't have children, wouldn't submit their babies to the torture that they themselves had gone through. "We don't get the choice, Kyra, of who we fall in love with. Fate is a cruel mistress."

He could see the horrified look in Kyra's eyes. Ryder moved so quickly, he knew she couldn't track his movements. He had her pinned to the bed beneath him in the span of a heartbeat.

"I neither need nor want your pity, Kyra. Love is a wasted emotion for idealists and lovesick fools. Neither of us are either of those things, so don't pity Trackers. We do just fine."   She shook her head. "No, it's not. Elements thrive on love. We couldn't live without it. It brings us light and hope. I often think it should be its own Element. Wars have been fought, lost, and won on love alone."

Ryder snorted. It was a cynical sound, even to him. "And how's that treated the races so far? Your precious Element of Light is lost to you forever. As a people, you are helpless against the world and its darkness because of it."

He could tell his words were hurting her, but he needed her to understand that he had nothing to give her. Although, he wasn't sure who he was trying to convince—her, or himself? Instead of trying to understand his feelings, Ryder went in for the kill. "You've secreted yourself away from the world because of it. Your entire race is in danger because of the love of one woman."

"Stop," she whispered, her beautiful blue eyes filled with tears. "Love and light are two different things. You love your brothers, and you're a Tracker, so you love the hunt. It brings you calmness and centers you. Call it whatever you want, but it is still love. Try as you might, nothing you say will make me believe you are heartless. You love just as powerfully as everyone else."

Ryder snorted. "I never admitted to being heartless, Kyra. I just refuse to share that heart with anyone. Love is overrated."

Kyra shook her head. "Everyone needs love, physically and mentally," she said passionately.

Ryder pressed himself against her. "I don't need love to satisfy my physical desires, and neither does anyone else. Ask the hundreds of Mortals and Others out there fucking anything that will stand still long enough." He was surprised when she didn't pull away. It drew him in. "Lust is a great substitute for love, Kyra."

Then he was kissing her, pressing his lips against hers, soaking up her warmth and light. He coaxed her mouth open and thrust his tongue in, tasting her, drawing her taste into him. It went straight to his head like the finest liquor. Stars burst behind his closed eyes. Ryder sank deeply into the kiss. He didn't need love from Kyra; he only needed her body.

She pressed herself into him, giving as good as she got, which only made Ryder want her more. The primal Tracker in him screamed for domination, the need to mark her building inside him to an overwhelming desire.

Ryder jerked away from her as his mouth filled with the pheromone that was unique to Trackers. It was a sign of how much Ryder wanted Kyra and how dangerous she would be to him. Ryder rolled away, trying to control the way his body reacted to her.

Kyra pulled away. Swinging her feet to the floor, she stood and walked to the door. "I would never pity you, Ryder, but neither will your cynical view on love taint the love I have shared with my people. We may be in danger because of the love of one woman, but at least we have the choice to love or not. And that is what I pity. You aren't even given the choice."

Ryder slammed through the house and out into the woods. The pheromone still drained into his mouth from the special gland in the back of his throat. He spat it out, growling and muttering to himself about Trackers and Elements. He stomped into the woods, following a trail that led away from the house. He needed to put distance between him and Kyra. He didn't stop until he was a good length from the house. He breathed, Kyra's scent not tainting the air around him.

"Trying to find peace when there is none?" Marcus asked, stepping up to stand next to Ryder. They both stood on the side of a small stream. Ryder had felt the Fallen move into step behind him an hour ago.

"What the fuck are you talking about?" Ryder asked.

"There is no peace to be found when women are involved." Ryder couldn't agree more. "But from what I know of the Trackers, you have all taken a vow against falling in love."

For some reason, the fact that the Fallen knew that information wasn't surprising. "We've watched our families and our people die," Ryder said. "Wouldn't you do the same to save your race?"

Marcus laughed quietly. "My race, Tracker? I have no race," he said with such finality that it tugged at Ryder. At least Ryder had his brothers. What did the Fallen have?

"Do you have anyone?" he asked honestly.

"There are several of us who fight against the darkness after being rejected from Elysian Fields." Ryder couldn't imagine what it would be like to be part of something like the Elysian Fields and then be turned away from it. "It drives us mad eventually," Marcus said. "And that is what we fight against. Not all of us have fallen because we are evil. We fall for different reasons. Angels can be very judgmental creatures."

Ryder snorted. "Wasn't that the point of the creation of Angels—to protect Mortals?"

"Ryder, how many Guardians have you seen on the Mortal plane lately?" Marcus asked.

Ryder thought for a moment. He had known a few but lately? "Not a lot." he admitted.

Marcus nodded. "They," he pointed upward, "have pulled back Guardians. Those Guardians should be here stopping this type of thing from happening."

"Why?"

"Only they can answer that question." Marcus shrugged, looking up toward the night sky again. "It is a point of contention within the ranks of Angels. On how exactly they are to interpret that mandate."

"That sucks." Ryder really had no idea what the Fallen fought against.

"I did not follow you out here to speak of our races. I have an idea on what can be done with the monster in the mountain. But in order to get what I need, I'll have to leave." Ryder was impressed that the Fallen had come to him.

"How long will it take?"

"A day, maybe more," Marcus said.

"If you think it will help, then, by all means." Ryder nodded.

Marcus lowered his head slightly. "Ryder."

Ryder turned to the man. "She is a bright shining light that gives love more than she takes. But she holds things in that you don't understand. Things that drive her to be what and who she is. If you kill that part of her, you might as well kill her. Do not underestimate the power she holds. You may think it makes her weak. Remember, strength comes in very different forms." And then he was gone Ryder let his words sink in calming him.

Chapter 6

"He's definitely going to kill something tonight." Kyra heard Skylar mutter to Lykar as they climbed out of the car. She was really beginning to hate this clearing. She turned to watch Ryder climb off her bike, which she'd noticed this morning. He'd gone back for it, which made her rethink the whole idea about who he was.

"He isn't the only one," Kyra snapped, causing Skylar and Lykar to laugh. She didn't think it was funny at all.

Sophie appeared and Kyra gave her a long look. "Did you find a way to release me? Where is the angel?" She looked around for Marcus. He wasn't there. He had left sometime during the night, telling Fiona he would be back.

"Sophie, unless we are able to find what you are tethered to, we won't be able to release you. I'm beginning to think you might not really want to be released." Sophie gave Kyra a look that could kill.

"And just how do you plan on killing it?"

"We will trap it and destroy it." At this, Sophie started to moan. Kyra shook her head and walked away.

"Woman is crazy," Skylar wiggled a finger around one temple. To him, it looked like Kyra was talking to herself.

Kyra swung around to face him. "I'm sorry, but did you have something to say to me?"

His black eyes snapped with amusement. "Sweetheart, don't even go there."

She was about to swing on him when Sophie bounced in between them. "Come with me," she urged, darting off in a fit of mist.

Kyra rolled her eyes and turned to Simon, who nodded at her. She Phased out, letting the wind take her ghostly form in the direction Sophie had gone.

Ryder screamed from somewhere behind her. He hadn't said anything to her all morning. What made him think she was going to stop and speak with him now, especially after last night? She had lain there, not sleeping, her body tormented with lust for a man she wasn't sure she even liked. He obviously didn't like her much, either, or he would've uttered a couple of words to her today. They were supposed to be partners in this, but the last thing she wanted to do was consult him on anything.

Sophie stopped suddenly. Kyra materialized alongside her. "See?" Sophie pointed to several overgrown bushes.

Kyra looked at the bushes, walking around them. "You have to get down to see," Sophie offered pointing at the dirt.

Kyra was about to drop to her knees when inky blackness seeped from the trees in front of her. She backed up as quickly as possible. Yesterday's ass-kicking by that thing had been enough—she didn't really want an encore today. Maybe running off without the guys hadn't been the best idea. Kyra thought for a moment about going back and then returning with the rest of them. Then she shook herself. She was capable of investigating this without them.

Sophie moaned slightly. "It can't come any farther than those trees."

Kyra turned to the woman. "Whose side are you on?" she asked bluntly.

Sophie flickered for a moment. When she solidified, Kyra saw anger and pain flash through her dark eyes. "I'm on the side that will free me."

"How long have you been like this?"

Sophie's black eyes bled to a cold steel color. "Too long."

The blackness pulsed as Sophie spoke. "My soul," It moaned.

"You've said that," Kyra was tired of being pushed around. Frankly, she was getting sick and tired of the whole scenario.

The blackness rushed toward them, but slammed against an invisible wall. Kyra stumbled back at the same time, not sure if she could believe anything Sophie said.

Sophie was tugging on Kyra's sleeve. "Look under the bushes, Kyra." Her voice tugged at the edges of Kyra's sanity, edged with menace and hatred.

Kyra threw caution to the wind and crawled forward as the blackness rolled, an angry cloud just inches from where she crouched. She pulled at leaves and twigs to see what Sophie was trying to show her. Then there it was: a glowing mound of earth next to the base of the bush. Kyra crawled forward, making sure not to touch the barrier between her and the inky blackness as it hissed and screamed just inches away.

"Sophie, what is this?" Kyra asked without backing out of the bush.

"It's what keeps him here." Kyra could've sworn Sophie's voice held more than hate in it. "He put them here so the blackness couldn't get out," Sophie whispered.

"He who?" Kyra asked. Were they fighting more than one monster here?

"Me." A voice boomed over her head. Kyra turned toward the inky blackness and found a pair of bare feet poking out from beneath the bushes.

Kyra scrambled from the bush, the twigs scratching at her exposed neck and face. "What the hell?"

A man stood in front of her completely naked, short, dark hair glistening in the afternoon light. Kyra blinked several times and then shook her head. She was seeing things. This wasn't happening. When she opened her eyes again, the man was still there. Black eyes glittered at her in a knowing way, causing chills to tickle up her spine. She couldn't stop herself from taking a step forward.

"Ryder?" she asked, breathless, feeling her body respond to him like it had the night before. Her eyes raked over him, unable to take it all in. He was more powerful than any man she had ever laid eyes on.

"I can be whoever you want me to be." Ryder's deep voice rolled over her like that familiar thundercloud settling deep in the pit of her stomach. It spread through her limbs like molten lava, warming her to a fevered pitch. She shivered, unable to control her reaction to him. Part of her brain screamed for her to back away.

"Isn't he wonderful?" Sophie asked from beside her. Kyra turned to her, shocked. She had completely forgotten that Sophie stood there.

Ryder stepped forward through the barrier and held out a hand to Kyra. Something in her brain snapped to attention and screamed. "This shouldn't be happening."

Black eyes glistened and he beckoned for her to move forward. "Kyra …" He drew her name out, rolling the *r*. The sound vibrated deep inside Kyra, causing her to moan with pleasure. Sophie giggled as she urged Kyra forward.

"I will show you pleasure unlike you have ever known before."

Yes, she wanted that. Wanted to walk into his arms and let the darkness surround her and let everything else just fade away. She desperately wanted to show Ryder the light and kindness she had grown up with. Wanted to experience it with him.

He took another step toward her, and Kyra reached out her hand. This was what she wanted, tossing that little voice in the back of her mind to where she couldn't hear it anymore.

"I'm your dream. I'm your every fantasy. Take my hand, Kyra." He offered his hand, palm up. "Come to me."

"What the fuck is that?" someone barked from behind her, shocking her into immobility.

Sophie screamed next to her as the man stepped back and the inky blackness wrapped around him like a cloak.

"I'll come for you, Kyra," It whispered.

"Kill it!" Another male voice.

Kyra launched herself toward the darkness. "NO!"

Arms wrapped around Kyra, turning her away. Gunfire erupted all around her. She struggled to get free but just as quickly, the body holding her jerked as the bullets came flying back out of the mass of black.

She screamed again as she looked into Ryder's pain-ridden face. This wasn't supposed to happen. Ryder's arms were strong around Kyra as he wobbled unsteadily on his feet. He coughed, spitting out blood and cursing. He took her to the dirt path with him as he fell to his knees.

Kyra lay beneath Ryder, trying to figure out what the hell had just happened.

"You can't fire into it," Ryder snarled. "You're going to get us all killed one day, you know that?"

"Knowing that would've been helpful about five minutes ago." Skylar sat up from where he'd landed after being pelted with bullets.

"Yeah, well, fire first, ask questions later is a policy we might have to revisit," Lykar said, still lying in the dirt.

"Are you hurt?" Ryder asked, running his hands over Kyra. She shook her head but was still unable to speak. She had been through so much in her life, had killed many evil things. Had been partner to deaths in the name of the Druids and the Light. But nothing, nothing in all that time had prepared her for the terror she had faced yesterday and then again just now. That blackness had her number, and she was beginning to think it was going to be her downfall.

She finally found her tongue. "Yes, I'm fine. Are you hurt?" She wanted to slap herself in the head for the stupid question. Of course he wasn't all right. He'd been shot protecting her, for God's sake. "Let me take a look at your wounds."

He shrugged off her hands. "I'll be fine."

"Doesn't mean it doesn't hurt like hell," Skylar muttered. "If you want to play nurse, I'd be happy to be your patient."

"Shut up, Sky," Ryder snapped. "What was that?"

Lykar laughed, finally picking himself up out of the dirt. "Looked a hell of a lot like you in your birthday suit."

116

"I swear I'm going to shoot you next." Ryder gave Lykar a nasty look. He turned back to Kyra. "Well?"

Kyra shook her head and turned to where the blackness rolled. "I have no idea." One minute she'd been looking under the bushes, the next facing whom she thought was Ryder.

She looked around for Sophie, and made a sickening realization. "I don't think Sophie wants to be freed from that thing."

"Ah, we finally agree on something," Ryder muttered. Screeching tore through the trees and cold wind whipped around Kyra at Ryder's proclamation.

Ryder took Kyra by the arm, pulled her to her feet, and led her away from his brothers. "Explain exactly what happened," he ordered.

"I don't know exactly what it was. But he crossed the line. Sophie said that it couldn't cross the barrier." She pulled on her braid, trying to sort it out.

"You took off into the woods in the misty thing you do, and we had no way of protecting you," he shouted, causing Kyra to step back. "That's twice in less than twenty-four hours that you've been in a situation where I've been unable to protect you."

That comment pissed her off. "I do not need your constant protection. I can take care of myself."

"Yeah, because you've done such a bang-up job up to this point."

"You have no reason to bite my head off." She stood up to him and jerked herself out of his grasp. "I'm an adult. And I've been an Enforcer for all my life. Regardless of what you think, I can take care of myself."

"We are supposed to be working together." He fisted his hands together. Kyra was sure he wanted nothing more than to shake her again.

"What more do you want from me?" she asked.

He did grab her shaking her once before pulling her in and kissing her hard, backing her against a tree. Kyra should've pushed away, but she wanted this as much as he did. She wrapped her arms around his neck and pulled him closer. She opened her mouth, letting him ravage her, his tongue delving in to thrust against hers. Kyra pulled herself as close as she could to him. Hiking one leg over his hip, she pulled him into her center. Her hands found their way into his shirt to his rock-hard abs. How she wanted to run her tongue along those abs. The very thought drove a moan through her entire body.

"Please," she begged as he moved to kiss her behind her ear.

"What do you want, Kyra?" he asked. His breathing was as heavy as hers. "You're going to have to ask for it." He rolled his hips against her and she was lost.

"Gods, Ryder, I need you inside of me," she begged.

Ryder jerked away from her, stumbling into a tree. He put his fist into the large trunk. The trunk split as if hit by a wrecking ball. Once his body was no longer pressed to hers Kyra felt the tell tell signs of the shock she had to be in. The monster was adapting to her, learning what she wanted. The thought scared her to death.

Ryder glared at the tree not looking at her. His chest heaving with each breath, he should have scared her but she was beginning to understand him. Although he would never admit he cared. His next words confirmed it. "How the hell can I protect you if you run off and try to get yourself killed?"

"I don't need you to protect me! I know how to protect myself." It was such a line of bull but she feed it to him, she needed to take care of herself needed to be more than just a pawn in the horrible game she had stumbled into.

Ryder turned on her. "What was that? Because it looked to me like whatever the hell that was had you wrapped around his bloody damn finger. It could've killed you any second."

Kyra couldn't argue that point, she knew that, so she kept her mouth closed. Ryder stomped around the woods and she let him work off his mad energy. When he finally stopped, Kyra approached him. "Is there anything I can do for your bullet wounds?"

He gave her a hard stare, his eyes glittering black. "No." He took her by the arm and they walked back to the cars. Everyone was waiting for them, but nobody said anything. They drove back to town quietly.

Kyra felt like she'd been ostracized and wanted nothing more than to crawl into bed. Once they'd returned to the house, everyone worked together to make dinner and eat. However, everyone avoided eye contact with Kyra. They all believed she had gone off half cocked putting everyone not just herself in danger. And she had to agree with them—which only made things worse. As soon as she could, she excused herself and went to her room. She showered and put on a tank top and pair of boxers. It had been several days since she'd spent any time alone. Sitting on her bed she attempted to force herself to relax and she was about to give up when Sophie appeared.

Kyra didn't want anything to do with her. "What do you want?"

Sophie smiled but it didn't show in her eyes, which had were nearly black. "Your soul, of course."

"I'm not quite done with it yet," Kyra said, standing. "So no more pretending? You've decided to come clean and show me your true colors?"

Sophie shrugged noncommittally and looked around the room. "Can you possibly understand what it feels like to wander without substance?" She pushed her hand through the lamp on the side table, showing that she couldn't touch anything. "He has promised me the ability to feel."

"But you've touched me before. How can you say that?" Kyra didn't understand the woman and wasn't sure Sophie was in complete control of her own mind anymore.

"He gives me enough power to reach out once in a while, when it suits him," she whispered, pushing her hand through the lamp again and sighing deeply. "There is only one other way for me to feel anything."

Kyra couldn't help it she actually felt bad for the woman. "How long have you been like this?"

Sophie shrugged again. "I used to keep track of time. I used to feel the pain of the souls that I heralded into the in-between. But time is relative if you can't feel anything, if you don't have substance or purpose. I had purpose once."   k Kyra sucked in a shocked breath when Sophie moved quickly to stand in front of her blocking her from moving. "I want to feel again. I want to feel the touch of a man's hands on my body. I've seen the way the Tracker looks at you. I want a man to look at me like that again. I don't want to be beholden to that thing for something as simple as a touch." She moaned in pain and agitation.

Kyra didn't know what to tell her. "What are you?"

Sophie smiled. "How many times have I been asked that question? It's something they always ask in the end." She moved off, trailing her fingers along the top of the bedspread, as if she could feel the material.

"What are you?" she whined the words. "Why are you doing this? Blah, blah, blah." For just a moment, her mask of sincerity fell away. Kyra could see that she was as much a monster as the inky blackness.

"We are going to find a way to destroy you both," Kyra said. She wasn't sure how, but she wasn't going anywhere until they were both gone.

Sophie leaned in so they were nose to nose. "Bigger men than you have tried and failed. But your soul shall feed my master for months. But not before I get the chance to use your body."

Kyra jumped back. "Excuse me?"

Sophie glared at her. "You don't understand. A Mortal isn't strong enough to endure my possession for long."

"Possession?" Kyra's voice squeaked. "Not interested."

Sophie laughed. "I really wasn't going to ask permission. Besides you always seem to be able to get away from him, so I know you are strong enough."

Sophie blurred as she moved, her body slamming into Kyra with a power Kyra had never felt before It happened so quickly Kyra was unable to protect herself or call for help

Within seconds, Sophie had bled into Kyra's skin and mind like a virus. Kyra tried to scream but Sophie was there, slapping her own hand around their now-shared mouth.

"Get out of me." Her hand muffled her words.

"Don't fight it," Sophie whispered. The pain sent Kyra to her knees.

Kyra felt as if her head were about to explode. She fought against herself and the woman who was trying to take over her body and mind. She fell onto the floor, her body feeling as if it was being pulled apart from the inside. The world was going dark as Kyra fought mentally to push Sophie away.

"This isn't happening," she heard herself say. Then her body fell lax under the onslaught of Sophie's attack.

Laughter bubbled from her throat and mouth as hands roamed over her own body. "Oh, but it's done. And what fun I shall have with it." Kyra's voice but Sophie's thoughts. Kyra felt walls slam in around her mentally and she fought for some hold over what was happening.

"Ah keep fight." Sophie moaned. "Your physical reaction is amazing."

Kyra instantly stopped, causing Sophie to laugh. And then Kyra was standing in a black void. She blinked several times, somehow she knew she was trapped—in her own mind. Kyra let out an ear splitting scream but the blackness surrounding her swallowed it. And she was plunged into nothingness.

Ryder hurt all over. His body ached from the bullets that had still not worked themselves out. He climbed into the shower and turned the water on as hot as he could stand it. He heaved a sigh of relief when the last bullet plinked down onto the tile. He stayed in the shower until the water was clear and he knew he wasn't bleeding anymore, letting his mind wander to what had happened that afternoon.

When he'd found Kyra, he had to admit that he had been surprised to find her with someone who looked eerily like himself. His brothers were still laughing about that one. Ryder had been able to sense her passion and lust from yards away. He wanted to be furious that she was so physically attracted to something that looked so much like him. But for that reason, it almost made him smile. He wanted nothing but to take her to bed, but he knew that he had to take this one small step at a time, or else lose himself in the taking. That wasn't something that was going to happen.

He stepped out of the shower and wrapped a towel around his waist. With Lykar and Skylar here, Ryder felt like he could relax and sleep tonight. Fiona was out doing whatever the old woman did. Half the time she wandered around, muttering to herself, the other half she was missing completely. Ryder was pretty sure she was bat-shit crazy, and wasn't sure exactly what the hell she was doing to help them out. However, Kyra and Simon seemed to worship the ground the old lady walked on, so he let it go. Plus she had brought Marcus, although Ryder wasn't sure what the Fallen was going to offer to the group yet.

He hoped Marcus would be back soon he and his brothers had no idea how to kill the damn thing in the mountain. And every time they went near that cursed mountain, it played with them. Or more specifically, it played with Kyra. And frankly, Ryder was way over that little game.

"Ryder." Kyra had breathed his name in a way that made him hard in an instant. He stopped dead in the doorway to his room.

"What the hell are you doing?" Ryder asked the woman who was spread out on his bed wearing a T-shirt and shorts. Every part of him wanted to throw the towel away and join her, the lust in the air so thick, you could cut it with a knife. His body reacted and his hands were on the knot of the towel before he stopped himself. This wasn't right. Something was different, but he couldn't put his finger on it.

She pushed herself off the bed, leading with her large breasts. His palms itched to cup them and bring them to his mouth. He fisted his hands at his sides. What was she up to now?

Stepping up to him, she placed her hands on his bare chest. He couldn't help the breath that he sucked in as she drug her fingernails down his chest and over his nipples, making them rock hard. "I can't stop thinking about you. About this afternoon. Touch me, Ryder."

Ryder couldn't stop himself. Something was wrong, but damn, she felt too good pressed against his nearly naked body to care. For the last couple of days, all he could think about was putting his hands on her. He placed his hands on her hips and pulled her into him.

It was her turn to suck in a breath as he pressed his erection into her stomach. It was the most erotic noise he'd ever heard.

"Touch me," she whispered into his ear. As she traced the appendage with her tongue, Ryder shivered with pleasure and thrust toward her again.

Ryder ignored the voice in his head that said something wasn't right. He lowered his lips to capture hers. She immediately opened her mouth beneath his and sucked his tongue deep into her mouth. Her forwardness shocked him, but his arousal overrode it. The few kisses they had shared before had been a mutual blending, but now she was taking control.

Ryder pulled away and looked down at her. Her eyes were closed and her swollen lips begged to be kissed. She arched into him and a little part of him was lost. But he wasn't going to allow her to be in control. He turned so that she was pressed against the wall. He wanted to be in control, and he tore his mouth away from her to trail his tongue and lips down the long column of her throat.

She fisted her hands in his hair, pulling at the root.

"Not so hard, sweetheart." His hands worked upward so he could pull free before she yanked his hair out at the root.

"No," she moaned the word. She pushed his hands away, her strength surprising him as she turned him so that his back was against the wall again. She pressed herself against him, rubbing her entire body against his. Her moan of pleasure cracked in the air like the break of a thundercloud.

Ryder finally let that little voice in his head out. This wasn't right. "Kyra," he said, pushing her back.

She launched herself back at him. "No." She ground her lips against his.

He wrenched his mouth away from her. "Bloody hell." He didn't want to hurt her, but he had to get her off him. In the end, he used some of his Tracker strength to push her away. She came flying back, thrusting her tongue into his mouth and then Ryder realized that she tasted nothing like Kyra. At first he hadn't noticed, but now the taste of sulfur was so strong, it made him want to retch.

She didn't budge. "Kyra." He pushed again. When she ground her pelvis against him, he realized there was a serious problem.

"Don't talk," she moaned the words. "Just fuck me."

How much did he want to do just that? Forget about everything else and mark this woman as his? He shoved as hard as he could, throwing Kyra back. He cringed as she crashed against the wall, caving in the drywall. She surprised him when bounced off and landed on her feet on the bed. Like something out of a horror movie, she shook her head her strawberry blonde hair flowing over her shoulders like an avenging angel then glared at him. She pushed back her hair—how he'd dreamed of running his fingers through it—and revealed her eyes. Ryder froze when eyes, black as death, stared back from Kyra's beautiful face.

"What the hell?" he barked as she launched herself at him. It was only his ability to move with lightning speed that got him out from her grasp before she was able to get her hands on him.

"If you won't take me, then I will find someone who will. This house is full of men," She headed toward the door.

"The hell you will." Ryder wrapped his arms around her middle as she tried to move past him. "Where are you, Kyra?"

"Kyra is gone," the woman screeched. "All that is left is me."

Tucking her under one arm, he threw open the door of his room. "Lykar! Skylar!"

He moved away from the door, ignoring the screaming and yelling of the woman in his arms. With one hand, he tore the sheets from the bed. Moving to accommodate her as she tried to hurt him.

"Let me go!" the woman in his arms screamed.

"Geez, bro, what the hell?" Lykar asked, coming into the room.

"Hold her down so I can tie her up." Ryder said, tearing the sheets into strips with his mouth and one hand.

Lykar didn't move from the doorway. "I'm not really into this kinky shit. And frankly I'm surprised you would ask."

"She isn't herself." Ryder muttered. Lykar finally looked at Kyra, who was writhing and groaning as if in pain. She screamed like a banshee while trying to escape Ryder's hold.

"What the hell happened to her?"Lykar asked staring at her. Ryder wished he knew.

"Let's get her tied up and then we can question her." Ryder motioned to the bed and the sheet now in shredded strips.

"I'll give you the night of your life if you get me away from him," she said to Lykar, black eyes glittering.

"Bitch, I'm not touching you with a ten-foot pole." Lykar took the stripped sheets so that Ryder could hold her down while his brother tied her up.

When she was tied to the bed, the brothers stood back. She screamed and cussed at them. "I don't think she likes being tied up."

Ryder felt like punching something. He was aroused and the woman he wanted was possessed.

Simon and Fiona stormed into the room then. They took in the scene, and Simon lurched forward. "You can't do this to her," Simon argued.

"Really?" Ryder gave the man a hard look. "If you touch her, I'll break you in half. Just look at her. It isn't Kyra."

Fiona reached forward, closed her eyes, and then hissed. "She is possessed by the Shade."

Ryder narrowed his gaze at the woman and snarled. Kyra's beautiful lips turned up in a heart-stopping smile. She looked past Ryder to Simon.

"You aren't going to let him do this to me, are you?" she asked.

Simon looked conflicted. "Kyra?" he reached forward. The woman on the bed strained to reach out to him as well.

"Help me, Simon," she moaned. "You know I've always cared. We can be together. He wouldn't take no for an answer. Don't listen to him, Simon. Help me. I need you."

Ryder grabbed the Element as he moved forward. "Don't make me hurt you."

"You can't do this," Simon argued.

Fiona placed a hand on Simon's shoulder. "She isn't Kyra right now, Simon."

Simon looked from Fiona and Ryder to Kyra, and then slammed out of the room. "I won't stand by and see her like this."

Fiona looked sad. "I don't know how this happened," she said to Ryder, then headed to the door. She turned back to Ryder. "Fix this."

Ryder rolled his eyes and raked his hand through his hair. This mission kept getting worse. He kicked everyone else out of the room. He grabbed a change of clothes and pulled them on in jerky movements. He was in physical pain and had nothing on which to vent his anger. He scooted a chair next to the bed.

"Who are you?" he asked, using compulsion.

She shook her head and laughed. "You can't use compulsion on me, Tracker. It won't work, and the only one you're hurting is her. But if you release me, I'll answer any questions you might have. Release me and spend the night in my arms. I know you want this body."

She smiled. It was something he'd wanted to see from Kyra for days now. "To answer your question: I'm anything you want me to be."

She writhed on the bed in such a sexual way, Ryder had to stand and move away from her. "This body is amazing. I can feel so much. The other woman didn't have nearly as much feeling as this body has."

"What is living in the mountain?" he tried.

"My master."

"And the women who were killed?"

"Sacrifices. He needs the blood and souls to live." She shrugged as if it were completely normal to kill and mutilate women in order to live.

"So why take over Kyra?"

She smiled at him again. Her eyes bled out to the clear blue of Kyra's eyes. "Don't you want me, Ryder? I felt your desire for this body. If it's about the eyes, I can leave them like this." She blinked several times, showing him the clear blue that had haunted him for the last several days.

"I want Kyra, and just because you have her body doesn't mean I want you." He stood, knowing he wasn't going to get anything else from her. And if he had to look into those crystal-blue eyes knowing it wasn't Kyra, he was going to do some physical damage.

He stopped at the door. "Enjoy it while you can, because your time in her is limited."

Kyra's laughter mocked him as he slammed the door behind him.

Marcus left the room, shaking his head. "First, I must apologize. I should've realized what she was before. But she had a great cloak around her."

Ryder agreed completely. "What is she?"

"She is a Banshee, and even more so a tethered Banshee. Making her a very dangerous entity." Marcus lowered himself into a chair. He looked like he had aged several years from when he'd walked into the room where

Kyra was tied to the bed and when he had left the room. He sighed heavily, leaning his elbows on his knees and resting his head in his hands.

"That isn't possible," Fiona said. "Banshees can't possess anything. They are meant to announce death. They work with the angels and reapers to ensure the souls find their way. How is this even possible? Is she actually feeding souls to that thing in the mountain? None of this is possible within our realm of existence."

"Be that as it may, she is a Banshee and she is tethered to whatever is living in that mountain. And currently she inhabits Kyra, using her body for her own benefit." Marcus shook his head.

"So there are good Banshees and bad Banshees?" Sky asked from the table where he was cleaning his gun. "And we are assuming she's a bad one. What do we do with her?"

"Get her out of Kyra," Ryder snapped.

Marcus shook his head. "It's not that simple. If indeed a spirit has possessed her, then it would be just convincing the spirit to move on. I could easily deal with that, be it an evil spirit or not. But this, this is a creature that knows exactly what it is and what it wants. And unfortunately, it wants Kyra. Or more aptly, she wants you."

Ryder snarled and advanced on the Fallen Angel. Marcus stood and didn't even try to defend himself as Ryder grabbed him by the throat and slammed him against the wall. "Do you have anything that is going to help us free her?"

Marcus shook his head and placed his palm against Ryder's chest. Ryder flew back, hitting the opposite wall with such force he left an impression of his body in the wall. He hadn't felt anything except for the pressure of Marcus's hand on his chest before he was flying through the air.

Ryder shook off the dust and bits of the wall. "If I were you, I wouldn't try that again."

"There is nothing on this plane that can be done to me, Ryder, that would satisfy your lust for vengeance," Marcus said with a calm that belied his obvious superior power and strength. Marcus held up a hand as Ryder advanced on him. "I suggest you take her to the mountain."

"Not bloody likely," Ryder growled.

"Take her back to what she is tied to. Hopefully, we'll find some answers. At the moment, we have no other choice," Marcus said.

"That's all you have?" Ryder asked. "What have you been doing for the last twenty-four hours?"

Marcus lowered his gaze. "Helping, believe it or not."

"We can't just take her back to the mountain and give her to that thing," Simon interrupted. "There has to be another way."

The silence in the room was palpable. "For the love of all the Gods, Kyra is in there somewhere," Simon pleaded.

Ryder looked around the room. Nobody else spoke. "Well, it looks like there aren't any other ideas."

Ryder headed back into the bedroom. Kyra lay spread out, hands and feet tied. She smiled as he entered the room. She looked as if she had all the time in the world.

"Now what?" she asked breathlessly.

"We're going to take a little ride." She eyed him before turning to mist and reappearing next to him. Ryder hadn't been prepared for her to use Kyra's abilities and he was momentarily stunned.

"I don't want to go for a ride." She weaved her hands into his hair. "I want to stay here." She rubbed her body against his. "I would make it worth your while, Ryder," she whispered into his ear.

"I don't know who the hell you are, but you have two choices." Ryder turned and took her hands, lowering them. He pulled them so that they were behind her, pressing her even closer to him. He sucked in a breath, trying to keep his body from reacting to her closeness, reminding himself that it might be Kyra's body, but it was not Kyra. And Kyra was the woman he wanted, not this shell. And then it hit him: the smell of old earth, dirt, and sulfur. She smelled nothing like Kyra. It bolstered him.

He held her tight. "I'm taking you back to your master."

Her eyes flared and glowed for a brief second, and he knew that was the last thing she wanted. She had unwittingly showed him her cards. She tried to pull away from him, but he jerked her back, causing her to growl low in her throat. If it had been any other time and it had been Kyra making the sound, he was sure that it would've driven him crazy. But with flat black staring back at him, he knew he would do what he needed to get Kyra back.

"If you sleep with me, I'll release Kyra." Ryder froze. "If you take me to bed, and give me a night I will never forget in my eternity of servitude, I will release Kyra and tell you how to kill the thing living in the mountain."

"Release her, and I'll give you what you want," Ryder tried.

She pressed against him. "How exactly will you give me what I want if I release her?"

Ryder hissed as she rubbed against him. "I won't give you what you want if you are in Kyra." It felt wrong on so many different levels. And even though he was a heartless bastard, this wasn't something that even he could do.

She misted out and reappeared several feet from him. His hands fisted, he would give anything to wrap them around that thing's throat. "Is she okay?" he gritted between his teeth.

The woman tapped on index finger against her temple. "She's fine. Pissed as hell, but she'll be fine."

"Can I talk to her?" He wasn't sure if it was possible but he wanted the chance.

"Nothing comes of nothing," the thing said in a singsong voice. "What do I get if I let you talk with her?" Black eyes glittered with the knowledge that for the moment, she held the upper hand.

Kyra was going to kill him. She was going to have him flayed out and whipped, and flogged and … she stomped her foot, trying to figure out all the bad and horrible things she was going to do to him. For the moment, however, she was just happy to have control of her own body.

"I hate you," she spat, stepping from the circle of his arms.

Ryder smiled. She couldn't remember seeing him really smile before, and it went straight to her stomach, setting off butterflies. And in spite of everything, it made her smile too.

"Don't you ever touch me again. This is your fault. Sophie wouldn't have possessed me if you ..." There was no way she was going to finish that sentence, and they both knew it.

Ryder smiled again. Kyra kicked him in the shin. He didn't even flinch.

"Why would you give into any of her demands?" He had kissed her, kissed her like she was manna from the Gods. Kyra was so jealous and pissed, she couldn't even think straight.

"Sweetheart, I'd do anything to get to see those blue eyes again." She huffed, his words taking some of the fight out of her.

"What is the plan?" she asked.

"How much control do you have?" Ryder asked, cupping her face. He stared into her eyes.

"Very little. She hasn't discovered everything I am capable of. However, she blocks me from seeing what is going on." That was the most frustrating part. Sophie seemed to be able to control what Kyra saw and heard. She only gave in at different times, giving Kyra mere glimpses of what was going on, never the full picture. It was making Kyra crazy.

"Do you think you'll be able to learn anything from her?"

Kyra felt as if she'd been run through the gauntlet and just wanted to lie down and not get up. "She has very strong defenses, but given some time," she shrugged, "I'm sure I'll be able to work though them."

"Don't let down your own defenses in order to learn anything," Ryder urged.

Kyra rolled her eyes. "Of course not."

"I don't want to see you hurt, Kyra." He dragged a finger down her cheek and along her jaw line before leaning in to place a gentle kiss on her lips.

His entire body leaned in so close. The gentle kiss made her breathless for a moment. She may be possessed with Sophie, but that didn't change the fact that she wanted Ryder. In almost two hundred years, she had shared passionate embraces and passionate nights with plenty of men, but the kiss Ryder had given Sophie had eclipsed everything from the past, even what they had shared the night before. The thought that he'd been holding back made Kyra want to know exactly what he could do in the bedroom.

Kyra shook her head, trying to focus on the issue at hand. Sophie had released power back to Kyra with a sigh and moan of pleasure. And as he leaned in again, she felt passion stir in the pit of her stomach.

She knew this wasn't the time or place to throw caution to the wind and take exactly what she wanted from the man.

Taking a deep breath, she pulled away. "How are you going to get her out of me?"

Ryder shrugged his shoulders. "We haven't figured that part out yet."

Kyra couldn't believe it. "What do you mean, you haven't figured it out yet?"

"We don't have a lot of options." He cupped her cheeks in what she assumed was his way of trying to comfort her. She jerked away from him. She hated to ask for help, hated to be at a disadvantage in anything.

Kyra tried to pull away, but he gently held her and stared into her eyes. "What are you doing?"

"I missed your blue eyes," he said. Leaning down, he kissed the corner of her mouth and she was damned if she was going to pull away from his touch this time. She would also be damned if she would admit that she really needed his comfort at the moment. Her entire body wanted this and the small part that Sophie still controlled pushed her to accept exactly what he was offering.

"What is happening between us?" she heard herself ask, knowing it was a question any man would run from.

Ryder continued to place small kisses around her face. "I have no idea and don't know if I can stop it from happening. Or even if I want to."

His answer shocked her in its honesty, leaving her more confused than before. This whole mission had turned her life upside down and sideways. And when Sophie had possessed her, Kyra had to admit, she may not be capable of winning this one. She looked at Ryder for a long moment, wishing she'd let him have her. Even if it had been under Sophie's influence, Kyra would've felt some of it. Like she had felt some of the kiss, she laughed.

"Final requests," she said, more to herself.

Ryder leaned back and looked at her, his dark eyes searching hers. "Don't give up now, Kyra. We are going to figure this out and fix it."

She was afraid for the first time, and she was sure that he could see it in her eyes. "Ryder, if it comes down to it, I would rather die than let them win. It's what I've been trained for, to eradicate this type of evil from the world. It's what I've lived my life for. This is all I know. If it comes down to me or her, to me or letting that woman and thing win, I want you to kill me and take her out."

He nodded. She grunted. "Well, you didn't have to agree so quickly."

This time he laughed. "It won't come to that, Kyra. So stop thinking so morbidly. We have several options. Marcus has figured out she is tethered Banshee."

"How does that help?" she asked. But then she stopped and chewed her bottom lip. Kyra pulled away and grabbed her cell phone. "I might know someone who could help with that. Banshees and Wraiths are similar."

She dialed. "Hey, it's me." She listened as the person on the other end screamed at her for a moment.

"I'm still older," she threw in, which only made the screaming grow worse.

"I've been possessed by a tethered Banshee. Wouldn't happen to have any advice on how to get out of this one, would you? Maybe check with Xavier and the others?"

More swearing and then everything went quiet. Kyra looked at the phone. "I think he hung up on me."

"He? Being?" Ryder was really trying not to be jealous, but the fact that she had gone to another man for help rankled him.

"Eric, last standing male heir to the house of Diamond … blah blah blah. And loving brother." She stuck her tongue out in disgust.

"And exactly what can he do?"

"I have no idea, but he has some contacts that may be able to help. We need all the help we can get."

"And why was he so pissed?"

"I was supposed to wait for backup," she shrugged. "Live and learn."

Ryder shook his head, his temper getting the better of him. "Let me get this straight. You were sent here to find out what was going on? Not to fight or destroy it?" The last came out in a shout. "If your brother doesn't kill you, I just might."

"The other Enforcers were busy. It was supposed to be an information-gathering mission, nothing more. But then you blew up my motel room and dragged me back into the mountain and I'm sure you're familiar with the rest of the story." Kyra sat down on the bed and rubbed her temples. She felt Sophie trying to kick her way free. "Trust me—if I had known what I was walking into, I would've brought the entire Druid army with me."

"I don't know if you are the bravest woman I've ever met, or just damn lucky and too stupid to understand the danger you've put yourself and the rest of us in."

His words struck home and she felt each like a knife twisting in her heart. She peeked up at him. "It wasn't supposed to happen this way, Ryder."

Ryder closed his eyes and she watched as he took several deep breaths. When he opened them again, the look he gave her was filled with an emotion she couldn't name.

"I'm sorry," Kyra whispered.

Ryder kneeled down. "You have done nothing you need to apologize for. We are going to figure this out."

His words might've meant something more, but at that moment, she felt as if a bolt of lightning shot from her head to her toes.

"I think Sophie wants to be back in control." She shook her head, so hard she tipped herself over. Ryder caught her, swinging her up into his arms.

"You know what's weird, Tracker?" she breathed the words against the side of his neck, sending chills down his back. "If we had met under any other circumstances, we would've gone to bed together. Fucked like rabbits and walked away. But now … you'll probably be the one pulling the trigger. Coulda, woulda, shoulda."

She felt blood trickle from her nose as she fought to remain in control of her own body. Ryder set her down on the bed and grabbed a tissue. "Does it hurt?"

Kyra tried to smile but wasn't sure if it reached her eyes. "I get it, you know. Why she is doing this. Banshees were picked to herald the death of a loved one. They were assigned to great families by Angels and Reapers to guide souls and comfort families, to let them know their loved one wasn't alone in death. We have adapted to the changing world, all of the Others. We can't blame her. What other choice did she have?"

Ryder snorted. "You will not feel sorry for that monster inside of you." He dabbed at the blood that trickled down over her full lip. "She says she will give up what we want." He couldn't pull his eyes away from the smear of blood on the cusp of Kyra's lip. To taste her blood, he would have all three: touch, taste and smell. She would never be able to hide from him again. Not on this plane or any other plane of existence for that matter. And the ability to get to her, find her anywhere, was so overwhelming he couldn't see for a moment.

"Ryder?"

Ryder shook his head and raised his eyes. "I'm sorry. What did you ask?"

"I asked you what she wants for her information."

This was his chance. He leaned forward and pressed his lips gently over hers, licking the blood that remained. He let it soak into the gland at the back of his throat, memorizing every cell of her being as he continued to kiss her passionately. She kissed him back just as passionately. Finally, he leaned away to give her the news.

"You need to get some rest." He stood and walked to the door.

"Wait. You didn't tell me what she wants for her information."

Ryder pulled the door closed so that just his head was inside the room. He wanted a quick escape, just in case Kyra reacted the way he thought she might. "She only wants one thing: she wants me to fuck her through you."

Chapter 7

Kyra couldn't sleep. She stared at the cracked ceiling of her room. In Kyra's mind, Sophie pranced through the dance studio where Kyra had attended classes during her time at the academy.

"I would've loved to have trained with the Elements," Sophie said as she spun around and around, the light from the candles playing off her dark hair and pale complexion.

"How did you become a Banshee?" The lore on how Banshees came about was sketchy at best.

"Does it matter?" She kept spinning. It was actually making Kyra dizzy.

"Why do you want Ryder? How will that change what you are?" At first she'd been furious, and then she'd felt sorry for the woman. Now she was just curious.

"Does it matter?" she asked again.

"Actually, this time it does." Kyra placed herself in front of Sophie and grabbed her by the shoulders to keep her still. "This is my body, and you can't use it for your sexual desires." Sudden pain racked Kyra's body and she bowed off the bed. She felt her mouth open and close several times as she tried to scream, but no sound came out.

"Would you like to rephrase that?" Sophie asked.

Kyra took several deep breaths. "I want you out!" she shouted, sitting up in the bed. Her entire body hurt.

Sophie laughed softly and then Kyra was standing in the dance hall looking into the mirrors that lined the walls. "How many times do I have to prove that I am in control? And that you will do as I say?" The other woman actually stomped Kyra's foot in agitation.

With Sophie in control, she stood from the bed shaking off any lingering tiredness and headed toward the door. "What are you going to do?" Kyra shouted.

"Anything I want. And I'm tired of waiting."

A chill worked its way up her arms, and Kyra felt a shadow close around her as Sophie gave into the anger she'd held back. Her anger was unbelievable and overwhelming making Kyra hurt. Kyra hadn't been prepared for the darkness that encompassed Sophie's soul.

"Time to get things moving," Sophie said. Kyra tried to wrestle control back, but in the end, she ended up with pain lancing through her head. Once Sophie was in complete control, she rolled her shoulders and laughed at Kyra's impotence.

Kyra ran for the door of the studio, wrenching it open. She stepped into a meadow. Eric sat in the corner, one arm resting on a bent knee. Kyra screamed and turned back to the mirror-faced room. Where the hell did she think she was going? She was trapped in her own mind while a psychopath controlled everything.

Sophie pulled the bedroom door off its hinges as she moved through it. Kyra screamed, not sure what was going to happen but knowing it wasn't going to be good. Sophie pulsed with irritation and wrath. She didn't like to have to wait for anything. People did as she asked them, not the other way around, and she was about to prove it.

Simon and Marlee were sitting in the living room talking when Sophie strolled in. Marlee launched into a defensive position she glared at Kyra and growled. Simon stepped in front of her, trying to protect Kyra.

Kyra watched helplessly in her mind, pounding on the glass for Simon and Marlee to run. To get as far away as possible. But they heard nothing.

"It's still Kyra in there somewhere," Simon urged.

"That's not Kyra right now," Marlee snarled. "She smells like death and destruction."

"She is still Kyra." Simon argued. "I won't let you hurt her." He was wearing his heart on his sleeve and even in her position Kyra knew he cared way too much for her.

Ryder and his brothers came through another door. "Ah, just the men I wanted to see," Sophie purred. Marlee snarled again and Sophie turned to her and snarled back.

Sophie stepped forward and wrapped her arms around Simon, who still stood with his back to her, protecting her from them. Kyra screamed harder, the glass shattering. It slashed into her, pain slicing up her arms.

Sophie screeched and looked down as blood appeared from the cuts. Suddenly, she was standing in the hall with Kyra. "I was just going to frighten them," she said, eyes black as death, "but you had to go and do this!" She lifted her bleeding arms. "You're not the one in control here. Maybe after this, you'll remember that."

"Please don't hurt any of them," Kyra begged. She grabbed a shard of glass and slammed it into her forearm. Sophie shook it off but more blood trickled from the new wound. She flung her arms out and they were in the clearing.

"You'll pay for this! What I say and do is all that matters. Do as you please here in your mind." She looked around. "You are helpless. I am the one in control. Of you, of that stupid monster. All of it is mine to play with and use as I want." Sophie laughed. Kyra swung at her, clipping her cleanly on the chin. Sophie's head snapped back.

Black eyes narrowed back to Kyra, bled of all emotion. "I herald death. What do you do, Element?"

"I destroy bitches like you," Kyra snapped.

Sophie shook her head and gave a sad look. "Your pitiful attempt to change my course of action is wasted. And the deaths of your loved ones will stain your hands for eternity."

Then she was gone again. Kyra screamed and searched for a weapon, anything she could use against the crazy woman but found nothing. She was completely helpless, drowning in Sophia's satisfaction.

"Please don't hurt any of them," Kyra again pled but Sophie didn't answer. The scene in the living room played out in the starless sky above her like a movie.

Ryder crossed his arms over his chest, looking at the blood on Kyra's arms. "You're not completely in control, are you? Let Kyra know how proud I am of her, or better yet, get the hell out of her and I'll tell her myself."

Sophie seethed with anger and rubbed herself against Simon, whom she had never released while fighting with Kyra. She caressed his chest and kissed him below the ear. "You have all terribly underestimated what I am capable of. Those women, they were nothing compared to what is going to rain down on this mountainside. None of you will be able to stop it. None of you can even decide what to do with me, and I've made my demands perfectly clear."

Sophie rubbed herself against Simon. Ryder took a menacing step forward. "Get off of him, Sophie."

Kyra could feel Simon reacting, could smell his desire. Sophie purred against him, rubbing her hips against Simon's backside.

"Thousands of years ago, one man would've been as good as another, but …," she looked over at Ryder, "not all men are created equal."

"What do you want me to say, Sophie?" Ryder asked between clenched teeth. Kyra could see a vein throbbing in his temple. He was way more pissed than she'd ever seen him. Kyra fought for control, making Sophie stumble back.

She opened her eyes and looked at the people in the room. Ryder leaped forward. She felt her nose start to bleed as a pounding in her head grew to the point it almost took her to her knees.

"Do what needs to be done," she screamed while she had control of her body. But that was all she was capable of before Sophie had her back in the clearing. A spectator to her own life.

Ryder stepped back when black eyes burned into him. "I've made my request," she purred. "And it doesn't seem like anyone is really listening."

"I'll listen to you," Simon breathed. Sophie smiled at the man and pulled him in close. Simon molded himself to her.

Kyra watched helplessly. She heard the words she was speaking, felt the actions taking place, but was powerless to stop any of it.

"Of course you will," Sophie moaned. But then she turned to Ryder. "But you aren't what I want." And then she wrapped her arms around Simon's neck and snapped it.

Simon's body fell to the ground with a quiet thud.

Kyra felt Sophie laugh. But it was slowly drowned out by her own screams. The sound echoed off the walls of her mind. Kyra felt the fringes of her sanity start to slip. Curling into a ball, she screamed and cried so hard, every part of her body hurt.

Sophie stood over her, laughing. "If you had all just listened to me, this wouldn't have had to happen."

"Go to hell," Kyra sobbed.

"Oh, I've been to hell and back, Element. Why do you think I do what I do? I know what's waiting for me, not in the Infernos but in the hands of Satan himself." She looked up at the sky, now filled with stars. "Honestly, I have nothing to lose."

She kneeled down and picked up Kyra's face so that they were looking at each other. "So as you can see, I have nothing to fear."

Ryder held back his brothers as they rushed the woman, but he wasn't close enough to Marlee. The Lycan let out a blood-curdling scream as she threw herself at Kyra. Kyra swept one arm out, catching Marlee in the center of her chest in mid-leap, launching the other woman backwards. Marlee flew through the room, crashing against the far wall. When she hit, Ryder heard bones break.

Lykar rushed over to Marlee, who now lay unconscious.

"What do you want?" Ryder asked. He could smell euphoria from Sophie but under that, he smelled remorse and pain. He knew Kyra was in there dying slowly for what had just happened. When he got the chance, he was going to kill Sophie very slowly.

Black eyes stared back at Ryder. "I told you what I want." She looked toward the window, the pinking of the rising sun shading through. "You have until nightfall, and then someone else dies."

Lykar laughed. "Bitch, the rest of us are imMortal. How you going to manage that?"

She stroked Kyra's cheek and gave them a malicious smile. "Elements are not imMortal. They can withstand a great deal. But a bullet to the brain …" She shrugged and kicked the body at her feet. "A twist of the wrists, he didn't survive," she made a jerking motion with her head, "so I doubt little Kyra will survive a bullet to the head. Oh, and let's not forget the old woman, or all those terrified townsfolk shaking in their beds in the hope that the Boogeyman doesn't make a visit to take away their mothers. Sisters. Lovers. The Tribunal thrives on the anarchy that would ensue, and everything here would be gone. All at the hands of an Elemental Enforcer."

She turned back to her room, stopping before pushing the door into its place. "Remember. Nightfall, Ryder. I'll be waiting."

"That bitch has to die," Lykar snarled as the door was pushed into place, the peal of her laughter the only other sound in the house.

"So let me get this straight," Ryder asked, still not believing the stupid-ass plan they'd come up with. When Fiona had been informed that Simon was dead, she was horrified at the turn of events. Now the woman wouldn't be turned from the course of action they were planning. Ryder wasn't quite sold on the idea, considering if it went wrong, Kyra would die, her soul would be tied to Sophie's, and they would both end up in the Infernos or worse, hell itself.

"You want me to go in and have sex with that monster?" Ryder clarified for what felt like the millionth time.

"It's Kyra in there somewhere," Fiona argued. "I know the two of you have grown close, but she would not like to be used in this fashion. It's one thing to use her body to kill others she is dying inside because of that. But to use her in the fashion that Sophie insists it will be too much for Kyra."

"I don't give a shit how close we've become. I'm not taking advantage of her like that." The very idea repulsed him. He wanted Kyra, not that psycho bitch in control of Kyra's body. Hadn't she been through enough?

"We need Kyra to take back control. After what happened with Simon I believe she is hurting and isn't going to fight. We need to get her to fight back, rile her enough to have her back in control. You said that she gained control for a moment we need to do that again," Fiona explained. Marlee snarled from where she sat leaned up against the wall she was wrapped up from her broken ribs but would be better by tomorrow. But the way she reacted to Fiona apparently, she didn't like this plan, either.

"In any kind of possession, there are elements of the host that remains. But the longer that bitch has control, the less Kyra there is. We should just put her out of her misery and kill her and that thing inside her." Marlee gave her opinion her eyes snapping with pain and anger.

Fiona shook her head. "I understand the associated risks. However, I would never be able to face Eric or the Enforcers again with her blood on my hands. We must try something, before it is too late."

Marlee slapped her hand against the table. "She's a liability. Has been from the beginning. She must die before she kills anyone else."

"What are you worried about? You're imMortal," the older woman asked, tears in her eyes. "Simon wasn't given the opportunity to defend himself. Kyra would understand and make the sacrifice if asked."

"So those little boxes." Ryder decided to move forward with the plan, even if Marlee wasn't on board. He had to give Kyra a chance. He motioned toward the intricate ironwork boxes the size of a loaf of bread. "Will these trap Sophie if we can get her out of Kyra?"

Marcus joined the conversation. "Yes, that is what I've been told."

"And who exactly told you that?" Marlee asked. She had been a real bitch since waking up. It'd taken Ryder and Lykar to keep her from going in and killing Kyra outright.

"I have connections with Reapers. And when something doesn't belong in the Infernos, or Hell, Dante places them in one of these," Marcus explained, patting one of the boxes.

"You mean they collect the souls of the turned Fallen when the Fallen fall," Sky said.

Ryder watched as something flashed in Marcus's eyes, but it was gone really before it materialized into something. "There are other creatures out on this plane of existence that do not belong in the Infernos or Hell. But yes, the turned are trapped in the boxes when we are able to capture them."

"Will you eventually end up in one of those boxes?" Skylar pushed.

Marcus didn't even blink. "Yes."

"It's not going to work," Sophie crowed from the doorway of Kyra's room. She leaned against the doorjamb, arms crossed over her chest. "I have complete control and nothing you do will cause me to falter."

Fiona stood. She was small in stature but Ryder could smell her anger and pain. "You are an abomination and should burn in the heart of Hell for what you've done."

Sophie laughed, her black eyes glittering. "Old woman, you have no idea what I've done to survive. You Elements have some absurd notion that if you stick your heads in the sand long enough, everyone will forget that you dropped the ball thousands of years ago."

Fiona took a menacing step forward and her hand rose, palm out. Sophie shrieked as she was picked up off her feet and thrown back through the door of the room. Ryder heard her crash against the far wall. Max was not going to like what they were doing to his house. He would have to pay to have the damn thing completely rebuilt.

Fiona closed her hand and the door that had been dangling on bent, twisted hinges, shutting Sophie away from the rest of them.

"Do you think that was a good idea?" Marcus asked, lowering himself into a chair. "Pissing her off is what got Simon killed."

"I feel remorse for hurting Kyra's body, but the woman needed to be shut up." Everyone turned to the room as the most horrible shrieking noise shook the very foundation of the house.

"That worked well," Skylar noted.

A round of "shut up" from everyone in the room had Skylar back to cleaning the gun.

"How are we going to do this?" Ryder asked.

"You will have to go in and seduce her," Marcus said. "If I know Kyra, she isn't going to like it. In fact, it's going to infuriate her, she will forget for the moment about Simon and go on the attack. We need her to fight, otherwise she is lost. The other Enforcers tease her and call her china doll when they really want to piss her off. So be really nice. Sophie will soak it up, and Kyra will hate it."

"So not a compliment," Lykar laughed.

Fiona stepped in. "When Eric was young and learning to Phase, they played a game. Phasing in and out all over the house and grounds. If they were able to capture each other, the winner would scream 'Boo!' It's a message—if you can get that one word to Kyra, then she would know to that she was to Phase in and out. I doubt that Sophie has mastered Phasing, even if she has done it once or twice since taking over Kyra's body. She won't be able to keep up with Kyra. Kyra's ability to Phase and Shift and a few other Elemental abilities is unprecedented in Elemental history. She's amazing at it. There's no way Sophie will be able to keep up with her. In theory, it would separate them and all we need is a window of opportunity." Ryder nodded taking all the information in.

145

Skylar tossed his gun on the table and everyone turned to him. "And just why does Ryder have to go in there and fuck her? Isn't there any other way to distract her?"

Ryder was surprised Skylar was defending him. Not something his younger brother normally did, especially in the last couple hundred years. "We need all her defenses down. Do you know of any other way to do that?"

Skylar grunted and picked up his gun again. "This shit is crazy, and if it works, I'll be surprised as hell."

Marcus stood, took the smaller of the two boxes, and set it next to the door to Kyra's room. "When they separate, you will have to put yourself between them and give us a signal. I just need to touch the Banshee to gain control of her."

Ryder stood and moved over to the liquor cabinet. It took a lot to get a Tracker truly drunk. He knew that being stone-cold drunk wasn't the best way to go into this, but he needed something. He was about to piss off a Banshee and a woman he wanted nothing more than to seduce himself. To top it off, his brothers and a host of others were going to be standing outside the door, listening to every move he made. He tipped the bottle of whiskey and poured half its contents down his throat, letting it burn into his stomach. Then headed for the room.

The sun was just starting to set. He wanted Kyra—that he wasn't going to deny. But the thing that had control of her wasn't Kyra. For some reason, he felt as if he was betraying Kyra. He wasn't sure how far things would go before Kyra had had enough and fought back.

The room was a wreck. Every piece of furniture had been turned upside down or torn to shreds. The only thing remaining was the bed and half a table. "Redecorating?"

Sophie immediately stopped screeching when Ryder walked into the room and pulled the door into place behind him. Sophie smiled and ran her hands across her shoulders and down her chest, cupping and squeezing each breast.

"Do you have any idea the power this body holds? What she is capable of? When you look at her, you have the look of someone besotted. Do you have any idea how long it has been since someone looked at me like that?" Sophie stepped over ruined pieces of furniture so she could stand in front of Ryder. She ran a finger along the collar of his T-shirt, just grazing his skin. He felt as if he'd been burned and stepped back.

Sophie's black eyes glittered. "I burn a little hotter than this semi-Mortal. She isn't the pure soul you think she is. She is heartless and will turn her back on you the first chance she gets. You realize that, don't you? You look at her like she is some type of angel, but the only thing she cares for is her people. You are a stumbling block in her way. To use and toss away."

Her hands had moved to her own waist. She continued to sway slightly, hands moving all over Kyra's body, gyrating in a manner that Ryder couldn't help but be turned on by.

He shook his head and raised his eyes to Sophie's black ones. "I need some answers before this …" He waved toward the bed.

Sophie threw her hands in the air in agitation and walked over to the ruined table. One of Kyra's Glocks sat gleaming on one of the pieces. She picked it up and placed it under her chin. "Did you know that if I kill her while still in her body, she will be connected to me? She will become a Banshee sentenced to herald death for eternity."

Sophie rolled her head on her shoulders, bones popping as she did so. "It sucks as a job."

"How did you get tethered? I've never heard of a Banshee being tethered before. Common occurrence for Mortals but an Other? You must have sucked as a Banshee." He couldn't help the jab.

Sophie shrugged, rubbing the barrel of the gun against Kyra's soft cheek. It took everything Ryder had not to leap forward and snatch the weapon out of the woman's hand. She laughed but it was a hollow sound. "He creates and builds ,splices and dices to his heart's content. Has been doing so for hundreds of years, if not longer."

"Lordus grew tired of the souls who would linger after he'd destroyed their bodies and decided a Banshee would be the cure to ease the souls out of this plane. I used to scream for the dead, herald the coming of death and the triumph of life. Now I am nothing." Her face twisted in pain.

"But not all of them wanted to go. They felt jilted and fought me. They were lost. Reapers wouldn't come for them, the souls hidden. So many lost souls." She finally sank down onto the edge of the bed. "I herald death and lead souls to what is next. I don't know what it is. But I've seen the faces of the ones who go to the Infernos and the ones who go to the Elysian Fields. They are two completely different places. But these souls didn't want to go." She pounded her fists against the side of the bed. "I got sick of trying to get them to the right place, so I convinced Lordus to create me something to feed the ungrateful souls to. So they had two choices—they could choose the Infernos or the Elysian Fields, or what is now in the mountain. Eventually, I got tired of even offering them that, so they all go to that thing."

"You're not tethered to that thing in the mountain. You're tethered to Lordus." Red and black swirled in her eyes as she watched him complete the puzzle.

"Lordus would bring me the souls of his experiments, of his attempts at creation. That worthless thing in the mountain? He was a shapeshifter with strange abilities. Well, that was before Lordus got hold of him. And now he will be anything I want him to be, take the shape of any creature I want in order to draw out the death cries. That is what I feed off. Then he gets the souls."

"But Lordus stopped bringing you souls, didn't he?"

Fury poured through her. "He promised to give me a Mortal body. To live out a life, and die, be given the choice I wasn't given when I died the first time."

"And that would be?"

She shrugged as if it really didn't matter. "I'm done talking."

148

Ryder wasn't done questioning her. However, Sophie distracted him by pulling off the T-shirt she was wearing, exposing Kyra's full breasts covered by a thin layer of practical cotton. He had imagined what her underwear would look like, but wasn't surprised that it was simple black. It seemed glued to her tight, strong form like it had been spray-painted on. His body immediately responded and he shifted his feet, trying to ignore his raging erection.

"If you take me from him, the wards will be broken and he will roam free. So if your plan is to kill me, you might want to try something else." She laughed at Ryder's expression.

Sophie smiled as she wiggled out of the tiny boxers Kyra wore to bed. Sensible black bikini bottoms hugged her so close, it was sinful. Ryder had seen hundreds, if not thousands, of women in their underwear, but the sight in front of him? He wasn't sure he was going to be able to resist taking her for his own, regardless of the fact that Kyra was possessed with a psychotic Banshee. He wanted her that badly.

"So, no moving me from the area or my witless pet will sweep through the town and beyond. Uncontrolled, that is, until the Tribunal finds out about him. You know it will only be a matter of time before they are notified, and you will all be held responsible. We all know what that means." Her voice flattened out at the last, no emotion, just facts.

"We all do what we have to in order to survive, don't we, Ryder?" She said his name the way Kyra said it—hard *R* and *D*. He wanted nothing more than to suck the words straight from her tongue.

Climbing off the bed, she moved to where he stood, wrapping her arms around his neck. She pulled him down, pressing her entire body against him. The heat she was putting off could've burned the clothes right off him. "You'll like it in a moment," she moaned, rubbing her belly against his erection.

Ryder closed his eyes, hating what he was doing. He wanted Kyra. With his eyes closed and his senses dulled with liquor, he could almost imagine it was Kyra. Maybe if Sophie kept her mouth shut, he could get this underway and get her out of Kyra, once and for all.

Kyra was in the dark. She could see nothing and she screamed in rage and pain.

She had killed Simon.

How could she ever go home, face her friends and family? She was sure that Fiona would kick her out of the Order. She would be ostracized for what she had done. A small part of her kept saying that it hadn't been her, that Sophie had been in control.

It still had been her body, and she couldn't get past the feeling that if she'd wanted to stop it, if she'd had any idea what Sophie was going to do, she could've stopped it. That was what hurt the most. What was it going to take to get this Banshee out of her? She knew the guys were planning something, but Sophie had kept it from her, sealing her away in blackness.

Kyra kept moving, not sure where she was going, knowing she was trapped in her own mind. Her only thought was to put one foot in front of the other. It seemed to be helping, staving off her feelings of going stark raving mad.

"When all else is lost, stop searching and the answers will come to you." Kyra stopped walking and wiped tears from her face. Eric had said that to her so many times, she felt it was tattooed on the inside of her skull. She missed her brother. He always calmed her when her temper was too much for even her to take. He was a hundred years younger than she was, but served as a constant calming influence. She briefly thought of Ryder and how he seemed to fill that role during this mission. Always a calm mind. When she wanted to blast away, he would hold her back. She may be older than Eric, but she learned from him every day.

Remembering Eric's words, she lowered herself into a cross-legged position and closed her eyes. The answer was there; she just had to slow herself down enough to figure it out.

150

Meditation had never been her strong suit in school. She was too jittery, wanting to be everywhere at once, but she forced herself to be calm. Part of her was totally freaked out that she was even doing this. The basics of trying to do something like meditate within yourself were so odd that she kept forgetting to count her breaths. Because she wasn't really breathing. Her mind couldn't wrap itself around it. Finally, she slowed her breathing down and focused, thinking about her feet and wiggling her toes slightly before moving up her body. She worked her fingers and felt the sensation of silky, short clipped hair slip through them.

Kyra's eyes flew open and she jumped up. "What the hell?" she screamed, some of the pain and remorse taking a backseat for a just a moment. Foggy glass surrounded her as she forced the blackness away and gained a little control. Sophie was distracted, and Kyra had a sick feeling she knew why. The fog on the glass cleared and she saw Ryder's face descend to kiss her. He was actually doing it. That son of a bitch—he was going to fuck Sophie through Kyra.

Among all of them, none had been able to come up with a better plan than this? When she got out of her mind, she was going to kick their collective asses.

Her fury was so vast, it cracked the glass she was staring at. Kyra took several deep breaths, concentrating and gaining back some control.

Ryder leaned into Sophie, praying to the Gods that this was going to work. Sophie grabbed and kissed him roughly. She pressed her body against Ryder, gyrating for all she was worth. It made him sick, and he was immediately turned off by her forwardness. Not like he didn't like to have his females as active partners, but Sophie wanted to be in complete control. Ryder was way too alpha to be turned on by that. However, he had a part to play and forced himself to wrap his arms around her, playing into her need for him. She radiated heat and he let her make the moves.

Suddenly, she stopped and moved back an inch, anger infusing her words. "Your participation is required," she said between her teeth.

"You seemed to want to be in the driver's seat," Ryder said dryly.

Sophie stepped away from him and walked back to the bed where she had left the gun. Ryder caught his breath. "After I kill her, I will pull all the children from this pitiful little town and feed them to him. And the best part? She will be forced to help me."

Ryder held up his hands. "Anything you want."

She smiled and lay down on the bed. "Give me a night I will never forget."

Ryder pulled off his shirt and unbuttoned his jeans, but didn't remove them. He was praying that things wouldn't get that far. He stretched his body out over hers, the base part of him thrilled at the feel of Kyra's warm body beneath him. After days of wondering how it would feel, he gave in slightly and kissed her as if she were Kyra.

Sophia moaned deep in her throat, wrapping her arms and legs around him. She was soon in control again and Ryder mentally pulled away, waiting for some sign that Kyra was in there and ready to fight.

Sophie was so engrossed in the kiss, Kyra was surprised how easy it was to switch places with her. One moment Sophie was in control and the next Kyra was kissing Ryder, and Sophie was bellowing to bring the heavens down deep in Kyra's mind.

Ryder felt the change. Kyra's lips softened. The hands that held him slackened so that she was touching him, not pressing him into her.

He leaned back and looked down into aqua blue eyes. "Kyra?"

"This was the best plan you could come up with?" she asked. "I …" Then she moaned and tossed her head back and forth in pain.

"Fight, Kyra!" Ryder demanded, climbing off the bed as she started to thrash. She cried out, her body bowing until he was sure that her spine would snap.

He kneeled at the side of the bed. "Fight!" he demanded, shaking her by the shoulders. Then he remembered what Fiona had said and screamed the word at her. "BOO!" Aqua eyes turned to him in recognition before black bled quickly back into place. Sophie shrieked and grabbed Ryder. Sinking her nails into his shoulders, she pulled him forward.

Ryder grunted in pain as her sharp nails punctured his skin. Leaning down, he placed a kiss just below her earlobe. "You're losing control, Sophie."

Sophie shook her head. "No." But it was more a plea than anything else.

She shoved Ryder away and he flew from the bed, hitting the wall and slid to the floor. He got to his feet, swaying just a little, but was able to maintain his footing.

Kyra/Sophie clambered from the bed. Black eyes battled with blue and her head kept shaking, and then she Shifted. One moment Kyra was standing there and the next she was standing next to Ryder, but she had two heads. Which, Ryder had to admit, freaked the hell out of him. But just as quickly she Shifted again, coming up next to the table.

Ryder had to take a second to wonder what type of game this had been for her and her brother.

"Boo!" he screamed at Kyra as she reappeared, this time more Kyra than Sophie. Both women screamed. Kyra was in control of the right side while Sophie seemed to have control of the left.

"Now!" Ryder shouted and Marcus and his brothers broke through the door. The fighting women didn't even slow down as they Shifted throughout the room, separating a little more each time.

Kyra finally ended up next to the bed, Sophie still connected by a thin strand of light. Kyra grabbed the gun, cocked it back, and held it under Sophie's chin. "How human are you now, bitch?" And then she pulled the trigger.

Sophie shifted and the bullet blew through a wisp of smoke that had been her head milliseconds before. The lead lodged in the ceiling. When Sophie reappeared, she was several feet from Kyra.

"Do you have any idea what that would have done to us both, you lunatic?" she howled, lurching toward Kyra.

Marcus stepped between them, wrapping his arms around Sophie. She struggled for a moment and then started to shriek when she saw the box at her feet.

"If you lock me in that and take me away from him, the wards will be broken and he will roam free, killing everything he comes in contact with." The words tumbled from her mouth in an attempt to change her fate.

Ryder pushed past the crowd, grabbing his shirt as he went. He handed it to Kyra, who pulled it over her nearly naked body.

"Thank you." She looked like hell.

"Not a problem. You okay?" He lifted her chin so he could look into her eyes. They were blue but a darker shade than before, her irises now outlined in black.

"My head hurts." She paused and leaned against the table. "Actually, my entire body hurts." She stumbled but when he reached out to steady her, she pushed his hands away.

Ryder turned to the others. "Put her in the box, but don't take her to the Infernos."

"No, please," Sophie begged. "I'll tell you anything you want to know. I'll help you destroy him, and Lordus, for that matter. They mean nothing to me. I was their pawn! Thousands of years a pawn," she begged.

"She's lying," Kyra said in a shaky voice. "You weren't the only one fucking with a mind. I got a good look at yours while you took me over."

154

"Get rid of her. I don't care how you do it. In fact, what happened to my gun? I'd like to shoot her again. Get rid of her," Kyra said the last to Marcus. The Fallen looked at Kyra for a moment before nodding. He whispered words that were drowned out by Sophie's shrieking. The box's lid flipped open and a dark mass oozed out, climbing up Sophie's leg. She kicked out, as if she could dislodge the inky blackness that now stretched up her thighs.

When it reached her mid-chest, she turned to Kyra and pierced her with coal-black eyes. "I will be back for you, Element. And when I do, you'll die slowly," she said with perfect calm.

Sophie was capable of doing just that. With one last shriek, the inky blackness swallowed Sophie and slid back into the box, the lid quietly clicking shut, cutting off the Banshee's screams.

"Is she in pain?" Marlee asked from the doorway. Marcus looked sad as he nodded.

"She'll live in constant pain with the darkness of the world."

"That's what that is?" Lykar asked, taking a step away from it.

Marcus nodded. "Holds all the evils of the world. When opened by a pure soul, they will be released. But opened with words of power that the Reapers have, they are able to direct the darkness to the soul being punished. It's a Pandora's Box."

"Not cool." Skylar backed away as well. "Now what?" he asked, keeping his distance.

"I'll take her to the Infernos," Marcus suggested.

"You can't move her very far from the thing in the mountains or it will release it," Kyra said. Her entire body hurt and all she wanted to do was sleep. She wanted to call her brother and cry because of what had happened to Simon. She wanted to drink until she was completely numb. Most of all, she wanted to wreak vengeance on the bitch who had possessed her. Kyra started to shake and had to lean into Ryder or completely fall on her face. He wrapped his arms around her. And for that moment, she felt safe.

Ryder agreed with her. "Sophie said something similar to me."

"Was that before or after you fucked her through me?" Kyra surprised herself. She didn't even realize she had the energy to growl the words at the man holding her.

Lykar and Skylar both shook their heads. "Awkward," they said together, and then headed for the door.

"Marcus, let's see what Fiona's up to," Lykar suggested, slapping the Fallen on the shoulder. The three men left.

Ryder turned to Kyra and she couldn't resist. Her hand snapped out and she slapped him across the face. He barely flinched, which just made her want to hit him harder, but she just didn't have anything left. Her tanks were totally empty.

"How could you?"

Ryder stepped toward her, making her back up until she was pressed against the wall. She couldn't help but be completely aware of the fact that he was shirtless and her body was still tuned into high gear.

"First of all," he gave her a look that could have melted the ice caps, "if I had fucked you, you would've known about it. Even trapped in your own mind. And second, when I do fuck you, and it's going to happen, mark my words on that one, you won't have to question it."

"But you would have, you would have whether I had wanted it or not," Kyra accused.

Ryder blew out of breath of air in frustration. "She killed Simon, and she was threatening to kill you. Was I supposed to let that happen? Stand back and not do anything? Let her win?"

Kyra faltered at the mention of Simon. "I am not worth the souls that have been lost because of her or because of her pet in the mountain. You should've just shot her, me, us."

"It wasn't your call, Kyra," he said, walking away from her. "Take a shower and get some sleep. You smell like Sophie and you look like hell."

Kyra wanted to throw something at him. Instead she sniffed her shoulder. "What the hell are you talking about?"

"Sophie smelled of sulfur, dirt, and death, and now you smell of it as well. It doesn't suit you. Take a shower and get some sleep. We'll discuss what our next plan of action will be in the morning." He slammed out of the room. Kyra jumped when the door vibrated on its broken hinges.

She slid to the floor and wrapped her arms around her knees and cried. She just couldn't help it. So much had happened. So much had gone wrong. Her fact-finding mission had blown up in her face, and all she wanted was the comfort of her own bed, her brother to make her laugh. And while she was at it, she wanted Simon to be alive. Which only made her cry harder.

Warm arms wrapped around her, and Kyra relaxed into Fiona's warm grasp.

"I'm so sorry I killed him. It should have been me, not him."

"The path of life often takes us on detours that we neither expect nor want. It's how we react to those detours that matter." Fiona pulled Kyra's face up to meet hers, pushing hair and tears away. "You did not kill, Simon. Sophie did. And regardless of what you say or do, nothing will change that fact."

"But I should have stopped it," Kyra hiccupped.

"Could you have?"

Kyra just looked into Fiona's gray eyes. "I stopped her from letting Ryder have his way with me."

"Maybe you should be thinking about why you were able to stop that and not stop her from killing Simon. Remember that it was Sophie who killed Simon," Fiona reiterated. "We all have a part to play in this life. Simon's part has ended for now. But that doesn't mean he is no longer with us or that his memory will be erased from time. He left a mark." She touched the center of Kyra's chest. "His light will remain."

"I have contacted the Haven. Eric would like you to call him, and Daemon is on his way to take Simon home." Fiona left Kyra sitting on the floor. She cried herself out and then dialed Eric's private number. He immediately picked up.

"Kyra?" She started to cry again when she heard his gentle voice, full of concern and love. "I wish I were there."

"I wish you were here too," she cried. "Everything that can go wrong has."

"Sometimes shit happens, china doll." Eric used the nickname she hated. She was sure he was trying to get her to stop crying, but it wasn't working.

"I should've married him and moved into a house with a white picket fence and given him children. That was all he wanted, why he became an Enforcer, to be close to me. And I killed him," she sobbed.

"Kyra," Eric's voice was strained when he spoke, "Simon made choices. We all make choices. I am sorry for what happened. You will never be able to change it, but it wasn't you."

No matter what Fiona or Eric said, she still blamed herself. "Eric, I have lived my life doing what I do so that I can make up for the fact that my family didn't survive, that they weren't given the gifts that I have. Now Simon ..."

"For the love of all the Gods, when are you going to live for you?" he barked. Kyra pulled the phone from her ear and looked at it. "Pick yourself up and dust yourself off. Daemon has a gift for you from me. And don't get yourself killed, or I will never forgive you."

Kyra smiled in spite of the pain she felt. "I love you, Eric."

"Yeah?" he asked, his voice now full of concern and apprehension. It was something they shared—the need for the other's love. Sometimes they felt like it was the two of them against the world. Regardless of the other Enforcers, they had a very special relationship.

"Yep, I do."

"You're going to be okay. Just make sure to come home safe."

Kyra shook her head. "I'll do my best."

They said their goodbyes and Kyra pulled herself to her feet. She moved slower than usual, her entire body hurting. She climbed into the shower and made the water as hot as she could stand, scrubbing her skin raw. She didn't want anything of Sophie remaining, but knew that what was in her mind and soul would be there for a long time.

Ryder listened at her door, knowing she was sleeping, but couldn't stop himself from going in and pulling up a chair next to the bed. He wanted to check on her, wanted to ensure that she was still Kyra. Just sit and enjoy the silence and her. He leaned down and took a deep breath. The underlying smell of sulfur was now gone, but something else lingered from what she'd gone through. She'd been changed forever by what had happened. It upset him that she felt so much pain. He knew she was strong and could handle just about any situation. He had pushed her past her limits and though he wasn't a man who often felt guilt, he felt a great deal now. He'd pushed her too far.

Her eyes opened. They were dark and filled with so much pain, it was palpable. She stared at the ceiling, her breathing catching slightly. Ryder leaned back.

"I can feel him leaning into me, trusting me," she whispered, tears slipping from her eyes. She looked at her hands as if they didn't belong to her.

Ryder didn't say anything, didn't know what to say. How do you comfort someone in this situation? It just wasn't possible. She might not have been in control but he knew she felt the death of her friend and that it weighed heavily on her conscience.

"How long have you been an Enforcer for the Elements?" he asked instead, getting her mind off Simon.

Kyra rolled over so she was facing him. "Forever. I know that sounds relative when we live so long. Or in your case, as an imMortal." She sighed heavily. "When I showed signs of being Elemental, I was taken from my family and placed in the Academy."

"How old were you?"

"Five."

"Do you have any memories of your family?" Ryder couldn't imagine not having the closeness of his brothers and his mother and father.

"General memories. They were Mortal. The Druids tried to explain what I was and why they needed to take me away." She shrugged but he could see the pain in her eyes. "It was normal back then to find a strain of Element in families all across Europe. Enforcers and Lookers were sent out to scout towns and people. If they didn't find you and take you someplace safe, it was likely that eventually, you would be accused of witchcraft or heresy and killed."

"Did you have any brothers or sisters? Any family who remained?"

"I had one younger sister, but she didn't make it to adulthood. So many didn't back then. My parents died shortly after my sister. Their cottage caught fire." Ryder could see the pain in her eyes and wished he could erase it for her. "The members at the Academy became my family. Then they moved me to The Haven where the Enforcers live, and they became my family. Simon followed when he came of age."

"And what of this Eric who you call brother?"

She smiled through her tears. "I adopted him as my brother when he was a child. He has a very complicated history. I think he was born angry and pissed at the world. Nothing anyone says or does will take away the fact that we didn't come from the same parent. We are brother and sister."

"So how many Others have you killed?"

"I have no idea. Why?" Her blue eyes sparked in indignation.

"Because being an Enforcer, or a Tracker, in my case, we hunt down things that people, especially Mortals, don't want roaming the world. How many friends have you lost in your job?" Kyra couldn't even begin to count how many friends and people she considered family had been lost in the last century.

"What's your point, Ryder?"

"We kill. It's what we do. Because it's either us or them. And I have a very strong will to survive. You can choose life, or you can choose to hide in terror of the things that go bump in the night." His realism stung. At that moment, she would rather have hidden under her bed from those horrible things.

"Would you kill one of your brothers?"

"No. I would kill myself first," he said honestly.

"Then you know what I am going through. I would give my life to bring Simon back. He didn't deserve to die at my hands. He was protecting me from Marlee, and Sophie took advantage of that and killed him with my hands." Kyra looked down at them again in disgust.

Ryder reached out and took her hands into his, and she felt a jolt of electricity shoot up her arm. It shocked the hell out of her, and she sucked in a breath. That meant something in the Elemental world, but she wasn't about to say anything to Ryder.

He squeezed her hands, ignoring the electricity. "It might have been these hands that killed Simon. But it was not you who killed him. You need to figure out how to separate the two things."

He released her and stood up. "Killing is what we do, Kyra. I'm sorry your friend died today. But at the end of it all, I will not regret the fact that you are still here." He leaned down and kissed her gently on the forehead. Another sizzle of electricity shocked them.

"A lot of electricity in the air tonight," Ryder muttered as he left the room. She desperately wanted to call out to him to stay with her. Even if it meant he would just hold her for the night. But she knew that he wouldn't just hold her, and as much as she wanted the sex, she needed to work through this pain before she could offer anything to anyone else.

She lay in the dark for several hours wondering how she could've changed the outcome, but she could find no answer, except from a small, hideous voice in the back of her brain. It laughed at her, eyes black.

"Maybe, just maybe, you wanted him dead," it whispered before disappearing back into the shadows of her mind.

Kyra rolled over. She didn't think she had any tears left, but they came, anyway. She cried herself to sleep.

Chapter 8

"Where is Lordus now?" Marcus was talking to someone on the phone when Kyra came out of her room.

"Here." Ryder handed her a plate piled with eggs, bacon, croissants, and a bowl of fruit.

"Thank you." He shrugged and turned back to Marcus.

"If the bloodsucker won't give us the information, then he is useless to us," Ryder barked.

Marcus placed a hand over the receiver. "And if you talk to him like that, he is less likely to help,"

"Damn moody vampires. Can't trust them for anything," Ryder mumbled. "Most useless race created."

"Hello, hello?" Marcus threw the phone down and glared at Ryder. "He heard you and I doubt he is willing to help us. Can't you just keep your opinions to yourself for a little while? Instead of insulting everyone and everything you come in contact with?"

"Was the vampire our only lead?" Kyra asked around a mouth full of eggs.

"No, but he was our best lead." Marcus looked pointedly at Ryder as he said it. "The King of the Vampires and Lordus have a long and complicated history. They've been trying to kill each other for over two hundred years."

That was all new information to Kyra. She wondered if there wasn't anyone in the Other world that Marcus didn't know.

"I will not kiss the ass of the Vampire King, or a Fallen for that matter. We can deal with this ourselves."

"Who is Lordus?" Kyra asked. She hadn't heard the name before but he was someone that both Ryder and Marcus obviously knew.

"He claims to be a Descendent."

"As in 'a Descendent'?" Kyra asked, choking on her breakfast. She had never met a descendent of Atlantis before. The origins of the world both Mortal and imMortal were tied to descendents from Atlantis. But to claim you were actually a pureblood descendent meant something. If that was the case, then you had the means and power to pretty much destroy and rebuild worlds. A descendent would be a God unto himself.

"But if that's the case, why hasn't he destroyed everything he doesn't like and rebuilt the world in the image he wants?" It was told that is what destroyed Atlantis—the Gods and deities in charge wanted to build their own worlds, be Gods in their own right. They branched out to be their own Gods, taking power away from the collective that was Atlantis, leaving it vulnerable to the plague that ultimately destroyed it. Kyra shivered remembering the story. A brilliant scientist had fallen madly in love with a nightwalker. They were shadows of beings, created in the in-between, neither of the Mortal plane nor any other plane for that matter. Their one weakness was that they did not produce platelets; when attacked, one small cut would kill them. Today they were housed in the Lake of Souls, kept safe by the Infernos.

But back in Atlantis, the scientist couldn't stand the thought of her nightwalker being killed or harmed in any way. She broke all the rules cavorting with this nightwalker. But like so many Atlantians, she thought she knew better and worked day and night to find a cure for him and his race.

She created vampires in her quest for imMortality for her love. Before Atlantis could get reinforcements in from the other Gods, the city had been wiped out. They say the only two to walk out of the ruined city was the scientist and her lover. From there, they created their own race of vampires.

Kyra had thought it a romantic story when she had been little, to love someone so much that you would give up everything you knew and understood and in the process, wipe out a civilization. She couldn't remember the last time a guy had opened a door for her, much less helped to destroy a civilization and create a new one in the process. But she also understood now that love was important, though it had its limits. She couldn't help but look at Ryder as that thought passed through her mind.

"Legends demand that in order to create and destroy worlds, you have to have certain objects. It's not something that can be done by one man. He must have a following," Marcus explained. "Lordus is a vampire and has been trying to create a new race to lord over for several hundred years. The Others and Councils of Others have ignored him because he dabbles, but as yet has been unable to create anything of substance. Unfortunately, the Tribunal finds him interesting, so they clean up after him when he does something really bad."

Kyra snorted. "Until now."

"Yes," Marcus agreed. "Lordus has been playing in creation. But everything he's ever created has been an abomination that even he couldn't stand. This is different—he left this thing in the mountain with Sophie. It doesn't make any sense. He has to have another plan."

"Do you think he will come back for them? Is he waiting for something to happen to them?" The thought made Kyra sick. Anyone trying to create a race by torturing other living things was horrible.

"According to Sophie, he has left them to fend for themselves," Ryder added. Kyra had to admit she was just a little jealous of what Ryder had shared with Sophie where it was through her body or not. He had touched her and kissed her and Kyra didn't remember any of it. It bothered her more that it should have.

But she remaindered herself he was a Tracker and had told her that love was for fools. And she wasn't going to waste her time on someone who felt like that, no matter how sexy he was.

"What?" Ryder leaned in and whispered so that only she could hear him.

"Excuse me?" Kyra asked, turning back to her plate.

"You just gave me the strangest look." He raised a questioning eyebrow.

Kyra bit the inside of her cheek. She was not going to tell him she was jealous. It was pointless. After this mission they would never see each other again. And damn it all to hell, the last thing she was going to do was pant after this man.

When she didn't answer, Ryder leaned in and sniffed.

"What the hell?" Kyra barked. She moved away so fast, she almost fell out of the chair. Everyone in the room stopped talking and turned to the two.

Ryder smiled and steadied her so she didn't fall before replying. "Nothing."

"Don't do that," Kyra said under her breath.

"You know that Trackers can practically smell emotions," Marlee offered, stuffing eggs into her mouth.

Kyra felt her face grow hot and turned to Ryder.

"Shut the hell up, Mar," Ryder snapped, not making eye contact with Kyra.

Kyra stood and walked out of the kitchen. She was not going to be sniffed by anyone, especially Ryder. She was able to read air, but apparently her Elemental abilities took a back seat to what the Trackers could smell. She bristled with anger.

"Don't take it personally. It's what they do," Marlee said, following Kyra.

Kyra turned to the Lycan. "How did you end up with the Trackers, Marlee?"

Marlee smiled but it didn't quite reach her eyes. "I am a female Wer without a Tribe. I am open game for any male Wer looking for a woman."

Kyra understood enough of the Wer laws to know Marlee's was not a position any female wanted to be in.

"Ryder found me half dead after being attacked by a rogue male tribe. I was out of my mind. He nursed me back to health and I've stuck with him ever since. I've grown to love the independence of not answering to a man and the brothers don't ask anything of me that I won't willingly do." Marlee shrugged. "You can't pick your family, but you can pick your friends, right?"

Kyra couldn't agree more. "So why the sniffing thing?"

"You don't know much about Trackers, do you?"

"No, not really. Until I met Ryder, I thought he was a myth," Kyra admitted.

Marlee laughed. "Aren't we all. Trackers have special senses; the strongest being taste, touch, and smell. They have a special gland in the back of their throats that gives them the upper hand in those areas. So if they get a taste or smell of something, they can track it anywhere."

. "Does anything stop them?"

Marlee shrugged. "Funnily enough, cloves. They are highly allergic to cloves. It kills their senses. And the amount and length of contact will determine how they'll react and how long it'll take them to recover. The original Trackers were nomads. They moved around, never in the same place for long. Basically they're the same now. Hard to find, and even harder to hire. You have to have a pretty good reason for them to pick up a track. The Reapers use them. Creeps me out."

That sent a chill up Kyra's spine. "Why was he sniffing me?"

"One of two reasons: he either likes the way you smell or you were telegraphing your mood in your scent and it interested him." Marlee patted Kyra on the back. "You'll get used to it if you hang out with them long enough."

Kyra was furious. "So is nothing private?"

Marlee smiled it was more wolf than human. "Not really. Not unless you can learn to mask your scent or always be downwind. If worse comes to worse you can use the cloves, like I said their allergic but only as a last resort. The last thing you want is a pissed off Tracker."

Kyra had the strongest urge to walk back into the kitchen and punch Ryder in the face. He wouldn't be smelling anything if his nose was broken. He couldn't just go around sniffing her. She thanked Marlee and walked to the front of the house instead, putting distance between them rather than slamming her fist into his face. She pushed open the front door and stood in a ray of morning sunlight. She soaked it up, trying to put the horror of yesterday behind her.

"You look deep in thought," Fiona said, striding up the porch stairs. "Would you like to talk about it?"

Kyra sighed heavily. "How will I explain to Simon's family what happened?"

Fiona's silver eyes sparkled in pain. "Sophie killed Simon. That's all anyone outside of the Enforcers needs to know. You had nothing to do with Simon's death."

Fiona patted her shoulder. "Killing yourself with self-doubt will get you nowhere, Kyra."

They watched as a black SUV pulled into the gravel drive. Daemon, dressed in the browns of an Earth element, a solemn look on his face, climbed from behind the driver's seat. Kyra took one look at him, this man she'd lived with for over a hundred years, and ran into his arms.

Ryder stepped from the house just as Kyra flung herself into the arms of a strange man. He heard himself growl and was about to lurch over the railing when Lykar grabbed him and Fiona stepped in front of him.

"Daemon is another Enforcer. He is no competition to you for Kyra's affections," Fiona urged, holding up both hands. As if that would be enough to stop him.

"Then tell him to get his bloody hands off her before I break them off and kill him with them," Ryder snarled.

Lykar jerked Ryder back into the house and slammed him against the wall. "What the fuck is your problem?"

Ryder shook his head unable to control himself. "Back off, Lykar,"

"Let's get out of here." Lykar headed toward the back door. Ryder followed, knowing that if he went through the front and saw Kyra in the arms of another man, he might not be able to stop himself this time.

"You need to get control of yourself, man."

"No shit, Lykar. I don't know what the hell is going on. When it comes to her, I can't control myself." Ryder rubbed a hand over his short hair. He didn't even want to say her name right now—he wanted so badly to go back and tear apart the man who'd been touching her.

"I think the little Element is working her way under your skin. You want me to call in Falcon?" Damn, that was the last thing Ryder wanted. The oldest out of the eight, he was the strongest and most jaded of them all. He showed little to no emotion, happy or sad. Frankly, Ryder didn't think it was normal.

"Hell no. I'll control it."

"Yeah, you better hope so. 'Cause anything else is a death sentence. And I won't let you go out that way. I'll kill her first." Ryder would've snapped at his brother if he didn't know he was utterly serious. If he cared at all for Kyra, he would stay away from her.

Kyra couldn't hold back the tears as they performed the death rites on Simon, packing him in earth and then wrapping him in clean cloths. They placed the four major Elements within each layer of his death shroud, and then Daemon placed the body in the back of the SUV. When he shut the door, Kyra's legs shook so hard, she wasn't sure if she'd be able to stay upright.

"Daemon ...," she started.

"I've got it, china doll," he said with a sad smile.

She looked into his lovely amber eyes that glistened with tears, but she knew he wouldn't allow them to fall. "I can't thank you enough, for coming for him. I should go back with you. I should be the one to face his family."

"His family knows, Kyra. I spoke with Adelaide last night," Fiona interrupted.

Kyra felt the knife twist in her heart. "How ..."

Fiona rubbed Kyra's arm. "They are mourning the loss of their son. But they also knew this was a possibility. After all, he was an Enforcer."

Kyra buried her face in her hands, wishing she could take their pain away. "I'm so sorry," she moaned, her heart breaking.

Daemon gathered her into his arms. "This is not your fault." He tilted her face so she was looking into his eyes. "Keep fighting, Kyra. Never stop. Stopping is giving up, giving into the evil, letting it win. Is that what you want? Do you want Simon's death to mean nothing?"

She shook her head.

"Do you need anything else?" he asked. She shook her head again. He smiled and pulled a brown bag from behind the driver's seat. "Eric," was all he said. She took the package and held it close to her chest.

"You're going to be late," Fiona said, checking her watch. It was a Druid and Element ritual to have the body in the ground within seventy-two hours, and they were pushing it.

"I have the plane ready." He hugged the two women. "Promise me you'll both come home safe and sound." It was more emotion than they typically shared with each other, which told Kyra they all understood how dangerous this mission had turned out to be.

"I promise to come home safe if you promise to go out on the next intel mission. Because this shit was supposed to be a look-and-see." Kyra tried not to let her eyes linger at the back of the SUV.

"Okay," Daemon smiled. Kyra gave him a dirty look. "I can only hope it has something to do with the Amazons," Daemon said with a wink. "I could intel the Amazons for months."

Kyra rolled her eyes and wrapped her arms around him. "Take care, Daemon."

"You too, china doll." She couldn't resist that last one and hit him right in the stomach. He grunted and laughed.

"Thank you." She walked back to the house as Daemon said his goodbyes to Fiona. The house was empty. She had no idea of anyone's whereabouts or what the next plan was. She put the bottle of liquor down and cleaned up the mess created by her possession. When everything was back in its place, she went to look for Fiona.

The older woman was kneeled in the shade of a large redwood. Kyra kneeled down next to her and took several deep breaths, but she couldn't seem to focus.

Sighing deeply, Fiona turned to Kyra. "You have never been any good at meditation, Kyra. Why this afternoon?"

"I'm trying to find peace in a world that has flipped upside down on me," she said hopelessly.

"Sometimes peace is not meant to be had until the actions of anarchy are taken care of." Kyra barely controlled her snort. Truer words had never been spoken.

She leaned back on her heels and rubbed her temples. Fiona reached over and threaded her fingers into Kyra's hair above her right ear.

"She has left part of herself inside you. You will have to learn to live with that. You will never be able to get rid of it," Fiona said sadly, dropping her hand.

"But what will that make me?"

Fiona smiled. "It will do only what you allow it to do. You have control, Kyra. Just because a minuscule piece of that abomination remains doesn't mean she has any control or any say in anything you do. She only has whatever power you give her, and nothing more."

Kyra nodded. She didn't want any part of the woman left inside her, but she also knew there was nothing she could do about it. Except to push it as far back as possible and move on with her life. She stood and went back into the house. It was still silent, so she headed to her room. The bag her brother had sent contained a bottle of tequila. Eric always knew exactly what she needed. And the oblivion of liquor was something she really needed at the moment.

"We have an idea," Fiona offered as Ryder, his brothers, and Max came in via the back door. Fiona, Marcus, and Marlee sat at the kitchen table. The intricate box they had trapped Sophie sat in the center.

171

"Interesting, because we have an idea as well," Ryder said.

"That's wonderful. What's your idea?" Fiona motioned to a seat.

"Where's Kyra?" Ryder asked.

"She is indisposed at the moment," Fiona said noncommittally.

Marlee snorted and Marcus lifted one questioning eyebrow at Fiona, which made Ryder question all of them.

"We don't have time for her to mourn," Ryder snapped

Fiona held up a hand. "Let her have this evening, Ryder."

"Is she a part of your plan? Because she's a part of ours. And she will be part of the decision-making if she's involved," he said angrily. Yes, she'd had a bad couple of days. But she couldn't hide from the world forever because of it.

"Of course she's part of the plan," Fiona sighed.

"Then she should be part of this conversation," Ryder said, heading out of the kitchen toward Kyra's room.

"Good luck," Fiona called to him from the kitchen.

This time it was Ryder who snorted. He wasn't going to make a decision about their next move without Kyra.

He pounded his fist against the closed door instead of walking in like he wanted to do. "Kyra, get your ass out of bed. We have some plans to make."

He turned back toward the kitchen but stopped when he heard a thump from Kyra's room. It brought him to a dead halt. This time he didn't knock but threw open her door. Kyra was face down on the floor.

"Good hell." Ryder raced over to her. She was trying to pick herself up and started to slap at his hands, which only sent her back to the floor.

"I can do it," she slurred. Ryder took a deep breath. Was she possessed again? He got a sniffer full of alcohol fumes.

"Are you drunk?" he asked.

Kyra turned to look at him. "Oh, it's you. You can help me. If you don't make me want to punch you in the face." She blinked several times, as if she wasn't quite seeing him correctly.

"Really?" Ryder leaned back on his heels. "And what makes you want to punch me in the face?"

"Seriously?" she asked, a twinkle in her alcohol-glazed eyes. "Pretty much everything you do ends up with me wanting to punch you in the face. What does that mean, do you think?"

Ryder grunted. He didn't have an answer for her and didn't really like the thought that she wanted to punch him so often.

She offered him her hand. "You may help me if you don't make me feel helpless about it. Because frankly, I'm sick of that as well," she said in a stage whisper.

He took her hand and pulled her to her feet. "Why are you drinking?"

She held up a bottle of blue liquor. "We performed the burial rights for Simon. My brother sent me a gift." She took another swig from the bottle. "He always knows what I need."

Ryder was confused. "Your brother sent you a gift for doing burial rights?"

"Argh," Kyra sighed heavily, making her lean forward. "No, he sent it so I could drink it, silly. Like I said, he knows what I need."

Ryder didn't like the fact that another man, regardless of it being her brother, was sending her gifts. And knew her better than he did.

"How much of that have you had?" he asked, trying to hold on to his anger as she swayed. Damn, she was a cute drunk.

Kyra lifted the bottle. It was three quarters gone. "That much," she said, smiling at Ryder as if she'd done something amazing.

Well, at least she could hold her liquor. That much alcohol would put a grown man on his butt. But there she was, standing there. Sort of. He reached out to steady her as she tilted to one side. He attempted to take the bottle. "Maybe you've had enough for the night."

Kyra clutched the bottle to her chest. "I need it." She stumbled back and fell onto the bed.

Ryder kneeled down and reached for the bottle again. Kyra rolled over, trapping the bottle underneath her. "Mine."

"Kyra, I don't ask twice."

Her words were muffled as she spoke into the covers of the bed. "You say that a lot, but you never explained what would happen. And I think that I should fully understand what the consequences would be if I made you ask twice. Oh, and I've heard you break that promise several times." She giggled; he growled.

"You do that a lot too," she said, rolling over. She pulled the lid off the bottle and took another healthy drink. "Don't get me wrong. I really like it, but I don't understand what it means." She drew the last word out, as if she were thinking very hard about it as she said it. "I don't do well with people I can't read. I'm good at that. Reading people, I mean."

"Yeah, because you read Sophie so well," he said, and then wanted to pull the words back as soon as they came out. Pain flashed through her eyes. He shouldn't have said it. But the moment the words were out, the damage was done. The bottle went back to her lips.

"She did pull one over on me, didn't she?" Kyra's words slurred a little. "When Simon and I were young, he used to tell me that he was going to outdo me in everything. That way I would fully understand that he would be able to take care of me when I finally agreed to marry him." Her words caught at the end.

"Maybe I should've married him and convinced him to do something normal. But I chose to become an Enforcer and he followed. Then I killed him." She finished off the bottle with one long, last pull. And in a fit, she flung the bottle as hard as she could away from her. Ryder ducked as it flew past his head and slammed into the wall behind him, shattering into a million little pieces.

"Would you've been happier if you'd married him and lived a quiet, suburban life?" Ryder asked.

"Hell, no!" Kyra shouted. "I want adventure. I want to live life to the fullest. I want to experience everything I can." Tears filled her eyes. "I want to experience everything my Mortal family missed out on. Even though I don't really remember them, I think they deserve that, don't you? And now Simon." She held up a finger. "I'll have to fit a couple of things in for him now as well."

Ryder shook his head. "And exactly when will you fit in time for Kyra? Be who you want to be?"

Kyra laid back and stared at the ceiling for several minutes. "Never. When they took me from my home, they said it was a gift, the skills I had. That if I didn't come with them, my gifts would be wasted. They said I would do good things, that I would help make the world a better place. Now I've killed one of the gentlest, kindest men I know. Someone who truly did make the world a better place."

She sat up suddenly. "I need more alcohol." Bounding off the bed, she weaved her way down the hallway toward the kitchen. Ryder stayed close enough to catch her, but far enough to keep out of her way.

He made it into the kitchen just as she noticed the box on the table. "BURN IT!" she screamed, pointing at the box. Then she turned, searching for something. She found the alcohol in the cabinet and took out a bottle of tequila, put it aside, and reached for another, a small bottle of whiskey.

"Yep, this'll do," she said over her shoulder to Ryder, as if he knew exactly what she was talking about.

Fiona took the opportunity to intervene. She gave Ryder a stern look before turning to Kyra. "Kyra, you should get some rest. The next couple of days will be busy."

"Really?" Kyra said, still searching the kitchen for God only knew what. She tucked the bottle of whiskey under her arm. Ryder leaned back and crossed his arms over his chest. If anything, she was entertaining.

"And what exactly will we be doing, Fiona? Ah, ha!" Kyra screamed. Several people in the room jumped. Ryder didn't see what she was so happy about. She turned to everyone sitting at the table. "Are we going to bury someone else?" she asked drunkenly. "Will Marlee be doing Max in?" She pointed at each of them with the whisky bottle. "Those …" She motioned to Ryder and his brothers. "Oh, they can't die. Will you bring in more Enforcers? Because we know THEY die." She looked Fiona dead in the eyes. Fury and unadulterated pain colored her eyes a dark midnight blue. "I'm sick of death," she said quietly, but her words were lined with steel. Then she threw the bottle of whiskey as hard as she could at the box on the table. The bottle shattered, and everyone scrambled.

"Bitch needs to burn in Hell!" Kyra shouted over the chaos she was creating. She pulled matches out of her other hand. Ryder wasn't quite fast enough as he lurched forward, realizing too late just exactly what she was doing. She struck a match and threw it on the table, which went up in a spectacular blue and orange flame.

Ryder tackled her, turning so that he took the brunt of the fall as they hit the floor. With Kyra being as drunk as she was, she was dead weight and hit him like a ton of bricks.

Everyone else scrambled to put out the fire. Ryder dragged Kyra away from the group and the danger, swearing as he moved. She fought him off, screaming that Sophie should burn in Hell. Tears streamed down her face.

"You should be locked up, do you understand me?" he barked.

She nodded. "I agree completely," she said, wiping tears from her face with the back of her hand. She looked so childlike in that moment. It broke Ryder's heart.

"Get her the hell out of here," Lykar said as they worked at extinguishing the fire. "We'll take care of this."

Ryder nodded and flung Kyra over his shoulder. He headed for her room and tossed her on the bed, shocked to see that at some point, she'd grabbed the other bottle of tequila and was taking a drink.

"I'm not a good person, Ryder. I left my family and they died. I kill Others who have broken the Council laws in secret because Gods forbid, the business we do cannot be known to everyone. I have done things I am not proud of. And now I've killed Simon. I am not a good person." She took another swig.

"When exactly do you think you will pass out?" he asked, lowering himself onto the bed next to her. He was tired, but he also knew that she needed to get this out or it would eat at her, eventually make her crazy or even worse—turn her to the dark side. He watched her stare at the ceiling, taking a drink every few minutes.

He tried to imagine her as a dark Druid, but he couldn't see it. She'd asked him to kill her instead of being possessed by a Banshee. No, she would do anything she could to not turn. She was better than she thought. She just needed to give herself some credit.

He rolled over and brushed hair from her face. "You are a good person, Kyra. Think of all the lives you've saved by taking out the bad guys."

Tears streamed down her face. "I knew she was going to do something bad. I could see everything she was doing. When she was in control and nothing was happening, she shut me out. But then she let me see and I knew something horrible was going to happen, and I didn't do anything. I sat in my own mind and cried. How pitiful is that?"

"Pretty bad," Ryder agreed with her.

She huffed and rolled over so she was facing him. He was struck by how beautiful she was. He wanted this time with her. Even knowing the consequences and the promises he had made to himself and his brothers, he wanted this and her.

She cradled the bottle between her breasts.

"I think when you're trying to make someone feel better, you shouldn't agree with the thing that's making them feel bad." Her eyes were growing sleepy and he smiled. Even drunk as hell, she was gorgeous.

"Is that what I'm doing? Trying to make you feel better?" he asked quietly. Unable to stay away from her another second, he leaned forward and kissed her.

She held back for a moment before wrapping her arms around his neck. She opened her mouth for him, making a sound in the back of her throat that made Ryder mindless with wanting.

He removed the bottle and rolled on top of her, touching her with every inch of his body. She was soft where he was hard. She was warm and fit him so perfectly, it was painful and yet felt amazing. Thousands of women and this little Element had him falling to pieces. The moment they were sharing so night and day to the kisses and groping he had shared with Sophie.

He leaned up on his elbows, running his hands through her soft hair, and then leaned down. He kissed her below her earlobe and then took a deep breath. There, at the base of her hairline right behind her ear, was the pure essence of who she was. He took a deep breath, feeling every inch of his body with her smell, her very essence.

"God, Kyra, you smell so good." He kissed her again, almost frantic to have her taste on his lips.

"I need you Ryder. I need this so bad." She arched up, pressing against him. However, her words were like a cold bucket of water on his ardor. She needed to be loved, needed to feel human companionship because she felt pain. He couldn't fill that place for her. It would be wrong and it would put her life in danger. He desperately wanted to comfort her. She was mourning, for God's sake, and all he wanted was sex. And maybe if he told himself that a million more times, he would believe it.

"Kyra." Her name came out as a moan and she tried to pull him closer. He hated himself for what he was about to do. He shook her. "Kyra."

178

Her eyes opened. "What?" Her aqua eyes burned with passion and need.

"I want this so badly," he couldn't stop himself from saying.

She only raised an eyebrow, and then recognition darkened her eyes.

"But …"

"But you need to rest. You don't need me mauling you." And he knew he didn't have enough control to do anything short of just that.

She closed her eyes again, a single tear slipping down her cheek. She turned her head away from him, basically shutting him out. He was surprised how much that hurt. Ryder's body protested as he rolled away, swinging his legs to the floor. He put his head in his hands, trying to gain control. He'd never had to be chivalrous, never had to be the gentleman. He took what he wanted and walked away. He couldn't bring himself to do that with Kyra. She deserved so much better.

"Ryder, I know that there is no way you and I would ever be more than …" she faltered. "Anyway, I understand that, but please, please don't leave me tonight. Just hold me."

"Damn it, Kyra," He wasn't sure if he was capable of that. But he wasn't sure he was capable of saying no, either. Swearing, he turned and lay down next to her, pulling her in as close as he could.

"Thank you," she whispered around the silent tears that fell, soaking his neck and chest.

He thought it took an inordinate amount of time for her to fall asleep, but she finally did. Ryder was able to relax somewhat next to her, her breathing soft and even. He kissed the top of her head, wondering what the hell he was going to do with her.

Chapter 9

"Why the hell don't you just fuck her already?" Marlee asked, taking one look at Ryder as he joined everyone in the yard.

"Shut the hell up, Marlee."

"You look like shit," Skylar offered. As if Ryder didn't already know that. He hadn't slept a wink last night and had finally pulled himself away from Kyra only to take a ten-mile run and a cold shower where he actually released himself. He hadn't done that since he was a kid over two thousand years ago. Now, even thinking about what he'd done, the images he'd conjured up, had him hard again. He'd never been so tied in knots over a woman before. He needed to get the hell away from her. But he couldn't leave, couldn't get far enough away from Kyra, to not want her. The thought of being with someone else made him feel sick.

"Let's just get this mission over with and then we can all move on," Ryder snapped.

"Yeah, 'cause at this point, we can all just walk away," Sky muttered.

"Exactly what is that supposed to mean?" Ryder snapped.

Skylars sarcastic laugh grated on Ryder's last nerve. "I'm not sure a whipped dog can walk away from his bitch."

Marlee and Lykar exchanged a look and then both took a step back.

Ryder turned on his brother, slamming his fist into Skylars face. It didn't seem to relieve any of his tension, so he did it again. They were soon both in the dirt throwing punches and elbows, knees, and insults.

After several minutes, Lykar grabbed hold of Ryder, and Marlee stepped in front of Skylar. "Don't you want to hear the plan we came up with?"

"No. I want to make Skylar cry like a bitch," Ryder snapped, trying to push past Lykar.

"It's going to take a lot more than you," Skylar snapped, picking himself from the dirt. "Go fuck your bitch and then maybe you'll be able to hit me with some power, 'cause right now, you're hitting like a damn girl. Who would've thought that not getting into a woman's pants would make you such a pussy?"

Lykar threw his hands up. He wasn't going to get hurt. And Skylar had crossed the line with those words, pushed Ryder over the edge. Ryder flew past him and slammed into Skylar with bone-breaking force.

"How long are we going to let them go at this?" Marlee asked, stepping out of the way as one of them flew past. She turned and headed back to the house.

"Until one of them is unconscious. Then, by all the Gods, we can get this damn mission over with," Lykar swore.

"How are you feeling this morning?" Marcus asked, handing Kyra a cup of coffee as she came into the kitchen.

"Like my head is about to explode. What the hell happened to the table?" There was a huge burn mark in the center.

"Well, actually, you set it on fire."

Kyra nearly dropped her cup of coffee. "What?"

"Sophie's box was sitting there, and I think you said something about the bitch should burn. Bashed a bottle of whiskey over it and set it on fire." Marcus smiled as he told her. "You're not a very good drunk, did you know that?"

"I'm sorry," Kyra moaned. She couldn't believe that she'd done that. Typically when she drank, she was in a completely controlled atmosphere. She did things and went places she wasn't supposed to when she drank. She couldn't remember a lot about last night, just little bits and pieces. Ryder had been there but she didn't remember what exactly had happened. She probably had done something completely embarrassing and would never be able to look him in the face again. She was afraid to ask what else she might've done but was saved the embarrassment when Marlee and Lykar came in through the back door, laughing.

"What's so funny?" Marcus asked. Turning to the sink, he deposited his coffee cup and then froze as he looked out the window. "Is that Ryder and Skylar fighting in the yard?"

Kyra pushed past Marcus to look out the window. Ryder and Skylar were definitely kicking the ass out of each other. "Holy shit."

She turned to go out, but Lykar grabbed her around the stomach and pulled her off her feet. He hugged her to his chest. "You do not want to go out there right now, Kyra. Just let them fight it out."

"But they're going to hurt each other." Kyra tried to pull away from him.

"Kyra, if you go outside right now, you'll make the situation worse." This could only mean that she was the reason for the fight. She turned to look out the window and wanted to cry. Ryder was bloody but still standing. Skylar was in the dirt, but picking himself up.

"So, do you want to hear the plan?" Marlee asked, sitting down at the charred table. Lykar set Kyra down on her feet.

She swallowed the pain she felt and turned to face the group. "Yes, let's get this mission over with."

"Okay, so we're going to the mountain to draw it out and get it in a box of his own? Or convince him that he should join forces with us in order to take down Lordus?" Kyra asked. "And what if he doesn't want to work with us?"

"We'll feed him you. He seems fixated on you, so that should distract him until I can blow the caves he uses to travel to Hell and back, trapping him in that mountain forever." Marlee didn't even crack a smile when she said it.

"Well, that makes sense," Kyra said, pushing away from the table. "So I'm bait?" She looked around the table. Lykar and Marcus wouldn't make eye contact with her.

Marlee, on the other hand, nodded as if this kind of thing happened every day. Which, in Marlee's world, it probably did.

"I hope you have enough explosives. That mountain is like a giant anthill for that thing," Marlee laughed at Kyra's statement Lykar shook his head. "Stupid right?" Kyra asked him.

"I always have enough explosives, sweetheart," Marlee answered.

Kyra sighed and pushed herself up from the table. Bait it was. "I'll go get ready."

Everyone here hated her. She couldn't blame any of them. She'd killed Simon; none of them could trust her. Ryder was fighting with his brother. Fiona had disappeared last night after Kyra had lit the kitchen on fire and nobody knew where she had gone or if she was coming back. Not even Marcus knew where she had gone. And he was really the only one speaking to her at the moment. She stepped into her room and closed the door. That was as far as she made it before the tears started to fall.

Her entire life she'd dedicated to everyone else. To ensure the safety of the Druids, and the Elements. If they hadn't saved her, she would've died with the rest of her family, or worse, been burned as a witch. She owed them her life, and every day she lived to make her dead family proud.

She pushed herself away from the wall. It was funny, really. The moment she found something or someone else worth living for, she became bait in a deadly game, a game she knew she couldn't win.

She washed her face and dressed in her typical black pants and T-shirt, slipping on her weapons before pulling on a leather jacket. She just wanted it over and done with. She couldn't continue to walk the line she was walking with Ryder and the rest of the team.

Something deep in her chest heaved. The thought of walking away from Ryder made her physically ill. But she would do it, because she didn't really have another choice. He thought love was for sentimental fools. She knew enough about him to know that she wasn't going to change his mind on that issue.

She looked at herself in the mirror, pulling her long hair back in a braid and pinning it out of the way. Unfortunately, Ryder was the one. She couldn't hide from that fact. When they'd touched, there were sparks. It was the Druid way of knowing you'd found your one true mate. Why it hadn't happened until after the possession, she couldn't understand. She couldn't remember if it had happened the night before.

Maybe her senses were all screwed up because of everything going on. She nodded to herself in the mirror. That was what it had to be. She was just off-center. Steeling herself for what was going to come, she put up a wall around herself using old Druid magic. It wouldn't make her stronger or give her anything useful, but it would bolster her confidence. And best of all, it would render her feelings unreadable to anyone else. Anyone who looked at her would see a strong, confident Enforcer.

When she left the room, the only one left in the house was Marcus. "Where is everyone?"

"They said they would meet us in the clearing." When he spoke, though, he wouldn't make eye contact.

So they were going to ignore her, were they? The sacrificial lamb to the slaughter.

Marcus finally looked at her. "Trackers are very complicated creatures. They were hunters and nomads. They roamed where no one else would or could. They were the power of nations. They could've ruled this world if it wasn't for their one flaw."

"It's a pretty big flaw, Marcus."

"To love and not be loved in return? I could think of nothing worse." Something flashed in his eyes that pulled Kyra up short. He had felt that before—unrequited love. She wanted to wrap her arms around him but knew it wasn't any of her business. "Druids and Elements thrive on love. You are all brought up to love unconditionally. Eric and the Enforcers are slightly jaded to that, but you," he reached out and touched her cheek, "you still hold true to the faith and purity of love."

Kyra shrugged. "I don't know, Marcus. I'm becoming more and more jaded each day."

"Trackers, on the other hand, despise the weakness of love. The stronger and more jaded you are, the better. Otherwise, they would not have survived as long as they have," Marcus continued.

She felt her heart skip. "What exactly does that have to do with me, Marcus?"

"He cares for you. He is fighting what that might mean, not only for him but for the other Trackers as well. Bonding with you would break a thousand-year vow made between the remaining Trackers. A promise that has kept them alive when they should've died out," Marcus said honestly.

"Yeah, well, the bullet he tried to put through my forehead the day we met says otherwise on the caring issue. I don't see a problem with them continuing on exactly as they have been for the next thousand years." She started to walk away and Marcus fell into step beside her. "I don't care." And maybe if she told herself that over and over and over again it would be true.

Marcus laughed quietly. "Much has happened since that day. Even you cannot disagree with that. And maybe, just maybe, Kyra," he pulled her to a stop, "the more times you tell yourself he doesn't care, there is more of a chance you might actually believe it."

He grabbed the gilded boxes as they walked out of the house, tucking one under each arm. "By the way, I won't allow them to feed you to that thing."

She snorted. "Does it matter now? I wouldn't blame any of them if they just threw me in and let that thing have his way with me." Marcus gave her a strange look. She moved forward. "Let's just get this over with already. I want to go home."

Ryder checked his face in the rearview mirror; the swelling was already starting to go down. Skylar, however, was still in the back of the SUV, unconscious.

"Should we wake him?" Lykar asked.

"Nope. He should learn to hold his own. Then he wouldn't miss out on all the fun. Besides, he knows the plan. When he wakes up, he'll know where we are." Marcus and Kyra pulled up next to them and everyone climbed out. Ryder refused to look at her. He wasn't going to let her pull him in today. She was a distraction that none of them could afford and frankly, it scared the hell out of him how badly he needed her.

After this was all done, then he would deal with her.

When Kyra reached for the box, Ryder halted. "What the fuck?" She didn't look up at Ryder, but at Marcus.

"We'll wait for the signal," Marcus said. Kyra nodded. Throwing on her backpack, she turned and headed toward the forest without taking a backwards glance.

Ryder couldn't believe what he was seeing and started to go after her. "This wasn't the plan,"

"Plan changed," Lykar said quietly.

Ryder turned to his brother and knew instantly that Lykar had lied to him. "Marcus was supposed to take the box in."

"We didn't think it would come out for Marcus. Marlee is hiding in the woods. She'll give the signal when we can head in," Lykar said, his voice deadly quiet.

"Is that before or after that thing kills her?" Ryder bellowed.

"Before," Marcus interjected.

Lykar shrugged. "The important thing right now is to trap that thing."

"You're sending her in there to die!" Ryder yelled. He turned toward Kyra and shouted with as much compulsion as he could. "Kyra, stop."

She stopped, one foot suspended mid-step before shaking herself and moving forward again. Goddamn her for her ability to ignore his compulsion.

When that didn't work, Ryder started forward. Marcus and Lykar each took an arm.

"She's going to die in there." Ryder actually pleaded with Lykar. For the first time in a long time, he begged. "Please don't do this, Lykar."

Lykar stared at Ryder as if he'd never seen him before.

"That thing is going to kill her," Ryder said, his emotions bleeding into his voice. "Don't let this happen."

"No, she is doing her job," Fiona said, stepping up to the group.

"Where the fuck have you been?" Ryder demanded. "Are you going to let her walk into the den of that monster?"

Fiona looked up at him, her eyes sad. "Ryder, what did Sophie do for this monster? This genetically manipulated Shapeshifter?"

Ryder thought for a moment. "She brought him food." Goddamn it! They were sending Kyra in to die! He tried to shove away from his brother and Marcus. He felt like his brain was short-circuiting and all his training was taking a leap out the preverbal window. All he could think about was the fact that Kyra was being put in danger and he needed to save her.

"And it has been several days since he has eaten. He will be confused and disoriented. If we go in guns blazing, the only result will be bloodshed. Kyra can take care of herself. She needs to do this," Fiona reassured him.

"Aren't you some type of mentor to her? Why would you do this?" Ryder demanded.

"You have pulled her ass out of the fire many times in the last week, She needs to stand on her own. Let her do this." Fiona looked at Kyra's retreating back.

"No way." Ryder growled.

It took both Marcus and Lykar to keep Ryder from going after her. In the end, they had to knock him out in order to ensure he didn't go.

Kyra walked toward the forest and hesitated at the line between what she knew was safe and where that thing was. She could hear Ryder bellowing about the change in plans. As she turned to see what was going, she watched as Marcus knocked him out. Probably for the best. Ryder didn't have a great deal of faith in her ability to protect herself. She picked up her foot to cross the line and hesitated, remembering the last time she'd been there. Her mind started to reel. Each time she'd had Sophie with her; now she wasn't sure if Sophie had helped or hindered them. That night in the tunnels, Sophie had disappeared. The sudden realization that Sophie had been distracting the monster while they explored made sense to her. She wanted to lead them to where they would find the old lab. Sophie had been pulling the strings the entire time. She looked down at the box in her hands.

"I really hate you," she muttered, shaking the box. In response, the box quivered slightly. This was the way it had to be. They all knew the monster didn't show up for any of them but Kyra. She was the bait, whether she wanted to be or not. The writing had been on the wall from the beginning, when Sophie had appeared to her that first day. Kyra stuffed the box into her backpack, making sure she could still reach her guns and her knives. She took a deep breath. She wasn't going to lie down and die. She wasn't going down without a fight.

"Are you ready for this, you bastard?" she asked the woods. Then she stepped over the line. When nothing immediately happened, she started walking toward the caves, knowing she had a four-mile hike ahead of her. Maybe the monster was so hungry, it was incapacitated. She could use that to her advantage.

She had been walking for several minutes when the ground shook slightly and inky blackness surrounded her so quickly, she almost didn't respond. She Shifted a few feet back and the blackness again tried to encompass her. Then she tried Shifting to the side. "We could do this all day, but I want to talk."

She tried to keep the tone of her voice calm and even, despite the fact that she was a frightened. She Shifted again moving just out of reach again.

"So hungry," the mass gurgled. It finally stopped trying to catch her.

After a long minute, the mass contracted and she was staring at the man, the same man from the day she'd had her ass handed to her. She braced herself. She had Sophie in the box—that was her one ace. She glared at the man, worried because the other three aces were either in play or the thing in front of her held them.

"Who are you?" she asked softly.

"Does it matter?" he asked. "When I was recreated, my identity was stripped from me, along with many other things." His were sad words and pulled at the love Kyra shared for all things good or bad. "What have you done with Sophie?" he phased into shadow for a moment before solidifying again. When Kyra didn't immediately answer, he tilted his head to the side in a way that Eric used to do as a child, when he was trying to figure out an incantation. It brought tears to her eyes. She would've liked the opportunity to say goodbye to her brother before leaving on this mission.

A maniacal smile played at his lips. "You've destroyed her, haven't you?"

"What is your connection with her? You know she isn't a very good person." Kyra felt almost as if she were scolding a small child. Rather, she was scolding a monster that could probably kill her fairly easily, and quickly, for that matter.

"She made one too many demands from Lordus and he left her here." He shrugged, as if it didn't really matter to him. "She served as a go-between in order for me to feed."

"Really, and how is that?" Kyra asked.

He leaned forward and sniffed her. Now this thing was sniffing her? She was getting really tired of that. "You should know. She possessed you."

Kyra didn't understand for a moment and then started to put the pieces together. "You mean, she possessed those women and brought them to you to feed on?" The thought made her shiver.

"Not a complete possession. That would've killed them. Mortals can't handle her type of power. She possessed them enough to bring them here. It was much easier than going out and looking for my own food and risk the Tribunal wreaking havoc on our heads." He Phased again, reappearing within inches of Kyra. It took everything she had to not back away from him.

"But I think that might've been her plan. If the Tribunal had come down on this mountain instead of us …" They would have destroyed this thing and everything else they found that wasn't Mortal.

The shadow growled. "She was a bitch, and I wouldn't put it past her. So now what do we do?" he swirled around Kyra, his words coming at her in different directions. "I'm starving, Kyra. And your body and soul are calling to me. Regardless of what that bitch did, I still need to feed, and your soul is ripe."

"We want Lordus," Kyra said, trying not to flinch as the dark mist caressed her cheek.

"Don't we all. The creatures he experiments on all want him flayed alive. What makes you different?"

"He didn't destroy you or Sophie. He must still have a use for you," she said. He Phased into a man again and laughed.

"You have no idea how many of his creations are out in the world roaming wild," he growled, making the hair on the back of her neck stand on end. "So, what did you do to Sophie?"

"Before or after she told us that you were her pet, and had you under her ultimate control?" Kyra pressed. The man flickered.

"Those stones she showed you? They kept her trapped here, not me. I choose to stay within the woods because it suits me." He swirled out, covering several trees and bushes. "She brought me food because it was the only way she could feel. It was the only way she could be human, even if only for hours at a time."

Kyra held up her hands in supplication. "You don't have to live like this anymore. What's your name?" she asked again.

He seemed to grow slightly in stature and anger rolled off of him. "I told you. I don't have a name. He took it from me because I was not worthy of it."

"I think you are," Kyra said gently. If she could just get him to trust her a little, their plan might work. And she would be walking out of these woods instead of being carried out in a body bag.

He dissolved into the inky blackness and was on her before she could take another breath. Kyra hadn't expected the attack; she'd let her defenses down for half a second. But that was all it took to be engulfed in blackness. Kyra expected pain, but surprisingly none came. All she felt was an increasing tiredness. She didn't want to fight against the blackness anymore. She wanted to sleep and then when she woke up, everything would be okay.

Ryder woke up in the dirt, Skylar standing over him. His brother did not look happy. Ryder pulled himself up, pushing away the dizziness that threatened to send him back down. He reached for a gun, but Skylar stopped him.

"Just take a moment," he offered, in a rare show of concern.

Ryder took a bottle of water out of a cooler they'd packed and downed the entire thing. Skylar watched him the entire time.

"What?" Ryder finally asked. "We're losing daylight and Kyra could already be dead."

Skylars next words shocked the hell out of him. "Why is she so different from Felicia? What makes her more special?" Raw emotion coated each word.

Ryder took out another bottle of water and sat on the tailgate of the car. "You didn't truly love her, Sky. I didn't want you to throw your life away on something that wasn't real."

Sky stomped several steps away. "But that wasn't your decision, brother," he finally said, turning. "And fucking her to prove it to me was definitely uncalled for."

Ryder stood. Everything in him wanted to run into that mountain and save Kyra, but this conversation was three hundred years overdue. "She was Mortal, Skylar. If you had given her any of the pheromone, it could've killed her. I wasn't going to let you throw your life away on a Mortal who didn't care for you. She told you exactly what you wanted to hear and nothing more. I didn't sleep with her. I only wanted you to catch us kissing. As soon as that happened, I left your sweet Felicia and never looked back." It was the truth. The woman disgusted him, and what she had done to Skylar.

"And what exactly did you do?" Ryder asked. "You saw us kissing and turned and walked away. If she was meant for you, you should've stayed and fought for her. Why didn't you? Why didn't you stay and fight for her, Sky?" Ryder knew that anytime another man came within arm's reach of Kyra, he wanted to murder them. If he caught her kissing someone else, it would kill him.

Skylar took a deep breath and looked up into the bright, cloudless sky. "I had two thoughts when I walked into the room that night." He turned to his brothers, his eyes black as coal. "My first thought was that you had betrayed me."

"And you're second?"

"That if that was my first thought, then I didn't really love her. So I turned around, and I walked away." Sky let out a huge puff of air. "Part of me has hated you ever since because of that. Especially now, with her."

"Why, Sky? Why hate me for showing you the truth?"

Sky was suddenly on Ryder, holding him by his shirt collar. "Because I could've been happy. She could've survived. Just because you sorry bastards don't want to feel anything doesn't mean I have to follow that dictate. Hundreds—no, thousands of years of roaming, never settling down, never letting anyone close. Doesn't it get to you? Because it sure as shit gets to me."

For the first time in several hundred years, Ryder had to agree with his brother. "Do you really think you would've been happy with Felicia?"

"No, but that wasn't your choice to make." Skylar released him and stomped away. He started to strap on weapons, handing some to Ryder as he went.

"Sky, I regret what happened with Felicia. I regret how it turned out. But it had nothing to do with the pact, and everything to do with the fact that I wasn't going to watch another sibling die. I am the oldest. It is my responsibility to ensure your safety." He sighed deeply. "If I could've thought of another solution, one that would've saved you from pain, I would have."

Sky turned and looked at his brother for a long moment before going back to loading himself with weapons. "I believe you, but if you ever interfere with me like that again, I'll walk away and you'll never see me again." It was the worst sort of threat that Sky could throw at Ryder. He would give everything and more for his brothers.

"You never answered my question," Skylar said. Stepping back, he looked at Ryder. "What makes Kyra different?"

Ryder turned and looked into the woods. He couldn't hide it any longer. Not that he was sure he'd been hiding it before. "The only answer I have for you is this: if I caught you kissing her, I would kill you both, and in the process, myself."

Skylar gave him a hard look and then a smile spread across his still-bruised face. "Shit, dude, you got it bad. Can I be there when you tell Falcon? 'Cause he is going to blow a gasket."

Ryder ignored his brother's sick humor and took off into the woods. Skylar easily caught up to him. "How long have they been gone?"

"Thirty minutes. The signal never came. They don't know what happened, so Marcus and Lykar went in search of Marlee. Fiona headed toward the caves."

Thirty minutes. Ryder felt like the world was closing in on him. That was more than enough time for that thing to maim and murder Kyra. He wasn't sure he would be able to just clean her up like he had the other bodies. In fact, he knew he wouldn't. If she died, he was pretty sure it wouldn't be long before he followed her.

They caught up with Marcus and Lykar. Marlee, in wolf form, lay in the dirt.

Ryder kneeled down his world tilting on its axis, Kyra and now Marlee? "Is she …" She couldn't be dead. It just wasn't possible. The crazy bitch was going to outlive them all and scream and yell and chomp her gum, blow up shit while dancing and laughing on their graves.

Lykar looked up. "She's just unconscious. I'll stay with her while you guys go help Kyra."

"Why does it seem that the plans always go out the window? We improvise this shit like piecing together a Goddamn puzzle blindfolded," Sky said as they moved off toward the tunnels.

"Shit, if I'd known that, I would've stayed home," Marcus grumbled, but there was no real conviction in his voice. Ryder had to give it to the Fallen he didn't give in.

Sky grunted. "Well, you're stuck with us for the time being, brother, so get used to working on the fly."

Fiona stood at the entrance of the tunnel where Kyra had gone. When the men stopped next to her, she whirled on them. For the first time since he'd met the woman, she was angry, and showing it.

"Who planted the explosives?" she demanded.

Ryder stood there, not sure what the woman was talking about. Sky, on the other hand, took a tiny step away from his brother.

Ryder turned to Sky. "What the fuck did you do?"

"We didn't know how this was going to turn out, so Lykar, Marlee, and I came out last night and planted explosives at the entrance of all the caves. If we can't beat it, maybe we can trap it. Kyra knows about them." Like that was going to make it okay.

"If you set off those explosives, there's a really good chance you could bring this entire mountainside down." Fiona looked like she wanted to scream and cry at the same time. "Do you have any idea what that would do to the town, to anyone else living here?"

Sky shrugged sheepishly. "It was a last-resort kind of action."

Fiona shocked everyone when she stepped forward and slapped Sky upside the head. "That is the stupidest answer I've ever received from a grown man. Do you actually think that thing wasn't going to see or notice two men and a wolf running through the forest?"

"We came here to do a job. Kill it or trap it forever," Skylar said.

"She's in there?" Ryder said, looking at the darkness in front of them. He could smell her. She'd passed here within the last hour. But her scent was mixed with something that smelled like burned-out brakes.

"Now what?" Marcus asked.

Fiona sighed heavily. "You two," she pointed to Marcus and Skylar, "get rid of the explosives as quickly as possible. Ryder will have to go in and find Kyra."

"And what about you?" Skylar asked. "Aren't you going to be joining this fight?"

It was Marcus's turn this time to slap the Tracker upside the head. The fallen shook his head in disgust. "You just can't help but open your mouth and stick your foot in it can you?"

"It's who I am man." Skylar smiled at Marcus and turned a dubious look at Fiona.

"I will return to where Marlee is and send Lykar to help you. Will that satisfy you?"

"Just didn't know if you were going to wander off into the woods like you did yesterday. We need to know who we can count on." Sky explained.

"Just because you don't see me Tracker does not mean that I am not working on this issue just as diligently as the rest of you." Her answer seemed to mollify Sky and he nodded.

Fiona gave them all a sad smile before, taking hold of Ryder's shirtsleeve. Marcus and Sky headed toward the entrance of the tunnel to disarm the bombs they'd placed there.

"I know you think that I sent her in there to die." Damn straight, he did. "But she has a part to play in this, and neither you nor I can stop it. Regardless of how much we care for her, it will be up to Kyra on how she comes out of this, whole or broken. But by all the Gods, Ryder, please bring her out." A single tear slid down Fiona's cheek before she straightened and walked away.

"Once we disarm the bombs, we'll head in from different angles," Sky explained as he stood up, dusting his hands off. He pulled his pack from his back and gave it to his brother. "Extra ammo and water."

Ryder nodded and turned to Marcus. "As stupid an idea as this was," he motioned for the explosives, "if something goes wrong, you need to be the one to do something about it. And if that means trapping us down there, do it."

Marcus nodded. "I know just want to do. But I would much prefer that you bring Kyra from the mouth of the beast prior to that action."

When Kyra woke, she was laying on a cold metal table. She drew in a breath, choking on the death and destruction she sucked into her lungs. She scrambled off the table like it was about to devour her. "Where am I?"

The cavern was lit with torches sending the already creepy room into shadow. The inky blackness gurgled something incoherent and rolled and seethed on the floor for several moments before the man appeared again. "Home."

Kyra tried to take a deep breath, but the stagnant air stuck in her throat. "I can't breathe down here." It was a flat statement. The man stopped pacing for a moment and glared at her.

"I'm an Air Element. The air down here," she looked around, "I can't breathe down here," she explained trying to hold onto her sanity.

He moved again so quickly, she was engulfed again. "What did you do to Sophie?" Just as quickly, he backed away again.

"I thought you didn't care about Sophie?" Kyra felt like the cave was closing in on her. The images and the voices in the air were pulling at the edges of her sanity. She grasped at the table at her back holding it in order to stay on her feet.

He backhanded her, throwing her up against the cave wall. For a moment she saw stars. Shaking, she glared at him.

"Where is she?"

Kyra pointed to the backpack. The man picked it up and shook it out. Supplies and the gilded box fell onto the metal table.

Pushing herself to her feet, she spat blood. "Ever heard of Pandora?"

His eyes narrowed, and then he stepped away from the box. "I guess that's a yes." Kyra couldn't keep the sarcasm from her words.

"Wanna join her?" she said as she Phased, knowing it would gain a response. Blackness slammed against the wall where she'd been standing. Dust and rock crumpled to the floor.

He returned to his human shape and turned to her. "Open the box."

That was the last thing she'd expected to hear. "Excuse me?"

"I said, open the box," he moved over to the metal table. "You can't smell it, but there are souls in there. I need them. It's them or you."

"I can't open the box," she said honestly.

The thing laughed. "Now you're just lying. Of course you can. I can smell how pure your soul is. The goodness that seeps from you. You're the perfect vessel to open a Pandora's Box."

Vessel—because whatever came out of that box would attempt to inhabit her. "You open it."

He hit her again. She slammed against the empty cabinets, pretty sure a couple of her ribs cracked.

She was done losing the fight and she Phased, ignoring the pain as she moved to stand behind him. She leveled a side kick right across his back, throwing him forward onto the table.

Inky black shadow rolled off the table like smoke. "Damn it, what are you?" she screamed, backing up so that she was against a wall. That way, he couldn't move behind her.

He solidified on the other side of the table, a wicked smile at the edges of his lips. "I am whatever you want me to be," he said, his voice changing as he morphed into Ryder.

"What would you do for your love?" he asked.

"Fuck you." Kyra launched herself over the table and took him to the ground when he didn't immediately turn to smoke. She pulled out one of her guns and pulled the trigger.

The bullet went through his chest and imbedded in the rock floor of the cave.

Laughter filled the room as he turned to ink and surrounded her. Unlike the time in the woods, she was now filled with pain. Every inch of her body, inside and out, burned with agony. She might've screamed but wasn't sure. When the blackness receded, she was on her hands and knees on the floor, gasping for air that wasn't there.

The edges of her reality started to go a little fuzzy. "Open the box, Kyra."

"No," she gasped. When he came at her again, she pulled a knife from each wrist gauntlet and started to slice through the blackness. He bellowed in pain and backed off, returning to the form of the man. He was cut in several places.

"So, not indestructible?" It was her turn to smile.

"Open the box. Or I will kill you here and now," he bellowed, shaking the room. Glass shattered in shelves; a large fridge tipped over. Dust and rock rained down around her.

"Go to hell."

Chapter 10

Ryder could smell her, taste her terror. It swamped him from every direction, making him lightheaded with worry and fear. He should've told her how he felt. Should've let her know that he cared. But he had let his anger and need dictate his actions. Now it might be too late. He couldn't imagine a world without Kyra in it.

It didn't matter, he realized, what became of the world outside these tunnels if Kyra wasn't with him. He stopped and took a couple of deep breaths, trying to get his bearings. After two centuries he had done what he'd sworn he would never do. He had fallen for a woman. He thought it would hurt. He had watched his brothers and sisters die from the pain of loving. She was the one for him; if she didn't return his feelings, he'd be damned. But he knew he didn't want to live in this world without her.

"Who is the sentimental fool now?" his own mocking voice bounced around in his head.

And he couldn't argue with it.

When he finally made it to the cavern with the makeshift lab, he found Kyra bleeding from a wound on her chest and several on her arms. But she was Shifting, Phasing and slicing, keeping pace with the monster, now in human form, who was also bleeding from several places.

Ryder didn't hesitate. Dropping his packs, he ran, launching himself on the man. They rolled, arms and legs tangling. When they finally stopped, Ryder was on top and threw a punch into air. He struck the stone ground and felt bones crack.

He scrambled away, grabbing Kyra by the arm as he moved from the black shadow. "Are you okay?"

She nodded but didn't take her eyes off the black mist as it again swirled into a man's body. Ryder pushed Kyra behind him. "Don't let it touch you!" she warned.

The monster growled. "Your soul will do just as well as hers, except I'll make it hurt more for you."

Ryder tried to move away as blackness climbed up his legs. Everywhere it touched felt like needles shooting into him. He threw himself away as pain lanced through his legs.

Kyra jumped forward and slashed at the blackness, screaming, "Stop! Don't hurt him."

Ryder fell to his knees, the pain too much. He looked into Kyra's beautiful blue eyes. "Run,"

"Please," Kyra begged. Ryder could see tears streaking down her face as she continued to fight off the blackness that devoured him. "I'll open the box."

Everything stopped. Ryder wasn't even sure he was breathing anymore, it hurt so much. Then the blackness started to recede, though its leaving was as painful as its infiltration. Once Ryder was free, he scrambled back, sucking in great gulps of air. He checked himself for actual wounds; it felt like he'd been burned from the waist down.

"Do it now," the blackness bellowed.

Kyra scrambled forward and threw herself on Ryder, who wrapped his arms around her.

"Are you okay?" It was her turn to ask.

Ryder nodded. "What is it?"

Kyra shrugged. "There isn't enough air down here." She said it quietly, giving Ryder a glimpse of the pain she was in.

"Do it now, or I'll kill you both."

Kyra pressed a knife into Ryder's hand.

"Stall," Ryder whispered.

She stood and moved to the large metal table. She reached for the box. "This isn't going to solve anything. You know that, right?"

The man stepped out of the black mist next to her. He

leaned in, his eyes on Ryder as he did it. "Yes, but I'll feed, and that is all that matters."

Kyra picked up the box. "You and Sophie deserve each other."

The blackness actually laughed, the sound filling the cavern. "That's exactly what she would say when I killed the Mortals for her."

Kyra paused. "What?"

He whispered in Kyra's ear, sending chills down her spine. "She was the one trapped here. I stayed because I loved her. Now open the box and let her out."

Kyra picked up the box and stepped away from the thing next to her. "The two of you have been working together this whole time?"

The man shrugged. "When Lordus found out about us, he trapped her here fifty years ago. It took me that long to find out what he had done to her. And as soon as I did, I came for her. But being trapped here like she was, you can only imagine what that might do to a person."

"Why didn't you just remove the wards?" Kyra asked, taking small steps around the table so that the thing was between her and Ryder.

"Only a witch or a Druid, or some Other with significant power is capable of breaking the wards. Lordus, of course, has a Dark Druid with him. We knew if we made enough noise, eventually something like that would show up." He smiled.

"But what if the Tribunal had come instead?"

"Then there wouldn't have been a problem. They would have destroyed us."

"That's a pretty big gamble you were making." Kyra shook her head.

"We had no other choice." He looked down at the box hungrily. "Now open it."

"Do you even need to feed?" Had this all been about these monsters freeing themselves?

He phased into black smoke and back again. "Yes, but I can survive for a great deal of time without feeding. Sophie, on the other hand, enjoyed the deaths. Now open the box."

"You have no idea what else is in this box," Kyra said, picking it up.

"Sophie is inside and that is all I need to know."

"Nightwalker," Ryder rumbled the words.

The thing turned. "Partially. I was born a Shapeshifter. But you never stay what you are if you live with Lordus for any amount of time."

Ryder had pulled himself to his feet. He watched both the man and Kyra, who looked pale, her eyes going from blue to silver like mist shifting over a lake. She was losing control with the stagnant air. She didn't have a lot of time.

"She isn't opening that box," Ryder said.

The thing threw its head back and laughed, filling the cavern with the horrible sound. Kyra visibly shuddered, her eyes the color of mist. Not blue, not silver.

"Oh, she will open it, or she will die slowly. And you will watch." The thing moved so that he was standing in front of Ryder before Ryder realized he was moving.

Ryder watched over the thing's shoulder as Kyra shook her head and took several breaths. She was losing it.

He needed to get the two of them the hell out of there. Ryder gave the thing one of his own maniacal smiles. "Not only is she not going to open that box but we are leaving. And you … you will be trapped in this mountain like your psychotic lover FOREVER."

It opened its mouth to three times its size as it advanced on Ryder. He dodged it as it attacked, barely making it out of the way.

Several other attempts at Ryder and the thing stopped. "If you think your explosives are going to do anything, you're wrong." His voice was quiet, which only made his words that much more horrible.

Kyra stepped beside him. "I don't think you will be able to kill us both," she taunted.

Ryder turned to her in astonishment. "Not really the time to poke the bear with a stick."

She gave him one of her beautiful smiles. "I will not go down without a fight."

Marcus stepped into the cavern from the only other entrance. "I think that's a fine idea."

The thing hissed and backed away from Marcus, as if his mere presence was painful.

Marcus smiled. He wasn't carrying any weapons as he advanced on the thing.

Kyra scrambled to the other entrance as it made a go for her. She slashed at it with her knife. It roared and moved to the center of the room, morphing back into the man.

"All the explosives were already removed," Marcus said, his eyes fixed on the man.

The monster laughed. "Did you really think I could allow that?" Then, without warning, he attacked Kyra.

Ryder launched on to the thing as it encompassed Kyra. Kyra screamed in pain, her body arching forward before she fell to her knees.

Marcus rushed forward as well. Ryder slashed at it with the dagger he held. Marcus shoved his hand into the mass and it recoiled.

When it solidified in the corner, he was sucking breath. "I want the box opened!"

"Tough shit, asshole," Kyra bellowed back.

Marcus pulled the other box from his backpack. "How about this box? I'll be happy to open it for you."

The whole thing shook, and growled again.

Kyra leaned into Ryder, unable to hold herself up any longer. "I need to get out of here."

Ryder looked down at her, his eyes dark, he communicated no emotion.

The blackness threw open several cabinets, exposing all the explosives.

"Damn, that Marlee—she's going to blow us all straight to hell one day," Ryder snarled as explosives tumbled from the cabinets.

"How about Kyra opens the box or I blow this entire mountain down around our ears? I'll survive," he mocked, and then looked at Marcus. "You'll survive, Fallen. And you, Tracker, you'll survive."

Everyone turned to Kyra. "But our beautiful little Element will die. Who would like her blood on their hands? Because I couldn't care less."

"Go ahead, you slimy bastard," Kyra said.

"Shut up, Kyra." Ryder pushed her behind him.

Kyra pushed past Ryder. "No." She advanced on the thing. "I'm not going to hide behind anyone. And I'm sure as hell not going to reunite him with his crazy lover. So blow the mountain down." She slashed at its throat when she got within arm's reach, but it phased into mist and moved away.

Kyra phased, shifting with it, slashing as it attacked. Ryder tried to get her out of the fight, or even join, but they moved so fast, it was impossible. One minute they were on one side of the cavern and the next they were on the opposite.

"Bloody hell, do something!" Ryder snapped at Marcus.

Marcus fiddled with the box. "Working on it."

Kyra shifted so she was standing next to Ryder. She was bleeding from her nose and a wound on her shoulder. She tried to smile. "I think I might be done stalling."

"Christ, Kyra." Ryder wrapped his arms over her shoulders and swung her around as the thing solidified next to her. Ryder snapped out and punched it in the nose, smiling when he connected. He really needed that.

Marcus slid the box onto the floor so that it was in the middle of the room. "Get it close and we can trap it."

It phased into black shadow again. Swarming through Ryder, it attacked Kyra and pushed her against the metal table. Kyra reached behind her and grabbed the box. "Is this what you want?"

The thing stopped and glared at Kyra. "Open the box."

Marcus moved up behind it, whispering words. The box at his feet clicked open.

As the thing realized it was trapped, it bellowed and tried to Phase into shadow, but the blackness from the box already had a hold of him.

In its last attempt, it grabbed Kyra.

Everything happened so fast; Ryder was powerless to do anything. Kyra had a hold of the box but as the thing attacked, she fumbled with it, throwing the lid open as she went down. The box splintered into pieces in her hands. Ryder threw himself toward her as screeching filled the cavern. Smoke and black shadows rushed from the now open Pandora's box. Kyra screamed and scrambled away.

"Marcus, you know what to do!" Ryder screamed as he moved toward the exit. He grabbed Kyra, forcing her to her feet. "We need to MOVE. NOW"

Marcus nodded and held up a hand, focusing a beam of power directly over Ryder's head. He barely made it through before the tunnel collapsed behind him.

Kyra didn't look good, but he didn't have time to stop and see what was wrong. The mountain was coming down, and they needed to get out before it trapped them.

Screaming and horrible noises followed them as Ryder half dragged, half carried Kyra down the tunnel.

"Kyra, MOVE!"

The mountain trembled around them so violently; they could barely stay on their feet. Ryder did everything he could to protect Kyra as they flew around the tunnels like the ball in a pinball machine.

Ryder grabbed her as the mountain shook brutally, sending them both to the dirt. This time Ryder was able to take the brunt of the fall. He rolled her to the side and pushed her to her feet.

"Keep moving!"

He pushed her forward, only to pull her back as the tunnel in front of them collapsed. They had one more way out.

As they turned, that escape also trembled and came down. Kyra ran forward, anyway, digging at the rocks with her bare hands.

"Kyra, stop." Ryder pulled her away from the wall of rock. She jerked away from him and threw herself at the wall. He grabbed her, wrapping his arms around her before she hurt herself. If he had to judge, he would say they'd come very close to the entrance when the final wall had caved in.

Kyra screamed, and then started to cough violently as she sucked in dust. "NO … AIR." she barely said between coughs. She searched through the wall of rock, her hands running over the surface.

"Ryder, we have to get out of here," she cried.

"I know, sweetheart, but we aren't going anywhere for the moment." Some of the dust had settled and the mountain had stopped quaking. Ryder shook himself, sending out a dust cloud.

Suddenly, a small beam of light appeared just over Kyra's head. Ryder looked at it in shock.

"A little trick I know," Kyra said, pure terror on her face. "How far down do you think we are?"

"I saw the opening right before it collapsed." He motioned toward one of the blocked tunnels. At least he had thought he had seen the entrance but he couldn't be sure.

"Okay," Kyra said, her voice trembling. "I can maintain the orb for a little while. Unless…"

"Unless you can't breathe." She nodded when he finished for her.

He pointed in the direction he believed was the exit. "That is the way out, Kyra. I will get you out of here."

"At least the mountain has stopped shaking."

Her hands ran gently along the wall. He watched for several minutes, wondering what she was doing and realized she was looking for any type of breeze, any type of air movement.

"Kyra." She turned her eyes bright with fear. Ryder moved up and cupped her face. "I will get you out of here."

"I opened the box." She pushed away from Ryder. She paced for a minute and then tilted her head back and screamed. Really screamed, screamed to bring the heavens down. She then turned and pounded her fists against rock. When he saw blood, Ryder moved in and took her into his arms. She stomped and pounded her bloody fists against his chest.

"So much evil." She pushed back from him. "I feel it! I hear it! And now I've released it. It took something." She pointed to her chest. "Ripped something from deep inside of me," she cried. "You wouldn't think there was anything left, but it found it. Something came out, something far worse than what we were fighting, there at the end. And I am responsible for it."

Ryder felt rage well up from deep inside. He forced it back down; there was nothing he could take his rage out on at the moment. And Kyra needed him.

He cupped her face. Wiping tears away, he looked deep into her eyes. "You are going to be okay."

She gave him a watery smile. "No, I won't. It will never be okay again." She pulled away from him, moved to a corner of the space, and slid to the dirt. She hugged her legs against her chest and put her head on her knees, her orb of light going out.

Ryder looked around. They were in a tight spot but there was enough space for them to have a little room to themselves in the dark. His hope was that his brothers and Marcus were able to get out of the mountain. Kyra had slowed him down, but he'd rather be here with her than safe on the outside.

He pulled off his pack and dug through it. Two bottles of water, a granola bar, and an extra set of clothes. Not much, but it would be enough. At least his emergency kit had a blanket. He wrapped it around Kyra's shoulders.

"Kyra, I'm going to move some rocks around." She looked up and nodded, but didn't say anything else.

Ryder pulled rocks free, making sure to move them to the opposite wall from where he was digging and as far away from Kyra as possible. After an hour or so, he stopped, tired and covered in sweat and dirt.

He pulled off his T-shirt. Turning it inside out, he wiped himself off. That was about as good as it was going to get.

"Kyra, are you with me?"

"Yes. Would you like me to take a turn now?" He heard her stand.

"No, I've got it. I just wanted to make sure you were okay."

"You know something, Ryder," she said angrily, "last time I checked, I didn't need a keeper or a watchdog."

Ryder smiled to himself. At least she wasn't crying anymore. Maybe a brawl with him would give her some fight back.

"Really? Then why have I had to save your ass so many times in the last couple of days? From where I'm standing, Blue, you not only need a Goddamned keeper, you need a watchdog, possibly a guardian, and definitely a bubble to live in." He heard her huff and turned to her. She was standing with hands on hips.

"I never asked you to save my ass, you pompous son of a bitch. And why is there no freaking air in here?" She bellowed the last part, her head tilted to the ceiling.

"Now that's just mean, Kyra. You don't know a thing about my mother," he said sarcastically.

She Shifted so that she was standing face to face with him. He didn't have a chance to step back as she slapped him.

"Not fair," he muttered, flexing his jaw. She hadn't hurt him, although, he had to admit, if she had wanted to, she could, and without trying very hard.

"Oh, really? 'Cause I once asked you what your superpower was and you disappeared," she mocked.

"I moved fast, Kyra. I do not disappear."

"It's called Shifting," she said more calmly.

"And the misty ghostly thing?" he asked.

"Ghosting, or Phasing. Depends on who you talk to. But only Air Elements can do it. And I don't want to talk about it."

Her orb reappeared. She shaded her eyes as she grew accustomed to the light. "How fast can you go, anyway?"

"Depends on the situation."

"But fast, right?" She was going somewhere with this, and he wasn't sure he liked it.

"Fast enough."

"So, you could've gotten out of here if I hadn't slowed you down?" It was a statement, not a question. "One more to add to the list." The last was said more to herself than to him.

"Kyra, could you phase or shift out of here?" he asked instead. "And what list, Kyra?" Now he was starting to get angry. She wasn't making any sense.

"One more person who I'll have to redeem." Ryder was so shocked, he couldn't speak for a moment.

"What the hell are you talking about?" he asked.

"When you die down here, I'll have to redeem your soul," she explained.

"Come again?"

"My family. The lives I've taken in the name of the Druids and Elements. Simon. You. And now I've opened a Pandora's Box so now the list will include anyone harmed by that. My list is getting very long."

He grabbed her and shook her. "For the love of all the Gods, you make no sense. I am going nowhere. ImMortal, remember? What the hell are you talking about?"

When he stopped, she moved back. "Ryder, I lived. I've survived in situations I shouldn't have, partially because of training. The other part was sheer luck." That part he totally understood. "But that doesn't mean that those people didn't deserve redemption. I was taken from my family to train, and they died, Ryder. If I'd stayed with them, I would've died too. I've skirted death by mere inches so many times, I can't count."

"So you think all those people who died—your family, the ones you killed because they were evil—are all waiting in Purgatory for you to redeem them?"

Kyra nodded, as if he finally understood everything.

"That is the stupidest thing I've ever heard."

Her mouth dropped open. "Excuse me?"

"You need to live your life for you, Kyra. Not anyone else. Not a single soul other than your own. If all you have is the constant reminder of what has been lost, then you have nothing at all," he said.

She gave him a sardonic look. "Pot, may I introduce you to kettle? And the why and how I fight is none of your damn business. The minute this mission is over, we'll never see each other again." Her words cut into him like a knife.

He wanted to scream that she would never get away from him, that he would never let her go. The thought of losing her made him slightly crazed. Words evaded him, so instead he kissed her.

The moment his lips touched hers, she was lost. She wasn't worried about stagnant air, the murmurs of the trapped souls. Her worries over all the souls she needed to redeem. All she knew was that the man she loved was kissing her. The man who was meant for her was holding her in his arms.

He felt so amazing pressed against her. In the darkness, she'd heard him moving those rocks, grunting and moaning, and it had taken everything she had to not let it turn her on. The noises he had made had kept her sane. She hadn't worried about the air, the murmurings of the tortured souls. Her only thoughts had been of the play of muscles and tendons that she was missing because of the dark. She hadn't wanted him to know how much he affected her. But now, she let all the pent-up sexual frustration loose and clung to him as her own personal lifeline.

And then, the stagnant air was replaced with the unique smell of passion and desire. Kyra breathed it in, letting it erase her pain.

She wrapped her arms around him, pulling him in as close as she could. They'd almost lost today. They still might lose, and she wasn't about to give up this opportunity. She had wanted him from the first moment she'd laid eyes on him.

"Damn, you taste good." He licked the column of her throat, sending chills up her spine. Kyra leaned her head back so that he had better access. He buried his nose into her hairline just behind her ear and licked her. She had never thought that was an erogenous zone, but damn, it felt so amazing she couldn't stop the moan that escaped. Thank the Gods he was holding her tight because she was pretty sure her legs were useless at the moment.

Ryder chuckled and did it again. Kyra felt a tightening in her womb. "More," she pleaded. He did as she asked. Kyra twined her legs with his, rubbing herself against his hard, long cock. "Damn, Ryder, I've wanted you so bad," she moaned.

Kyra let her hands roam over his body. She tried to memorize the way he felt under her fingers. The play of muscle over his back as he moved his arms forced her closer. He pressed his erection against her stomach, and Kyra's knees weakened.

He wrapped his arms around her, holding her up. He took several steps back until she was pressed against the cold stone. She wrapped her legs around him, grinding against him. "I can't get close enough, Ryder."

He groaned, "For the love of the Gods, woman. You're making me crazy."

She smiled. Never in her life had it felt like this before. She ran her hands over his back again, electricity sparking off her skin and into him.

He jerked. "What the hell?"

"It's an Element thing," she explained, not really giving him the complete reason.

He shrugged and kissed her harder. Kyra felt like crying. If only he knew. She sucked in the pain and pushed it down deep inside where she could hide from it.

"Kyra?" Ryder leaned back, feeling her withdrawal. "Do you want me to stop?" he asked, his voice low and raspy.

"I don't think I like that you can smell my emotions," Kyra said, looking up into his face. His eyes, typically black, were a dark blue. He'd told her countless times he thought she had beautiful eyes, but she couldn't remember ever seeing anything as beautiful as his eyes at that moment.

"I would never force you." He went to move away. Kyra locked her feet around his waist, not letting him go. This was her opportunity to have the one man who was meant for her before they went their separate ways. He'd never lied to her about what he thought of love. She would never try and change his mind. He had reasons that went back thousands of years. She could never compete with that.

"Please make love to me, Ryder," she asked.

"Damn it, sweetheart." He kissed her again. She opened her mouth to accept him, his tongue delving in to explore, only to pull back so he could suck on her bottom lip. His hands were everywhere, touching and massaging her.

Kyra needed to feel him, skin to skin. She tugged on her T-shirt. Ryder was more than willing to help. He pulled the shirt over her head and had her bra off in record time.

Kyra laughed. "You've done this before."

Ryder's only reply was the raising of one eyebrow. He leaned down to take one nipple into his mouth. Kyra's head fell back again as she moaned, her entire body jumping with electricity. She pressed her hands to the wall so that she wouldn't shock him.

He didn't seem to notice as his hands went to her lower back, pressing her close to him. Then moved one hand to massage and tweak a nipple.

"Gods, what I wouldn't do for some light. I want to see your face when you come for me." Immediately, a blue orb appeared over his head. Ryder looked up and smiled a slow, sexy smile.

"Ryder." She barely recognized her own voice. She slapped the wall behind her. She wanted him so badly, she wasn't sure she could stand much more foreplay, and they hadn't even gotten their pants off yet.

"Breathe," he whispered against her lips, instinctively knowing what she needed. Kyra sucked in the air he gave her. Before moving to her neck again and then back to her mouth, he breathed over her.

Kyra was in paradise. Never in her life had she felt so protected and alive, so wanted and needed at the same time. Ryder wasn't asking for anything but her body. No redemption, no promises. Just her. She would give him that and anything else he asked if he promised to never stop touching her.

Without thought, her hands rose to rest on his shoulders. Electricity weaved down her arms, causing small blue sparks to blink off the ends of some of the hairs on his arm where her hands touched.

Ryder pulled away. "Kyra? Is this electricity thing going to get worse?"

"Is it very painful?"

"No. You?"

How did she go about telling him that to her, it felt like a slice of heaven? "It doesn't hurt me at all." In fact, it turns me on the more it happens. She kept that part to herself.

She fisted her hands. "I'll try not to touch you, but I can't promise anything."

"Gods, Kyra, I want you to touch me." He kissed the corner of her mouth, breathing into her. "I need you to touch me, sweetheart."

She felt embarrassed, an interesting feeling with Ryder. She'd felt a lot of things with this man, but embarrassment hadn't been one of them. He leaned back, putting several inches between them.

"Touch me, Kyra."

Kyra hesitated but the need to touch him overcame every other sense she had. And with one index finger, she reached up and touched his collarbone. Blue sparks shimmered before going out in a blink. Ryder sucked in air.

Kyra's eyes flew to Ryder's. "Does it hurt?"

"No," he swallowed, "it feels amazing."

Kyra placed her finger back on his collarbone and the same thing happened. Ryder groaned, his hips thrusting forward. She dragged her finger down his chest, blue light sparking as she went.

She circled one nipple and then the other. When he didn't protest or move, she leaned forward and sucked one of his flat nipples into her mouth. Little electric blue sparks flared off her lips and tongue. She pressed her hands to his rib cage just to feel his abs contract as she touched him.

His hands had found her breasts and were massaging them as she licked and ran her hands all over his chest, memorizing every inch of his skin. He had a scar on his right shoulder, and another one just over his waistline that dipped down around his hip. She tracked it with her finger, causing him to jerk violently.

"Bloody hell," he stepped back, gasping for air. "That little trick is going to kill me." He stripped out of his pants. "Gods, what I wouldn't do for a bed right now. I'm sorry, Blue." He laid out the emergency blanket and their clothes, then moved back to her on his knees. He kissed her flat stomach as she ran her hands over his short hair.

His breath whispered over her belly button as he dipped his tongue in. She couldn't stop the sounds coming from her at this point. Her voice didn't sound like hers anymore as she moaned and begged for more.

His hands roamed over her legs. Sliding up the back, he cupped her ass, pressing her closer to his tongue. She watched as he grabbed the button of her leather pants between his teeth. Eyes glowing, he looked up into her eyes as he bit off the button and spat it out. It was the most erotic thing she had ever seen. She would've folded to the ground but he held her up. She would never have imagined something like that to be such a turn-on. And then he was dragging the zipper down with his teeth. She felt more alive at that moment than ever before in her long life. Her entire body shook with emotion and need.

"I've wanted to do this from the moment I saw you in them," his breath whispering over her hip. Kyra jerked in anticipation. Fisting her hands, she rested them on his shoulders, taking deep breaths as he peeled her leather pants from her legs.

"Dreamed of it every night." He palmed the back of one thigh. Squeezing, he gently bit the outside of her leg.

"God, you had me jerking off in the shower just thinking about peeling them off you."

That surprised her. She looked down at him. "You've brought me to my knees," he said humbly. Tears stung the back of her eyes and choked her throat. She couldn't make a sound at the moment. Otherwise, she was going to scream out how much she loved him.

And Gods, the thought of him touching himself while thinking about her almost had her coming herself. Ryder placed a hand on her belly, holding her up.

"I'm not nearly done with you yet." He peeled her panties down next, taking as much time as he had with the pants. Her entire body was on fire. She was barely able to think when he lifted one thigh over his shoulder and placed his mouth where she burned for him the most.

 The first swipe of his tongue had her screaming her release, her entire body quaked around his mouth as she came so hard, she saw stars. Her body fell back against the wall of the cave.

"Dear Gods, you're so wet." Then he stopped speaking. His tongue slid around her, making her moan and scream in pleasure.

"Ryder," she moaned his name over and over again, her head twisting back and forth against the cold rock wall as he made love to her with his mouth.

"You taste so wonderful, Kyra. I don't think I'll ever get enough of you," he whispered, piercing her heart.

"My turn." Kyra pushed him down onto their makeshift bed and ran her hands up his legs, lighting the way with her blue electricity. Ryder arched his back, thrusting his hips to the heavens. Kyra pressed his hips down, making his erection stand tall and proud. She was amazed at its size and wrapped her hand around the base, causing Ryder to shout her name.

Leaning down, she ran her tongue from the base of his sack to the tip where a drop of liquid had collected. She lapped it up and then sucked him in as far as he would go. It was his turn to make incoherent sounds. One hand buried in her hair, he called and moaned her name, whispered it as she made love to him with her mouth.

He sat up, suddenly lifting her so that she straddled him. "You're going to have me coming like an untried teenager. Time to slow it down," he whispered as he suckled her breast, tonguing the nipple until she was almost climaxing again.

When he moved to enter her, she stopped him. "Ryder."

He leaned back, his eyes dark with lust. "Stop?" His voice was so guttural, it gave her chills. That he would even ask made her heart hurt.

"No." Relief washed over his face. Kyra wrapped her arms around his head and leaned down. "But frankly, you're huge."

He nuzzled at her neck. "For the love of all the Gods, please do not tell me you're worried I won't fit?" His head had fallen back and his eyes were closed, the look on his face somewhere between pain and pleasure.

Kyra closed her eyes, wishing he didn't see so well in the dark because she was sure he could see and smell her embarrassment. Finally, he looked up, eyeing her warily.

Then he chuckled. "I'll fit, sweetheart."

She slapped his shoulder. "Don't go getting a big head over it."

He raised an eyebrow in a way that was so endearing; she couldn't help but lean down and kiss the eyebrow. "You know what I mean."

He pressed himself to her opening and the breath was stolen from her lungs. "Yes, Kyra, I know exactly what you mean." He breathed into her mouth as he kissed her.

"Just breathe." She took what he gave her as he eased into her, sucking the breath from his lungs as she opened for him, her entire body tightening with her need.

Ryder was nearly mindless with passion, but she was so tight and resisting him. He didn't want to hurt her, but he only had so much control.

"Breathe, Kyra," he whispered into her mouth and felt her relax. He slipped a little farther into her. She felt amazing. Tight and wet and his.

His brain screamed. The gland in the back of his throat started to secrete fluid into his mouth. He swallowed it, knowing if he consumed too much, it could poison him. He desperately wanted to mark her as his, desperately wanted to claim her in every way possible, but he needed to speak with Falcon. He would walk away from his brothers if he had to, but he was never going to let this woman go.

Instead, he kissed her, breathing into her. She relaxed the last little bit and he slid home, deep inside of her. Clenching his teeth, he waited for her to adjust to him, waited for her to make the next move.

It was almost too much to take. Although it was less than a minute, it felt like hours to Ryder. Then she shifted slightly. Ryder couldn't hold back his moan. Her hips moved forward, then back. He was so close to losing it all, he grabbed her hips. Stopping her for a moment, he took several breaths.

She pulled his head back, running her tongue along the seam of his lips, and then kissed his cheek. She moved to the pulse on his neck, biting at his collarbone. She moved her lips and sweet tongue up the side of his neck to just behind his right ear, licking and kissing him just the way a female Tracker would do during the bonding. It was his undoing, her tongue running down the side of his neck only to come back up as she licked him behind the ear.

"Kyra," he moaned. He flipped her over while remaining deeply seated inside her. "I can't wait any longer."

218

She nodded and rolled her hips in a way that pressed him deeper. He shouted her name and ground his hips into her.

He eased himself out gently, not wanting to hurt her, before slowly pressing back into her. She arched up to meet him. He moved slowly, making sure she wasn't in any pain.

It was her plea of "Ryder, please" that was his total undoing. His mouth filled with saliva mixed with the pheromone of a Tracker male. He leaned down and licked the side of her throat at the base where her heart beat, laving her with his mark as he pounded into her.

Kyra wrapped her legs around him, never wanting him to leave her. He feverishly pumped into her as he kissed and licked her, wrapping her in a scent that was all male and all him. Ryder didn't disappoint. He gave her exactly what she needed.

Her orgasm this time was so fierce, she thought briefly that her heart would stop. She heard herself scream out his name over and over again, the sound bouncing off the small space.

Ryder pulled one of her legs up and placed it over his shoulder. He rolled his hips, hitting a spot that prolonged her orgasm to the point of pain and set her off again. Shudder after shudder of pure ecstasy convulsed through her body.

As she started to roll from the expanse of her orgasm, Ryder moved to a faster pace, his eyes locked with hers. As every muscle in his body tensed, he called out her name before releasing himself into her. She felt every inch of him contract from deep within her body, over and over again. Finally, he collapsed on her, sucking in air. He pulled her into his arms and wrapped the remainder of their clothes around her.

He leaned down so that his breathing was mixed with hers. The generousness of that pierced deeply in her soul. Tears slipped from her eyes. She was in big trouble with this man.

"Don't think," he breathed. "Just sleep."

He was right. Tomorrow they would find a way out, and then they would go their separate ways. Kyra pushed the thought away and snuggled closer into him. Ryder wrapped one long leg over hers, pulling her as close as he could so that his heat wrapped around her like a blanket. She burrowed into him, wishing they could just stay here forever in this little bubble.

Chapter 11

Kyra stretched, feeling tight and sour in too many places to count.

"If you keep that up, I will have no choice but to have my way with you," Ryder whispered over her face before nuzzling her behind her ear. He licked her again.

Kyra didn't want to move and didn't think that being ravaged by him first thing in the morning was a bad idea. She wrapped her arms around him and arched into him.

Ryder moaned, making his chest vibrate against her. She felt her nipples harden and joined him in the moan.

"Damn it, Kyra." He rolled her over, entering her so quickly, she gasped.

He froze. "Did I hurt you?"

Kyra shook her head. It felt amazing. She arched up to prove it. "Don't stop, Ryder," she said breathlessly.

He started to move. Sensation welled up from deep in the pit of her stomach. She dragged her fingertips down his chest. Blue sparks flew in every direction.

"Damn, that feels good." He leaned down to kiss her as he started to move faster.

Kyra pulled her mouth away to gasp for air. She dug her fingers into his shoulders as her orgasm unfurled around her. Ryder moved faster, extending her orgasm. She panted and nearly screamed in pleasure when he went taut, his entire body flexing as tight as a bowstring.

He collapsed on top of her. "I think you might end up killing me one day."

That would imply they would be together for longer than this mission. She didn't know if she could stand to be with him and know he would never love her. Although if the sex was this good, she would almost be willing to give up everything she knew, loved, and believed in. She'd been raised to love and be loved in return. She wouldn't settle for anything else from a life mate. And if her life mate couldn't give that to her, then she would live a life without him and that love. But the thought felt like a spike driving into her heart.

He finally rolled away. "We should get dressed and see about getting the hell out of here," he said, oblivious to her thoughts.

Kyra lay staring into the pitch-blackness, trying not to feel anything. She didn't want him to sense her feelings.

Sending up her orb of light, she looked around and gathered her clothing.

She stood and shook out their clothes, handing Ryder his. He pulled a clean T-shirt from his bag.

"Your shirt was ruined from your fight with that thing. Wear this one instead." She smiled and took it. It swamped her but once she had her gun holster on, it cinched the shirt against her.

Once they were dressed, Ryder pulled out a bottle of water for each of them and a granola bar, which he handed to her. She broke it in half, but Ryder was already shaking his head.

"You eat it. I'm fine."

"But you need to eat just as much as I do." She offered the piece to him again.

He leaned down so that his nose touched her. "I want you to have it." Then he kissed her sweetly and gently.

Kyra felt tears well up in her throat. She wanted to scream. This couldn't be happening. She quickly extinguished her orb and turned away from Ryder. She knew he saw perfectly in the dark, but it made her feel better to cover her feelings.

She took several breaths of stagnant air, the familiar feelings of terror swamping her. She pushed back at them and breathed out. She ate the granola bar in silence, trying to not feel as if her world were coming to an end.

"Are you okay?"

"Yes, just the air," she lied.

He turned her around. "I'm getting you out of here today. Think about the cool breeze that blows through the forest, the smell of the trees and bushes, the clean air of the mountains surrounding you." He spoke quietly with a sure, calm voice that had her envisioning it. She took a breath and felt better.

"Let's get this done." It was difficult because she wanted desperately to stay right there in his arms, but she pulled away and went to where he'd been digging the night before.

They didn't speak as they started to pull rocks away. With each rock she dislodged, she felt some of her hopes and dreams die a quiet death.

Kyra had no idea how long they had been at it when Ryder grabbed her arm. "Do you hear that?"

She stopped moving, even stopped breathing. Please, please, her brain screamed.

And there it was.

Sounds of digging through rock that matched their own, accompanied by arguing, a great deal of arguing.

Kyra couldn't help but laugh. "Do all of you fight like that?"

Lykar and Skylar were going at each other like vapid fish wives.

Ryder smiled. "We do enjoy a good fight, but Lykar, Skylar, and I enjoy a fight more than the other Trackers."

He leaned down and kissed her. "I told you I would get you out of here."

She smiled, swallowing the tears that threatened to spill. It was just a matter of time before they were going to be free and he could walk away from her. Kyra wondered what it would be like to go back to the Haven and live a life without him. Pain sliced through her heart, and she stumbled back.

"Kyra?" Ryder grasped her. "Kyra, are you all right?"

"I can't breathe, Ryder," she lied. He leaned down and breathed into her, knowing this would be it. This would be the last moment they would have together. She wrapped her arms around him and held him close.

"Would the two of you shut the hell up?" They heard Marcus say. "If you'd put as much energy into digging as you do into fighting, we could've found them by now."

"Yeah, well, this is the fourth tunnel, asshole, so forgive me for being a little grouchy," Skylar barked back. "All I gotta say is they better be in here or dead, 'cause I'm going to kill Ryder as soon as I find him."

"I guess the jig is up." Ryder leaned back and smiled, then kissed Kyra deeply. She was swamped with emotion and pushed everything away. "When this is all done, we have a lot to discuss. You and me, Blue."

She nodded, unable to really do anything else. If she opened her mouth, she would shout that she loved him. Loved his strength. The power he exuded, and the fact that he pulled her back from the brink of danger every time she stepped in front of it. She loved how loyal he was, how much he loved his very odd brothers.

"Stop fighting and dig you morons!" Ryder shouted, letting them know they were here. Everything went silent on the other side of the wall.

"Bloody fucking hell," someone said.

Kyra laughed through her tears and dug at the rocks, not caring that her fingers were bleeding. She dislodged a rock and a beam of light shot into the dark cavern. Kyra pushed her face into the air that rushed in. Breathing it in, she felt herself fill with energy and life again.

Marcus's face appeared. "Kyra!"

Kyra smiled, "Hi."

"Thank the Gods." Marcus reached in and she reached out through the hole they'd created. Their fingertips touched and she felt warmth spread up her arm before she was pulled back, Ryder growling something under his breath about damn Fallen. He stuck his head into the hole.

"Can we just get the hell out of here already?"

"Of course," Lykar said. "It's not like we haven't been digging in tunnels all night or anything. Hey, it smells like—"

"Shut the fuck up," Ryder barked, "and dig."

Kyra blushed. Their noses were way too sensitive for their own good.

The hole was almost big enough for Kyra to crawl through when the entire mountain vibrated. Ryder jerked Kyra out of the hole and pushed her against the wall, shielding her as rocks fell all around them.

"No!" Kyra screamed but when the shaking stopped, the opening was still there.

"Thank the Gods."

"What the hell was that?" Ryder barked into the opening.

"We weren't able to contain everything that was in the box," Marcus said.

"What?" Kyra asked.

"What exactly does that mean, Marcus?" Ryder yelled as the mountain shook again.

"Sophie?" Kyra asked.

"Oh, Sophie and her companion are gone," Marcus said. "However, the thing that took them was more than we can contain." The mountain shook again and something pounded at the fallen rock behind them like a battering ram. "And I think it knows this is the way out."

"We need to get out of her now!" Ryder bellowed. He pulled out rocks as the mountain shuddered and the screams of something unearthly pounded at their backs. Finally, the opening was big enough for Kyra.

"Wait." Ryder grabbed her before she crawled out. The mountain shuddered again. Once it settled, he nodded.

"Now!" He pushed her into the hole. Marcus reached for her at the same time and she was pulled free and into the arms of the Fallen.

"Damn, Kyra, I'm so glad you're okay."

Kyra smiled. "You're not the only one."

She turned to Lykar and Skylar who were both staring at her like they'd never seen her before.

"Mother of all that is holy, in this world and the next. What the fuck has he done?" Lykar swore.

"Shut up." Skylar slapped his brother on the back of the head.

Kyra looked down at herself. What had Ryder done? She couldn't see anything.

Fiona was next. "Oh, dear. I had no idea how I was going to tell Eric that we'd lost you. The boy has such a temper."

Kyra hugged her. "Well, let's not tell him about this, then."

Fiona laughed and hugged her back.

A crashing noise from inside the hole Kyra had just come through stopped everyone cold.

"Get me the fuck out of here!" Ryder shouted.

Everyone rushed forward, digging with everything they had, ignoring the growling and screeching that was now coming from the inside. Ryder grunted as he started to squeeze through the hole.

"I don't know what the hell that is, but it's coming." He popped through and they all stood back as the mountain shook. Dust belched from the new hole and Ryder rushed forward, throwing rocks back into it. Everyone joined in.

But it was too little, too late. The mouth of the cave blew apart, sending everyone flying in different directions. Fiona held her hands up and created an invisible barrier between them and what was about to come out of the tunnel. All Kyra could see were black wings and yellow eyes.

It battered at the barrier and screamed in frustration. "Kyra, Marcus! Right now!"

Kyra looked around. Marcus lay still several yards away. Kyra crawled to him, shaking him. "Marcus?"

He opened his eyes. Blood oozed from a wound over his right eye; he looked from her to Fiona and pushed himself to his feet.

"Reapers, NOW!" Fiona said, and Marcus disappeared.

Kyra stood up and rushed to Ryder. He was pulling himself to his feet. When she got to him, he grabbed her and turned her around.

"I'm not hurt. Are you okay?" Ryder nodded, looking back at the mouth of the tunnel.

Yellow eyes glowed from the darkness of the cave as it rushed, throwing its body against the barrier. Fiona stumbled back as if she'd taken the blow herself.

"Shit." Lykar rushed over to the older woman and wrapped his arms around her, helping to hold her up as the thing rammed against the invisible wall.

Skylar and Ryder joined in.

"Not much longer," Fiona moaned in pain.

"What is it?"

"One of the First," someone said from behind her.

Kyra jumped and turned around. Two cloaked figures stood behind her with Marcus.

"Holy shit!" She scrambled away from the Reapers at her back, standing so close they could've taken her and she never would've known what happened.

The one that had spoken walked up to the barrier and tilted his head in thought as the thing continued to pound against the barrier.

"How did this happen?" the one standing with Marcus asked.

"Explanations later. Action now!" Ryder barked as Fiona began to falter.

The Reaper standing at the barrier turned. "Lower it when I say."

The other Reaper moved to stand next to his comrade. They exchanged words under the shadow of their hoods, and then nodded. "He is going to be so pissed," Kyra heard one say.

"Not a pound of my flesh," the other one said.

The thing in the cavern had noticed the two Reapers and had backed up. The only thing they could see were the yellow of its eyes.

It was said so calmly that Kyra almost missed it, as if ordering tea instead of asking Fiona to lower a barrier and release something horrible.

"Now!"

The Reapers rushed in, one extending a sword Kyra hadn't even seen, the other a long chain it whipped back and then disappeared into the darkness. A howl of pain pierced her ears and she covered them with her hands.

Fiona collapsed and Kyra rushed over to her, covering the older woman with her body as rocks flew from the mouth of the tunnel. She felt someone encircle them both and knew it was Ryder.

After several long minutes, the fight stopped. Kyra turned to see something horrifying fly from the mouth of the tunnel and disappear into the horizon.

The two Reapers emerged from the tunnel, their cloaks in tatters. Kyra could only stare for the moment. They were beautiful: one was blond, the other sandy-brown, his hair curled around his temples. They looked as if they'd just had their asses handed to them, but neither looked defeated.

"You can stop staring at them anytime, Blue," Ryder growled in her ear.

"But," she pointed to them, "they should look like death," she whispered.

Ryder grunted. "And what exactly does death look like?"

She imitated his grunt and made claws with her fingers, eyes wide. "Scary."

But she looked back and they were anything but scary. In fact, besides the tattered clothes, they could've been pulled from a *GQ* ad.

The Reapers regarded each of them individually. "The Air Element, and the Fallen."

Ryder lurched to his feet. "NO!"

"What?" Kyra asked, standing. "What's going on?"

Ryder, Skylar, and Lykar all moved to stand in front of her. "The three of us for her," Lykar offered.

The sandy-brown-haired one smiled. "But we don't want you, Tracker."

It hit her like a ton of bricks. They wanted payment. They wanted Kyra as that payment. "But it got away," she accused. "How can you ask for payment of any kind when you didn't do what you were asked?"

The three Tracker brothers turned to her as if she had lost her mind. Marcus slapped himself on the forehead.

"Shut up, Kyra," Ryder snapped.

The Reapers laughed. "We were told that something had escaped a Pandora's Box. And so here we are to see what it was. We now know, and we demand payment."

Kyra pushed through the brothers, and put her hands on her hips. "And exactly what was it?"

"I said before, it was one of the First. Its name is Calliope."

"That's not a Reaper. That was a Muse," Kyra explained.

"It humored Dante to name the Firsts after Muses," the blond one said calmly. Kyra wanted to slap the bland look off his face.

"So, it's a Reaper?" Kyra asked.

They both nodded. "And now what is it going to do, now that it is free?"

Kyra might have been mistaken but she thought she saw sadness in the blondes eyes as he spoke. "It will do what Reapers do."

They were so calm, she wondered if anything ruffled their feathers. "And what exactly is that?"

"Reap souls." They turned to Marcus, as if that were the end of the conversation. "And you're responsible."

Marcus nodded, falling into step with them as they moved away from the tunnel.

"I'm not going," Kyra barked.

"Damn it, Kyra," Ryder said again. "You're going to get us all killed, you know that?"

"Who opened the box?" the blond one asked.

"Technically?" Kyra started. "I did. But it was an accident."

"But only a pure soul can open the box, intentional or not. And therefore, you must answer to Dante for what you have done," they explained. His black eyes pierced through Kyra.

"Three Trackers. Dante would be very impressed," Ryder said, moving forward.

"Yes, however, it would not answer the question of what happened here, would it?" They were being so damn calm, it made Kyra want to scream.

Kyra wouldn't allow the three brothers to give their lives for her. She would never be able to live with herself if that happened. However, she doubted she was going to live that much longer anyway. This wasn't expected. Out of all the outcomes, this wasn't even on the list.

"Borrowed time," she said, more to herself than anyone else.

Ryder turned on her, fury blazing from his black eyes. "Don't you dare give up! Your life means something, and you have nothing to repay."

She threw her arms around him. "Thank you," she said. He wrapped his arms around her, holding her so tightly, she was afraid he might crack her rib.

She pushed away from him. "Will you make sure Fiona gets help?"

"No, don't do this." Ryder's voice was quiet and deadly. When he realized she wasn't going to give in, Ryder advanced on the Reapers. Kyra reached for him, trying to stop him but the Reapers didn't even blink. One held up his hand, stopping Ryder in his tracks. He lifted him off the ground and made a fist. Ryder screamed in pain, his entire body folding in on itself.

Kyra screamed. "Stop! I'll go with you. Just stop."

The Reaper dropped his hand and with it, Ryder. Kyra rushed to him. Blood ran from his nose and mouth. Tears streamed down her face. "I won't carry you and your brothers on my conscience."

She looked up at Lykar. "Please take care of him and Fiona." Lykar nodded. Ryder tried to rise, but the Reaper pushed him back down with a flick of his wrist.

Kyra swung on the Reaper. "I said I would come with you. You don't have to torture him anymore."

The Reaper smiled. "But that's what we do, little Element."

When she turned back to where Ryder now lay unconscious, she nodded to Skylar. She smiled past the tears. "We all knew this was the ultimate answer, didn't we?" she asked the cynical Tracker, desperately needing some validation. "Whether the thing in the mountain or the Reapers, I was never supposed to survive this mission," she admitted.

"Yes, but I would not have my brother so hurt in the process." Sky looked from Kyra to where his brother lay.

She turned to the Reapers as they opened a portal. She looked back before stepping through, and whispered the words she hadn't dared say before.

"I love you, Ryder." She then stepped through the portal into Dante's Inferno and the pathway to Hell.

Chapter 12

Never before, throughout two thousand years of life, had he been in as much pain as over the last several weeks. The Reaper had pretty much broken every bone in his body. And damn his Tracker blood—he healed so quickly that they had to be re-broken several times just so he'd heal correctly.

Emotionally, he was worse. He wasn't speaking to anyone. He hadn't been conscious when they'd cleaned up the mess and explained away half a mountain exploding. He'd woken in one of their homes far away from Marshall, Montana, and that horrid mountain. Marlee had sat with him as his brothers had taken care of what needed to be done. Fiona had been taken away by the Druids that lived there. But none of that mattered to Ryder, the only think he cared about had disappeared into the Infernos. And he was to hurt to follow.

When they had eventually made him home Sky sat with him every day. Lykar, Falcon, Marlee and his other brothers visited but he didn't speak to them. She was gone. Sky said she walked into the Infernos. His heart had broken at the thought of her there, unprotected.

"She's gone!" Lykar had screamed at him after two weeks of silence.

"I know." Ryder bellowed back, trying to climb from the bed to attack his brother. That had caused his right leg to need to be re-broken for the fourth time so that it would heal straight. After that, none of his brothers mentioned Kyra, and Ryder lay in bed, wishing for death.

After four weeks, Ryder was finally able to get out of bed without crippling pain. He climbed from the bed, wondering if it was even worth it.

Sky brought in breakfast and found Ryder staring out the window. He sat the tray down on the bed and watched Ryder, until Ryder couldn't stand it anymore.

Ryder turned on him. "What?"

"Are you going to die now?" Sky asked. Ryder looked at his brother and saw the small boy he'd been so long ago. It was the same question he'd asked their father when their mother had been killed, dismembered and disemboweled by a rival Tracker tribe.

Their father, incapable of any further emotion, had wandered into the woods. Ryder found his body several days later, burning it where he found it. He then took his four brothers and two sisters and they had moved, as far away from that evil place as possible.

"No." Ryder's answer was very quiet and full of the same amount of pain their father had been in so many years ago.

"Are you going to go after her?" Sky asked.

"No."

"Do you love her?"

"Yes."

"Then you will die."

"I marked her but I didn't perform the bonding ritual. I had to speak with Falcon before breaking that bond." But now he wished he'd spoken the words. Dying would be easier than feeling like he did now.

"What does it feel like?"

Ryder stopped and turned to his brother. He knew for the first time in his life that he was wearing his heart on his sleeve. "It hurts, Sky. It fucking hurts."

Sky put an arm around his brother. "Thought so."

"Get your ass out of bed." Falcon demanded as he slammed into Ryder's room two weeks later. Ryder struggled to open his eyes. He'd started drinking two weeks ago and really hadn't stopped. Being unconscious was far more appealing than reality.

"Why?" Ryder asked, his voice raw. He wasn't going anywhere, except to grab another bottle.

"I got you access to the Infernos." Ryder couldn't help it. His mouth sagged open.

"How the hell did you do that?" he pushed himself up, suddenly very interested in what Falcon had to say. He pushed through the fog of the liquor.

"Doesn't matter. And it also doesn't ensure that you will be granted an audience with Dante. But it's better than sitting here drinking yourself into a hole," Falcon said. "Find out what happened to her."

He stormed out with the same force with which he'd entered. Ryder sat in his bed, staring at the door. It was his chance to find out if they'd killed her, or worse, made her a concubine. He didn't know if he'd be able to handle it if it were the latter. But not knowing hurt like hell.

Pulling himself from his bed, he showered, shaved, and put on clean clothes. If anything, he felt better being clean and completely healed from his wounds. Now if only he could fill the hole where his heart had been.

When he entered Falcon's study, a hooded man stood to the side. "Is this him?" it asked, his voice raspy as burnt paper.

"Yes," Falcon nodded.

"He will take you to Dante's Fortress. From there, you will have to wait to see if Dante will even grant you an audience."

Ryder nodded. It was worth a try. He followed the hooded man through a portal and into a large courtyard of stone carvings. The hooded figure shuffled forward to a large gate.

"You will wait here." He opened the gate and closed it before saying, "Do not touch anything."

Ryder looked around, knowing that the life-size stone carvings of people were not carvings at all. Yeah. He wouldn't be touching a damn thing.

Kyra stepped through the portal and felt as if she'd stepped into her own personal hell. Dry, acrid heat blasted her from every direction. She stumbled as the voices and cries of the dead beat against her. Marcus held her by the arm.

"Are you going to be okay?" he asked.

"Do you hear them?" she whispered.

Marcus looked over the wasteland that was the Infernos. "Yes."

She stumbled to her knees. "So much pain." She retched, emptying her stomach of what little it had in it.

Marcus pulled her to her feet. "It's too much." She grasped her head.

Marcus held her by her arm, pushing her forward. At some point, he had acquired the two Pandora's Boxes, which he held under his arm.

The Reapers led them down red rock-lined passages, the sky a strange orange-red combination that rolled and pulsed with the sounds of the damned. Kyra felt each pulse deep inside like a knife slicing through her soul. Her heart stuttered and pulsed to the beat of the dead. Tears raced down her face unchecked.

Without Marcus, she would've never made it to the Fortress. He held onto her, not letting her fall, standing by her side when she threw up again and again. At one point, they stopped and allowed Kyra to rest against hot red stone. If given the choice, she would've curled up right there and let the death cries carry her to her final resting place. But the Reapers soon pushed her forward again.

Kyra looked around and tried to break the sounds and images from her mind. She had to admit that it was beautiful. She'd pictured the Infernos to be a place of darkness. It was horrible, but in a beautiful way that she probably would never be able to explain to another person without sounding crazy.

They stopped before a dark lake over which stretched a long stone bridge. The Reapers turned to the two.

The blond spoke. "This is the Lake of Souls."

"There are people in there," Kyra said as she looked down into the water.

"If you fall in, you are lost."

So don't fall in, Kyra thought. But just as the Reapers started to walk along the bridge, a gust of wind created from the waves blew their cloaks aside, revealing a wealth of weapons. She had no idea they were carrying so much. It explained their caution.

Marcus motioned for Kyra to go first. "If you slip, I'll be right behind you."

Kyra smiled. "Thank you, Marcus. For everything."

He nodded and nudged her gently forward.

Several times the wind picked up, almost sending Kyra over the side, but Marcus never wavered himself. He was there for her every second of the way. It felt like it took forever to get across the lake. She hoped that if she were somehow able to get through this, perhaps there would be an easier way out.

When they finally stepped onto the opposite shore, Kyra let out a breath she hadn't realized she'd been holding. "I don't want to do that again."

"And the alternative?" Marcus asked, stepping from the bridge himself.

"We could just avoid the Infernos altogether," she said with a small smile.

"Do you love him?" Marcus asked, surprising her.

Kyra knew what he was talking about. Felt a stab somewhere near her heart. "Yes."

"What does it feel like?"

Kyra was shocked at the question. "Marcus, you were once an angel. You knew limitless, unconditional love."

He nodded. "Yes, that is what most people think. It was beautiful to be an angel. However, the love Mortals share is something completely different. Being in this Mortal body, it feels different than the love an angel feels."

That made sense. "Well, right now, it hurts. But before …" When they'd been in the cave … "It felt wonderful, and utterly confusing."

"But as a Tracker, what future is there?"

236

"I have no idea." Kyra sighed heavily. "But I love him, anyway. I would like to have thought I could've loved him enough for the both of us."

Marcus nodded sadly. "You love with all your heart, Kyra. It is an amazing quality, not one that many creatures possess." The way he said it revealed a little more about who the Fallen were. He had loved someone, and they hadn't loved him back. The woman had to have been insane.

"Do you want to fall in love, Marcus?" She knew he'd taken a vow of celibacy. But that didn't mean he didn't want to find someone.

He gave her a sad look. "Love is a strange emotion, and even after spending two millennia among Mortals, I do not fully comprehend love. I have seen it kill people, drive them to do things you would never imagine. I have seen it heal, and calm. It is both beautiful and horrifying."

Kyra looked around, and smiled. "A lot like the Infernos."

Marcus chuckled and wrapped an arm around her as she faltered. "Are you going to make it?"

"Does it matter?" She didn't expect to live through this. Just being here was slowly killing her. Each scream, each image of death chipped away at her soul, the air thick and suffocating, no Ryder to breathe for her. She leaned into the strength and light that Marcus radiated, the only thing keeping her alive at the moment.

Marcus gave her a sad look. "Not everyone taken by the Reapers is condemned."

"Name one." She closed her eyes and tried to block the visions of death that danced at the edges of her vision.

Marcus did not speak again for some time, leaving Kyra with her own thoughts.

Finally, she answered his question. "I don't think that we are meant to understand love, Marcus. I think it is something that is either there or not."

He nodded thoughtfully. "Are you afraid?"

She was too tired and hurt to lie. "I'm terrified."

Marcus pulled her a little closer. "Do not be afraid, Kyra. Dante may rule the Infernos, but he does not have the final say. And often he can be reasoned with."

That is not exactly what she'd heard of the man. Nevertheless, she was going to let Marcus try to ease her fears if it made him feel better.

"Aren't you afraid?"

Marcus shook his head and sighed heavily. "Unfortunately, this is not the first time I have broken the rules of the Reapers. They cannot kill me or take my soul." He stopped, pulling Kyra to a stop with him. "Whatever happens, Kyra, do not argue. It will only make things worse. Insolence is one thing Dante will not tolerate."

They finally stopped before a large gate. At first, she thought it was intricately entwined wrought iron. But as she looked closer, she realized that it was made of blackened bones. One of the Reapers spoke something and the bones groaned and unwound, making an opening for them to walk through.

Kyra moved back as screams emanated from the bones. "They're still alive."

Marcus pulled her forward, but it was too much and her legs gave out. Marcus swung her into his arms. She was too tired, hurt too much. She relaxed against the safety of Marcus.

They followed the Reapers into a courtyard, gravel pathways leading to several houses. Interspersed in the gravel were tall statues depicting different scenes from not only human mythology but Other mythology as well.

They stopped as the gravel gave way to what almost looked like white marble streaked with blood. Kyra followed the path with her eyes. At the top was a large round domed building. If she hadn't known better, she would've put it in the category of a coliseum. Dante's Fortress.

The Reapers turned. "You will wait here."

Marcus nodded and set Kyra down on a stone bench.

"Don't touch anything." The second one offered.

"No shit," Kyra muttered.

Marcus gave her a hard look, but she could've sworn the first Reaper smiled as he turned away.

Marcus folded his arms and closed his eyes. He could've been one of the statues, he was so still.

She needed to fill the silence or go mad listening to the cries of the damned. "Marcus, how many times have you been here?"

He didn't even open his eyes as he answered her. "More times than I would like to count. The Fallen and the Reapers have an understanding."

"What type of understanding?" she couldn't help ask. She'd never heard about a pact between the Fallen and the Reapers.

"We help each other out." He shrugged, as if it wasn't a big deal.

"In what way?" she pushed.

He finally opened his eyes, the clear blue giving her hope where she thought all had been lost. "They can go places the Fallen can't and vice versa. We often work together. They may be Reapers, but that doesn't necessarily make them evil."

Kyra felt her mouth fall open in shock. Marcus shook his head and explained. "The old race of Reapers, very evil. That thing that got away today—evil as it gets. However, Dante realized what he'd created. He couldn't control it, couldn't undo what he'd done. Like most of the Gods eventually did, Dante realized that controlling the creatures he'd created was an impossibility. Once you give a creature the right to live and make choices, you give up the ability to control it. Unfortunately, the creatures Dante created to rule over the Infernos with him were born of evil. Therefore, they *were* evil. Would you like to hear the story?"

Kyra nodded. His voice drowned out everything else and when he started to talk, she closed her eyes and just listened. "When darkness parted from the Light—I don't mean when the Keeper was lost, but before that—the reason Light and Dark were added to the Elements. Atlantis still reigned over the Mortal plan. The original inhabitants were shocked to learn that there was a need for the departed souls of Mortals. It was a surprise to the inhabitants of Atlantis that Mortals had souls. For how brilliant they were, they were also idiots. The Original Descendents, not the Mortals. We, I mean the Angels, knew the Mortals would one day rule this plane and so we offered to guide the departed souls to where they needed to be, whether that was to Hell or Heaven. But the Dark did not want the Angels to have all the power. They wanted a piece of it. And so Dante offered to create a race that would guide souls as well. But what he created here in the Infernos bred evil. There were originally nine Reapers, one for each Level.

"But each one turned against Dante, giving into the evil that bred them."

"That must have been horrible." Kyra couldn't imagine it.

"Yes, well, they had to be contained. And it was up to Dante to correct the matter. So he created the first of many boxes. One at a time, he trapped his creations, his sons, in those boxes, containing what was known as the greatest evil in the world at the time."

"But then where did the current set of Reapers come from?" Kyra asked, enthralled despite their precarious position.

"Ahhh, that is the thing, Kyra. This is the third set of Reapers. However, they have been the longest standing of the Reapers. I believe that Dante may have gotten it right with this group."

"But how?"

"A pact between the Angels and Dante."

Kyra's mouth dropped open. "They are Angels?" She looked at where the Reapers had disappeared.

"No, Kyra, they are Reapers. They are Dante's spawn. Angels volunteered and he impregnated them. They lived here in the Infernos until the child was born," Marcus said the last as if it pained him to admit it.

"When they returned, their souls were tainted and they were unable to live in the Fields. They became the first of the Fallen. And their sons? The ones they'd volunteered to carry were the beings who reaped their souls when they turned against humanity."

Kyra felt a tear roll down her cheek. "I am so sorry, Marcus. Did you know any of them?"

Marcus shook his head. "That was even before my time, Kyra. But it still saddens me, the sacrifice made and taken."

"So now there are two factions always vying for the souls of the dead?" Kyra asked.

"Not really. If you are a good person, you go to a good place and wait to be reborn. If you are evil, then a Reaper will come for you, but not just a Reaper—it could one of many minions that the Reapers control. Way too many deaths for the nine, but if a Reaper, not a minion, comes for you?" Marcus shook his head sadly. "Then you are truly damned. And if you are in-between? You go to Purgatory until your name is called. There is both a Reaper and an Angel who hold Purgatory."

"Called by whom?"

Marcus looked very mischievous as he answered. "Dante, and Helena, an Archangel."

"And do they fight for the souls?"

"Of course not. Helena wouldn't lower herself to fight Dante. No, they give the soul the chance to argue its case. What it did during its life. Whether it should be given a second chance at life or spend eternity in one of the levels of the Infernos."

"So none of them are sentenced to hell?" Because even she knew there was Hell. That was a place you never came back from. Like Heaven, if you were granted access to either, you never came out.

"If you are evil enough to go to Hell, then you go straight there, escorted by Dante himself, it's said." Marcus shivered. "Dante leads you through the gauntlet of Reapers."

That made Kyra quiver, to be tortured so horribly, to end up suffering even worse in the depths of Hell was not a fate she cared to experience.

They didn't speak again until the blond Reaper came back down the pathway.

Marcus helped Kyra to her feet. "Be strong, Element, and if things do not go our way, think of me while you are in Heaven." He leaned down and kissed her cheek.

They followed the Reaper and entered the domed structure into what looked like a Victorian manor house. She couldn't control her reaction. She stopped in her tracks and stared. The oppressive heat was gone, as was the wind that carried the screams. Kyra instantly felt better.

The Reaper noticed her reaction. "Just because we deal in death and evil doesn't mean we have to live that way." His eyes twinkled with pleasure at her reaction.

"It's the angel in them," Marcus added.

The Reaper grabbed his chest, as if in pain. "Never allow Father to hear you say so."

He turned them down a short hallway and grabbed a cloak, throwing it around his shoulders. He pulled up the cowl in one fluid motion as he threw the door open. Kyra was stunned at his grace, but her astonishment soon turned to horror when she looked around. Nine cloaked figures ringed the room, and at the head sat a simple-looking man on a dais.

He could've been any twenty-something man sitting at a bar or coffee house, waiting for an order. Brown hair, slight figure, dressed in slacks and a pressed white shirt halfway unbuttoned. She saw muscle ripple as he motioned to someone next to him.

However, he exuded such strength and power, Kyra knew instantly that she was looking at Dante. People didn't come back from talking to this imMortal.

She forced her feet forward, her hands fisted at her sides trying to dampen her terror. If she was going to be held accountable, she was going to do it on her own two feet. She just wasn't sure her feet and legs had gotten the memo.

"My boxes?" his voice boomed. Marcus stepped forward and laid the boxes at Dante's feet. One was beautiful, with gilded edges. The other, however, was dull and tarnished and currently in several pieces.

"Which one of you gave him two boxes?" he asked the ten figures standing around him.

One cloaked figure stepped forward. "It was I, Father."

Dante shook his head in disappointment. "They are not to be trifled with." His voice boomed and Kyra had to lock her trembling knees.

Standing, Dante kicked the pieces of the broken box. They sailed through the air and shattered against the far wall.

"And now Calliope is loose. Do you have any idea what that means?" Everyone was silent. "Who opened it?"

Kyra breathed out as she stepped forward. "I did."

Dante looked at her for a long moment, his soft brown eyes belying his power. He moved off the dais and walked toward Kyra. She'd never wanted to run from something so much in all her life, but she remained, rigid in place.

"An Element?" he laughed. "Now that is funny. You didn't do it alone. Who made you do this?"

"It was an accident, actually," she explained.

Dante laughed but it was a humorless sound. "That is what they all say, my dear."

He pierced her with black eyes. Kyra realized she was looking into the eyes of eternity and if she stared long enough, she would be lost forever. Her fate lay at his feet. She sent up a silent prayer that he would be merciful.

Dante turned to the Reaper who stood forward. "What do you require?"

"Calliope must be brought back," a soft male voice came from the hooded figure. "And of course, the requested pound of flesh."

Three hooded figures moved forward, two taking Marcus by each arm. They led him to the side where two huge columns stood, metal shackles hanging from each.

Realization hit with the force of a Mack truck and her frozen mind and body snapped to.

"Stop!" Kyra screamed. "Oh, please, stop. I opened the box—I should be punished. I did it." She rushed over to where the Reapers continued to strap Marcus into the shackles.

"Step back, Kyra," Marcus demanded, his voice soft. He showed no fear. That he was so calm only upset her more.

Someone grabbed her by the arms and moved her away. Kyra wanted to scream and yell but remembered what Marcus had said. Nobody in the room moved except the three who had Marcus.

"Your punishment will come," Dante whispered in her ear. She froze. Dante was holding her. It was then that she felt the cold grip on her upper arms. When he let her go, she rubbed at her skin. His hands were freezing. Two bands the width of a man's hands encircled her upper arms. She had been marked by Dante himself.

Kyra locked her knees again as a whip was unfurled. She looked into Marcus's wonderful eyes. She wouldn't look away. She promised herself. The least she could do was be there for him.

Marcus, silent throughout the ordeal, was whipped until unconscious. Kyra stood and cried quietly for her friend. They'd brought him into this fight and he was suffering for it.

When they were done, she was surprised at how gently he was taken from the restraints. Six women filed into the room from a door Kyra hadn't seen. They helped as the Reapers picked Marcus up, placing him face first on a long board and carrying him from the room. The women clucked in concern after them, along with one cloaked figure.

Kyra turned and glared at Dante. She couldn't help it. "Now what? Would you like a pound of my flesh for opening the box?"

Dante gave her a sad look. "Do you know the story of Pandora's Box, child?"

"Of course. A Greek legend …" she started, but Dante waved her off.

"Yes, of course, the Greek version." He rolled his eyes. "The Greeks seem to get a great deal of credit for history that does not belong to them," Dante said. Soft murmurs of assent issued from the hooded occupants.

"Nevertheless, Pandora was given the box because of her inquisitiveness. Her punishment was the knowledge of the evil she had released into the world, but she kept one small thing. Do you know what that was?"

Kyra swallowed. "Hope," she whispered.

"As you have explained, my dear, the opening of the box was unintentional." He moved to his seat on the dais. "Your punishment is to have become a marked soul." He motioned to the bands of dark skin around each arm. "What you choose to do about that is up to you. Of course, the knowledge of releasing evil into the world is also punishment. But," he stopped and gave her a hard look, "of all the creatures that have graced my halls, I see hope in you that is pure and great. You have released evil, but your fight against it, past and future, shall free you. But you need to allow it. I would suggest you help in the efforts of finding and destroying Calliope before he can destroy the balance of the planes of existence."

"I would rather you whip me," Kyra said.

"Ah, but if I did, I have a feeling I would have a very angry Tracker knocking at my door. And that is bad business," he said.

"Is this all a game to you? Pieces to be moved around a board willy-nilly?" Kyra felt like a pawn, like she'd been used and was now being sent to bed without dinner.

She stomped over to him. "You scared the bloody hell out of me and whipped my friend! These are lives you are playing with, you bastard."

Someone in the room gasped, but Kyra was too far gone in her anger to stop now. She was in pain, had suffered through the Infernos listening and viewing the misdeeds of countless souls, hearing the screams of pain and death. She'd witnessed Marcus's whipping and had been marked by Dante. And she had released a horror upon the world that could destroy the planes of existence. Frankly, she'd had just about enough.

"How can you be so cruel?"

He moved so fast, she wasn't even able to take a breath before he was nose to nose with her. "I am the ruler of the Infernos, and I answer only to Satan himself. This game, as you put it, balances on a precarious perch that an Element, the closest race to Mortal of all the Others, couldn't hope to fully comprehend. If anyone knows how to play this game, it is I. You, child, should understand that. The Elements have hidden their heads in the sand for far too long. It is time they take part in the ultimate outcome of imMortals and man. You shall be that ambassador. As my Touched you will carry my mark and your soul will belong to me when you pass. You will answer to me when I request it."

"So I am to be you're what…" she stammered.

"My Touched." He said. "Like I explained the Elements have long been observers of the world. It is time for them to come out onto the field of battle and fight for what they believe in. With one of their own my Touched I think it will sway them toward fighting."

"Now leave before I change my mind and have you whipped. Or worse, turn you over to one of my sons as a concubine." Someone grabbed her where Dante's hands had burned her. She flinched but let the Reaper drag her out of the hall.

"You should be thankful. He could've had your soul ripped straight from your body. Not a pretty sight," snapped the Reaper who held her.

He led her to a set of doors. "What about Marcus?"

The Reaper removed his cloak, revealing he was the blond. "I am Victor, and I promise that he will be cared for and returned to the Mortal plan when he heals."

She followed Victor. "Marcus knew the punishment if something went wrong," he said over his shoulder. He held her back as a small, cloaked man shuffled past.

Victor opened a side door. She was amazed to see the cottage they'd been staying in ahead of her.

"We can open portals wherever we want," he explained.

"Then why did you lead us here the way you did?" Kyra asked incredulously.

"Because it was so dramatic," Victor smiled.

"You're a bastard too," Kyra snarled. "I'm an Air Element and the way we came was torture for me."

Victor laughed. "I am sure we will see each other again, Element." Kyra certainly hoped not and stepped through the Portal.

"One more thing," Victor said as he closed the door. "Once in the Infernos, we can manipulate time. It moves differently within each plane. Reapers are able to travel ahead, but not back—only forward and, of course, present."

"What does this have to do with me?" Kyra asked, so tired she couldn't think straight.

"You've been gone for six weeks."

She swung around but the portal was closed. The laughter of the Reaper drifted softly on the wind.

Kyra was left alone on the dirt driveway in Marshall, Montana staring at the house she'd shared with a team that had destroyed a monster, only to release an even worse horror onto the world.

Ryder felt like driving his fist through every single one of the stone statues in the courtyard. He'd been there for hours, which meant only God knew how long in the Mortal world. Reapers and Dante could bend time at will.

Ryder's patience almost spent, the small, cloaked man made his way down the path. It took everything he had not to shake the man.

"Dante will not see you," he said, his voice gravelly.

"I won't take no for an answer. I want to speak with him." The cloaked figure looked up. Ryder stared into a partially skeletal face, the other half burnt beyond recognition.

"Dante thought that might be your answer and bid me to tell you that the Element you seek is no longer with us." Ryder's heart skipped a beat.

"No longer with him? As in he sent her on her merry way? Or no longer with us because he sent her to Hell?" Ryder couldn't contain the rage of his words.

"Dante doesn't actually send souls to Hell. They are predestined for Hell, or not." Ryder grabbed the robed man.

"I don't really give a damn about any other soul than the one that belongs to Kyra. Where the hell is she?" he shouted unable to control himself.

"Put him down, Ryder," Victor said, coming down the walk.

"Where is she?" Ryder dropped the man and approached the Reaper.

"She received her punishment and we sent her back."

"She's alive?" Ryder almost couldn't believe it.

"Yes, the last time I saw her," Victor said.

"What was her punishment?"

Victor gave him a sad smile. "I am unable to give you that information, Tracker. Good luck finding her."

Victor reached out and touched Ryder on the shoulder, and Ryder felt as if he was jerked backwards right off his feet. When he landed, he slid across the hardwood floor of his bedroom, crashing against a bookshelf.

Chapter 13

She really had been gone for six weeks. And after she walked the six miles to town, Max was so shocked to see her, he actually fell off his stool.

He let her use the phone. Eric screamed at her for half an hour before he agreed to have the plane sent up for her. Max drove her to the private airport.

When he stopped, she thanked him for the ride. He grabbed her arm before she climbed out of the police car. "Ryder was really torn up when they took you."

"Really?" Kyra asked. Tears she could no longer control streaked down her face. "Did he try to come for me? What did he do after it was all done?"

"They left. All of them," Max said honestly. "Cleaned up and we told everyone it was an earthquake. Then they were gone. I didn't really see Ryder a lot during that week. He was hurting pretty bad."

She nodded. "But he left. They all left."

"Kyra, was he supposed to sit on that mountain and wait for you to come back? He didn't even know if you were alive." She hadn't expected Ryder to wait for her. He hadn't promised her anything. She shook herself.

"Thank you, Max, for everything. I'm glad your town is safe." She climbed from the car and walked to the tarmac.

Max watched her until the plane came, refueled, and then took off. She had been broken. Anyone could see that. He felt horrible for her. She had sacrificed a part of her soul to save his town.

Taking his phone out, he punched in Ryder's number, praying he was doing the right thing.

"What."

"Ry?" Max asked.

"No, it's Lykar. Who is this?"

"Lykar, it's Max. Is Ryder around?" Only silence met his inquiry.

"Hello?"

"If you have another monster, you'll have to find someone else to take it on. Ryder isn't available," Lykar said. Max could hear the fatigue in the Tracker's voice. Had any of them come out of this intact?

"No, nothing like that. But I thought … well. He's done so much, given so much, I thought …" Max closed his eyes and remembered the pain on Ryder's face the last time he'd seen him, and the pain on Kyra's face as well. "She came back today."

"WHAT?" Lykar shouted so loud, Max had to pull the phone away from his ear.

"She just walked into the police station like she was on a Sunday stroll. Except she was dressed to fight. I fell off my damn chair."

"Where is she now?"

"She left, Lykar. I saw her get on a plane not more than ten minutes ago."

"Why the fuck didn't you call us before that?" Lykar blasted.

"They both looked so broken," Max explained. "Broken in a way that tears at your heart. I didn't know if he would want to open that wound again."

"Thank you, Max. I'll relay your message to Ryder. You did the right thing."

"She's broken, Ly, and I don't know what or who she's going back to. Ry has you and the others, but my heart broke just looking into her eyes." He shook his head.

"Thank you, Max."

"RYDER!" Lykar shouted for his brother, doing it several more times before Falcon came out of his office.

"He went to the Infernos," Falcon said in his calm way.

250

"What?" Lykar raked a hand through his blond hair. "How long?"

"'Bout a week ago. If Dante grants him an audience, it'll be another week or so before he comes back." Falcon turned back to his office.

Lykar grabbed his older brother. "You don't understand—Max just called. Kyra was in Marshall today."

Falcon didn't say anything for several minutes, making Lykar want to shake the hell out of his brother. "Be that as it may, there is no way of contacting him now that he is in the Infernos. When he returns, we can give him the news."

With that, Falcon returned to his office. Lykar watched him go, wondering if anything ever ruffled Falcon's feathers.

"Are you going to get out of bed today?" Astrid asked, poking her head into Kyra's room.

"Maybe," Kyra replied but she highly doubted it. She hurt both inside and out. She had been home for four days, and each of the six Enforcers had come in to give her the what-for. She was so tired of getting screamed at to get out of bed, only to climb back in and cry some more.

"Daemon says that girls are nuts," the nine-year-old said, climbing onto the bed. She pushed Kyra over so she could lie down next to her.

"He's probably right," Kyra agreed. "Most girls are nuts. However, I am not a girl. I am a woman, and an Element Enforcer, and that makes me different."

Astrid giggled. "But we're girls. We have to stand up to the boys."

Kyra pulled herself up. "And just how do we do that?"

Astrid's little face screwed up hard in thought. "I have no idea," she finally said. "You're older. You should know more about these things."

Kyra tapped a finger on her chin in thought, then shook her head. "Nope, I have nothing."

Astrid jumped off the bed. "I'll go do some research on the Internet." She skipped from the room.

Two months ago that would've made Kyra smile but right now, it brought tears to her eyes. She wanted to be that innocent again.

She wanted Ryder.

She rolled over and screamed into her pillow. She'd promised herself that she wouldn't think about him, say his name, even think it.

Eric walked in without knocking. Kyra glared at him. "What if I'd been naked?" she asked.

"I would be scarred for life," he uttered

"I'm done being lectured, Eric. I'm older than all of you, and I'm being lectured like a child. I'm done with it." She crossed her arms over her chest.

"Yeah, and saying that with Daffy Duck pajamas on makes it so profound," Eric said, holding back a laugh. She stuck her tongue out at him and threw a pillow at his face. He Phased out and then back.

"Spring equinox is in two days. Do you think you can pull your fat butt out of bed by then?" he asked, leaning against one of her bedposts.

"I do not have a fat butt," she said defensively.

"You will if you stay in bed any longer."

"Of course I'll be there. Have you heard from Fiona?" She'd gone to stay with the Druids who were close to Marshall when everything fell to shit.

"Yep. Last night. She'll be back day after the equinox." He smiled and flung himself onto the bed next to her, tucking his hands behind his head. His bright blue eyes stared up at her ceiling.

"Love sucks," he said.

Kyra snuggled down and put her head on his shoulder. "Yes, it does."

"Let's you and I grow old together, single and grumpy and fighting off the world."

"Okay," she said sadly.

252

Eric rolled over so he could look at her. Kyra looked at her brother. His blond hair curled at the ends, hung down just a little long. While she thought it needed cutting, it seemed to drive all the women nuts. He had kind blue eyes and broad shoulders perfect for leaning on.

"You going to be okay?"

"Yes," she said around the tears that choked her.

He jumped off the bed. "Just remember. Your butt gets bigger every second you lay in that bed."

She threw a pillow at the back of his head, which hit him perfectly because he couldn't see it coming.

The morning of the equinox was bright and beautiful. Kyra stood at her window, watching the sun rise over the hills of the Haven. She opened her window and took a deep breath of the fresh air.

She'd forced herself to get out of bed yesterday. And then again this morning, if only so her butt didn't expand any further.

Astrid came sliding in on stocking feet. "Guess what?"

"What?" Kyra asked.

"We have a visitor for the party tonight," she said, jumping up and down with excitement.

Kyra didn't know anyone was coming to celebrate the new spring with them.

"Really? I hadn't heard of anyone coming." She headed for the door. Eric had some explaining to do.

"He showed up real late last night. Daemon thought I was asleep. He's a looker," Astrid whistled.

Kyra stopped and looked at the nine-year-old. "Excuse me?"

The little girl fanned her face. "You know, hot …" Astrid raised an eyebrow and touched the tip of her tongue with her finger before flipping out her hip and sizzling that finger against her rump.

"Where did you learn that?" Kyra asked.

"TV."

Kyra only shook her head. "You have school, my dear."

"But I want to meet him too."

"After school will be soon enough." The little girl huffed and turned back down the hall.

As Kyra headed to Eric's study, she heard two male voices. Although it wasn't in her nature to be timid, she knocked politely.

"Come in."

Kyra swung the door open and froze.

Marcus rose from his chair and smiled at Kyra, who promptly burst into tears and flung herself into the Fallen's arms.

"How are you?" he asked, laughing.

"When did you get back?" she hiccupped. "Are you in any pain? Sit." She pushed him back toward the chair.

"Kyra." He grabbed her hands. "I'm fine. ImMortal, remember?" Kyra nodded, brushing tears from her face. "I just wanted to stop and see how you were doing."

"Ohh," she waved, "you know me. I'm fine. All healed up and ready for the next fight against big bad evil."

Marcus raised one eyebrow, and then exchanged a look with Eric. "Let's go for a walk." He took her hand and led her from the room.

They didn't say anything until they were outside, the sun shining down on them. Kyra soaked it up.

"What are you doing?" Marcus finally asked.

"What do you mean?" Kyra asked, pretending to be whole.

"I mean, why aren't you with Ryder?" She flinched when he said the name. "See? You can't even stand to hear his name." She closed her eyes.

Kyra turned to Marcus, pulling him to a halt. "I'm hanging by a thread here."

"I know where he is." Kyra stumbled back as if he'd threatened her. "If you ask, I will tell you. I understand that you might not have known where he was when you got back.

And that is why you aren't with him, happy, right this second."

"He didn't want me." The words burst out.

"What are you talking about?" Marcus asked incredulously.

"I mean, he wanted me. But not a forever type of want. He lusted after me. We made no promises to each other." Kyra started walking again. "I will not ask where he is because I will not go out and find him. If he wanted me, he should've tried to come for me in the Infernos. But he didn't, did he? Nope. He cleaned up the mess and went home, wherever the hell that is."

She continued walking and finally turned to see Marcus hadn't moved. She walked back.

"What?"

"You don't always have to lose, you know."

It struck like a knife, because it was so close to what Ryder had told her. "Fighting for what you want," he poked her in the chest with his finger, "isn't a bad thing, Kyra."

"I have no idea what you're talking about," Kyra said, trying not to cry.

"You fight for everyone, every cause that needs a champion. Except for yourself." Marcus shook his head. "You should try that once, and see what happens."

"He didn't want me, Marcus." And then she was crying and turned around and walked back to the house, tears streaming down her face.

She grabbed two bottles of tequila and headed for her room. Eric stopped her on the stairs.

She shook her head. "Get me when it's time for the equinox."

"Don't do this to yourself," Eric said, his words laced with the pain he felt for his sister. "I love you too much to see you hurt so desperately. Marcus can help you find him."

She was so tired, so physically and mentally tired. She wasn't sure her legs would hold her much longer. "We didn't make any promises to each other, Eric. He explained to me before we even got involved that he didn't need love, just the release for his lust."

"Maybe things have changed," Eric said.

Kyra popped the cork from one of the bottles and took a healthy swig. "Yep, everything changed. I am in love with a man unable to love me back."

Eric growled. "I'll kill that bastard if I ever get the chance."

Kyra laughed but it was a hollow sound. "Do you really think that would make anything better?"

"I can't stand to see you like this," he said.

Kyra took another drink. "Between that monster, the Infernos, Simon, and Ryder," she choked on his name, "this is all that's left, Eric."

Eric took her by the shoulders and shook her. "Bullshit! Don't let the darkness win."

One lonely tear coursed down her cheek. Her legs wobbled. If she didn't make it to her room soon, she wouldn't make it at all.

Kyra pulled away from her brother and took several steps up the staircase. "I think it might be too late for that." She didn't look back as she moved away from him.

Eric had to carry her out to the clearing where the equinox ritual would be held. The moon was full and there was a slight bite in the air. Kyra swigged more tequila; it was keeping her plenty warm.

"Damn girl," Daemon swore when Eric placed her in the chair they'd brought out for her.

"Shut up," she tried to say, but it came out more like "ut'p."

She watched the ritual as the darkness of winter was erased while the beauty of spring was reintroduced to the earth. Spring would win out over the death of winter. They danced and drank and sang and then Eric gave his blood to the earth, providing it with the nutrients it needed to thrive. That had always been Kyra's place, but she was too drunk to stand up. She shook her head and guzzled the remaining liquor in her bottle.

She leaned back and stared up at the stars, closing her eyes when they started to dance and swirl in their own pattern. When she opened them again, they were moving so fast it made her dizzy. "Eric, the earth is spinning."

Eric laughed. "Nope. That's just you." He helped her into bed and tucked her in, just as she used to do for him when he was little.

"Sleep it off, china doll." He kissed her forehead. "Tomorrow is another day, and the sun will rise and bring with it light and love," he promised.

Kyra prayed to the Gods that he was right. She really needed a little light and love in her dark life.

Kyra stared up at her ceiling, imagining the stars and patterns that had danced for her just an hour ago.

"Oh, Ryder, I need you so badly," she whispered. Curling into a ball, she passed out.

"I need you, Ryder," Kyra moaned. Ryder's eyes snapped open and he looked around his room. He'd just climbed into bed after returning from the Infernos. Kyra was alive, and tomorrow he was going to find her.

Then he heard it again. "Ryder, I need you."

The words whispered across his cheek. He jerked back as something moved next to him. He turned to see Kyra lying on her side, her beautiful blue eyes sparkling in the dark.

"I need you, Ryder," she said again.

"I'm dreaming," he told her, barely able to breathe, afraid that the slightest movement would cause her to disappear.

She smiled that perfect, beautiful smile and sat up, letting the covers fall away, revealing her naked form. Ryder felt his entire body respond. She held out her arms. "Then let's dream together."

"Bloody hell." Ryder couldn't turn from her. He'd worked so hard in the last couple of weeks. He knew this was a bad idea but he hadn't dreamed about her at all, not once, not since she'd walked into Hell. And now here she was, naked, her arms wide open.

He gathered her in his arms and kissed her. She tasted so damn good, it was intoxicating. It filled every inch of the emptiness that had consumed him.

"I've missed you," he breathed into her mouth. His tongue delved in to taste her, swirled around hers, as he sucked it into his mouth. "Missed your taste, Gods, your smell," he moaned.

She pulled back and smiled. "But I'm right here, Ryder."

He kissed her, covered her body with all of his, soaking up every inch of heat she possessed, trying to suck her right into him. He would never let her go. He would fight his brothers or anything that came knocking at the door. The Gods themselves wouldn't take her from him again.

Kyra kissed his cheek, then each eye. She slowly covered every inch of his face. He fell back as she straddled him. She kissed his throat, her hands roaming everywhere at the same time. Blue sparks of light ignited and fired into the night. She kissed his shoulders, his chest, moving down his body. She bypassed the part that needed her the most and continued to his feet.

"I need to memorize you. Commit you to memory forever," she whispered against his foot. "There is never enough time to encompass you totally."

"Why would you need to memorize me?" Ryder moaned. Not sure why she would say something like that. But his brain wasn't functioning clearly; she was driving him insane with her hands, her lips, and her tongue. Then she had him by the base of his cock, and he felt like his world was coming apart. His eyes shot open as she kissed the head, a blue spark flying from her lips to the head of his penis. Ryder nearly screamed in pure ecstasy. He'd never felt anything as wonderful as a single touch from this woman.

She suckled him until he was out of his mind and pulled her up so he could kiss her. She smiled against his lips. "Need to love you, memorize you."

"Yes," he promised her, not sure exactly what he was promising, but he didn't care. The rational side of his brain screamed this was only a dream. But that didn't matter, she was here and in his arms and he was never going to let her go. He didn't know how he was going to do it, but he wouldn't lose her again, he didn't think he would be able to live through it a second time.

Ryder kissed her drawing in her smell and taste; he gave her the same treatment, kissing every inch of her body. Memorizing her as she had done to him. Once he reached her toes, he moved up to the juncture between her legs.

"Ryder," she moaned, her head tossing back and forth. Her golden hair spread across his pillows, and her body bowed up, thrusting her beautiful breasts high. He grabbed one, tweaking the nipple as he sank his tongue into her.

She moaned, and he felt her orgasm roll over her as he made love to her with his mouth.

He lapped it up, thanking the Gods for her, promising that if they didn't take her away, he would treat her the way she should be treated for all of eternity. He would spend the rest of his life making love to her, making her smile, making her happy. He moved so that he was between her legs, his cock throbbing to the point of pain. He would make up for ever hurting her, for fighting with her. For not understanding how much he loved her before he lost her. For not going after her like he should have. For not fighting for her. That was what tore at him. He hadn't fought for her like he should have. He believed he didn't deserve this love, that it was a wasted emotion. Ryder leaned back and looked down into her face. How stupid he had been. The only thing that had been wasted was time.

"I'm never going to let you go, Kyra," he said as he slid into her. She gripped him like a vise as he slid home. "You belong to me for eternity," he snarled in exotic, pleasurable pain.

"Mine," he moaned into the crook of her neck. He licked her behind the ear, breathing in the scent that was uniquely her. "Mine, forever. Never letting you go!" he shouted as he came, pumping his seed into her.

When his orgasm passed, he fell to the bed next to her. "You belong to me now, Kyra," he whispered.

She laughed. The soft sound made him smile in return. "But you already let me go." Her words whispered over him like an arctic breeze. He reached for her and came up empty-handed. His brain screamed with the knowledge that she wasn't actually there. Pain erupted in his chest where his heart lay.

"Kyra?" Ryder sat up in his bed searching for her.

"Memorize you," she whispered. Appearing on the other side of him, she cupped his face, kissing him deeply.

He pulled back. "Kyra?" He felt like his world was unraveling as she Phased out again, disappearing for a moment.

"I would have given you my heart, my very soul. Everything I am and everything I will be." Her words barely a whisper on the heavy air of the bedroom.

"Kyra!" Ryder shouted. He stumbled from the bed, the sheets wrapping around him. He fell to his knees. By the time he gained his feet, there was nothing left. Not even a trace of the mist of her Phasing.

"I love you, Ryder." He felt the words brush against his cheek, and then he was alone. He felt it all the way to his soul.

Alone in his room, he looked around frantically. He smelled the pillows where her scent lingered. He had dreamed it? He threw his head back and hollered at the pain that lanced through him. And for the first time in his adult life, he cried. For what he had lost, what could have been. He lay back down, crushing the pillow her head had lain on. He crushed it to his chest and face, trying to soak up the ghostlike smell of her. When nothing remained, he rolled over and stared at the ceiling.

She belonged to him, and damn it, he was going to get her back. He should've done more, went to the Infernos sooner. What had he been thinking?

It struck him like a bullet to the head. He hadn't thought he deserved her, had languished in pain knowing he deserved every second of it. She was pure light and love and after two millennia, he didn't believe he deserved her. He was an utter fool. The dumbest lovesick fool in the world.

He was going to have to pay for that. But he would pay anything he had to just hold her again. He chuckled. If he knew Kyra, she would make him pay and pay.

He jumped from the bed and jerked on a pair of boxers. He left his room, pounding on doors as he went. "Everyone up. Time for a meeting."

Doors opened and several of his brothers looked out as if Ryder had lost his mind. "Get up and meet me downstairs in ten minutes."

Falcon stepped from his room, tying his robe. "What the hell is going on, Ryder?"

"I'm going for her, Falcon. She is mine, and I won't live without her." Several of his brothers stood staring between the two.

"At least you've made up your mind. But it's going to take all eight of us. Find Cameron," Falcon said, turning back to his room. "I'm going to get dressed."

Cameron threw an ice pack to Ryder as he came back into the dining room. Ryder nodded and put it on his knuckles. Lykar lay passed out on the floor. It took everything he had not to kick his brother while he was down.

Max had called him over a week ago, telling him she had just appeared and then flew away on a plane. It didn't matter that he'd just come back from the Infernos himself. Lykar should've been waiting for him, to tell him that he knew she was back. After Ryder called Max and got the full story, he felt like a bigger ass than before. She'd felt abandoned when she had come back to Marshall and they were all gone, as though they'd never been there, like they didn't care whether she returned from or died in the Infernos.

Skylar came into the room and flung a large file on the table. Papers flew everywhere. A sealed plastic bag slid over to Ryder.

"So I've put together everything I know about the Elements and Druids." Everyone turned and stared at Skylar, as if they'd never seen the man before.

"What? I'm good for some things, you Neanderthals. Research interests me. I have a file on everything we've done."

Ryder whooped. "Damn, Sky, you rock." He sorted though the papers, mixed with pictures of Kyra. Ryder traced the soft line of her jaw. He wanted her so badly, he couldn't think straight.

"I've been able to track them to Illinois."

"The state of Illinois?" Ryder asked.

"They are as secretive as we are. So, yes, the closest I could come was the state of Illinois." Skylar looked hurt. "I figured once we got that close, you'd be able to sniff her out."

"You know what? You're right, Sky. Thank you."

They made a plan and discussed options. The sun was just rising when they had the basic plan set up. "Let's get a couple hours of sleep. It will take that long to get a plane."

Ryder gathered the information and stood. The Ziploc bag hit the floor. As he bent down to pick it up, he noticed it held a piece of black cloth.

Sky grabbed it. "You don't want that," he said, shoving it into the papers he had.

"Why?" Ryder asked. "What is it?"

Sky took several steps back. "Don't get mad."

Ryder growled deep in his throat as Sky talked. "Geez, you're always so easy to set off. You should work on your temper. Having a bonded mate should calm him down, shouldn't it?" Sky leveled the question at the rest of the brothers, who all shrugged. None of them knew what would happen with Ryder taking a mate.

"What is in the bag, Skylar?"

"Evidence."

Ryder's eyes narrowed. "What type of evidence?"

"We are Trackers, man. The three senses are what we rely on. If we don't have that, we don't have anything, right? Touch. Taste. Smell." Sky looked around the room again for affirmation.

Ryder scrambled over the table, tackling his brother as he went for the bag.

He tore open the plastic and the smell almost knocked him out. He saw stars for a moment. His gland swelled, choking him. He leaned over and threw up, the pheromone making him ill.

"That's just disgusting," one brother said, though Ryder wasn't sure which one. The contents of the bag spilled onto the floor. A black T-shirt, a wad of hair, and a toothbrush.

When they all got a look at what Ryder was holding, another brother added to the conversation. "Well, that's just creepy."

"Like, stalker creepy," another brother agreed.

"Damn it." Skylar untangled himself from Ryder, who was still trying to recover from the assault of Kyra's scent. Ryder buried his face into the T-shirt. "It's research and information," Skylar said.

Ryder gave his brother a hard look. "Thank you, Sky." He helped him to his feet.

"Wait," Lykar interrupted. "Sky steals a toothbrush, hair, and a T-shirt from your mate and he gets a handshake? I tell you she's still alive, and I get knocked out. What Sky did was way creepier than me not saying anything."

Skylar disagreed and the three started to argue.

"Same fight, different topic," Falcon said, pushing himself away from the table. "I suggest the rest of you get some sleep. I sure as hell am," he said over the brothers.

He was heading up the stairs when he heard wood crack and then splinter apart. Falcon shook his head. A houseful of men wasn't always a good thing.

263

Chapter 14

"Damn, how big is this damn state?" Cameron snarled.

"Much bigger than I originally thought." They'd been searching for two days. And not a scent of her anywhere. Ryder was becoming a little insane.

"What next?" Cam asked Falcon.

"We wait to hear from the others."

The phone rang, making Cameron jump. "Sup?"

"Where is Ryder?" Lykar asked.

"North."

"Good. I got something. I'll call in an hour. Get everyone back to base."

"Sure thing." Cameron relayed the message to Falcon and they called the brothers. Hopefully, their wild goose chase would soon be over.

Cameron didn't understand what the big deal was. Women were interchangeable. One was as good as another. Why Ryder had gone all primal on this one, he would probably never understand. And it would probably kill him. Cameron would miss his brother, but you choose your own fate. Cameron couldn't think of a single woman who was worth this type of trouble.

The sun was just setting when Lykar pulled up to the side of the road where the other SUV was parked.

Ryder climbed from the vehicle. "What do you have?" Sky pulled out a topo map.

"Okay, so the estate is basically a circle. The center is where the house is located. You can't get to it unless you go straight down the driveway. They have this place locked down—like, Fort Knox locked down."

Falcon nodded. "Cameras, motion detectors, lasers.

Everything you can think of, they have. If we so much as sneeze within ten feet of the estate, it's going to set the whole damn place off. They do not want anyone to know they are here."

"So what's the plan?" Ryder asked.

"Only one option. Straight in, guns blazing."

Ryder shook his head. "They're Elements, and therefore not imMortal. Guns blazing will injure someone. That is the last thing I want to do."

"I know this sounds crazy but what about knocking? Why do we have to break in?" Lykar asked.

"Tried to make contact this afternoon. They wouldn't even answer the inner come." Falcon offered looking over at the trees that surrounded the estate. "Pretending like no one is home is going to get them Trackers on their front door step whether they like it or not."

"Okay so guns blazing?" Cameron reaffirmed.

Ryder shook his head, "No guns."

Cameron moaned. "Where's the fun in that?"

Ryder slapped him upside the head. "Don't make me shoot you, puppy."

"Let's wait till full dark. That will give us a small advantage. Ryder, you're the fastest so you'll reach the house first. You and Marlee will set up a charge to get their attention. But I bet by that point, they'll already know you're there." Ryder nodded and rolled his head on his shoulders. He stood and looked out at the estate through a pair of binoculars. She was there. He could smell her on the wind. He was going to get her and never let her go.

Her door was thrown open and Eric stomped in.

"I'm done!" he shouted.

"Congratulations," Kyra said sarcastically. When Eric didn't say anything more, she looked up at him from her window seat. "What the hell are you doing?"

He grabbed her hand and dragged her down to the living room. The room was busting at the seams with everything that Kyra liked.

"What did you do, Eric?" Her eyes filled with tears.

"This is something to make you smile, not cry." Eric threw his hands in the air. "Damn it. Now you're crying."

Kyra walked into the room, running her hands over the fluffy bunny that was as tall as she was. A set of soft flannel pajamas and new bed sheets. Extra pillows, imported chocolate.

"Eric, why did you do this?"

"Because I would give anything in the world to see you smile again. You do things for everyone. This is my way of saying thank you." Eric stepped up to her and cupped her cheek. "I miss your smile, Kyra."

She tried to smile for him, but she just couldn't do it.

"Oh, now I'll have to pull out the big guns," Eric said dramatically. He picked up a Bugs Bunny pillow by one of Bugs' ears and swung it around, hitting Kyra upside the head.

Her mouth dropped open. "What the hell?"

He hit her again. "Smile, damn it."

She hit the pillow away as he swung it back at her. "Stop hitting me."

"Smile." This time it was Tweety along the other side of her head.

"Damn it, Eric, this isn't funny." He was swinging the pillow wildly now and she screamed, scrambling for a pillow to protect herself. She ended up with Elmer and slammed it into her brother.

"Ah, you hit like a girl, china doll."

She felt her eyes bug out and Eric started to really laugh. She hit him so hard, he stumbled. She hit him again. He tackled her down to the floor. Kyra screamed as he held her down. Straddling her, he pinned her arms under his knees.

"Eric, get off me," she struggled beneath him. She might be older but he was definitely bigger.

266

Her brother tapped an index finger on his chin. "Now that I have you where I want you, my pretty, whatever shall I do with you?" he said in his best villainous voice. He curled a pretend mustache.

"You are not ten anymore, Eric." She wiggled under him but knew from past experience, she wasn't going anywhere until he let her go.

He tapped her forehead. "Kyra, are you in there?"

"Stop."

"I would like to speak with my sister Kyra, not grumpy Kyra," he said while making a face and sticking his tongue out at her. "Grumpy Kyra sucks."

Kyra pierced her lips together. "Ah ha!" he yelled. "I think I might have her!"

He made another face and released her arms so he could tickle her. She screamed and tried to scramble away, not even realizing she was laughing.

"It's not fair! You're bigger than me!" she screamed, picking up anything she could reach to fling at her brother. He was laughing too. He let her go for just a moment, flipped his hair out of his eyes, and let loose a war cry that would wake the dead.

Kyra screamed out in laughter, curling to protect herself as her brother tickled her relentlessly.

After several minutes, they were both breathing hard and lying on the floor. Kyra sat up and grabbed a box of chocolates. Opening it, she offered him a piece. Eric popped one in his mouth. Kyra did the same.

She laughed. "Don't you think it odd that a brother and sister would be best friends?"

"Nope," Eric said, grabbing another piece of chocolate. "Besides, who else would be friends with you?"

She slapped him on the shoulder. "Honestly, you were the grumpiest child I'd ever met."

Eric shook his head. "I don't recall it that way at all."

"Yes, because as far as you're concerned, you were born a full-grown man with all the strengths and abilities of the house of Diamond." She waved her hands dramatically.

"Yes, well, I do have a reputation to maintain," he said with his best British accent.

Kyra laughed so hard, her sides hurt. "What else do you have in here?"

She sat up on her knees and started digging through the pile of goodies. "Eww, cream soda?" She grabbed a bottle out of the ice bucket and handed another to Eric. She popped it open and took a big slurp, and then belched.

Eric let out a whoop of laughter just as every alarm in the house went off. They stared at each other for a moment.

Realizing what was happening, they jumped to their feet, soda falling to the ground and bursting into twin foam geysers.

"Freaking hell!" Eric Phased out and back on the other side of the sofa.

Kyra stared at him for a moment. "Are we under attack?" she screamed over the sirens. She couldn't help but laugh. She was coated in cream soda, surrounded by mountains of stuffed animals and cartoon characters, alarms blaring loudly enough to shatter glass.

She couldn't stop laughing as she climbed over the sofa, moving toward Eric and their stash of weapons in the sideboard. Eric handed her two guns and took out a couple for himself.

"You can stop laughing now," Eric said as he checked to make sure they were loaded.

"I just think this is so weird. How can we be under attack? Nobody can get within a hundred feet of The Haven."

The blast picked them both up and threw them across the room. Kyra flashed back to a motel room in Marshall as she flew through the air and slammed against a wall, only to have another wall slam against her.

However, the wall against her was breathing. In fact, he had his head buried behind her right ear. Without thinking, her chin dropped and she inhaled his exhalation.

"Gods, you smell good," Came an unexpected voice she never thought she'd hear again. "But a little sweeter than normal."

Kyra couldn't move, could barely bring herself to breathe as Ryder pressed against her. His body jumped several times and she realized Eric was shooting him.

She threw her hands up, pointing her guns to the ceiling. "Stop shooting!"

"Then tell him to let you go!" Eric snarled.

"Ryder?" Ryder inhaled, but when he didn't release Kyra, Eric shot him again.

"Stop!" Kyra screamed. She knew being shot wouldn't kill him but it definitely hurt him. Wait—she didn't care about this man. She'd convinced herself of that, hadn't she? They had no future together.

"Ryder, you need to let me go," she said quietly into his ear.

"Do you have any idea how much I've missed you, Blue?" he inhaled again. "And I'm not moving an inch until the psycho behind me with a twitchy trigger finger puts down his guns."

Kyra leaned over Ryder's shoulder so she could see her brother. "Put your guns down."

"When he lets you go."

"Eric, he will release me the moment you put your guns down," Kyra said calmly.

"And just how the hell do you know that?" Eric asked.

"Trust me."

Eric said something foul and lowered his guns. The moment they were no longer pointed at his back, Ryder released Kyra, turning to her brother.

Kyra leaned against the wall for support. "Um, Ryder, what the hell are you doing here?"

When he didn't immediately answer, she turned to Eric. Had she fallen down the rabbit hole *again*? "Would you mind pinching me?"

Eric gave her the strangest look and then stepped up to her and hit her not very gently on the forehead with the butt of his gun.

She made a very unladylike sound. "Pinch, you dumb ass, not pistol whip."

"Let's get back to the fact that we're being attacked," Eric said as three more men clambered through the man-sized hole now where the front window had been.

Kyra jumped in front of her brother. She held up her guns. "Don't shoot."

The alarms went off and she could hear shooting in other parts of the house. She ran to the intercom, screaming into it. "EVERYONE! STOP SHOOTING!"

Still rubbing her forehead, she turned back to Ryder. He was rubbing his shoulder where Eric had shot him.

"Ryder," she said very calmly because she felt as if she might be losing her mind. "What the hell are you doing?"

Now that he was standing in front of her, he was speechless. She was dressed in crazy cartoon pajamas, which he had to admit looked damn sexy on her, surrounded by stuffed animals and cartoon characters, food and beverages. In fact, Kyra was dripping something sweet and wet.

"You're Ryder?" Eric asked, fury lacing each syllable.

Ryder nodded. Eric raised his gun and shot him again, this time in the leg.

"That hurts," Ryder pinned Eric with a dark look.

"Good." Eric smiled. "Now get the hell out of my house. You are not welcome here."

Kyra jumped between them again. "Have you heard of a door?"

"Wasn't sure you'd let me in," Ryder groused, rubbing his leg and glaring at her brother.

"Idiot. I should shoot him again. You might've tried the door first before blowing a hole in the side of my house," Eric growled. He was nearly speechless, he was so angry. Kyra had never seen him this mad before. Throwing his hands in the air, he swore, "But now you're bleeding all over my Persian rug." Eric stomped over to a pile of new cartoon-character towels.

Kyra jumped forward, waving her gun. "Not Daffy." She grabbed the towel out of his hands and handed him another. "He's not an idiot, by the way," she said.

"Seriously?" Eric threw the towel in the general direction of Ryder and looked at Kyra. "He just busted through the wall with explosives and you're defending him?"

Eric swung back to Ryder. Ryder knew that Kyra and Eric weren't related by blood, but they looked a great deal alike, with the same eye color and similar hair. They fought like he and his brothers did, which made him smile.

"You're a lunatic," Eric said when Ryder smiled. "Now get out. Just use the way you came in." He pointed at the broken window and sizable hole in the wall.

"I'm not going anywhere without Kyra."

"Not likely." Eric took on a predatory stance.

Kyra's mouth dropped open and just as quickly snapped it shut. She gave Ryder a mutinous glare.

"How did you find me?" she asked.

"Um, Tracker, remember?" he asked in return.

Eric barked. "You aren't so much as touching another hair on her head, much less taking her from this house."

Ryder rolled his eyes. "For the record, you're not at the top of my list of people I like right now, either."

Kyra rolled her eyes. "Are the two of you going to have a pissing contest now?"

The door to the room flew open as she said it, through which walked every single occupant of the house, including their old cook, who looked ready to faint from terror. They were herded in by four heavily armed men. Xavier was bleeding from the shoulder and Daemon was holding Astrid close. Marcus, who was still staying with them, sauntered in at the end of the group like he owned the joint.

Kyra looked around the room. "Have you all lost your minds?" She glared at Ryder's brothers. "Put those guns away right now. There are woman and children in this house."

One guy dropped his gun immediately. The others looked to Ryder before holstering their weapons.

"Good hell, Bowen, get a set, would ya?" Skylar shook his head in disgust as he holstered his weapon.

"And all we're missing is the mouthy Lycan," Kyra threw her hands in the air in agitation.

Marlee chose that exact moment to stick her head through the gaping hole. "I don't like to be shot at." She climbed in, outfitted in a red leather cat-suit.

"Seriously, Marlee, a cat-suit? Isn't that an oxymoron?" Kyra asked, shaking her head.

Marlee shrugged. "Only to anyone who really knows me." Her eyes changed and went feral for a moment. Then she winked at Kyra.

Kyra narrowed her eyes. "Bag?" She held out her hand.

Marlee smiled, reached through the hole in the wall, and grabbed a large duffel bag, dangling it from her fingers.

"How much exactly do you have in there?" Kyra wasn't sure she wanted the answer.

"Enough to level the house," Marlee said, grinning.

Kyra grabbed the bag and turned to X. "Lock this up. And if she asks for it back, shoot her."

Marlee laughed. "Plenty more where that came from, sweetheart."

Kyra turned to Ryder. "And why couldn't you use the door?" she practically screamed. It was either that or grind her teeth to dust. When Ryder didn't answer immediately, she turned on Marcus. "And why haven't you done anything to stop this … this … attack?"

"Honestly?" he asked, looking from her to Ryder. She nodded. "Because when I realized what was going on, I couldn't wait to see how Ryder was actually going to explain his actions." Marcus looked at Ryder as he said it. "Because this is a little crazy even for a Neanderthal Tracker."

Kyra felt her eye start to twitch. There was just no way this was happening.

One of the brothers snorted. "Has a point."

Ryder had at least put his guns away. "Kyra belongs with me."

"The hell she does." This from Eric.

"Bad choice of words, bro." Skylar grumbled.

"That was just stupid." Kyra wasn't even sure who said that or who said: "Over my dead body."

Kyra was totally overwhelmed, so she did the one thing she had control over: she turned and walked out. It was too much, Ryder was there in her home and he was fighting for her. Just the thought of it turned her stomach. She wanted nothing more than to throw herself into his arms but then the pain lanced through her he could never love her the way she needed him to. Had the entire world lost their freaking minds? She thought as she stomped up to her room. Maybe if she climbed in bed, when she woke up, the world would make sense again. Regrettably, it was the same thought she'd had for several weeks now.

"You have your answer. Now get the hell out of my house." Eric glared at Ryder.

Ryder couldn't believe she had walked away from him. "I just need five minutes with her." He headed toward the door.

"No." Eric blocked his way. "Do you have any idea what shape she was in when she returned from the Infernos? The Infernos, you prick. Not to mention the bullshit you put her through."

Each word was like a knife in his heart. Ryder looked at the door, willing it to open, for her to come back and just speak to him.

"In his defense, not that I'm taking sides," Marcus said, folding his arms over his chest, "he really had no choice in the matter. Plus, if I'm not mistaken, he was gravely injured, trying to keep her from that fate."

Ryder dropped his head. "I admit, I didn't do enough. It will be a decision I will regret for the rest of my life. And I did go after her, after a time."

"Don't you dare make me feel sorry for you. She is the strongest, hardest female I know. She fights better than most men, has a will of iron. And somewhere along the line, from what you did to her and the Infernos and that mission, she broke. I won't give you the chance to do it again, damn it. I actually got her to smile for the first time tonight, until you barged in."

What Ryder would've given to hear her laughter. He turned to his brothers.

"Your call," Falcon said.

They had followed him, all of them, to fight for him and the woman he loved. Ryder straightened his shoulders. He'd be damned if he was going to leave without at least speaking with her.

"Get everyone back to where they belong. Lock the house down." Ryder headed for the door. Eric pulled him to a stop. Ryder drew his gun and placed it at the other man's temple. "I just want to speak with her."

Eric's eyes, so like Kyra's it hurt to look at him, were glazed with fury.

"You wouldn't dare hurt me. I'm her brother and if you did, she would never speak to you again," Eric said, pressing his head against the barrel of the gun.

"Damn it," Ryder lowered his weapon exasperated.

Skylar stepped up to one side of Eric and Lykar the other. "Give him a chance, man," Lykar pleaded on his behalf.

Sky tried to grab him, but he Phased just like Kyra.

Eric was now standing in front of the door. "You have ten minutes."

Ryder didn't even stop to thank him, just pushed him out of the way. He followed her scent, taking the stairs two at a time. He nearly beat her door down when he knocked.

"GO AWAY."

"Open the door, Kyra."

"No."

He didn't have this kind of time, so he did what he knew and kicked in the door. Kyra was standing next to the window, arms crossed defensively over her chest.

"Somehow I knew you were going to do that," she said.

Ryder was bombarded by her smell. The only thing he could think to do was touch and taste her. It made him mute for a moment. As he gathered his wits, he replaced the door and slid a heavy chair in front of it.

"What are you doing?"

"I don't want to be disturbed," he said, looking at the barrier.

"Do you know anything about me?" Kyra asked and disappeared.

A slight knock on the door.

"Would you like to move the chair now?" He pushed it out of the way and opened the door so she could reenter her room. "You have five minutes."

"Damn it, Kyra. What was I supposed to do?" Ryder asked her. It wasn't like the two months had been easy for him.

"Exactly what you did. You weren't given a choice, Ryder." He looked up hopefully into her eyes but flat, emotionless blue stared back at him. "You had no idea if I was ever coming back, or where I would pop out when or if I did. Marcus at least popped out at home."

"Tell me what happened."

"No." She shook her head. "It's over now."

"What happened to you, Kyra?" he couldn't help but ask. She had been strong, a fighter, but right now, she was exactly as Eric had said.

Tears filled her eyes. "I have no idea what you're talking about. Why don't you go downstairs, apologize to my brother, and maybe the two of you could talk it out. Because he keeps asking me the same damn question."

She walked away from him into what looked like a bathroom, slamming the door behind her. He listened as she started to cry. He moved to the door but couldn't bring himself to break through another one to get her. He heard her shower turn on and before his body took over, he left the room and headed downstairs.

Ryder walked up to Eric. "My sincerest apologizes for breaking into your home the way I did. I will, of course, pay for the repairs."

Eric looked at him, one eyebrow rising slightly. He finally nodded. "Thank you. I accept your apology, although because of Kyra, I still don't like you."

Ryder couldn't blame him. "I understand, but you have to know, I'm here because I love your sister and would do anything in the world for her."

They stood staring at each other, neither willing to break.

"Good hell," Marcus finally said, "everyone sit."

"Who the hell put you in charge, Fallen?" Ryder said.

"Ryder, take a seat or get the fuck out," Marcus said with a great deal of feeling.

Ryder sat down. Marcus was the last one standing. "For the Trackers, do you know that Air carries with it the memories of what was?"

"Cool," Skylar said.

"An Air Element with Kyra's abilities is able to not only see but hear what is carried on the wind. She heard things, sensed things, in the windy valleys and over the Lake of Souls. That tore at her," Marcus started. "She was in so much pain by the time we got to Dante's Fortress she wasn't even able to stand without assistance." A shadow passed over Marcus's face. "It's too fucking windy there. And we walked for miles."

Marcus had a dark look in his eyes before he shook himself and continued. "When we were finally granted access to Dante, she was spent. It was like they knew what would happen by walking her through the valleys. It was part of her punishment. I have never appeared in the Infernos so far from the Fortress."

"What happened to her?" Ryder demanded.

"Dante laid down the sentence. A pound of flesh."

Eric and Ryder both shot to their feet. "He whipped her?" Ryder was barely able to get the words out.

Marcus sighed. "No, but he made her stand there and watch while they took a pound of my flesh. I found out after I'd recovered that she was made to watch. You both know her, and can imagine what that did to her. Especially after Simon. To top it off, Dante touched her."

"That would explain the long sleeves," Eric said.

"Her punishment is what was originally handed down," Marcus said sadly, "which, for Dante, is lenient. But she took it as she is now responsible, heart and soul, for the damage that Calliope reaps on the world."

Eric sat down, his head in his hands. "This is worse than I thought. It was bad enough that you broke her heart, but this ... how much is one woman supposed to carry?"

"None of it, damn it," Ryder bellowed. "None of it should be on her shoulders. She is a pure and innocent soul, God-dammit. I won't allow her to punish herself for the rest of her life for the sins of others, for deaths she cannot prevent."

Ryder turned on Eric. "What the hell! Are you all taught to be martyrs?"

"Of course not, but she feels things so deeply, she can't separate them from her own feelings. They had to remove her from the other Elements and bring her here because she felt so much, she was literally tortured." Eric started to pace. "It's why she was trained as an Enforcer instead of taking her place with the other Elements. She had to be taught to control some of it or it would kill her. The discipline of becoming an Enforcer strengthened her so that she was able to handle it, control it."

Ryder turned to Eric. This wasn't going to be easy. But he wasn't going to give up—he loved her too much. "Can we possibly work together?"

Eric looked at Ryder's extended hand for a long moment, and then placed his own hand into Ryder's. "If you hurt her again, I'll kill you myself, do you understand?"

Ryder nodded, knowing that it would take him and one hundred of his best men to accomplish it.

"Awesome. Where do we sleep?" Cameron asked.

"Not here."

"What about Staten?" a man with a shoulder wound asked.

"Staten will work."

Eric turned back to Ryder. "Elements really covet their privacy. I own everything within ten miles. There is one other estate with a home on it. It will need some work, but it is attached to the Haven by a system of tunnels."

"How far away?" Falcon asked.

"Exactly across from the Haven, six miles between the two front doors."

"That would be perfect," Falcon said. "Thank you."

The dark-haired man with the shoulder wound stood. "I'll take you over and show you the security system. I'm Xavier."

"Is it anything like this place?" Bowen asked with a light in his eye.

"Exactly. I designed both." Ryder smiled. Xavier might not know it yet, but he'd just made a friend for life in Bowen. The kid wasn't a fighter, regardless of how hard his brothers tried to make him one. He was a gentle soul and only wanted to play with gadgets.

Ryder followed his brothers and Xavier to the front door and turned to look up the stairs. He wanted to see her one more time before they left.

"Go say goodnight," Eric said, his arms folded over his chest. "If you leave again without saying goodbye, you might get flogged."

Ryder took the stairs again two at a time. He was going to fix this and if he couldn't, he was going to love her enough for the both of them.

He didn't bother to knock. She would just deny him again. She was curled in a ball in her bed and looked so tiny, it pulled at his heart, a heart he thought had been dipped in iron a thousand years ago.

He climbed onto the bed and gathered her into his arms.

"Please, Ryder, I don't have the strength to fight with you," she pleaded.

"I don't want to fight, Kyra." He held her, took deep breaths of her scent, combed her wet hair through his fingers, and kissed her forehead.

"Why are you here?" she whispered. "Why did you have to come here?"

He tipped her chin up with an index finger so he could look into her blue eyes. "Because. I realized I couldn't live without you."

"But you didn't even know if I was alive or not." Kyra sighed and pulled her face away. She laid it down on his shoulder. "Max."

"Yep, that—and I went to the Infernos," Ryder explained.

Kyra pulled back, surprised. "Why?"

"Because I couldn't stand to not know what happened, Kyra. Victor broke nearly every bone in my body. It took weeks for me to heal."

"And then?"

"I have to admit, I wallowed in self-pity." Ryder was embarrassed to admit. "But it cost you. I wish I could've gone after you immediately. I'm going to fix this, Kyra."

She pulled away from him and curled up in her bed. It didn't matter what he'd done. They still didn't have a future together. Even he had to understand that.

"There is nothing here that is broken, Ryder." Her words were muffled into her pillow.

Ryder leaned over her and kissed her forehead, basking in her touch and taste. "Sweet dreams, sweetheart." It took all of his strength to climb off the bed and walk out of the room, but he did it. He'd had two months to come to grips with losing her, and she'd left the Infernos only two weeks ago. She needed time, and he had plenty of it for the both of them.

Chapter 15

When Kyra opened her eyes the next morning, she pulled a pillow over her head. It was pounding so hard, she didn't think moving was a good idea.

She was surprised that Astrid hadn't come in to visit her, as she'd done every morning since Kyra's return home.

Kyra pulled herself up into a sitting position and pulled the blankets up. She wrapped her arms around her knees.

Ryder had come for her, part of her was thrilled, the part she thought the Infernos had killed. She should be thrilled and throw herself into his arms. But then she remembered it wouldn't be forever.

She was shocked when her door flew open and Ryder walked in carrying a tray. Kyra sunk down into her bed. "Seriously? Why can't you just leave me alone? Or at the very least, knock?"

"Not going to happen, Blue." She peeked out of the covers to glare at him.

"Don't call me that. You lost your privilege to call me that."

Ryder snorted. "When exactly did that happen?"

"Ten minutes ago, when I woke up with a headache."

"Sit up," he demanded. She didn't know why, but she did as he asked. He handed her the tray of food and pushed her forward.

"Hey." She juggled the tray as he settled in behind her. She now sat with her butt pressed against his groin and a strong leg on either side of her. She should've felt trapped, but for the first time since coming back from the Infernos, she felt safe. "I can't eat like this," she lied.

She tried to pull away but he grabbed her shoulders. "Kyra, just relax, and eat your breakfast."

He started to rub her shoulders and neck and damn it all, she couldn't resist the urge to lean into him.

"Eat," he whispered into her ear. She looked down at the plate of food.

It was her favorite. Waffles with bananas, whipped cream, and caramel sauce. Scrambled eggs on the side, sprinkled with her favorite hot sauce, and a cup of coffee. She curled her toes, refusing to admit to the man at her back that she was in heaven.

"How can you eat that?" Ryder asked over her shoulder, his words whispering over her skin. She breathed in his scent. "It's so sweet." His voice was low and throaty. Kyra stuffed her mouth with eggs so she didn't sigh as he continued to rub her shoulders.

"It's actually wonderful," she said. "You should go down and ask Cook to make you some."

"Or," his hands ran down her shoulders, "I could have a bite of yours."

"Nope." Kyra shook her head. "Nobody touches my waffles. Go ask the other Enforcers. They all know."

She felt him laugh from deep within his chest. "I'll make a mental note of that."

He continued to rub her arms and shoulders as she ate and finally, her conscience got the better of her. She stabbed a fork full and offered it to him over her shoulder.

"Here. Try."

He laughed. "Are you sure?"

"Just take the bite."

She watched out of the corner of her eye as his head tilted forward and his mouth wrapped around the fork. Kyra wasn't sure what it was about that movement, but suddenly she was so turned on, she couldn't breathe.

Ryder hummed behind her. The sound vibrated through her back and into her chest. "You're right. It is delicious." He murmured so close to her, his lips brushed the shell of her ear.

He nuzzled her with his nose, right behind her ear, and then licked her there. "You are the most beautiful woman I know, but this …" He kissed her again behind her ear. "This part of you? I'll never get enough of your scent here. It is so strong, I can breathe deeply and draw your scent right into my very soul."

She leaned back. She couldn't help it. Everything in her wanted this. She had missed his touch so much, missed the feeling of safety he gave her. Leaning her head to the side, she offered him better access to her neck.

"Ryder," she breathed, trying to remember that she didn't care anymore.

"Hmm?" he asked.

Kyra sat up abruptly, pulling away from his heat. She mentally shook herself. She wasn't going to be his pawn anymore. "I need to pee," she blurted out, and then wanted to kick herself for saying something so crass. She moved the tray of food and climbed out of the bed, tripping over Ryder's leg as she tried to get away from him.

Ryder helped her so she didn't actually fall on her face. Then she forced herself to walk calmly toward her bathroom.

"Kyra?" She stopped at her bathroom door and looked back. Now that she had the length of the room between them, she could breathe normally again. "I like your pajamas."

She nodded and walked into the bathroom, shutting the door a little harder than necessary. She could imagine him laughing right now. She was wearing pink Betty Boop pajamas with lace and a bright pink bow across the butt. She was going to have to start sleeping in her fighting gear if he was going to stick around.

She chewed on a fingernail. Trackers were nomads. They roamed and tracked but they never stayed in any one place for very long. He would have his fun and then he would be gone.

And she would be left with another broken heart. She didn't know if she would be able to live through that again.

Ryder lay in her bed for a moment, listening to her pace in the bathroom. He'd gotten to her this morning. He knew he had. His raging erection was proof as well. But he also knew it was going to take some time to get her to trust him. He grabbed the breakfast tray and left her room.

His brothers were down in the kitchen eating faster than the poor cook could prepare the food. Lykar did what he could to help her.

"I'm home," Bowen said. Leaning back, he patted his stomach. "Either that, or we are taking this wonderful woman with us when we leave."

The elder woman blushed. Ryder rolled his eyes. His brothers were making themselves right at home. Staten didn't have power, so they'd come over at first light.

"Why have you taken over my house?" Eric demanded as he walked into the kitchen. He looked around in disgust.

"No power at our place."

"That will be corrected by the end of the day. In fact, I am sure that X is working on it now."

"Oh, he is. I talked to him this morning," Bowen said, shoveling eggs into his mouth. "I should go and check on his progress and see what I can do."

Falcon snorted. "Probably won't see him for the rest of the day."

"Don't you have something to track?" Eric asked the rest of the room.

"Well, we all dropped what we were doing to get Ryder to his woman." Cameron waved a fork in Ryder's direction.

"And just how is that going?" Eric turned to Ryder.

"Progress." Ryder smiled. He took a plate that Lykar offered him and sat down at the table. Eric did the same. Marcus soon joined them. They sat silently, eating and glaring at each other.

Soon they were the only ones left in the room besides the cook, who was humming as she cleaned up.

Ryder looked at Falcon. "Adapt or die."

One of Falcon's eyebrows rose in question. "And what is that supposed to mean?"

"The time of being nomads has passed. We need to

adapt to where we are, who we are, and what we are. Adapt or die."

"He has a point," Marcus said, taking a drink from his coffee.

"We have fought side by side for thousands of years, brother, to keep our race alive only to reduce it down to eight." Ryder placed his hands flat on the table. "Adapt or die," he said again.

"Wait a moment," Eric interrupted. "What does this mean for me?"

"I think you might have permanent neighbors." Marcus laughed at the look on Eric's face.

"I don't want a neighbor. That's why I bought all the damn property to begin with," Eric uttered.

Falcon raised his hand. "I would never think to impose upon your gracious hospitality by overtaking the home you have loaned to us." But then he looked at Ryder. "But I do agree with my brother. The bonds we made have made us weak. If we are to survive as a race, we must adapt."

He thrust his arm to Ryder, who took him by the wrist and squeezed. "Thank you, Falcon." Ryder had to admit, his brother was making a great sacrifice. Falcon had roamed the world for centuries and Ryder wasn't sure he would be capable of staying in one place for very long.

"Bloody hell. If you can get Kyra to bond with you, then you can have the damn house. But you may not interlope here as you please." Eric shook his head.

Falcon smiled. It was a slow and easy show of emotion, something he rarely did. Ryder often wondered if it hurt him to smile because he did it so rarely. "I will pay for the house, Eric. And when we are settled, you won't even know we are there."

Eric pushed himself away from the table, snorting and swearing under his breath. "Famous last words. I'm going to go beat something up."

Marcus smiled at the two men. "This is a good beginning. I am lucky to have been here for it."

"You're leaving?" Ryder asked. He'd had little contact

with Fallen and hadn't really liked any of them. But Marcus was different. Ryder would always be grateful to the Fallen for protecting and caring for Kyra in the Infernos when he wasn't able to do so himself.

"Yes, Calliope is out there. And I have been charged with finding him before he wreaks havoc on the Mortal plane." Marcus pushed himself away from the table.

"We will help," Falcon said, also rising. "Cameron is not tasked with any Tracks right now. He will enjoy the hunt for this monster."

Marcus nodded. "Thank you. The ranks of Fallen are few at the moment."

"Few, as in …?" Ryder asked.

"I only have two who are loyal to me at the moment and not on the verge of turning," Marcus said honestly.

"Damn." Ryder shook his head.

"But Angels fall every day. It's just getting to them before evil does." Marcus looked haunted.

Ryder stood. Marcus extended his hand but Ryder took the hand and pulled the Fallen into his arms. "Brother," he said, releasing him.

"I would be honored to be considered as such," Marcus said.

Falcon slapped Marcus on the shoulder. "Let's go find Cameron."

Ryder eventually left the kitchen and sniffed. Kyra was no longer in the house, but she was close. He followed his nose and found the gym.

He found it impressive. A full-size track, inside Olympic-size pool, weights in the center of the track. But what impressed him most was the woman dressed in all black, sparring on mats to the left of the door. He folded his arms and stared at her. She moved with such grace and fluidity.

She sparred with Eric. Ryder's first instinct was to jump in there and stomp Eric into the ground for daring to touch her, but he tamped down the caveman in him, knowing that Eric would never intentionally hurt Kyra. He might just love her as much as Ryder did, but Ryder was doubtful of that. However, if he spilled one drop of her blood, Eric would bleed as well.

Eric taunted her as they circled. Ryder could see she was getting frustrated with her brother. He moved closer so he could hear what they were saying but not interrupt them.

"Holy cow! You've gotten so slow," Eric taunted. Stepping in, he slapped her gently on the side of the head.

Kyra threw an elbow but Eric moved out of the way before it connected.

"Slow … like molasses in winter." Eric laughed his voice dropping to a deep timbre as he spoke. He bounced around her on the balls of his feet. He looked like an excited kid on Christmas morning.

"Two weeks on your butt, and you're toast." He slapped her on the shoulder this time.

"Oh, for God's sake," Kyra muttered.

If he hadn't seen it with his own eyes, Ryder wouldn't have believed it. One second she was there, and the next, there were two of her.

Eric swung at one Kyra while the other kicked his feet out from beneath him. Then the second Kyra slammed him square in the chest with the flat of her hand as he went down, pounding him into the mat so hard, it would've left a Mortal man broken.

Ryder blinked and there was only one Kyra again.

"Cheater," Eric gurgled. "Projecting is cheating." He curled up, holding his chest. He was taking short, gasping breaths.

Kyra smiled. "But you're not dancing around me like an idiot now, are you."

"Cheater," Eric said again. Kyra just shrugged.

Ryder had seen enough. His thoughts went back to four nights ago and the very vivid, very real "dream" he'd had about Kyra.

"How do you do that?" Ryder demanded, walking onto the mat.

Kyra looked up, surprised. "How long have you been standing there?"

"Long enough."

"She projects," Eric moaned from the floor. "She's the only Element currently with that type of power. And she uses it to cheat." Eric tried to yell the last part, but he was still gasping for air.

Kyra kicked her brother. "Shut up."

"See?" He rolled out of her reach.

Ryder's eyes narrowed. "How far can you project?"

Kyra pursed her lips.

"Kyra?" Ryder warned.

"It's none of your business and it takes a great deal of strength. I rarely use it," she said, folding her arms over her chest. She gave him a look that said she wasn't going to say another damn thing. But she had another thing coming, because he was going to get some answers.

"Yes, but that's not what I asked you," Ryder said quietly.

She stomped a foot, which under other circumstances would've made him laugh. "If the Elements and the Gods are kind and everything is aligned, I can project myself anywhere in the world. But the farther I go, the less time I can hold the projection, and sometimes I am phased."

"And why didn't you use this ability while we were hunting that thing, while you were fighting it?"

"It was never necessary."

Ryder's mood exploded. "You could've sent the projection into the mountain instead of the real you! You could've been saved from all of that if you'd used that ability."

He wanted to shake her. It could've been so much easier. "Why do you do things the difficult way?" he demanded, raking a hand over his short hair.

Eric finally pulled himself to his feet. "She's like that."

"Shut up, Eric," Kyra snapped. Eric threw up his hands.

"What happens if the projection is injured?" Ryder asked Eric, knowing he would get the answers he sought faster than trying to squeeze them out of Kyra.

"Kyra receives the same injury wherever she is. It's not as useful as you think," Eric offered, ignoring Kyra as she told him to shut up again. "When she projects, the real Kyra is susceptible to attack. Completely unable to protect herself while she is projecting. She did just now because the projection was so close. But anything more than a few feet puts her physical form in danger because she has to go into a trancelike state to hold the projection and control it."

"So, if the projection is injured, the real Kyra sustains the same injuries?" Ryder put the pieces together, and some of his anger diffused.

"Once," Eric snorted, "she got drunk and projected herself all the way to the Academy in Chicago. She ran through the halls banging on doors and screeching like a crazy person."

"Shut up, Eric!" She stepped over to him but Eric moved away.

"They tried to stop her but they couldn't catch her because she kept phasing out. After an hour or so, they figured she was projecting. Called me to wake her ass up." He slapped his knee, laughing. "You do a lot of stupid stuff when you're drunk."

That, Ryder agreed with completely. "Maybe she shouldn't drink." Ryder gave her a hard look.

"What if you don't know where you're going?" Ryder asked Eric, who was still dancing around Kyra.

"Oh, she doesn't need to know where she's going. It's not like shifting where you have to know where you're going and to have been there before. She explained it once—she follows energy trails on the wind. Right?" He stopped and Kyra swung a fist at him that he didn't block, obviously not expecting it.

Blood gushed from his nose. "Shit, Kyra." He covered his face and walked away.

Kyra turned and walked out of the training area. Ryder followed. "Where were you four nights ago?"

She missed a step and almost fell when he asked the question. Then her steps increased and she suddenly took a left turn. Ryder realized she was walking on a path where the wind was now at her back. Little minx was learning, but she still had some questions to answer.

"Um, I was here," she said over her shoulder casually. "It was Spring equinox. Ask anyone. I was here celebrating the coming of spring."

They made it to the house and she threw open the door. "I'm going to go get in the shower. I'm sweaty. Have a nice day."

"Kyra." It was said as a demand rather than a request. She stopped and turned to him, innocence written all over her face, forced innocence, he noticed.

"Did you happen to have anything to drink on the celebration of the Spring equinox?" Ryder asked, moving closer to her.

She backed away a step, and her brow furrowed as if deep in thought. "I might have had a little to drink." She nodded.

"Yeah, two bottles of her favorite tequila," one of the other Enforcers said, coming out of the house. He must've overheard Ryder's question. "Had to carry her down to the grove. She was passed out completely by the time we brought her back to the house."

"Thanks, Daemon," she said sarcastically.

"Was it a secret?" he asked, pushing past Ryder. "Is Eric in the gym?"

"NO, and yes," Kyra said.

And then Daemon was gone. Ryder turned slowly back to Kyra. He approached her, drawing in her scent. "Kyra, sweetheart." He spoke slowly, as if talking to a child. He did not want her to misunderstand anything he was about to say. "You know that I don't ask twice, but on this one occasion, I am going to make an exception. And I've already made quite a few of those in your regard."

She covered his mouth with her hands, shaking her head wildly. Her mouth opened and shut like a fish out of water, and then she shifted and he was left standing in the doorway alone.

Ryder ran for the stairs. Her door was closed and when he pushed on it, he realized she had barred it somehow.

"Kyra, open this door," he demanded.

"I'm getting in the shower," she said. He heard the bathroom door close. Now he had two doors he had to get through. Frustration made him kick the door.

If he were a betting man, and he had been known to lay a few down on the tables, he would bet she'd passed out and projected herself to him that night. And she was going to admit it, damn it. But he had to get in there first.

"Hello."

Surprised, Ryder looked down at a young girl standing next to him in the hallway. He smiled down at her.

She stuck out her small hand. "I'm Astrid."

Ryder took her tiny hand in his large one and she shook it. "Daemon is my brother," she explained.

"That's nice." Ryder turned back to the door, trying to figure out if he was just going to bust through it or not.

"I'm going to marry Marcus when I grow up. He is so dreamy." Ryder stopped and looked down at the little girl again. She couldn't be more than eight or nine, but spoke with an authority far superior than her age implied.

She smiled. "Are you trying to get into Kyra's room?" Astrid looked over his shoulder at the door. Ryder took a deep breath.

"As a matter of fact, I am. But she's locked me out."

"Yeah, Daemon said you two were fighting a little," the girl explained.

"Yeah, just a little," Ryder agreed. If that wasn't the understatement of the year, he didn't know what was.

"But you know what?" she asked, lowering her voice to a whisper, "I'm a romantic at heart." She patted herself on the chest.

Ryder was so shocked, he just stood there. In all his life, this was going to go down as the strangest conversation he'd ever had.

"Would you mind coming with me?" she held out her tiny hand. Ryder looked back at the door and then back at the little girl. She smiled so brightly, he knew he couldn't deny her. Placing his hand in hers, he glared at the door. He was not admitting defeat.

She skipped and talked about the house, sharing with him its history. "There's a scary wraith that sometimes stays here. You should avoid her at all costs."

"I'll make a note of that."

Astrid led him to the third floor. "So the Enforcers are Druids. They typically don't have Elemental powers. They were entrusted with keeping the Elements safe. Kyra is the first female in history to be both an Element and an Enforcer. I mean, there have been female Enforcers before but not a female Element," she said with such adoration, Ryder could tell that the little girl idolized Kyra.

"And not only is she an Enforcer, but she is also an Element. Like Eric. They are very unique. I hope me and my brother have a relationship like theirs when I grow up," she said wistfully. "But right now, I'm too young to understand anything …" She drew out the last word.

"Now, because this has been the house of Diamond for so long, and the Enforcers' home base for just about the same amount of time, the Druid Enforcers who lived here didn't have the powers of Elements. So they had secret passages and escape routes built into the house." Astrid smiled when she explained it, as though it was the answer to all the mysteries in the world. She had led Ryder into a room full of boxes and old furniture.

She tapped the floor with her sandaled foot. "This trap door leads directly down into a closet."

Ryder was finally catching on to what the girl was getting at. "Whose closest, Astrid?"

She motioned him to come closer. Ryder kneeled down so they were face to face. She leaned in to whisper in his ear. "I can't tell you that because my brother made me promise to stay out of grown-up business. But giving you a tour of the house isn't butting in, and being a romantic isn't bad, either."

Ryder kissed the girl on the cheek. "No, being a romantic isn't a bad thing, Astrid."

She grabbed his hand as he stood. "Please don't make her cry anymore."

Her words tore at his heart. "I don't want to see her cry, either, little one."

Astrid smiled at him, as if that solved the problem.

"Okay. Have a nice day." She skipped out of the room as Ryder searched for a way to open the trap door. It took a minute but he finally found the lever and slid it open. He looked down into a well-kept walk-in closet. Black apparel hung from every hanger.

"Gotcha." He smiled and jumped down into the closet, closing the hatch behind him. He had her now. He took a minute to sniff the air. She was still in the shower, oblivious to the fact that she was now cornered.

Kyra stuck her head under the hot stream of water and turned on the second shower nozzle so she could relax under the power of both. She held her breath and tried to figure out what she was going to do.

She hadn't meant to project herself to him. She'd woken up in such terror the next morning, it had made her sick. The first time she had projected while asleep, Fiona had researched ways to keep her from projecting when she didn't want to. But she hadn't found anything. Kyra was going to have to do some of her own research. She couldn't have that happen again, not with him so close now.

What had Eric been thinking to lend them the Staten? They were nomads, barbarians. She flipped a switch and classical music filled the shower stall. It also doubled as a sauna and she cranked the heat, trying to flush her system of the man driving her absolutely insane.

Without warning, the shower door was thrown open. She squeaked and covered herself, jumping back as Ryder, completely nude, climbed into the shower with her. For just a moment, she thought about shifting away, but she couldn't bring herself to do it. She wanted him too badly.

"How in the world did you get in here?" she demanded, trying to maintain some anger.

"A little birdie flew me in," he said, advancing on her. She backed up until she was pressed against the wall of the shower.

"Ryder, what are you doing?"

"Where were you four nights ago?" he asked again. She felt her mouth drop open. He had asked twice. He had broken one of his rules and asked her twice.

But just as quickly, she snapped her mouth closed. "I was here, at Haven. Now get out of my shower." She shoved at his large chest but she might as well have been trying to move the Empire State Building.

"And your projection?" he asked, crowding her, not quite touching but close enough that she could feel the heat rolling off him. She should've been more self-conscious standing there before him, naked and wet.

"Why do you want to know?" she countered.

"Kyra?" He used his compulsion voice, but because it wasn't really a question, she just felt a little shiver. "I will only ask this one more time."

"And then what?" she interrupted.

One eyebrow rose sardonically and he flipped water out of his face. "You, my lovely, do not want to know." He leered at her in such a suggestive way, her knees weakened.

"It might have wandered away for a little while. But I had no control of her. None!" she said.

"Then who had control of her?" He actually had her on that one. Ryder must've read the look on her face and he

294

pounced. "I knew it." Then he was kissing her, pulling her body into his. She fought him for all of two seconds before her hands wrapped around his neck and held on for all she was worth. She'd missed him so much, and she'd shamelessly taken advantage of him several nights ago, making him think he was dreaming. Except it hadn't been the same as her physical body pressed against his.

"Gods, you feel so good." He ran his hands down her back, pressing her against him. He cupped her ass and squeezing each cheek, he lifted her so that she straddled him. Kyra locked her feet behind him. She wasn't going anywhere. The only problem was, she didn't know if she was capable of ever letting him go again.

He hiked her up the wall, holding her with his body as he suckled each nipple until they were rock solid. He let her slide down, licking and kissing her as she did. Her moans of pleasure bounced off the walls.

"I will never get enough of you, never tire of the taste of you, never feel anything sweeter or more wonderful than the brush of your fingertips against my skin, the gentle glide of your body against mine." He licked at a trail of water that slid down between her breasts, his tongue following it all the way up to his favorite spot behind her ear. "Never tire of the sweet sound of your breath mixed with mine." He breathed out and she inhaled his exhalation. It was almost a caress for the both of them, sharing a breath. Kyra wanted to cry, she loved this man so much, wanted him so badly. She wondered if she would ever get enough of him, if a person could die from pleasure and wanting.

His hand slid down to move smoothly between her legs. Even his groan of pleasure turned her on. He groaned her name against the side of her neck. His other hand cupped her face, his thumb rubbing circles on her cheek as he plundered her mouth with his tongue. With his other hand, he drove her toward a climax that she wasn't quite ready for.

Pulling her mouth away, she begged for mercy. "Ryder, oh, Ryder, I can't take much more." She twisted her head back and forth as water splashed and steam enveloped them.

"I will protect you with knife." He thrust one finger deep inside of her, making her scream in pleasure.

"Ryder," she moaned.

"I will protect you with sword." His thumb flickered over her sensitive bud, and she felt like her body was coming apart.

"I will protect you with my very soul." He moved down, placing kisses on her stomach as his head dipped in to replace his fingers.

She was so out of control with pleasure, she couldn't think, could barely breathe. Her world had become this one man in this one moment. Steam filled the shower, encasing them, creating a world of ecstasy. And for the moment, this one moment in time, they belonged together. She was going to hold onto him with everything she had.

Ryder spread her legs for better access, making Kyra limp as she grasped for purchase. He held her steady, just as he always did, making sure she neither fell nor stumbled. And in that manner, he held steady as her world spiraled out of control with Ryder at the center, holding her, keeping her safe. He slowly stood, licking every inch of skin as he went.

He looked deep into her eyes. "By the touch of the Tracker." He dragged a finger down the column of her throat to the tip of one turgid nipple. His breath caught, his entire body shaking. He leaned down to take the nipple into his mouth.

"Ryder, please …" She begged. Wrapping her legs around him again, she reached down and palmed him.

He jerked in reaction as the shock ran from her hand into his sack. He closed his eyes, taking deep breaths as she rolled him in her hand, driving him as crazy as he was driving her.

"Gods, Kyra." He seemed to be searching for control but she wanted to be in the driver's seat, if only for a moment. She wanted him as mindless as she was. Kyra leaned forward, nipping at his muscular shoulder. She licked his neck in the same fashion as he'd done to her so many times before. He threw his head back, gripping her hips as she dragged her hands down his torso. Leaving her mark, she licked every inch of exposed skin as she moved upward. When she moved back to his neck, she sucked on the spot where his pulse beat strong and hard, driving life though him.

At this point, he was gripping her hips so tightly, she knew that she would carry his mark for several days, but she didn't care. "Yes, Ryder, please …" She begged for more.

"By smell." He kissed her, sucking in her very breath and then breathing it back into her. She sucked on his earlobe, keeping him close, and ground her hips against him. He rotated his hips against her, grinding her against him but not entering her. She needed this more than her next breath as he guided her toward another orgasm.

Her head fell back against the tile as she moaned his name. "Yes, the smell of your climax." He was physically shaking. He pressed into her neck just behind her ear as he finally pushed deep inside of her. Kyra couldn't control her scream as he entered her. It felt so amazing. He covered her mouth with his own, plundering it with his tongue as he seated himself completely inside of her.

Tearing his mouth from her, he moaned, "By taste." He licked her again behind the ear and then kissed her deeply, thrusting his tongue deep into her mouth. He tasted different but it only turned her on more as he slowly started to thrust in and out of her while kissing her.

She was mindless and finally tore her mouth away. She called out his name as a third climax drove her over the edge.

Ryder thrust several more times. "I claim you as mine. Mine by the grace of the Gods and the bonds of eternity." She watched in amazement as his entire body arched into this one final thrust so deep, she could feel him touch her womb.

"Mine," he said finally before shouting her name and pouring his seed deep into her.

He held her against the wall for several minutes, placing small kisses on her face before moving back. They washed each other, and then he dried her off and carried her to the bed where he made love to her again, slowly, drawing out the pleasure to the point of pain. Kyra wouldn't have it any other way. She clung to him with everything she had. And when they were sated, she fell asleep with him still inside of her.

"Ryder?" she poked him in the shoulder with her index finger.

He muttered and rolled away. So he was a heavy sleeper, was he?

She smiled, reveling in the knowledge that he was here, that they had spent the day making love to each other. She refused to think about what was going to happen next. Kyra promised herself that she was only going to think about the here and now. And for right now, the man she loved lay in bed next to her, sound asleep. She leaned back and tried to come up with a way to get him out of bed. She was hungry.

It came to her in a blink, knowing a sure way to get him up. She took several deep breaths and then shouted. "Oh my God! We're under attack!"

She couldn't believe how fast he moved. He was up and out of the bed with a weapon in his hands in a blink.

"Damn, that was fast."

Ryder looked around, blinking the sleep from his eyes. He narrowed them at her, dropped his gun, and lunged at her. She laughed, scrambling back onto the bed.

"Where did you get that gun?" she asked over her shoulder, kicking her legs so he couldn't get hold of her.

"Sweetheart, I always know where my gun is." He smiled suggestively, finally capturing her leg.

He had her by the ankle and slowly dragged her back and under him. He pushed himself into her. Kyra gasped and held onto his shoulders before she spiraled out of this world and into one of pleasure.

"Waking me that way … not funny," he said, nuzzling her neck. He slowly moved in and out of her. "And now, you will have to be punished."

Kyra giggled, lifting her hips. "Just remember that I give as good as I get. Besides, you wouldn't wake up," she accused, "and I'm hungry." She arched up to meet him as his thrusts became more urgent.

"Fuck now. Eat later," he said. As he kissed her, she forgot that she wanted anything but this man inside her.

"Ryder?"

"Hmm?"

He was drowsy and so was she, but she had some questions. The sun had set long ago. Eric had knocked earlier to make sure they were still alive but other than that, they'd been undisturbed all day.

But now that she was fully awake and he wasn't driving her nuts with passion, she had some questions she needed answered. And she was pretty sure the answers were going to piss one of them off.

Steeling herself, she asked, "What were those words in the shower? They were beautiful." And specific, very, very specific. Now that she wasn't in the throes of passion, she had a sinking feeling they were something more than just words whispered during passionate lovemaking.

Ryder opened his eyes and looked at her. They weren't black but a soft gray that gave him the appearance of calm and serenity.

"They were the Tracker bonding ritual," he said it so nonchalantly, for a second, she thought he was kidding. But when his expression didn't change, her temper flared.

Kyra quickly climbed from the bed so she could slug him directly in his smug face. Instead, she stomped into her closet for her robe. Ryder was still in the bed, hands behind his head, like he had all the time in the world.

"Have you lost your fucking mind?" she shouted, totally losing her temper at his blasé attitude. "Did you think for a moment about asking me first?"

Ryder raised an eyebrow and sat up. "Excuse me?"

"Why would you bond yourself to me?"

"Because I love you, Kyra, and I'm never going to let you go," he said gently, as if talking to a child.

She pointed an accusing finger at him. "Don't you patronize me. How could you do this?" She couldn't believe he'd done something so stupid. For several moments, she wasn't sure what she was supposed to say or do. She picked up a book and flung it as hard as she could, striking him directly in the chest.

Ryder made an oomph noise and climbed from the bed. "What the hell is your problem?"

"You! You are my problem. Why would you bond to me?" She barely avoided death on a day-to-day basis. And if she died, then he … she couldn't bring herself to think it.

He moved up to her slowly, as if she would bolt at any second. "I love you, and I refuse to live my life without you."

"You said love was for the weak, the sentimental, and simpleminded. For fools," she accused. It was just too much. The very thought of him dying because of her hurt so deeply, she wanted to curl into a ball.

"Can you reverse it?"

Ryder growled so low, it was menacing. "No. It cannot be undone. I'm sorry that the thought of spending our lives together is so abhorrent to you."

He was jerking on his clothes when Kyra touched his shoulder. She was surprised when he flinched.

"Ryder, you didn't even ask. And I'm going to die."

He swung around so fast, she stumbled back. "What the hell are you talking about? Did something happen in the Infernos? Why are you dying?" He seemed to choke on the last word.

Kyra shook her head. "No, Ryder, you don't understand. One day, I am going to die. I'm going to grow old and die. And that will kill you. I can't live with myself every single day knowing that I'm killing you. My conscience is loaded down already. I love you too much to sentence you to death."

"Say it again," he asked.

"I'm going to die," she said around tears that started to fall.

"Not that part—the other."

She peeked up at him with teary eyes. "I love you."

Kyra started to cry in earnest, burying her face in her hands.

Ryder gathered her into his arms and carried her back to the bed. He let her cry herself out.

"Sweetheart?" he asked gently, once she'd stopped crying.

"Yes?"

"I'm sorry to say this, but you're stuck with me."

Kyra pushed away from him. "But I don't want you to be stuck with me."

He chuckled. "Kyra, Trackers have an extra gland in the back of their throats that allow us a better sense of taste and smell. We're not sure how it increases our tactile functions, but it does that as well."

"Yes, I know all of this from Marlee," Kyra explained.

"Damn Lycan needs to learn to keep her mouth shut," Ryder muttered. "Anyway, it secretes a pheromone type of elixir when we find our true mate. If we ingest too much of it, it poisons and kills us. But if we share it with our chosen and she accepts it, it has a completely different effect."

Kyra jumped up onto her knees, her eyes flaring. "That was why you tasted different in the shower."

He shrugged. "I've marked you in several places with the pheromone." He reached over and touched her behind her right ear, the side of her throat.

Kyra was shocked. "That would explain all the licking."

Ryder looked immediately defensive, so she rushed to clarify herself. "Oh, don't get me wrong. I like your licking, really like it. But I've never been with anyone who liked to lick as much as you do."

When he jumped from the bed so fast, Kyra wasn't able to accommodate the quick movement and fell off the other side, striking her shoulder. She whimpered in pain. Ryder was by her side instantly.

He picked her up. "Tell me who they are," he asked, so low if he hadn't been speaking within inches of her face, she might've missed it.

Kyra rubbed her shoulder. "You hurt me," she said, trying to change the subject.

Ryder rolled his eyes and rubbed the spot where she'd hit. He then leaned over and kissed it. Looking up, he asked, "Better now?"

She nodded.

"Good." Ryder pushed her back on the bed so that he was leaning over her. "Now give me the names of the other men you've slept with so that I can kill them,"

"Damn, you're impossible." She tried to roll away from him. "It's not like you came into this mating ritual unscathed. How many women have you been with?"

Ryder huffed and settled back on his heels. "That's different."

Kyra couldn't believe what he was saying. "You're kidding, right?"

He looked so disgruntled, she couldn't help herself. She wrapped her arms around him, hugging him close. "The thought of you …" He trailed off.

"It doesn't matter, Ryder. What matters is that you're the only one from this point forward." She kissed his shoulder.

"You're not going to die, by the way," he said, wrapping himself around her. "What I was trying to get at before is that pheromone elixir we secrete prolongs your life, as long as we are together." He waggled his eyes suggestively and Kyra honestly couldn't help but laugh. "You shall remain as you are now."

"I'm imMortal?" she asked, incredulous.

Ryder growled. She was beginning to understand his different growls. This was the one that said, *Have you heard what I've been telling you?*

"No, so don't go out and do something stupid. It just extends your life if I die." She opened her mouth but he placed a hand over it before she could say anything. "And when you stop receiving the pheromone, you start aging again and eventually die. But only Others can handle the elixir. Mortals, when given it, die. We don't understand why."

"I would rather be imMortal," she said petulantly.

He laughed. It was a deep sound that filled the room and her heart. "Yes, well, we can't have everything we want, now can we?"

Kyra shrugged. "You know what I want right now?" she asked instead.

Ryder kissed her throat, licking his way up to behind her ear. "What's that?" he whispered.

"Waffles, actually."

Ryder leaned back to see if she was serious and then rolled his eyes. He pulled himself out of the bed and finished dressing. She didn't move.

"If you want your waffles, you're going to have to come down and make them with me," he demanded.

She smiled and peeled off her robe. His heart started to beat a little faster as she leaned back into the pillows. "I think the waffles can wait."

Ryder jumped on her fully clothed, burying his face in her neck. "You are going to make me crazy, you know that?"

She smiled and nodded. "It's what wives are supposed to do."

"You're my mate, not my wife. There is a difference," he corrected her. "Mate is forever. You can never walk away from me. In fact, spending more than a couple of weeks apart could be deadly for me. Not that I want you anywhere but by my side for the rest of our lives."

Kyra nodded, making note of that in the back of her head. He kissed her deeply and then let his lips drift down her neck and over her shoulder. She tried to pull her arm away, but he was much stronger than she was.

"Do they hurt?" he asked of the bands burned into her skin just above her elbows. They had turned a dark brown, almost like a suntan, on both arms.

"No, not anymore."

"I'm sorry, Kyra. You'll never know how sorry I am." He kissed the mark and moved over to her other arm to kiss that one as well.

"Ryder?"

He looked up, his eyes the color of a storm cloud. "Is it possible for us to have children?" He stared at her for the longest time. "I mean, we don't have to have any if you don't want to," she stammered.

Ryder shook his head. "I would be honored if you carried my child," he said, a catch in his throat. Kyra actually thought she saw tears in his eyes.

"I will, of course, stay an Enforcer until I get pregnant. But I want children." The smile he gave her was so brilliant she couldn't help but smile back.

She looked into his eyes and realized how lucky she was, how wonderful he was, and just when she thought she couldn't possibly love him more, he did something that surpassed the love she currently felt for him.

"Does this mean you're a sentimental fool?" she asked, laughing at the look he gave her.

"Would you like me to tattoo it on my forehead?"

"No, but you can admit it. I promise not to tell anyone that you subjugated to a woman." It was her turn for her eyebrows to waggle.

He growled, which made her giggle. "I was wrong, Kyra." He rolled over so that he was on top of her. "Love is not for sentimental fools. Love is a gift from the Gods that should be cherished, and anyone lucky enough to find what we have should thank the Gods." He finished by kissing her. She had never felt more loved or cherished in all her life.

Epilogue

Kyra looked around the room she'd spent the last hour cleaning and nodded. The Staten had to have a great deal of work done. It was a good thing she didn't mind getting dirty. She'd take time off from being an Enforcer to settle her home, and it was a well-deserved vacation. Except for the fact that Ryder kept hiding the key to the liquor cabinet where she kept her tequila. Marlee explained that it was a game he enjoyed playing. He hid her gum from her all the time. The two women had become close friends against the many men not only at the Staten but at the Haven as well.

When she learned that Eric had given them the home, she was so surprised and happy, she burst into tears and threw herself at her brother.

"Get her off of me! I have no idea who this woman is," he snapped.

Ryder peeled her off her brother. "Don't thank him yet. You haven't seen the place."

She had loved every second of making the Staten a livable home for her and Ryder. And all the other Trackers, whom she now considered brothers. They didn't know how to treat her, so most of them—with the exception of Lykar and Skylar—avoided her. But she was sure that she would get around their walls eventually.

Kyra pulled the bedspread straight. It had taken them two months to get Staten up to par and this would be their first night in their new home, to the great relief of Eric, who groused daily about the Trackers and their barbarian ways.

She smiled. All the brothers had rooms and had come and gone, knowing they now had a real home. It warmed her soul to know that she had built a home for them all. It helped to relieve some of the pain she felt over the past.

She felt as if she was taking a turn in her life, a good turn, and she felt like she belonged somewhere for the first time ever. She brushed a tear from her face when she heard Ryder coming down the hall.

Ryder came through the bedroom door and looked around, a smile playing at his lips.

Kyra smiled at him. "Welcome home."

"Kyra?" he asked, a little breathless as he noticed her attire. "What are you wearing?"

Kyra looked down at the long white negligee. He was always on her about the lack of color in her wardrobe, but the fact that she would wear Daffy Duck to bed boggled his mind.

"Ryder, it's a full moon." She motioned to the giant picture window. The full moon shone down in brilliant color.

"Okay," he said, stepping toward her.

"You performed the mating ritual for a Tracker." He nodded, taking another step. "But tonight, I would like to perform the Druid right to bond," she said. "Since the beginning of the Druids, every spring on the full moon between equinox and solstice, the woman of marriageable age would dance." She took his hand and led him over to a chair, pushing him down into it. "They would dress in virginal white to show their pureness to prospective husbands." She motioned to the lovely white gown she was wearing.

"Sorry to break it to you, sweetheart, but you're not a virgin. Either that, or I'm not doing my job right." She slapped his shoulder.

"It's a symbol. Now, are you going to be quiet and let me do this?"

Ryder leaned back. "By all means, please." He motioned for her to continue.

"On the full moon, they would dance, creating a frenzy and each woman of age would choose." Kyra had thought it barbaric herself, but she and Ryder were already bonded so this was for her own satisfaction. She really hadn't known they were bonding together when he'd done it. And she wasn't sure how she would one day explain to their children how their parents bonded. So she was going to perform this ceremony.

She whispered a spell Fiona had taught her and the lights winked out.

"We are going to have to talk about all these little tricks you have. Because at least once a week, I find out something else you do that I didn't know about."

Kyra put her hands on her hips, the light of the full moon illuminating the room and silhouetting her incredible body beneath the nearly translucent nightgown. "You need to shut up,"

Ryder's eyes rounded but he shut his mouth. After a couple of months with Kyra, he loved her more and more every day. When he caught her scent in a room, it brought calmness to him. It also made him want her. He said it the night when she projected herself to him—he would never get enough of her.

"On the night of the full moon, the men would be brought out to the sacred grove." Her voice was growing husky and Ryder suddenly wasn't in the mood to tease her anymore. "And the women would be brought out. They would dance for the men until the night pulsed with sexual tension. And then each woman would reach out and touch each man on the chest right where his heart should be." She placed her hand on Ryder's chest. "If light appeared, they called it the blue spark of life. The woman knew she had found her one true mate."

Ryder's mind reeled for a moment. "It happened the first time, the night after you were possessed. You knew then?" He jumped to his feet.

Kyra smiled. "Yes, but it wasn't our time yet." She forced him back into his seat. "Do you want to see the dance or not? Frankly, I'm starting to think you're not interested."

She crossed her arms over her chest in such irritation, he couldn't help but smile. One of the things he loved most about her was her short temper. It matched his and they often sparred verbally.

"Yes, I want you to continue."

She smiled and started to sway her body, flowing with movement from the floor up. He realized for the first time that the windows were open and air swirled in, catching her hair and dress, almost becoming her dance partner. Ryder watched as she started to gyrate, moving her body with the breeze stirring in the room. Her arms swayed in the air. All he could do was sit and stare as she started to glow. She moved closer to him, almost touching his knee, and he felt the breeze over the back of his hand as she twirled around him. Breath tickled the back of his neck. Hair brushed against his thigh.

He started to breathe a little heavier, wondering how much of this he could take before attacking her and taking her to bed.

"Kyra," he whispered her name as she swirled around him, wrapping him in her smell, in her love. He couldn't take it and as she spun around him, he stood and took her into his arms. Her blue light sparked before their lips touched. He pressed into her, kissing her deeply.

When he lifted his head, they were both breathless. Kyra smiled, her eyes alight with love. "I guess that makes it official. You're my one true love."

"Did you ever question it, Blue?" he asked, swinging her into his arms.

"There was a time or two," she admitted as he laid her on the bed and covered her body with his own.

"It will never happen again," he buried his head into her neck, kissing her.

"Never," Kyra agreed, drawing him in close.

Acknowledgment

This book would not have been possible without the help of a team of people.

Being an Indie published writer I get the chance to interact with so many people that broaden my horizons I wouldn't be able to name them all here.

However, I really need to thank my editor Jen she worked tirelessly with me to make this manuscript everything it is today.

Also I can't thank my beta-readers enough they see things that I miss even though I read through the manuscript hundreds of times. Thank you, Thank you, Thank you!!!

To Jaycee my cover artist and all thing art related you bring my visions to life.

To my twitter writing friends who teach me knew things every day.

To my husband and kids (yes AGAIN). You are so important to me. I couldn't do this without your love and support.

And last but certainly lost least. To my fans you guys rock and give me the drive to continue writing.

I am sure I have missed some one, so if I haven't mentioned you I sincerely apologize!!

--Christie

ABOUT CHRISTIE

Christie was born and raised in a suburb of Salt Lake City, UT. Where she still lives less than a mile from the home she grew up in. World traveler she is not. But what she lacked in travel she more than made up for in her imagination. Within her vivid imagination she has traveled the world over as well as different worlds and different times.

She works a full time day job to pay the bills but looses herself in books and her writing whenever possible.

She is a loving mother of two wonderful children that she admits she is obsessed with. She has been married for 18 years to a very tolerant man that is grounded in reality in order for her to fly to the heights of her own imagination.

She started writing when she was a teenager after reading a book that she didn't like the ending too. Took a hiatus to raise her wonderful children but has dedicated herself to becoming a published writer for the last several years.

FIND HER AT THE FOLLOWING:
www.author-christiepalmer.com
Facebook: http://www.facebook.com/christie.palmer.5011
Twitter: @christieauthor
Goodreads:
http://www.goodreads.com/user/show/11563672-christie-palmer

www.ingramcontent.com/pod-product-compliance
Lightning Source LLC
Chambersburg PA
CBHW060531180626
46817CB00002B/526